Vita's Prayer

A Christian Romance and a Quo Vadis Retelling

Grace Liu

Copyright © 2024 by Ge Liu

All rights reserved.

No part of this publication may be reproduced, distributed, or transmitted in any form or by any means, including photocopying, recording, or other electronic or mechanical methods, without the prior written permission of the publisher, except as permitted by U.S. copyright law. For permission requests, contact grace@vitasprayer.com.

The story, characters, and incidents portrayed in this novel are a work of fiction. While certain characters and events may be inspired by real historical figures and occurrences, artistic liberties have been taken for the purpose of storytelling. Any resemblance to actual persons, living or deceased, places, buildings, or products is coincidental and should not be inferred as factual.

Book Cover by Nour E

Library of Congress Control Numbers: 2023924321

ISBN: 978-1-961090-01-9

Acknowledgements

My heartfelt thanks go out to my cherished family, especially my husband, whose support sustained me through the twists and turns of this long writing odyssey.

I am deeply grateful to Pastor Gong, whose enlightening church history videos on YouTube introduced me to Henryk Sienkiewicz's novel "Quo Vadis," igniting the flame of inspiration that fueled my own writing journey.

I also owe a profound debt of gratitude to Henryk Sienkiewicz, winner of the Nobel Prize for Literature in 1905, author of "Quo Vadis," whose captivating narrative served as the springboard for this retelling version.

I want to express my deepest appreciation to the literary giants whose works have shaped my imagination and fueled my passion: Francine Rivers, Kate Quinn, and Charlotte Brontë. Your brilliance continues to inspire me.

I extend my sincere gratitude to Mary Beard and Alberto Angela, whose research into ancient Rome provided invaluable insight and helped me build a solid understanding of the world in which I set my story.

A special thanks to Sophia Ellithorpe, Emilyn Zhao, and Jessie McDonald, whose invaluable assistance and guidance have been a beacon of light whenever I stumbled in the labyrinth of language.

Enduring gratitude is extended to Yue, for being the first person to share the gospel with me, and to my dear brothers and sisters in BTU-Cottbus and Stanford Christian fellowship group, whose nurturing guidance and support have strengthened my young faith and ignited my dream of storytelling.

And finally, I humbly pay homage and offer my deepest reverence to the courageous first-century Christians and all those throughout history who endured persecution for their unwavering faith in Christ. It is through their sacrifices that the seeds of faith have been preserved, providing the fertile soil upon which my story blooms.

Preface

I never thought I would write a novel, especially in a language I'm not familiar with. If God had revealed to me how much trouble I would go through, I probably would have given up from the very beginning. Fortunately, He hid everything from me.

In 2013, I arrived in the US from China as an international student spouse. Due to my visa status, which didn't permit me to work, I dedicated much of my time to reading books and watching documentaries. As a recent convert to Christianity from an atheist background, I found myself captivated by the history of the early church. One day, while watching a pastor discuss this topic on YouTube, I learned about a novel set in first-century Rome. It delves into the formation of the early church and its challenges under persecution.

This book was Quo Vadis, written by Henryk Sienkiewicz in 1896. Despite needing a dictionary to read it, as English was not my first language, I fell in love with it right away. This was not only due to the beautiful romance within it, but also because of the profound spiritual journeys it portrayed.

The story captivated me so much that I wanted to share it with as many people as I could. However, when I tried to persuade my friends to read it, most of them were not interested, because the novel was very long and not written in a style familiar to modern readers.

As I tried to figure out a way to share this story, something I've loved since childhood came to mind—— manga. I've been enjoying reading manga since I was very young, and I can say that in my adolescent years, stories told in the form of manga greatly shaped my personality. So, I figured if I adapt this story into a manga, more people will find it easy to digest and will benefit from it. Thus, I started my journey.

I devoted a significant amount of time to preparing for this manga project, even teaching myself to draw from scratch. However, while drafting the script, a challenge soon presented itself.

Despite my deep affection for the original story, I still desired to infuse my personal touch into the plot. Being a female author, I found it more natural to connect with the female main character. Hence, I endeavored to narrate the story from the heroine's perspective, in contrast to the predominantly hero-centric original. However, I soon realized that conveying the story as I envisioned would require significant alterations to the plot.

Regardless, not one to be defeated, my writing continued.

As time passed, I noticed that the more I wrote, the more my characters seemed to come to life. Now, it felt as if they were choosing their own paths, resulting in a new story in which the main characters had totally different qualities than the original ones, although the original novel's influence remained discernible throughout.

Meanwhile, I had another painful realization that even if I worked hard on my drawing skills, I might still need ten years of practice before I could handle this job. This was the point at which I decided to turn my script into a novel first, so that I would have some "finished product" before tackling the challenging task of manga making, which might take decades to complete.

Initially I hesitated, because as a non-native speaker and an amateurish writer, my skills were nowhere near as advanced as those of Henryk Sienkiewicz, a Nobel Prize winner. So, I spent four years "doing research" and used it as an excuse to delay starting my writing. However, over time, I realized that even though my writing may be rough, my story would still possess its own unique qualities. And I believe someone, somewhere in the world will resonate with my story when they read it.

However, the process of completing the book was much longer and more challenging than I had anticipated. I have to admit that at my lowest point, I reached a stage of desperation and hired someone to create an outline for me. Unfortunately, it didn't go well; her writing fell far short of my expectations, so I abandoned her outline and rewrote it on my own. Fortunately, with lots of tears and prayers, I persevered and successfully completed the book.

What about my manga dream? Well, I have to say that even though my drawing skills are still not good enough, I'm very optimistic about rapidly advancing AI technologies. I won't give up on the dream. If it aligns with God's plan, I might have the opportunity to transform the story into a web manga or even create a film with AI in the future. So, if you are interested in the promising future of my novel, please visit my website www.vitasprayer.com and subscribe to our newsletter. I'll keep you updated on the progress.

Additionally, feel free to connect with me through the following social media platforms or via email:

TikTok: @vitasprayer
YouTube: @vitasprayer
Instagram: @vitasprayer
Email: grace@vitasprayer.com
Looking forward to staying in touch!

Contents

1. The House of Darkness — 1
2. A Little Tablet — 12
3. The Longest Wait — 27
4. A Desperate Decision — 35
5. To Rome — 42
6. A Dazzling Figure — 49
7. A New Home — 57
8. A New Friend — 62
9. Girl Talk — 65
10. Hit the Bottom — 71
11. A New Low — 76
12. Lady Cassia — 79
13. Birds Uncaged — 87

14. The Fish!	93
15. Get on the Stage	97
16. A Troublesome Pair	105
17. A Resourceful Friend	110
18. A Petrifying Glance	117
19. Secretly Kept Thoughts	122
20. Reunion	128
21. Promise Renewed	134
22. Hope Rekindled	140
23. Caius is Coming	147
24. A Surprising Act	151
25. A Secret Plan	157
26. The First Night	164
27. Are You a Christian?	169
28. A Tour of the Villa	175
29. Visiting the Barracks	182
30. Sabina's Banquet	192
31. A Statue with Memories	203
32. The Interrogation	218
33. The Last Night	226
34. Two Surprises in a Day	231

35.	A Pool with Ice	241
36.	Stay	249
37.	An Invitation to the Palace	255
38.	An Audacious Answer	262
39.	Orpheus and Eurydice	271
40.	Temptation Draws Near	277
41.	A Plan to Escape	285
42.	To the Rescue	290
43.	The Fisherman's Wife	294
44.	Little Achilles	298
45.	A Sudden Accusation	303
46.	Her Hidden Purpose	311
47.	The Symbol	317
48.	A Secret Gathering	322
49.	The Christian Community	333
50.	The Disease	345
51.	Journey to Greece	352
52.	Leaving Rome	366
53.	Fire!	376
54.	Baptism	383
55.	An Unexpected Encounter	387

56.	The Arrest	393
57.	A Royal Scheme	401
58.	A Plea to Nero	405
59.	The Empress' Offer	411
60.	Shocking Secret	414
61.	A Visitor to the Jail	419
62.	Apostle is Back	425
63.	Confronting the Empress	430
64.	The Arena	437
65.	The Final Battle	444
66.	Epilogue	449
	The Story Continues...	456
	Dedication	458
	Author's Plea	459

One

The House of Darkness

THE SEARING HEAT OF the Cypriot sun blazed down from a cloudless sky, causing beads of sweat to roll down our faces. The dry air left a constant parched feeling in the backs of our throats, prompting us to drink more than usual.

At this moment, we took a much-needed break from the heat, going off to seek our favorite spot in the village. "The House of Darkness"—as we had named it—provided a reprieve from the scorching sun. This grand villa had long since been abandoned, yet its grandeur remained unchanged to the local children.

The wild, towering weeds had completely taken over the roof at this point. They had grown so tall that they blocked the light that used to pour into the atrium, plunging it into an unsettling darkness. It was the eerie blackness of this section of the house that had earned the villa its creepy local name, and with each of our visits, that name seemed to become just a bit more fitting.

I stood at the corner of the atrium, facing the wall, hands covering my eyes. Other children had gathered around me, also covering their own eyes in anticipation.

"...five, four, three, two, one. Open your eyes. Time to hunt the rabbit!" Gato's croaky voice boomed as he commanded the group.

Being the son of the village chief, Gato was well-fed and much stockier than the other children his age.

At his command, we all opened our eyes. The group scattered in many directions, searching for the wooden rabbit toy that was only about the size of a palm.

But not me. I would not scatter, remaining in situ, not joining the hunt.

"Why aren't you joining the hunt for the rabbit, little Vita?" Gato asked, scratching his head. "You're usually one of the keenest out of us all. Is everything all right?"

"Yes, I'm fine. I'm just taking my time, thinking some things over," I replied with a grin as I paced back and forth in front of Gato. "It never hurts to take time over things."

"What are you doing really?" Gato bellowed, his tone growing impatient, not used to seeing a usually unruly child looking still and contemplative. We usually all ran amuck.

"Nothing. As I said, I'm just thinking." I smiled, repeatedly glancing away and then back at him. "No rules against that, are there? A girl can think. You ought to try it someday."

He was not appreciative of my cheekiness and scowled.

"Hey, nobody finds the rabbit by thinking. You must look for it! You need to use these," he said, pointing at his eyes. "Come on, you're wasting precious time. Get going!"

"Maybe, we'll see," I replied with a smirk, keeping my plan close to my chest. And it certainly was a plan, too. One I'd been thinking about for a while, in fact, ever since the year before when I had been five years old and failed hopelessly at this same game.

Today is the day to put the plan to the test, I said to myself eagerly.

My nervous energy consumed me while I waited, pacing back and forth. When I noticed Gato had stopped scratching his head, I immediately started chanting, "Antechamber... atrium... study... front yard... back yard..." At the mention of each section within the house, I'd shoot a glance at Gato.

"What are you doing, you sly girl?" Gato balled a fist in obvious frustration. "You think I'm as easily fooled as my father's old mule, and that I'll just tell you where our target is?"

He let out a laugh. "So, all this thinking you've been doing has come to nothing. See! You've wasted so much time and given all the others a head start. Like I said, you won't find it without looking for it. It's not just going to miraculously appear."

He seemed smug and self-satisfied. Well, I was still determined to wipe that stupid grin from his face. So, I ignored him, continuing in the same manner as I'd left off, mentioning other places within and around the villa while his face reddened with impatience. He thought he knew better. No, he *knew* that he did.

His grin spread wider, and it wasn't a pleasant one. Now, he must surely have been thinking how he'd shown superiority over a stupid girl.

My plan hadn't worked out quite as I had hoped, the answer remaining elusive. However, when I mentioned "dining room," his mouth twitched. It was a telling sign; I was confident he had made a mistake.

"Thank you," I called out and bolted toward the dining room. "What did I tell you?" I added, running toward the small chamber at the end of the atrium, near the study.

The room was sparse with little space remaining, but the rabbit had to be here. Gato had most likely confirmed it with his facial expression just a short moment ago, unable to suppress the awkward twitch from the corner of his lip. *Where do I start?* I thought, then searched through the first of the grimy couches, sneezing as I flipped over each cushion and pillow.

The minuscule specks of dust all seized the opportunity of leaving their old home, now swirling playfully in the shafts of light strobing through the shutter of the window.

I could have sworn I almost heard them laughing.

Moving onto the next couch, in between another sneeze, I spotted two tiny ears between a pile of embroidered cushions. "Aha! Found you!"

Grabbing the ears, I pulled out a little wooden rabbit, the target of our game.

"B-But you... you cheated!" Dashing into the room, Gato snatched the rabbit from my hand and raised his arm high up in the air. "I'll take this. You should know that cheating isn't allowed. It's not fair to the others. Thanks to you, we'll now have to start all over again."

"Gimme! It's mine!" my tiny voice squeaked as I jumped, trying to get *my* rabbit back. But the highest I could reach was the edge of his sleeve.

"It's not fair. I didn't cheat, and you know it."

Gradually, all the other kids followed Gato into the room. "Hey! Vita found the rabbit," Marcellus, a younger boy, exclaimed. "Where did you find it—"

"No, she *didn't* find it. Well, she *did* find it, but only because she cheated, tricking me into divulging its hiding spot. Cheat!" Gato yelled, puffy cheeks turning from red to purple.

"Cheat! Cheat!" the other kids chorused with him.

"No, I'm not a cheat!" I yelled back as tears began to well, but I refused to let go of Gato's sleeve. "You're only acting like this because you didn't believe in what I was trying to do! And because it worked, you're behaving like a spoiled child. Give it back!"

"What are you children doing?" A familiar voice sounded from behind the curtain. It parted, and a slender boy with chestnut-colored, curly hair came in.

He looked a little older than the rest of us, wearing a rough, wool tunic with patches. His tender, warm eyes glistened in the dark room, and the moment I saw them, a surge of peace filled my heart.

Then, the boy turned his gaze toward us and asked, "Who said Vita was a cheat?"

No one replied.

"Well, from what I can see, it seems like her secret plan worked. Well done, Vita, for coming up with such a clever plan."

"Rufus, the rabbit is mine!" Seeing Rufus made my voice grow louder in confidence. "*I* found it, but *Gato* stole it from me. Gato's a thief."

"No, *she* cheated!" Gato remonstrated again. "You are supposed to look for the rabbit, look for it with your eyes, that's all, not... not *trick* people. The way you went about it was all wrong! It was devious. It's not the game. It's not the rules!"

I was way too young back then to know what "devious" meant. But the fact that Gato could use such fancy words while I couldn't only fueled my frustration.

Meanwhile, Gato's angry voice stuttered as he stomped his feet.

And he hadn't finished yelling yet. "The rules—and you know them, Vita—are that you all stand against the wall with your eyes closed as I count down. Then, when I give you the signal, you open your eyes, and go *hunt* the rabbit. You don't pace about thinking, coming up with cunning ruses, trying to trick me into disclosing the hiding place."

As soon as I saw his hand lower, I gave another jump, grabbing hold of the rabbit from his fingertips, trying to wriggle it free. *Let go, let go, let go,* my mind said. *It's mine!*

"Well, gimme my rabbit," I yelled, but he still wouldn't let go, and we jostled for it.

Rufus, the eldest among us, stepped in to intervene, but as the curtain parted once more, a stout woman wearing a bright yellow linen gown barged into the room, her thick neck nearly concealed by a chunky gold necklace.

Next, she rushed forward, grabbing Gato's ear.

She wasted no time before dragging him toward the door. I worked out that this was Gato's mother, and his facial expression told me that he was not at all pleased at her appearance.

"How many times must I warn you not to play with dirty and malnourished rats? You are the village chief's son. Don't you forget that! And you lot"—she looked at the others—"should know better than to lead my son astray. If I catch you around him again—"

She did not end her sentence. Thankfully. This was because Gato interrupted.

"But Mom, I want to play with them! V-Vita might be sneaky, but she is so pretty!" Gato's voice sounded teary when he was roughly dragged away, kicking and crying out.

"Oh, by Juno! And you've just admitted you were tricked by that scrawny rat! Look at her hair, the color of a barbarian's! And she doesn't even know who her parents are..."

Rufus covered my ears with his hands.

The woman went on, "For shame on you all!"

As quickly as Eleonora's falcon taking flight, mother and son both left the villa, Gato being dragged behind his mama, protesting as he went.

The younger kids looked at each other, not knowing what to do now. Some of the older ones hung their heads low, looking dejected. It was strange when Gato was not around; he steered and commanded everyone.

Lifting me, Rufus threw me over his shoulder and called out to all the children, "That's it for today. Time to go home, younglings."

The young rabble naturally obeyed the older boy as if he were a big brother, and they set off walking toward the door. "Don't look too disheartened. Come on, raise up your head."

Little Marcellus was the first to reach the curtain, and suddenly, he turned and giggled. "Look, Rufus is carrying his little bride! Quick! Come see!"

The other kids turned their heads, and as they saw Rufus holding me upside-down, they all shouted together, "Little bride! Little bride!"

Days before, we had all been playing house together in this same abandoned villa, Rufus and I playing at being newlyweds. I hadn't felt anything special that day, but today, somehow, those same two words made my cheeks burn.

"Come on, you younglings. Stop teasing. We aren't playing house today. Now run home before I kick your little behinds." Rufus laughed and pretended to kick out at them, sending the kids scampering off in high-pitched squeals.

He supported me with one hand and headed toward the room's door. "We must go home too. Nana needs our help with those baskets."

"Put me down! I'm six years old now." I pouted. "I can walk without your help. Come on, drop me down please."

"No. If I let you walk all the way home, you'll get hungry and eat all the food we have for the day." Rufus chuckled as he walked. "And *I'm* hungry, so you're staying put."

"No, no, you eat more than I do!" I yelled, punching his shoulder and trying to wriggle free, but it was no use. Yes, I was six, but I wasn't strong enough to escape his grip.

"I can see our little Vita is really hungry now."

"No, I'm not," I scoffed. "I never said I was hungry."

Rufus laughed and said, "You don't need to say you are. Someone is always a little defensive when she has an appetite."

"No, I'm just annoyed. And what about the rabbit? It *is* mine, you know." I pursed my lips in protest when I thought about my lost booty. "Shouldn't we head to the village chief's home to get it back? I'm sure Gato will see sense and hand it over."

"I tell you what; I'll make one for you. More beautiful than that one. I promise."

"You will?" Knowing Rufus' crafting skill, I decided to let go of the one I didn't get.

"Of course. When did I ever not fulfill my promise?" Still on Rufus' shoulder, we entered the dimly lit atrium, shafts of light coming down from the tall, weed-infested roof.

Each of the many wall paintings was covered with thick dust and spider webs. Farther along, we passed a marble statue, and even though it was also covered with dust, I could still make out the form a beautiful matron, with olive-shaped eyes and braided hair tied high. With a blank look and no affection on her face, she held a baby in her arms.

Nana had once told me the villa belonged to an extraordinarily rich woman in Rome. It was built about eleven years ago, and she moved in with a man soon after. However, a few years later, she left. Since then, the villa had been deserted, providing us kids with an ideal playground."

"Is she the woman Nana mentioned?" I asked. "The one from Rome?"

"Could be her," Rufus replied mindlessly.

"She is so beautiful. But there's something I'm unsure of."

"What is that?"

"I just don't like the way she looks at the baby. What do you think?"

"I didn't really notice, but remind me to look next time."

I was still thinking about the Roman matron when Rufus crossed the threshold. Suddenly, a cluster of red gladioli caught my eye, blooming like fire near the steps.

"Rufus, look!" I exclaimed, my tiny fingers reaching out toward the blooms. "I want that."

"What, one of these?" he asked. "Which one?"

"The biggest one!"

Rufus leaned over, plucking the fullest blossom, and handed it to me.

"Did you know this is the place where I found you? Right here where the gladioli grow. I remember there were no flowers here before, but after we found you, the red gladioli bloomed every year. Maybe it's a gift from the angels to you."

Rufus' smile was as bright as the sunshine above our heads.

That story, even though he'd told it to me so many times, still made my heart cheerful. It was a story I'd never forget, and one I'd always be grateful for.

"It was the coldest winter night I ever remembered. I told Nana I heard a baby crying somewhere, but she didn't believe me. Her ears were failing back then—"

"And you begged her to go and take a look when the rooster crowed the first time," I continued the story. "You begged and begged her."

"Yes, you were so little and cried so much that you had no strength to cry anymore. Thank God, you let out a cry again when I came closer." Rufus inhaled deeply and continued, "Jesus must have seen you and sent angels to squeeze your little cheeks. Otherwise, I would never have found you, at least maybe not soon enough."

"No, you will always find me, because I'm your little bride," I whispered into Rufus' ear.

"You silly little girl. Do you even know what little bride means?" Rufus pinched my chin gently. "I think I need to explain it to you once again."

"Of course, I know!" I beamed. "It means Vita and Rufus, together forever, and no one can separate us."

The summer sun shone on my face, making me squint at the brightness.

I was six years old, wearing shabby clothes, always hungry, and despised by wealthy people, but with Rufus' and Nana's love, I was never scared to face the world.

As we arrived home, Nana stood by the door, her hands resting on her hips.

"I think I'm in trouble," Rufus said. "Wait for it."

"What took you so long? I told you to go bring Vita home, not join in and play with the kids," Nana said with a stern look at Rufus.

Rufus chuckled and was about to explain when I started talking, same as always. It was hard for anyone to get a word in when I was around. "No, Nana, he didn't join us. I won today, but they wouldn't let me have it," I started before Rufus dropped me. "They said I cheated, but I didn't. You know I wouldn't cheat, don't you, Nana?"

"Wouldn't let you have what?" Nana said, holding my hand, and we entered our house.

I shared with Nana everything that had unfolded that day, only pausing as my gaze landed on the generous bowl of soup and bread placed by the window. Giving her a hug, I hurried over to the table, quickly finishing my prayer. Then, I eagerly tore a chunk of bread and dipped it into the piping hot soup. "Vita, you shouldn't always be so bold like this. Gato is the village chief's son. You will get into trouble," Nana said after Rufus and I almost finished our meals. "And where were you, Rufus, when all this was afoot?"

"Nothing to worry about, Nana, and it all happened before he arrived. But Rufus will always protect me. That I am sure of."

"Rufus will be ten years old next month. And in a few years, he will be looking for a wife and starting his own family. He won't be there for you forever," Nana said matter-of-factly.

"But I'm his little bride!" I cried out. "He can't be looking for someone else. Isn't that right, Rufus? Even the others are calling me that now. Little bride, they call me."

"What a silly girl!" Nana ruffled my hair and pulled me into her arms, but I didn't like it that both she and Rufus kept calling me silly each time I said I was Rufus' little bride.

After dinner, Nana gave us both a little piece of extra bread as a treat and let us enjoy it sitting in the backyard. The soup was amazing, and Rufus had been right all along; I was hungry.

See, Rufus knows me better than anyone—because I am his little bride!

As the sun set, the forest and barns in the distance became bathed in a warm golden glow. The cool summer breeze danced through the trees, rustling the leaves and carrying with it the delightful scent of blooming flowers, bringing the sweet pollen on the wind.

The sky looked incredible, painted with hues of orange, pink and purple, creating a picturesque scene that was nothing short of breathtaking.

"Rufus, the sun is going down behind the forest! If you look carefully and focus on a point, you can see it lowering. Lower and lower... until it sinks into the treetops."

"Yes, it's beautiful, isn't it?" Rufus said. "It's so peaceful too."

"When it comes back tomorrow, is it the same sun or a different one? Are there so many that they take turns to come to different parts of the land?"

"Not sure. I guess it is the same one," Rufus replied. "God created the sun. Nana said our God is so powerful, and He created everything——the sun, the moon, the land, the sea and all living things."

"Rufus, if the same sun goes down and comes back again, why doesn't the day come back anymore?"

"Why? It does come back. Tomorrow, the daytime will be back." Rufus looked at me, perplexed.

"But it's not the same day. We have yesterday, today, and tomorrow, and they're all different days. This day, today, is but one day of my life. It never comes back. And I'll even forget about it very soon, not to mention others forget too," I said with a sigh. "Sometimes, I think, what if I can keep this day forever? So that it never leaves me, and I can live the same day for the rest of my life, over and over, catch it in my hands, not let it go..."

"Oh, you have me confused now. Sometimes, I don't understand what is happening in this little head of yours, sweet Vita." Rufus smiled and rubbed my temples playfully. "But that makes my little Vita so special, one of a kind."

Two

A Little Tablet

I PUSHED OPEN THE wooden shutters, and my eyes were drawn to the sun's gradual ascent behind the distant hill. Its slow rise only fueled my excitement, making me wish I could give it a little lift.

I just turned nine two months ago, and that day Nana had given me special permission to accompany Rufus on his trip to Paphos, the bustling city on our island. It would be my first time!

Every month Rufus would travel there to sell the baskets Nana had woven and bring back groceries. The amusing tales he would tell when he got back were something I always enjoyed hearing, and I couldn't wait for the day to experience them firsthand.

One such story that stood out in my mind was the tale of a trickster at the market. It was said that he could turn one coin into many. Rufus' eyes sparkled as he recounted the story of the man being singled out and given lots of money.

"I was standing right behind the chosen man that day, and I couldn't help but envy him. Oh, how I longed to be in his shoes, for if I were, I could have brought home a large jug of exquisite olive oil," he exclaimed. "Yet, I soon discovered they were in cahoots, merely pretending to dupe people into giving them money."

Apart from that, he also shared other tales with me, funny ones, thrilling ones——or sometimes both.

So, when Nana eventually told me I could tag along with Rufus on his next trip to Paphos, I gave her a big squeeze and danced around our little hut in circles.

"Thank you, Nana! I really cannot thank you enough!"

The trip to Paphos would require nearly two hours of walking from our village. When I said "walk", I meant that term lightly. Fortunately for me, I was seated on the back of Phoebe, our old donkey, while Rufus walked in front of us, holding her reins. Looking down, I noticed the sway of Phoebe's sturdy frame, her muscles rippling beneath her coat.

A gentle breeze ruffled the hem of my dress, my smile broadening. So excited was I about the trip that I'd had to wear my favorite dress. It was a beautiful, carmine gown, meticulously embroidered by Nana. The apricot flowers were carefully stitched by her skillful hands, disguising an old cut.

Thanks to that cut, Rufus managed to get it from a village tailor for only five copper coins last year.

Looking at my waist, a small satchel hung strapped there, containing three loaves of bread, a handful of dried figs and five silver coins, as well as twelve coppers. Nana had put them there before we left home, knowing we'd be hungry before the trip ended.

The coins had come from the sales of our family's basket-crafting business.

"Children, tomorrow we won't be selling baskets; all I want you to do is to visit Elder Flavius' congregation and give the silver coins to him. Be very careful. Hold them tight!" Nana had told us the night before.

"Five silver coins? But Nana, that's one month's earnings from our basket sales!" Rufus exclaimed when he watched Nana place the coins into the satchel.

"It's called offering. A way to show our love and gratitude to God," Nana said. "And He has blessed us abundantly! Look! Our baskets have been selling extremely well this year and we even have some extra copper coins for olive oil."

I loved olive oil. Gato, the village chief's son, the one who'd accused me of cheating, always used it on his hair. It smelled so delicious that I sometimes had the urge to lick his head. But, of course, I never did. Goodness knows what tales would have made it back to Nana if I had given in to my urge!

Our meals at home were not often cooked with oil, so I could already imagine the look of delight on Nana's face when she would smell the fragrant scent of the olive oil we'd bring back home. It would be such a delight and a rarity for all of us.

"Why won't Nana come with us?" I asked as I ruffled Phoebe's mane. "I wish she'd come savor this. It's a lovely day, and the sunshine is good for her aching bones."

"Well, Nana used to come to Paphos often," Rufus said. "But the trip has become too much for her in her old age lately. Besides, she knew you would like to see the city, and Phoebe can only carry one person. Otherwise, she would love to hear Elder Flavius preach."

"Who's Elder Flavius?" I asked, seeing Rufus grinning at my many questions.

"He's an elder of the Christian congregation in Paphos. Nana said he had learned from Paul the Apostle when Paul was on a trip to Paphos eleven years ago."

"Paul the *Apollo?* That's a very strange name for him!"

"No, Paul the *Apostle*... apostles, that means Jesus' chief disciples. Jesus sent them out personally to establish churches and tell all the people the good news."

"Yes, I remember now!" I exclaimed with delight, suddenly impressed at my own memory and feeling very clever. "I remember, I remember, I remember! Nana told us the story of the Apostle Peter. She said he fell into the water when he tried walking on it. When I heard that, I laughed so hard that I even dropped a bowl." I giggled again as the memory came to me.

At the time, however, I was not old enough to fully grasp the significance of what was happening, but just listening to Rufus' stories and observations brought me joy.

Before I knew it, it was almost noon, and we arrived at a spacious area where a grand temple stood at the center. In front of it was a statue of a goddess with golden wings and cow horns. Beside the statue stood a man dressed in a shining, white robe adorned with fringes and golden bells. In his right hand, he held a rattle-like musical instrument.

As he circled around the men and women kneeling before the statue, he shook the instrument and chanted continuously.

"He must be a priest from the Temple of Isis," Rufus said, his eyebrows furrowed in disapproval. "The elder people in our village told me that Isis used to be an Egyptian goddess, but she has become extremely popular these days in all the major cities. They also said that her priests sometimes buy young girls from the slave market to serve as temple prostitutes, just like in many other temples."

Suddenly, the priest turned his gaze in our direction, his eyes fixating on me.

Rufus noticed too and quickly pulled me forward, tugging my hand as he led us away, avoiding the priest's gaze.

"Here is the marketplace. Now, let's go find Octavius' stand," he said hastily.

Taking in my surroundings, I was overwhelmed by a wave of exhilaration, a sensation I had never experienced before.

Encircling the temple were buildings on all four sides, and alongside these stood a plethora of small canopies supported by wooden poles. Underneath each one, a long table had been placed, laden with all sorts of goods from fresh seafood to ripe fruits. And standing beside the tables, vendors called out to passing customers, showcasing their latest produce.

The market was alive with the salty aroma of octopus, squid, and red prawns, mixed with the sweet fragrance of figs and pomegranates.

"Stay with me at all times, you understand? As you can see, it gets extremely busy here, and the vendors are persistent in getting trade.

So, you may get distracted," Rufus said, taking the lead as we made our way through the market.

After navigating through a few twists and turns, we finally arrived at a petite stall, sheltered by a modest canopy upheld by two flimsy-looking poles. Beneath the canopy was a table, upon which sat terracotta jars of various forms and shapes, each one unique and captivating. I couldn't help but reach out and run my fingers over the curves and indentations of the jars, imagining the hands that had shaped them and the stories they could tell.

Suddenly, a plump man in his forties popped out from behind the jars and gave Rufus a heavy pat on the shoulder. "Well, look who it is! Rufus, you are growing into a strong young man now. I can't believe it!" Then his eyes cast toward me, and they brightened. "No, it can't be! Is that little Vita?" I nodded, and the man continued, "Dear child, you were only a baby when I left the village. Now look at you, such a charming young lady."

His greasy fingers reached for my cheeks, and I couldn't help but giggle, squirming away from his touch. As he noticed the shine on my cheeks, a bashful grin spread across his face, and he hurriedly wiped his hands on his apron.

"Sorry, I was just handling a spilled olive oil jar. But olive oil is wonderful for your skin, sweet Vita. When you are as old as me and still have no wrinkles, you will be thanking me."

We all laughed.

Then he asked, "How is Nana?"

"Thanks, Octavius. Nana is doing well. She always remembers your kindness to our family before you moved to Paphos," Rufus said, swiftly wiping away the remaining oil from my face with his thumb. "We are going to Elder Flavius' sermon today. Would you mind if we tied old Phoebe near your stand? We'll be back in about an hour to get her—as well as one jar of olive oil." Rufus pointed to a small plain jar with a pointed tip on the stand.

"Besides," he slyly added, "the olive oil is necessary for Vita's aging skin."

We laughed again, and I play-kicked his shin. He danced around, feigning a terrible injury. "Vita, you are a cruel girl!" he joked.

Octavius seemed to take great joy from watching our rapport. "Go ahead. My pleasure," he said. "And I'll get your olive oil ready before you come back. Perhaps old Phoebe might like some vegetables while she waits? What do you say?"

"That would be most excellent and kind," exclaimed Rufus. "She needs more meat on those skinny ribs of hers."

"Then consider it done, friend," said Octavius, leaning forward to pick a carrot from a basket under his table and offer it to the donkey. "After all, a man cannot have a guest and not feed her, can he? That would be rude of me." He patted Phoebe's neck.

Afterwards, he went about clearing up the space around a nearby pole and tying old Phoebe's reins to it. "Please send my greetings to Elder Flavius. And tell him I'll attend his sermon next week when the busy market season is over. I'm sure my absence has not passed unnoticed."

"Why can't Phoebe come with us?" I asked loudly and ruffled her mane, not willing to leave our old friend behind, not even if she would be royally fed and watered. "Please, let's bring her with us to Elder Flavius' place," I begged.

Rufus scowled, something I rarely saw from him.

"Vita, we are in Paphos, not our village. Horse thieves are everywhere. At least by leaving her at the stall, Octavius can keep an eye on her."

I didn't object. Phoebe was too important to our family to be taken by thieves.

Elder Flavius' congregation held their meetings on the second floor of a potter's workshop located at the secluded end of the market, near the city theater, behind a wooden partition. Nana had told us that the inaccessibility of the location was to keep curious eyes at bay, particularly those of neighboring onlookers.

"Christians aren't popular among the people in Paphos," Nana had warned the night before. "Especially after Governor Sergius

Paulus, who was also converted by the Apostle Paul, returned to Rome eight years ago. So, be careful when you go to the congregation."

"Rufus, why do people hate us?"

"Well, I can't say for sure, but this is what I think. It's because our God is different. He doesn't have temples or sculptures. He doesn't require altar sacrifices. People think it's so weird to worship an 'invisible' God."

"Oh." I sank into contemplation.

"And when we have bread and wine together, it's a symbol of eating Jesus' flesh and drinking His blood. But there are rumors that we really eat infants alive."

Rufus' voice became a little crosser, but when he looked down at my feet, his anger transformed into laughter. "Vita, caution is good, but you won't have to tiptoe the last mile of our trip." Rufus couldn't hide his amusement at seeing how I was standing.

I was about to argue. "But Nana said..."

A burst of chaotic laughter and teasing caught my attention a few feet in front of us. At the turn of the arcade, a group of boys gathered around a column, their backs bent as if focusing on something at the center.

"What on earth are they doing there? I need to see." I couldn't contain my curiosity and quickly moved forward before Rufus could stop me.

"Vita, wait!" Rufus called, but it was too late. I pushed through the wall of bodies, making my way to the center of the group. There, lying on the marbled floor, was a frail brown bird with a pale-yellow beak. It was limping, its leg dragging behind as it attempted to fly but failed, letting out pitiful chirps.

"Look how funny the stupid bird is."

"It crawls like a crippled street dog."

The boys teased and laughed, which filled my lungs with rage. Rushing forward, I picked up the bird and shouted, "Do not laugh at her! She's hurt already! Leave her alone!"

"Who is this?" a boy sneered. "Where did this stupid girl come from?"

"Look at the dress she's wearing! Who made that stupid flower? It can't even cover the patch." A chubby boy stepped forward and grabbed a corner of my dress.

I tried to push his hand away and shouted, "It is not stupid! My Nana did it for me and she is the best!" I shouted even louder when I saw Rufus approaching our crowd with hastened steps. "And you were so mean to this poor little bird!"

The boys became flushed with anger, and a few of them began rubbing their hands together eagerly, showing they were eager for a fight.

Rufus' voice boomed behind us. "Let go of her!"

Before the boys could react, the sound of a bell echoed through the area, causing them to scatter in a single direction. Rufus quickly came to my side, kneeling beside me, checking for any signs of injury.

"Vita, what were you thinking? That was dangerous! They could've hurt you," he said, sighing in relief and concern. "I told you to stay close. You should really listen to me."

"But you'll protect me, won't you?" I gave him a broad, trusting stare.

"Oh, Vita, you always keep me on my toes, you know?" Rufus shook his head in resignation and ruffled my hair fondly. "Now, how should we handle this little one?" he said, changing the subject and focusing on the bird I was still holding.

I looked around and then up and noticed a small brown nest perched on top of the column capital. The poor little thing must have fallen from there.

"Rufus, give me a boost!" I said, my eyes shining with determination.

He let out a sigh, understanding my request, then stooping. "Hurry up, we still have things to do."

"Got it!" I said confidently, quickly climbing onto Rufus' back. With a gentle push, he helped me up onto his shoulders. Regaining my balance and using one hand to steady myself on the column, I carefully placed the bird back in its nest. "There you go, little bird. You'll be safe here. May the Lord protect you."

"Is it done?" Rufus asked, breathing heavily.

"Yes, you can lower me now. We did it!" I exclaimed, giving a joyful twirl as Rufus set me back on the ground. At that moment, I heard the distant chanting of the boys, so grabbing Rufus' hand, I pulled him along as we headed toward the commotion.

As we approached, the voices were clearer.

It was the same group of boys we had encountered before, now gathered around a column at the next turn of the arcade. In the center was a middle-aged man, his posture stiff and erect as he sat beside the column.

Dressed in a light beige tunic, he had a thick gray beard, his face stern as he held the boys' attention. In his hand was a tablet, upon which he wrote with a wooden stick. Every time he finished writing, he would hold up the tablet for the boys to see and let them recite the words he had written.

"It's a school, which I've mentioned to you before," Rufus said. "Local families pool their resources and hire a teacher to educate their sons together. In our village, only the chief's household has one, for their family's use."

"Oh, so the one with a thick beard is the teacher." I tilted my little head. "Can I join them?" I begged. "Just to listen for a while."

"Well... One, they rarely include girls in this type of thing. Two, it is paid for, and we have not contributed. And lastly, Nana sent us somewhere and we don't have all day," Rufus said as his hands found mine. "We must hurry before the service is over. We don't want Nana upset. This is your first trip here, and I'm sure there'll be plenty more. So maybe next time. If we plan it correctly, we can build in time for it."

"All right." I followed Rufus reluctantly but kept looking back to the "school", the boys' reciting voices like a melody in my ears. *Rufus is right. Paphos is so different.*

Upon arriving at the city theater, we found a small red ochre house discreetly tucked behind a wooden partition, just as Nana had described it.

Its entrance featured a niche in which an array of pots and vases of varying shapes and colors were showcased on shelves.

"This should be it. Nana said the house belonged to a potter," Rufus said, pointing to the ceramics. He tried the door, finding it was unlocked. Giving a shrug, he opened the door, and we headed up to the second floor.

An old woman with thin, white hair pulled back in a tight bun welcomed us with a broad smile and received the silver coins from Rufus' hands.

The service had already started, the congregation singing a familiar song when we got there. I loved to sing, especially if it was one of my favorites among those Nana had taught me. However, something about "school" intrigued me so much.

Why was I unable to join in? Of course, Rufus had explained, but it was not as though a vast fence or wall prevented me from simply positioning myself beside the boys in their incantations.

It ought to be so easy, and the scene just wouldn't get out of my mind.

Peeking at Rufus, I could see he was already engrossed in worship. *Surely, I can,* I thought. Inching my way back from him, I stared up. He still didn't notice, his eyes shut tight.

Pausing for a few seconds, I then quietly made my way toward the door, sneaking out and hurrying downstairs, pulse racing. The idea that I could learn to read and write somehow expanded my imagination, leading me to fantasize about putting down on parchment the ridiculous stories that often popped into my mind.

"I'd be able to write stories. Oh my," I muttered, making my way back to the arcade.

On getting there, the boys were reading what was written on the tablet, but this time, without the teacher saying it first.

"Veni..." I joined in the chorusing, making sure I wasn't loud enough to be heard. Hidden behind a column to the rear of the boys, I occasionally peeked out to see the next word.

"Read it twenty times. Hopefully, you will remember it when I return," the teacher said. Ready to leave, he set his tablet on his chair—suddenly, his eyes caught me.

"What are you doing here, girl?" His brow furrowed even more. He had his arm raised and was pointing, so everyone around could turn to notice me. And they did exactly that.

I almost fainted, stepping out from the column behind which I was supposed to have concealed myself. "I-I want to know how to read and write."

I must not let fear drown my voice, came the thought. *I must be bold, act with courage.*

"I have never seen anything like this before in my village. I-I'm here in Paphos with Rufus. It's my first time here. A-a school is a wonderful thing to me."

"I am sure it is! But let me ask you then... What's the point of school for you, little girl? You'll get married in a few years and have children. It is of no use to learn these things," he said, rolling his eyes. "And where exactly is this Rufus? I don't see him. If he's old enough to bring you to the city, he should know better than to let you roam around here."

The boys, who had all turned to face me, burst into laughter. "Go back to your dolls," teased the chubby boy who grabbed my dress earlier, and the rest joined him.

As the teacher left, seemingly disinterested, the boys' taunts persisted. "Girls who think they can read and write are morons," one of them mocked.

This was the tipping point. My decorum and sensitivity abandoned me completely.

I pounced on the boy who said it. The other boys, however, quickly took the chubby boy's side. In a flash, one yanked my hair and lifted me from the marble floor.

"Get off me! You mean boys!" I screamed and kicked the air.

Suddenly, out of nowhere, the fat boy holding onto my hair landed face down on the floor with a thud.

It was Rufus who had saved me.

He was not any taller than most of these unruly boys, but they all backed down when they saw him readying his fist for whoever wanted it next. It must have been down to the look in his eyes; they glowered, like thunder breaking through the clouds, his pupils darkened.

The chubby boy who just received a blow from him was struggling to stand, covering his cheek with one hand. "How dare you! Don't you know my father works for the city council?"

He then shouted to the other boys, "Lucas, Tigus, Cyrus, let's get him together! The tickets for tonight's gladiator show are on me!"

My heart pounded wildly as I clutched tightly to the hem of Rufus' tunic. "Run, Vita," Rufus whispered urgently. "I'll handle them. Please just go and hide among the shops across the street. I'll find you."

"No, you'll get hurt," I cried out, my heart heavy with guilt for getting Rufus into trouble.

Suddenly, the teacher appeared, bellowing, "What's going on here? Does anyone crave a spanking so much that they cry out for one? Show your faces, those wishing to get in line!"

Rufus immediately shouted, "Run!" and pulled me along, darting out of the arcade and blending into the crowd like two rabbits fleeing from wolves.

After hurrying as fast as I could for several blocks, I was out of breath and stooped over. Rufus looked around to ensure we were no longer in danger, then bent down to wipe away my tears and smooth out my rumpled dress.

"Rufus, was I acting like an idiot?" I asked, my voice quivering.

"No, they're just mean boys. You must know that," Rufus said as he hugged me. "If God put the desire to learn into your heart, there must be a reason."

I nodded in agreement, but my spirits soon plummeted once

more. "We don't have the money to buy a tablet, not even to go to school."

"Not to worry, Vita. I shall buy one for you, and you can learn on your own," Rufus said, patting my head.

"But where will you get the money?"

"Let's just use the money Nana gave us to buy olive oil."

"But Nana will be angry," I said, worried. "No, we can't do that. That was one of the reasons we came here."

"It will work out, Vita. It will all be fine. I'll take on additional work at the village chief's farm at night to pay Nana back. Besides, Nana has never stayed mad at me for more than a day." He gently tugged my hand, leading me toward a small shop down the street.

The small shop had a quaint facade but was surprisingly spacious inside. Rows of shelves lined both sides, displaying an array of scrolls and parchment made from the finest papyrus and animal skins. At the end of one shelf on the left stood a stack of wooden writing tablets.

"I see you are drawn to these," the shop owner said, making his way over to us. "These are practice tablets," he added. "Ten copper coins each. If you wish to learn... it costs."

Rufus took the satchel from me, then handed over the coins and received the tablet from the shop owner's hand. When he gave it to me, I was overjoyed. With trembling hands, I carefully examined the tablet, tracing my fingers over its smooth, waxed surface. Then I carefully stashed it away in my satchel. With a heart full of gratitude, I wrapped my arms and legs around Rufus. "Thank you! Thank you so much!"

"Hey, stop that! You silly octopus!" Rufus exclaimed, giving me a hug back.

The skinny shop owner, sporting a goatee, gestured toward a small jar filled with pointed wooden sticks. "You'll need a stylus to write on it," he said. "These are five coins each."

"No, I'll make one for her." Rufus grinned and tugged on my hand as we left the store.

As expected, Nana was furious when she found out that Rufus had used the coins to purchase a writing tablet instead of olive oil. "Reading and writing are not useful for our family," she exclaimed in anger. "What are we supposed to cook our food with, Rufus? Explain yourself!"

I quickly interjected, "It was my fault, Nana. I kept asking Rufus and he just gave in because I was crying so hard and couldn't stop. But he did say you would only be mad with us for a day."

Nana shook her head, knowing I was right.

We continued to eat our meals without the use of oil. Although Nana never asked for repayment, Rufus took on an additional job as a night watchman at the village chief's farm for an entire month, and finally saved enough money to buy a jar of olive oil as an apology to Nana.

After returning from Paphos, I would rise early every morning and devote time to practicing my writing on the tablet.

Rufus taught me how to write numbers and letters, as that was all he knew. One day, as we stacked chopped wood together in the backyard, I asked him, "If we had lots of money, would you want to go to school with me? We could learn to read and write together. What do you say?"

"Absolutely, I would," he replied. "I've always dreamed that one day, I'd open up a little basket shop right on the busiest street in Paphos. And when someone comes in to place a big order, I figure I should at least know how to write his name."

"But beyond that," I said. "Don't you want to learn more? Like reading poems, comedies, and dramas. After all, I'll need someone to read all the stories I write."

"I've never thought about that. Nana said these things are not suitable for families like ours who can barely support themselves," he said and gently placed his hand on my shoulder. "But I'll work hard and make more money to buy scrolls for *you* to study. And if I get time, then I will also learn."

"You are the best, Rufus." I planted a kiss on his cheek.

I yearned to whisper to him that in the story I penned in my dreams, his name graced every page. Yet, at that innocent age of nine, an inexplicable longing urged me to safeguard these words, like a precious secret meant for my heart alone.

Three

The Longest Wait

Sparks danced above the shallow basin, adorned with glowing charcoals, filling our small hut with comforting warmth. Meanwhile, the wind howled relentlessly against the cracked walls, stealing the little heat we were meant to enjoy. As unusual as it was for Cyprus, Nana said this was the coldest winter in the past ten years.

Although our neighbor's rooster had yet to crow, Nana and I were already busy weaving baskets with dried gladioli leaves.

My fingers fluttered over those leaves like a butterfly, coiling and looping them into different shapes. Years of training under Nana's guidance had honed my skills.

But that day, I couldn't fully concentrate on my work. From the open door, I could see Rufus out in the front yard, loading baskets onto the cart. His bustling movements kept pulling my attention away from my weaving.

Just as old Phoebe suddenly sneezed, my fingers faltered, and the sharp edge of the leaf pricked my skin. In that moment, a fierce gust of wind blew by, sending the baskets tumbling to the ground with a soft thud, and they rolled away in different directions.

I set down my unfinished basket and dashed into the front yard.

"Do you have to go?" I asked, tugging at his sleeve. "There might not be many customers at the harbor because of the weather."

I hesitantly helped him stack the baskets back in place, then went on, "Do you think it'll be worth the effort today? This weather doesn't look as if it will give up anytime soon."

"I show up there every week, regardless of the weather," Rufus said. "That's how we build up our business. Each of my customers knows I'm reliable, and if I don't show, they will find someone else to buy from. It's taken hard work to get to where we are, and we'll continue to do the same. One missed market day, and it could be our downfall."

"I know, but I can't help feeling worried," I said, tugging yet again on his sleeve, an action I used to do when I was a little girl.

Rufus leaned in, planting a soft kiss on my forehead. "Look, if you must know, it's your birthday, and I need money to buy you some rouge," he said. "You're thirteen now, which means you can soon be my true bride, and every bride needs her rouge."

I blushed, feeling the warmth rise to my cheeks as I looked into his eyes. "I don't need any rouge," I murmured. "All I want is to be with you. We can wed without blushes."

He still had more to say.

"Well, it's not just the rouge. Don't you remember when you said you wanted a Greek prose scroll, so you could learn from it? If our baskets sell well, I'll be able to get one for you."

My heart swelled with affection. *Was he truly considering buying me a scroll? But I couldn't accept it.* "I was joking about that. Five pieces of silver for a scroll? Nana would be furious. I do believe it would be the end of her. Besides, I don't know more than five words in Greek," I said, touched that Rufus remembered my interests. "Moreover, I've heard the city is not safe these days. Last month, Old Aulus went there to sell dried fish and he was robbed and beaten by a gang outside the city gates. Haven't you heard about it?"

"Don't worry, silly girl." Rufus pinched my cheeks. "Old Aulus probably got drunk again. I'm much more careful than him. I promise you, no matter how many baskets are sold, I'll head back home before the crowds rush to the city bath in the afternoon."

Feeling his determination, I hurried back inside to retrieve a handful of fig pies from the table. Swiftly tucking them into his satchel, I pleaded, "Please, promise me you won't go hungry. Nana and I will wait for you to return before having dinner."

We embraced for a long moment before finally parting.

I watched as he secured the load on the cart, an unsettling rumble at the base of my guts, an ill feeling growing in my senses as he mounted and turned with one last smile.

"Lord, please bring him home safely," I whispered, offering a heartfelt prayer for reassurance.

When Rufus vanished at the end of the winding lane, I went back inside to help Nana with the cooking. That day was my birthday, or at least it was the day Rufus and Nana had found me, the closest thing I had to a real birthdate.

Every year on this day, Nana would do her best to cook something delicious for us.

Our home was small, and the kitchen, if you could call it that, was nothing more than a small brazier in the corner, with my favorite red bean stew simmering in the pot on top and two loaves of barley bread on the little table next to it.

Listening to one of Nana's stories, I placed a few more logs under the brazier. Nana's storytelling style was always captivating and spontaneous. Whatever she saw, she had a story to tell about it. So, when she was stirring the stew, she told the story of how Jacob, Israel's patriarch, had stolen his brother's birthright with a bowl of stew, probably made of red beans.

"Imagine that? A man selling his birthright for a plate of food. Humph!" she said before shaking her head. "You have to always remember what the most important thing to you is, my little Vita." She smiled and stroked my hair fondly.

I nodded with a blush, knowing there was nothing more important than my Rufus.

Being with him was undoubtedly the most important thing in my life, and just as sure as the sun rose each day, it would never change for as long as I lived. My thoughts were still musing on this when Nana's eyes spotted the barley bread. Now, she launched into a new tale, this one being of how Jesus had succeeded in feeding thousands of people with only five loaves of bread and two fish, one of my favorite stories from growing up. What she did not realize was that whenever she told me Jesus loved me, I only nodded, but I'd never taken these things seriously.

I had Nana's and Rufus' love, and that was enough for me. However, Nana's dedication was so contagious that I would sometimes say prayers like she did, just in case.

The sky turned dark, the rain threatening as thunder crackled. An ominous feeling was brewing in my gut, and my mind would also not settle. Not until Rufus came home.

If he'd headed back home in the early afternoon, he should have arrived already.

My palms became sweaty thinking about my earlier instinct.

"I'm sure he is fine and on his way. Might have spent too much time choosing just the right present for me," I said aloud to myself as if it would help. However, the uneasy feeling that something might go wrong only intensified, weighing down my spirits.

Nana had urged me to eat several times, and I finally gave in to her persistence. The food tasted like wax without Rufus' hearty laughter. It seemed bland, soulless, and as empty as I felt in his absence.

He would be telling embarrassing stories of my childhood if he were here. I would be blushing and trying to hit him, and he'd pinch my cheeks and make me giggle.

When the sky was as black as a raven's feathers, Rufus still hadn't shown up. My heart felt so heavy that it seemed to sink into my stomach.

Rufus was a considerate man and never delayed coming back home. He knew how much it meant to me and Nana to have him at the dinner table every night. Something must have gone wrong. Fear choked my heart.

· ♥ · ♥ · ♥ · ♥ · ♥ ·

Torches lit up the ink-like sky in the first hour into the night, and the panicked footsteps broke the serenity of the little village. With four neighbors by my side, I embarked on the search for Rufus.

Our cries calling his name echoed through the darkness, met only with silence.

We searched every abandoned alleyway and dark crevice along the route from our village to Paphos, fear gnawing at my heart as I dreaded the thought of discovering Rufus harmed or, worse yet, killed by the ruthless men preying on him.

For sure, his hard-earned money at the market made him an easy target for them.

When the eastern sky turned pale as a dead fish's belly, we arrived at the harbor where Rufus would go to sell baskets. The salty and chilly mist from the sea shrouded me like a cocoon which the rays of rising sun couldn't pierce. In the vicinity, fishermen were busy unloading their catch and mending their nets on small boats. A few shop owners were also dismantling planks from their closed shops along the seafront.

As my neighbors scattered to search for clues on their own, I rushed over to an elderly man struggling to open his fish sauce shop. "Sir, have you seen a young man around this height yesterday?" I gestured as I spoke. "He has dark, cinnamon-colored hair, and he was selling baskets."

"Let me think." He tilted his head, and his eyes narrowed suddenly. "Yes, I remember seeing a young lad who looked like that. It was yesterday in the early afternoon, and I was cleaning a big jar. The harbor was quite empty, so he caught my attention. He was driving a donkey with a cart loaded with baskets. Yes, I'm sure it was the same person."

"Did you happen to see where he was headed?"

"He came past, and then... That's right, he headed toward a merchant ship that had docked over there." He pointed to a dock behind us.

"And then what happened?"

Suddenly, his patience wore thin as I bombarded him with questions, something Rufus had warned me of so many times. "I don't know, young lady, do I?" he said with a shrug. "I'm a busy man trying to support my family; I do not have all day to sit here, eyeing strangers going about their own business. But now that I ponder on it, I do believe I may have seen him climbing up a rope ladder onto that ship. I think it was him, but it's a long way off, you know, and my eyes aren't what they used to be."

"Did he come out?"

"I don't remember. It's always a busy time for us. Now, if you don't mind..."

No doubt overhearing, a stout fisherman approached us. "We've heard, sometimes, pirates disguise themselves as merchants," he said. "They deceive people by pretending to be interested in buying their wares and lure them into their ship and capture them. They might have gotten your friend."

"You're right about that," the old fish sauce shop owner acknowledged, scratching his chin in thought. "Come to think of it, I've never come across that merchant ship before, which is pretty strange."

I let out a groan and slumped onto the clay paved ground, feeling the world around me turn dark. "I hope you find him," the shop owner said with a sigh.

My neighbors also came over, surrounding me, eager to figure out what had happened. "Vita, we are not sure about that yet. It's possibly only a rumor. Maybe Rufus will come back by himself in a couple of days," the compassionate Festus said, avoiding eye contact with me.

My mind raced with images of Rufus, possibly held captive on a pirate ship, chained and covered in blood. All this could have happened because he wanted to make my birthday special.

I felt devastated.

Two of my neighbors offered to go to the city council to get a report, while the rest accompanied me back to our village. On the way, regrets flooded my mind.

I should have held him longer until those evil men left.

Oh God, I should have made him stay no matter what the cost was.

The weight of my remorse pounded my heart into my stomach.

"Vita, let me accompany you home," Marcius, my next-door neighbor, offered as Nana's shabby little hut came into view.

"Thank you, Marcius, but I need some time alone," I replied.

Marcius glanced at the other two neighbors and nodded, saying, "All right, please don't hesitate to reach out if you need anything." With that, they left.

I settled on a large rock in our front yard. Even now, the weight of my anxiety still lingers as I recall how long I sat there, praying to a God I had never paid much attention to, asking for the strength to meet Nana's expectant gaze. I prayed so fervently that beads of sweat formed on my forehead.

Nothing appeared to change immediately after my prayer, but something deep within me was shifting. There was a moment when I suddenly found the courage to rise and knock on the door.

Nana didn't shed tears. Upon learning everything, she sat quietly by the window, sinking into a long prayer. I sat by her side from the afternoon until night, from night until the next morning, watching as her once-grey hair appeared to turn white, strand by strand.

·♥·♥·♥·♥·♥·

In the ensuing months, we searched tirelessly, rising before the sun, covering miles on foot, asking everyone, and leaving messages everywhere. "If you happen to see or hear of a young man who looks like this… If you hear of one held captive…"

The days, we spent praying, clinging onto a faint and diminishing hope that Rufus would return soon. However, all that happened was the passing of the days, vacant and hopeless.

With each passing night, Nana grew frailer. The woman who had once been tirelessly busy in our little garden, weaving, baking, and caring for the house disappeared. She had lost all interest in everything. Now, all she did was sit by the door, looking into the winding road where Rufus had last been seen, and from which he seemed to have disappeared. Sometimes, when a young lad passed by, she'd jump to her feet, rushing toward the startled boy. But of course, it never *was* him, never Rufus, never the one she believed her eyes had glimpsed. Then, it would not be long before she returned, her eyes filled with tears and her heart heavy with grief.

I had to take care of Nana during the day and work late into the night weaving baskets, trying to use my hands to make ends meet. But even with all that hard work, I *couldn't* make ends meet. The only silver lining was that the hardships of life kept me too busy to dwell too much on my loss. Life was slowly falling back into place, or rather, I was forcing it to; there was no other option.

Prayer became a part of me. I silently prayed in my heart whether I was cleaning, cooking, or weaving. I would pray each time a wave of sadness crept into my heart, hoping to hear a mystical voice whisper to me or witness visions and dreams.

But nothing of that sort happened. However, an inexplicable sense of peace began washing over me every time I prayed. It became my life force, my breath, my sustenance.

"Nana was right. With prayer and faith, nothing can destroy us," I said to myself. But despite my best efforts, it was impossible to shake off the feeling that something had been taken from my heart along with Rufus. Little did I know, three years later, another catastrophe would befall me—one that would almost destroy me completely.

Four

A Desperate Decision

THIS WINTER WASN'T NEARLY as chilly as the one three years back, but the constant downpour had been going on for almost a month. It was as if the sky itself shared the sorrow of every home on the island, where every house had its share of departed souls, and each one was drowning in a mix of potions and tears.

About a month ago, a worn-down-looking ship had docked in Paphos' harbor.

After three days of no one disembarking, the dock captain climbed aboard to investigate, whereupon he discovered every single man on that vessel was dead.

The dreadful news spread faster than the air, and within a few days, the dock captain was dead as well, with members of his immediate family following soon after.

We heard the story from our neighbor Darius, who had gone to the harbor of Paphos to sell his leather crafts. He also died shortly after. When I accompanied his family to bring his body to the cremation site south of the village, we were shocked to find five more families there.

In the following days, the clouds of smoke from the cremations shrouded our village.

Nana's ailing condition was all but inevitable. Three years of mourning had ravaged her constitution, and with each passing winter, her respiratory affliction worsened to the point where I questioned her chances of survival. Yet, year after year, she persevered. As this year dawned, I sensed that the impending struggle would be more formidable than ever.

Luckily, our village physician, Glaucus, quickly resolved a cure for it, a formula made from his garden herbs, but as cases increased, so did the cost of it.

"God has a plan for those he loves. He never forgets them," Nana had whispered into the open flame of our makeshift fireplace.

Silent wheezes and peppery coughs spotted her speech. We'd bought the first medicine dose with the money accumulated from the clearance of all our basket stock; it had worked but without a quick second dose to follow, her condition quickly slipped back.

"I could spare you the medicine but, you know, our shop is getting busy and I'm going to need a pair of capable hands to... hold things down around here," Glaucus had said, his eyes roaming my body as if to grab a hold of whatever curves my hunger had not already robbed.

"No, thank you, my lord. Nana won't make it without my care." I turned away and hurried toward his newly painted door with the image of Asclepius, the god of medicine with his snake-entwined staff, almost tripping over an amphora filled with herbs.

Now I had only one place to go, the last place I wanted to head.

Drusus of Paphos.

People claimed he had once been a slave in Rome, fortunate to have a benevolent master who granted him freedom after years of unwavering service. Upon returning to his hometown here in Cyprus, he established a prosperous career as a moneylender. Rumors about his involvement in an underground slave-trading business circulated throughout the village.

"Oh, he'll lend you the money all right, but often at a cost that will haunt you for years to come."

"A former slave returning to his hometown to trade slaves. The irony."

"I heard he even sold his own poor daughters."

Drusus' new villa had been built last year on the western hill of Paphos, by the side of the temple of Mercury. The cloud-shrouded sun was sliding toward the winged helmet of the sculpture of Mercury who was standing at the top of the temple.

I hastened my steps.

The chilling persistent wind whipped past my nose, dragging a few of my frazzled hair locks with it, so I tightened my grip around the loose wool of my threadbare scarf.

My muddy sandals splashed in puddles along the lonely market street.

It was empty, the market... devastatingly and expectedly so. A black cat meowed at me from the shellfish stand, its sunset yellow eyes staring at me expectantly.

"God always has a good plan for His own."

My footsteps splish-splashed in the gray puddles. "He never forgets them," I whispered to myself. "But what could be His plan for all this?"

I arrived at the gate of Drusus' sizable home just as the sun had half disappeared behind the temple. A doe-eyed young slave boy opened the door for me, instructing me to wait on a bench in the corridor. As he turned and hurried into the atrium to report to his master, I caught sight of a long, palm-sized scar on his left calf.

On his return, the last ray of the sun had been swallowed by the monstrous temple roof. He gestured to me to come into the atrium. "The master is in his study behind the yellow beaded curtain," he said with a stony face, then walked away as quickly as he could.

The ceiling of the atrium was at least twice as high as that of our little hut, and here, a hunchbacked man wearing a one-armed tunic stood on a scaffold, painting a fresco on the atrium walls. On closer inspection, I could see the painting was of four satyrs with horses' legs guarding a tree with golden leaves. Their lustful bulging eyes sent chills down my spine.

At the far-left corner of the atrium was a newly painted red wooden chest, standing on four sturdy legs and guarded by a tall, well-built young man whose eyes were much like those of the satyrs. People in my village had said that only the wealthy would possess such chests, as they were meant for safeguarding valuables and displaying them to guests.

They were an obvious sign of wealth, which I had hardly ever seen until now.

As I reached for the yellow beaded curtain separating the atrium and Drusus' study, it was suddenly yanked open from within, and a man with thin gray hair came rushing out. He wore a coarse burlap tunic, marked with stains and holes, and his forehead bore deep furrows.

His sunken eyes remained fixed on a small cloth satchel cradled in his hands, visibly bulging with coins. Yet, there was no trace of joy or relief in his demeanor; to the contrary, an unmistakable sense of sorrow and regret emanated from him. A heavy burden settled in my chest as I observed his profound anguish.

What had he needed to give up in return for the money?
And what about me?

The man turned his head as he passed by my side, his weary eyes meeting mine briefly. "May Fortuna bless you," he said quickly before his gaze fell back upon the satchel.

I walked into Drusus' study, my gaze fixed on the mosaic floor beneath my feet, which was adorned with patterns of coins of varying sizes. Drusus occupied a throne-like chair at the room's center, flanked by two burly slaves, one on each side.

He was much smaller in frame than I had anticipated, and his tiny, gleaming eyes reminded me of those of a weasel. But his radiant, white toga and the gem-inlaid rings on almost every finger of his hands all conveyed his great wealth. Spread in front of him was a long black marble table, its four legs intricately carved into the shapes of wolf heads. Resting atop it were three large silver dishes and an assortment of smaller ones, each brimming with a variety of delicacies.

Drusus sat, dipping a piece of bread into a golden bowl filled with soup.

"I've been expecting you, young lady. How is your Nana?" he inquired coldly with his eyes remaining glued to his plate as if he feared someone might snatch his food away. The slaves must have reported my purpose for coming when I was waiting outside.

"She…" I swallowed, blinking rapidly to suppress the sudden wave of tears. "She could be better, my lord. Th-That's why I'm here."

"And how many gold coins do you need?"

Well, no one could accuse him of wasting time on frivolous talk.

Drusus finally raised his head from his feast, his eyes squinted and eyebrows raised. The table between us gleamed like a mirror. Suddenly, a group of trembling young boys rushed in, swiftly clearing the half-eaten plates to the kitchen, leaving only a cheese plate in front of him. My mouth watered profusely when the dishes were taken away. Once the last slave removed the oil-stained table runner, a young, curled-up girl emerged from beneath the table, apparently engaged in giving Drusus a foot massage.

I gathered all the courage I could muster and swallowed the excess saliva filling my mouth. It had been days since I'd had a proper meal.

"Twelve gold coins, my lord. That is what I require."

"Hmm," he acknowledged, gently brushing away stray breadcrumbs from his scraggly beard. "I can understand how dire your need might be, given that your desperation has led you here." He paused, picking up a coin from the small wooden chest by his hand and rubbing it between his fingers. Then he turned his gaze toward me again.

"I'll lend you the money no problem."

I let out a deep breath before realizing I'd dug my nails into the skin of my palms. Immense joy and exhilaration filled up my insides. *Finally, I will be able to pay for Nana's medicines!* I thought blissfully, and the image of her recovery flashed across my eyes, filling my heart with utmost delight and relief.

"Thank you, my esteemed lord." I gave him a deep bow. "Your kindness and nobility are beyond praise. And I promise that I'll pay you back in a month, my lord." A massive smile now graced my face.

Drusus raised an eyebrow. "And how do you plan to repay me?"

Suddenly, my smile vanished, and an icy feeling spread across my whole body. "My lord, what do you mean?"

"What's the guarantee you'll be able to pay me back after a month, young lady?" He lifted a piece of cheese from the plate in front of him and leaned back against the embroidered cushion of the chair. "Perhaps a bit of collateral as assurance?" he added, kneading the cheese into a squashed ball between his fingers.

A heated quarrel between what sounded like two young girls arose somewhere in the building, something about perfume. Drusus' face tightened in distaste as he beckoned a slave from behind him. "Tell my daughters to please exercise some semblance of decorum. I'm in the midst of a meeting with a client," he commanded in a composed yet menacing tone.

I suppose he never sold off his daughters after all. What a silly rumor.

The man trotted away, and after a brief moment, the much-needed silence was achieved.

I cleared my throat. "I plan to sell our hut, my lord."

An amused look sparkled in his eyes. "Your hut?"

"Yes, my lord."

"Well, that *is* a fair and noble sacrifice, all things considered," he said, brushing away invisible food crumbs from the table. "But I'm afraid that won't be enough."

My heart dropped. "Won't be enough? Our hut is worth at least fifteen gold coins."

"You have a lot to learn, so let me explain," he said, raising his chin to look me square in the face. "You may have realized a certain steady drop in the population of your village, so to speak. Even someone as young as you would have noticed this. Am I not correct?"

I had noticed. After all, who wouldn't? Funeral services were becoming a daily occurrence, with the number of attendees dwindling with each passing day.

"So, listen and learn. A drop in population numbers brings about an increase in the availability of housing and a corresponding decrease in price," he rushed out, traces of a smirk dancing on his lips. "I estimate your hut will be worth about... Well, have a guess."

"I-I don't know. Maybe twelve gold coins?" I replied hesitantly, my hope faltering.

Drusus laughed. "Ha! Twelve gold coins? That's an optimistic guess, for which I applaud you. But, from someone who knows how the market works, I estimate your hut to be worth five gold coins—if not less—when you *do* decide to sell it in a month."

I swallowed hard.

God always has a plan for His own. He never forgets, a silent inner voice told me.

"How much would a slave girl of my stature cost?"

My words gushed out, burning my throat and scalding the tip of my tongue.

Drusus' eyes lit up immediately, his gray orbs scanning me from top to bottom. At this point, he could no longer hide his smile.

"Easily twenty gold coins."

The memory of Nana's frail body huddled up by the fireplace flashed before my eyes. If Nana survived, she could resume basket weaving with me again. I had come up with some new designs before the disease broke out and they'd sold very well; coupled with the money from selling the hut, we could make it. We could survive.

"If I am unable to pay you in a month, my lord, you can have my freedom."

Drusus stared at me, sighing, excitement flickering in his eyes.

"Great Mercury, you are my witness today. I didn't trick her or force her into this. She willingly offered her freedom as collateral."

Five

To Rome

NANA HAD NOT SURVIVED.

The herb had initially proven effective. Nana had got better but remained still weak, and day and night, I had slept on a mat by her bed. Whenever she came to consciousness, I'd try to squeeze some water and medicine into her mouth. In the beginning, she would swallow some, but later, she always threw up everything she took in, so the benefits weren't absorbed.

On a rainy night devoid of visible stars, Nana had breathed her last, just like so many others in our village. It was inevitable but still hurt a lot.

Nana had taught me so much in our limited time together, and no matter how much time would ever slip away from me, I would never forget it, never quell those memories.

Now came even harder times.

With so many people deceased, all the families had no choice but to dispose of the bodies in an open pit on the outskirts of the village.

It had torn my heart to imagine my beloved Nana rotting there among countless others. So, I dug a hole behind our hut and laid her to rest there. To describe it as simply "digging a hole" would be an understatement; it was a laborious process, consuming many days and nights. By the time I had finished, Nana's body had undergone a disturbing transformation, displaying various colors, festering, and bloating with the passage of time. I had been on my hands and knees, grappling with the weighty corpse—skin and bone, yet incredibly difficult to move—then shoveling compacted earth back into the grave, laboring late into the night.

In the days to come, on the soil above where I'd buried Nana, I would often stretch out my limbs to feel closer to her. But all I ever felt was the soil's coldness freezing my blood.

Nana was all I'd had, and she was gone, cruelly torn from me way ahead of time.

"Why, Lord? Why?" I cried out. "Why did you have to do this? First, you took Rufus, and now Nana! What did I do to deserve this? Is my sin so terrible that you must put me through all this pain?"

I lay there, wishing the ground would swallow me too, letting me join Nana. But it didn't, and I had to get up and sell our hut, with the deadline for my deal with Drusus now around the corner. Regrettably, just as Drusus had predicted, too many had died recently, leaving numerous properties uninhabited. No one was willing to buy our hut, even at the lowest asking price.

On the last day of our deal, just before the rooster's crow, two burly men barged in, fastening ropes around my wrists, and forcibly pulled me out the door. One of them snatched the satchel from across my shoulder.

"Please! There is no money in it!" I shrieked.

He spat and flung the satchel wide open.

My writing tablet dropped on the ground, as well as the stylus Rufus had made for me. "Please, let me keep them. They are the only things my family left me," I begged.

"Nonsense, girl."

The other man stepped on the tablet, and with a crisp snap, it broke into two pieces. "Slaves don't possess property." Then they dragged me toward the entrance of our village.

Soon, I saw a trek of villagers with shabby clothes tied together. Drusus was there, with more golden rings on his fingers and a swollen pouch on his waist. A middle-aged man with a pockmarked face and a permanent sneer stood by his side, and I guessed it might be the slaver. Drusus took a quick glance at me and patted the man's shoulder. "This one should be the last of this month. Start today and you'll arrive in Rome before the festival dedicated to Mars. The slave market usually makes an appearance at such festivals."

The slaver took a stride toward me and squeezed my chin. "This one is only bones covered by skin. I doubt she'll survive the trip."

"She will survive it." Drusus grinned, revealing his golden teeth alongside a few gaps. "This girl has some spirit. She may prove to be difficult but die she will not. Not en route."

"Spirit or not, it all depends on the smile of Fortuna." The slaver shrugged, taking a whip and cracking it at the first man. "Let's move, sluggards. It is a long way to Rome."

Maybe I should thank God. If Nana had survived but we still couldn't pay back the debt, how would she come to terms with the fact that I had sold myself to save her?

At least she went in peace.

My nose tingled, and I raised my head to stop the tears from falling.

The west of the sky was still dark like the soot in the fire pot, but on the east side, orange-colored light gilded the cloud with a golden rim.

"Lord, if you are still there, please keep me alive on this road to Rome," I whispered my prayer.

The route to Rome should take no more than a month by ship and on foot. But because the wind was somehow against us on the sea and as some in our train were too old and weak to walk fast on land, we moved slower than expected. It took us two weeks to even reach a place called Fair Havens on the island of Crete, then another two weeks to Rhegium on Sicily, where we boarded a ferry and headed for Puteoli.

Our train's initial count had been about sixty, but as we disembarked from the ferry at Puteoli and began our journey to Rome on foot, the slaver was now counting only thirty loaves of moldy bread each morning. "I should've never have paid so much for those dying old wretches. Drusus is such a scoundrel," he cursed every now and then on the way.

We had been bound together in a long train with the strongest, thickest twine I had ever seen.

My wrists oozed blood from the tight rope, and my feet were numb from the endless journey. A deafening whooshing sound rushed past my ears, followed by the sickening crack of a whip striking human flesh, all accompanied by a woman's harrowing screams and sobs.

"Move! You're sluggish!" the slaver yelled. "We'll never get to Rome at this pace."

Thud. Thud. Thud. I had to shut down all my feelings to move forward.

Nighttime was the most relaxing part of the day.

We camped around the fire. No trudging in the cold wind, no whips falling on our bodies, and no harassment from the slaver, just warmth from the campfire.

In the flickering firelight, Nana's pallid face emerged, flooding my mind with memories of her final moments.

·♥·♥·♥·♥·♥·

After slipping into a coma for several days, she abruptly regained consciousness, filled with distress and fever, urgently calling out for me. Her strangely warm, bony fingers tightly gripped mine.

"The Lord gave me a vision and I saw Rufus. Vita, listen closely and remember what I say!" she whispered, her voice faint and muffled, yet infused with a desperate urgency. I put my ear close to her mouth, even though I thought her murmurings were just because she missed Rufus too much.

Her bloodshot eyes darted from one corner of the room to the other. "Yes, Vita, it is Rufus, our Rufus! He's taller and stronger, but I know it is him. I wish you could see him."

I've heard that just before people died, they would often see their deceased family members, as if the visitations had come to kindly usher them into the next realm.

I cuddled her further into my bosom, unshed tears blurring my vision. "Oh Nana," I whispered. "Why do you leave me so swiftly?"

"Rufus!" she chattered on. "Rufus is alive."

Not wanting to extinguish her last flicker of hope, I held her hands and said, "Yes, Nana, Rufus is alive, and he'll come home soon. We'll all be together again. Now, please take some rest, my dear Nana."

Her hand jerked away from mine with surprising strength, her gray eyes locking onto mine for the first time in weeks, filled with life. She vigorously shook her head. "No, my child. You must believe me. I'm not seeing things. Rufus is alive, more alive than I've ever seen him. The Lord carried me into the sky, and I saw him in a place with seven hills. Seven hills and lots of columns. The Lord told me you will meet him again. Seven hills—there he is, waiting."

Seven hills.

My heart raced suddenly, like a hare pursued by a golden jackal, as I recollected a neighbor's tale of Rome. He had mentioned that the great city was renowned for its seven hills.

Did Nana hear about it from someone too, and the image came as a hallucination before she passed, or did she truly receive a vision from God?

"Nana, please, tell me more," I urged her.

The light in her eyes dimmed and her body fell back onto the threadbare woolen blanket. "Water. Please give me water." She panted heavily.

As I turned my back to fetch the bowl, she took her final breath.

❦ · ❦ · ❦ · ❦ · ❦

"I've heard that in Rome, if you have a talent, even as a slave, there is still a chance for you to amass a great fortune."

"But the catch is you have to be lucky enough to have a kind master."

Suddenly, the heated discussion from two men nearby pulled me back to the present.

If Nana had truly seen this vision, could it mean Rufus is still alive and is somewhere in Rome? Shaking my head, I suppressed the hope stirred by this idea. My heart couldn't take another blow of disappointment.

"No, God, please don't tease me like this," I murmured, burying my face between my knees. "Please spare me from such torment."

"Are you praying to your god?"

Hearing the voice, I raised my head. It was Sofia, a young widow from Paphos, who was bound behind me on our journey. She'd been widowed swiftly and suddenly during the outbreak. Her late husband's family had deemed her of no worth and had sold her to the slaver soon after.

"Yes, I'm praying to my God," I said.

She stirred the campfire with a twig and sighed. It was clear she had much to say.

And say it she did, right away.

"Look, my husband's house has three altars dedicated to the household gods. And we made offerings to the temples of all the gods and goddesses in Paphos at every festival. None of them saved my husband, and none of them saved me. So, I very much doubt any god shall be coming along to save you either."

Then she shifted her lifeless gaze on me and carried on, "If your god is so capable, why did you end up here? Surely, he would have prevented it. Surely, your god would have been more benevolent. So, why waste time praying to him now, to the one who so obviously let you down?"

"I... I don't know," I stammered, searching for the last shreds of faith I held, much like a man with empty pockets might still pat them down. "My God always has a plan for His children. He won't forsake me. I have faith in Him."

She looked at me, her mouth twitching as if to convey, *silly little girl*.

"Well, I do hope your god doesn't forget his plan since there must be a lot to remember," she said at last.

"No, He doesn't... He won't..." I wanted to talk more, but a deep anxiety buried in my heart was now stirred up by her words.

What if He does forget me?

That night, after the snoring sounded from every tent around, I prayed in my heart.

Lord, do you still remember your daughter? Why can't I sense your presence? Why is there no answer every time I feel hopeless? My faith is weak these days.

I want to trust you, but it is so hard with all that has happened to me.

Please help me. Show your kindness to me in my despair. Please, show me your presence.

Six

A Dazzling Figure

THE MORNING FOG HAD just dissolved when the gate of Rome suddenly loomed over us. A tall monstrosity it was, supported by even larger and more formidable looking walls. The gateway was like the mouth of a giant, ready to swallow the throng trying to enter the city.

"This is Porta Capena, the southern gate," the slaver announced, chomping loudly on some nuts, saliva flying from his lips around his words. "Hurry up! We need to get to the Forum by noon. We haven't all day; we are not tourists here."

On reaching the gates, he saluted the guards, stopping to conspicuously slip a pouch into a hand. The guard grinned broadly, waving us through, eyes narrowing in his helmet under the sun. As for me, I cast my first glance of the great city toward the sun's direction.

It was dazzling and scorching, offering no respite to my sensitive eyes, but rather, a burning sensation.

I beheld a vast and towering forest of columns in the distance.

Wherever we went, marble columns competed for space, some even thicker than the oldest cedar tree trunk in my village and walking under them made me feel like a sparrow fallen from her nest.

In each direction my eyes reached, there were hills covered with clusters of buildings.

Suddenly, Nana's words came back.

"Rufus is in a place with seven hills and lots of columns."

"Maybe Nana did see a vision," I murmured, failing to suppress the rising hope. "Maybe Rufus is here alive."

When we walked past a giant building with curved walls, the slaver pointed to it and exclaimed, "That is Circus Maximus. Gladiators fight here. Prisoners die here. If you dare to run away from your future masters, this is where you'll find yourself." With that, he scanned our faces, and seemed to find great satisfaction in the fear his words had aroused.

"So heed my warning," he continued, "you really don't want to end up in there."

Hisses emanated from our train, which elicited a laugh from the slaver. "Imagine your flesh being torn by those hungry lions!" he added with a cruel, amused tone, his chuckle mingling with the sound of his loud nut-chewing.

Thud. Thud. Thud. Our steps became heavier than ever.

Soon, I saw a thick human river flowing in front of us and the slaver led us, joining the end of the flow. "We are about to arrive at the Forum now. This great market is the place where we bid our farewells and where you will be sold. It is time to pray to goddess Fortuna for kind masters," he advised.

"Now is your chance, otherwise you could end up with someone like me." He laughed again, a humor that none of us found amusing.

I looked around, and exhausted as they were, every head bowed in prayer, including Sofia's. Only the tops of their heads were visible, shining in the sun.

"Lord, I need a kind master too," I whispered, my interlocked fingers growing icy cold.

Trudging forward, my eyes almost half-closed from exhaustion, when suddenly, my feet stepped on something slimy, causing me to jerk awake.

I looked down to realize that we had reached an open area where the ground was covered with animal excrement, the appalling filth reaching my ankles. People, carts, and animals darted in all directions, pushing and shoving through the unruly throngs.

The cacophony of sounds and smells overwhelmed my senses. The pungent scent of droppings emanated from a nearby stand selling the noisiest turkeys. Meanwhile, the spicy aroma of shattered perfume wafted from a stall where a snorting pig had knocked over a jar. Just as I was catching my breath, a carriage led by two horses flew by us, splashing a wave of foul mud and grime onto our already filthy tunics.

"By the gods!" the slaver cursed. "How naïve was I to think that I could save my ten copper coins of cleaning cost." With a great deal of grunting, he pushed us through a small door next to the turkey stand. "Get those wretches cleaned up so I can make a good profit off of them," he grumbled as he dropped coins into the palms of a plump woman by the door.

"Absolutely, my lord. All slaves washed by me are guaranteed to fetch a high price." The woman's face radiated with pride. After an hour had passed, we emerged from the bathhouse feeling refreshed and clean, our woolen tunics scrubbed of dirt and grime.

The slaver gave each of us a heavy knock on the head as a warning. "Behave yourselves. If I can't recoup the extra coins I spent on your wash and clothes, you'll be dead by tonight!"

Guided down a narrow lane, hemmed in by the cozy clutter of grocery stalls, we made our way to a wooden platform that marked the lane's end. Before us, a broad thoroughfare unfurled, lined with the gleaming displays of blacksmiths and silversmiths, showcasing their crafts, parallel to the platform's prominence.

We climbed up the platform and price tags were put around our necks. I read mine: *100 gold coins.*

Drusus must have made a fortune out of me.

By this time, it was about an hour past noon, and yet more litters—wooden covered carrying couches, each comprising a bed plinth carried by one man in the front, one in the rear—stopped by our stand. Men and women with bright colored togas and dresses alighted from the litters, scanning every one of us with scrutinizing eyes. I bowed my head and kept praying silently for a kind master. As the corner of a gleaming white robe, adorned with fringes and golden bells, entered the edge of my vision, I heard the slaver's flattering voice.

"Oh, good priest, how goes the business in our divine goddess' temple?" The slaver grinned broadly, baring his golden tooth.

"Thanks to the patronage of our revered empress, our temple has witnessed a surge in the number of worshippers this year," proclaimed the white-robed man, all the dry ravines on his cosmetic-covered face radiant with pride.

"We have a few girls here with good looks. Make them the helpers of the goddess and you will make a lot of money." The slaver pointed at me and some other girls. My heart tightened. White robe, fringes and golden bells. *He must be a priest of the goddess Isis.*

Memories of Rufus came back in a flash.

He'd told me that some girls were sold to them to become temple prostitutes.

I tried to figure out a way to avoid the dreary fate as sweat formed in my palms. "Oh, Jesus Lord, please don't let him pick me!"

The priest came nearer. My heart was already in my mouth as he scrutinized me up and down, squeezed my cheeks, and couldn't hide his smile.

"This one could do. How old is she?" the priest asked.

"She's woman enough as you see for yourself." The slaver smirked.

The priest surveyed me once again.

"Needs some meat on her bones," he murmured to himself. "But it's nothing that can't be fixed. I'll give you sixty gold coins for her."

"Ninety is the least I can do for this one. She's a hard worker, a lot stronger than she looks," the slaver grunted. "And she's ebullient, stubborn as a mule, a spirited one. As you know, although such girls can be hard to direct, they fetch the best prices and never fail."

"Nonsense. Seventy or nothing. I can happily walk from a trade with you. Two ships loaded with barley were taken by pirates before reaching Ostia last month, so the food cost will go up." The priest looked away, but I could sense his peripheral sight was still on me.

The slaver sighed deeply, palms showing upward as if he relinquished. And he did.

"You're a hard man. But fine, it's a deal."

My heart raced along with my mind.

I can't possibly do this! Anything but this. Suddenly, I envied the slaves that had been sold to the arena. At least they'd die with dignity. What could I do?

My sight wandered to a gray-haired beggar in the audience; he gave a wide-eyed stare at nothing in particular whilst hysterically laughing, a little strand of foamy spittle hanging loosely from his lips. Suddenly, an idea struck me. Seizing my shoulders upward, a tense look of shock overwhelmed my face, and I shook violently. Sticking my tongue out, I let a little spit roll down the side of my mouth.

Shock and disgust appeared on the priest's face. "What's wrong with her? Seizure? You're not trying to sell me a fraud, are you?"

"No way. She's just tricking you. She's as strong as a cow. Nay, as a male ox," the slaver yelled and slapped my face. "You'd better stop this act, or I'll sell you into the arena."

I ignored him and kept faking madness, even though my heart was almost leaping out of my throat. It was now or never.

The priest's piercing gaze bore into me once more.

"Oh Lord, protect me," I whispered under my breath, lowering my head even further, pressing my chin tightly against my collarbone.

Suddenly, the sound of women shrieking and pottery shattering broke out from the throngs in the narrow lane in front of our stand. As I looked up, I saw a man in black forcefully shoving and elbowing his way through the bustling crowd, knocking over jugs, jars, and baskets from stands along the way.

"Catch the thief! Catch the thief!" someone behind him shouted.

Before I had time to realize what might have happened, the thief emerged ten paces in front of the slaver stand with a gray satchel tucked under his arm.

The gleam of the dagger in his hand made my blood run cold.

But with everyone, including the slaver, now focused on him, my heart raced. "This might be my opportunity for an escape!" Unfortunately, the tight ropes around my wrists reminded me of the absurdity of such a notion.

As I lamented my vanished hope of escape, the thief approached our stand. Glancing in the direction where the sun was setting, his face blanched and he sprinted the opposite way. However, before he reached the third blacksmith stall on our right, he let out a sudden scream and collapsed, grasping his ankle in which a bloody arrow shaft was lodged.

Wild bursts of applause exploded from the crowd near the thief and rippled throughout the entire street wave after wave.

As every face turned to my left, I followed their gaze until my eyes alighted on a striking figure, backlit by the glaring sun. He was mounted on a white horse while the sunlight cast a radiant halo around his gleaming silver breastplate and red-crested helmet.

His broad shoulder bore the weight of an ink-black crossbow, which he held with both hands in a stance of focused readiness.

Although his face was mostly in shadow, his sharp cheekbones and defined jawline still held the gaze of all the females in the vicinity. The man calmly parted the cheering crowd and, still upon the horse, made his way to the thief.

Meanwhile, two armor-clad soldiers went up before him and bound the thief with ropes.

"That poor thief had bad luck today," the slaver said with a shrug. "Falling into the Prefect Aemilia's hands. Probably cheated the gods with fake offerings."

The drama held my attention for only a moment before my worry about the future took hold of me once again. Looking around anxiously, my eyes sought out the Isis priest, but to my surprise, I could no longer see him.

"Hey, where is the Isis priest?" the slaver yelled, mirroring my thoughts. He scurried through the crowds, craning his neck and searching for any sign of him. After some fruitless searching, the slaver stopped with a sigh. "Hmm, scared away by the prefect? That old fox probably got some smelly fish on their tax roll."

Hearing this, my shoulders sagged, the heavy burden suddenly seeming to lift from me. "Thank you, God," I murmured under my breath. "Is this man an angel you sent to rescue me?"

The horse-riding man and his soldiers headed away from our stand with the thief at the end of the line, hands bound.

Sofia suddenly said in a dreamy voice, "If he could buy me and let me help him put on those shining armor plates every morning, I'd give up twenty years of my life."

"Stop daydreaming, girl," the slaver jeered. "He is Caius Aemilia, the emperor's most trusted praetorian prefect, sole heir of the Aemilia family whose bloodline is said to go back to Romulus and Remus. A man like him *never* buys market slaves. So, get that ridiculous notion out of your head. His house is probably full of war hostage barbarian princesses."

A crooked-nosed man mused, evidently having overheard, "Rumor has it that he has bedded half the patrician matrons in Rome. Even the empress herself is said to have summoned him to her chambers on occasion."

No wonder the villagers always say Roman patricians lead debauched lives.

At that moment, a middle-aged woman with deep wrinkles etched into her forehead and around her mouth approached the platform. She was dressed in an emerald-smooth silk dress and adorned with two jade wristbands, one on each hand. Her gaze swept across the slaves on display, eventually settling on me. With a stern expression that accentuated the furrow between her eyebrows, she inquired, "Are forty gold coins enough for the blonde girl?"

My palms grew sweaty, but the thought of being in her possession rather than the priest's gave me some solace. In my anxious state, I whispered a prayer, "Dear Lord, please let this woman take me."

"Forty? No fewer than sixty. She's got good looks when she is not so scrawny. A temple priest almost got her for seventy if it had not been for the—"

"Well, take it or leave it. Forty-five is the best I can do," the woman interrupted, handing a purse to him. "Good looks have no use in our household."

"Fine, she's yours now." The slaver looked at the setting sun, gnashed his teeth and took out a parchment from his satchel. "The deed!"

He grudgingly handed it to the woman, then untied the rope from my hand.

"Girl, you better mind your manners. This is Rome, and any thoughts of running away will land you in the arena, just as I warned you on the way," the slaver said, the gold inlaid on his teeth glinting as he spoke.

Before I could even respond, I was roughly shoved into a waiting carriage and whisked away.

Seven

A New Home

My posterior was pleasantly surprised to feel the soft cushion beneath it as I settled into the seat opposite the woman who had purchased me. The carriage was dark with the curtain drawn, so I couldn't make out her face.

"Can you cook?" She broke the silence abruptly.

"Uh... Nana taught me... I can make porridge and—" I searched for the best word.

"We never cook poor people's food in our house," she interrupted coldly. "Anyway, your position is in the kitchen. Do whatever the chef asks. Outside the kitchen, you answer to me. My name is Diana, remember?"

"Yes, Diana," I replied in a low voice, feeling a bit intimidated by her sternness.

A kitchen slave. My new identity.

Anyway, it's far better than a temple prostitute. I uttered a silent prayer to thank God.

After some clamoring and jolting, the carriage stopped. I got out after Diana and faced a small double wooden door, flanked by two pine trees meticulously trimmed into the shapes of bears.

The door creaked open at Diana's knock and a strong young man with olive-hued skin shuffled out. "Publius, lead the horse away to the manger and give him a good brush," Diana commanded.

"Follow me," she then instructed me.

As I entered the hallway, I nearly cried out when I stepped on a mosaic piece featuring a fierce-looking dog, its mouth wide open, with a red tongue hanging down. It appeared voracious and malevolent.

"No need to panic, girl. There is no dog in this house. This is just to prevent thieves," the woman said without looking at me. "Come on, stop wasting time and follow me. I'll show you the house. Learn quickly and pay attention. If you go the wrong way and offend the master, you'll be cursing the day you were born," Diana said, having taken a few big steps already.

I quickly followed her through the narrow hallway. Suddenly, the space opened up into a large square room with an opening in the center of the roof, allowing light to cascade down. Below the opening was a shallow pool built into the ground, reflecting the clear, cloudless blue sky. A young boy, most likely a fellow slave, held a small, porous stone in his hand as he diligently scrubbed the mosaic floor around the pool.

The four walls of this room were adorned with colorful frescoes depicting various deities and landscapes. Along the western wall, there were three large wooden chests, intricately inlaid with all kinds of precious stones of which I couldn't tell the names. I surmised that these chests were strongboxes, like the one in Drusus' house, though significantly larger. *It is astonishing. I can't believe it. This household appears even wealthier than Drusus',* I thought, still captivated by the vastness of the property and its many treasures.

I marveled at the house's beauty with every step: the mosaic floor, the marble columns, the brilliant and vivid frescos... Everything reminded me of "the Dark House", except that here, everything was much cleaner, brighter, more vibrant, and alive.

Thoughts of the Dark House were great memories from my childhood, but they suddenly brought with them recollections of my dearest Rufus.

My eyes were blurred with tears that welled up now. I lifted my gaze, letting the tears flow back, while shaking my head to rid its cruel and yet beautiful memories. Being emotional was not what I needed right now. I had to be strong and to survive. Crying was not the way.

We bypassed the marble pool, proceeding along the frescoed wall. Here, several painted, false doors alternated with genuine entrances that led into the atrium.

As I marveled at the intricate design, two large panels of heavy silk curtains, embroidered with winged, staff-wielding figures, suddenly loomed before us. I recognized the image as Mercury, the god of merchants and travelers, whose statue I had seen in Paphos.

"This is the master's business chamber," Diana said. "You are not to enter unless summoned, and that is unlikely as he has his designated slaves to attend to him."

Suddenly, harsh curses and a girl's screams could be heard emanating from within the room. The curtains were briefly pushed aside, and a young girl was violently thrust out, tumbling to the ground. A middle-aged man, his hairline receding, emerged from the behind the curtain, furiously gesturing at the girl and bellowing, "Idiot! Can you even imagine how much that vase was worth? It could have bought you ten times over! And now—now you have broken it—you are worth even less!"

"Master, please forgive me. I'm sorry, truly sorry," the girl managed to say through her tears.

"Forgive? Can forgiveness fix my vase? Or can it move Mercury to give me a new one?" the man scoffed. He turned his head to glare at Diana and snapped, "Diana, how did you train these girls? One of them broke a corner of my Corinthian vase. I spent three hundred gold coins on it, wrapped it with thirty sumptuous layers of silk, and brought it back all the way from Ephesus, handling it with the utmost care. Now it's ruined. From this day on, I shall deduct five silver coins from your monthly wage. You'll pay it off in sixteen years!"

Diana stood stiffly and nodded.

"Give her ten lashes and hurry up. Don't let her get in the way here," the man barked again before entering his room.

"Yes, my lord," Diana replied and shouted toward a door at the corner of the room. "Tychicus! Take this idiot to the discipline room and give her ten lashes!"

At her command, a young man with blond hair and two wide armbands came out and dragged the girl away. Diana then turned to me and said, "As you can see for yourself, in this household, people sometimes pay for the mistakes of others. So, watch every step you take and stay away from anything or anyone troublesome, or you'll get more lashes than her!"

Oh, Lord, give me wisdom and strength to survive this horrible place!

Diana still murmured angry words. Walking ahead of me, she led me to a large backyard filled with vast colonnades. In the center of the yard stood a beautiful garden, resplendent with red gladioli and other flowers in bloom.

"Not gladioli, please. Especially not the red ones," I whispered, struggling to contain my emotions.

Diana pointed toward a small door that faced the garden, beside which a stack of wood and several jars were neatly arranged. "Kitchen's here," she said. "Meet the chef tomorrow morning and he'll assign you tasks." She paused a little and added with unnoticed hesitation, "Just be warned, his name is Gala and he's known for being ill-tempered. Don't make the mistake of looking him in the eye and giggling. He hates it when girls do that. Sadly, they do it often, paying the price."

Then Diana took me to a door with black burlap curtains on the opposite side of the kitchen. "This is the slave quarters. Once you step in, the pallet on the far right is yours. Come to the kitchen at the first hour tomorrow morning and expect punishment if you arrive late. Understand?"

"Yes, ma'am."

Seeing the back of Diana's gray head stained golden by the last ray of the setting sun, I realized my first day in Rome was almost over. All my bones screamed of fatigue and soreness which made me lean on the wall for a second. I looked at the curtain leading to my new home and whispered, "No matter what tomorrow brings, tonight I have a bed to sleep on!" The air was filled with the sweet and spicy fragrance of hope, causing my nose to tingle. But as I parted the burlap curtains, a girl's suppressed groaning reached my ears.

Eight

A New Friend

THE ROOM EXUDED A dim glow, illuminated solely by the faint natural light streaming in through a small opening on the wall. A blend of musty sweat and the scent of lingering food, possibly from the kitchen, pervaded the air. Narrow pallets lined the wall on the opposite side of the door, spaced just enough for a single person to stand between them. Most of them accommodated someone in slumber, except for the far-right one, which stayed unoccupied with a neatly folded blanket.

I assumed it was meant to be mine. Nevertheless, in a pallet right next to mine, a young girl lay with half her face under the blanket, letting out soft groans.

Another girl with an angular face and prominent cheekbones held a jug, slowly pouring water onto her blanket. Giggling, she said, "Your wounds must be burning. Let me cool them down." A pained cry sounded from beneath the wet fabric.

On the neighboring pallet sat a curvy girl with beady eyes and arched eyebrows. Leaning forward, she sneered, "Who asked you to rush to pick up errands in the master's study? Do you think he will lay his eyes on you and make you his mistress?"

I recalled what had happened outside the master's study. Then I realized the groaning girl must have been the same one that was to be punished with ten lashes.

At this point, my feet were so sore that they could barely support my body, and as a newcomer, I really didn't want to invite trouble, so I walked directly toward my pallet.

However, the melancholic eyes of the bullied girl suddenly stirred something deep in my stomach. Another pair of eyes came to my mind—the eyes of the little bird I had saved with Rufus on our way to Paphos.

I paused my steps and lamented inwardly. *Oh, my Lord, can't I still be that brave girl when Rufus is not with me? Without him, am I a weakling?*

"What are you staring at, newcomer?" the angular faced girl snapped at me.

I stepped forward and grabbed the jug from her hand, saying, "She was just beaten, have a heart."

"Hey, newcomer, mind your own business." The curvy girl scowled.

The angular faced girl glared dangerously at me, her eyes fixed on mine as she continued to point accusingly at the groaning girl. "Antonia and I are teaching her a lesson," she said. "She's a siren in disguise, a master at tricking people. You'd better be careful, or she'll sell you and make you count her coins. Show her mercy, and you shall soon learn."

As anger boiled inside me, bringing an urge to lash out and punch the bully in the face, Diana's warning echoed in my mind, allowing me to resist the impulse. Instead, I chose to ignore the bullies and approached the distressed girl.

"Are you feeling all right?" I asked softly. The hair on the girl's forehead was damp and clung to her eyelids as I tried to brush it away.

"Fine, thank you," she managed, biting her lip in evident pain.

"Let me take a look," I said, lifting her wet blanket, and to my dismay, the clothes underneath were drenched with blood and water.

"You can sleep beside me," I offered. Under the scrutiny of the other two menacing stares, I gently helped the girl stand and guided her toward my pallet. Meanwhile, I noticed a spare tunic under her pillow, still dry. Carefully, I helped her put it on, yet an involuntary "ouch" still escaped her lips.

"I'm sorry. Did I hurt you?"

"It's fine." She managed to put on a weak smile. Gasping in pain, she said, "I-I'm Julia. And your name?"

"Vita." Right after, my stomach let out the loudest growl.

"Didn't you have dinner? There's still some bread in my parcel. Grab a bite, help yourself. If not, you'll be too weak to work tomorrow." Julia managed to say it all in one breath, as if fearing she might never get the chance again.

"You're so kind. And yes, I do feel hungry." I hurried over and opened the parcel on Julia's pallet. There was a piece of bread in it, and its enticing aroma led me to stuff my mouth without a second thought. After devouring half of it, I suddenly remembered that maybe I should leave some for Julia; it was hers, after all. When I was about to ask Julia, I noticed her tightly closed eyelids and rhythmic breathing.

Poor girl.

I put down the bread and offered a silent prayer. *Lord, you have also been whipped. You know her pain. May your nail-marked hand smooth her sorrow. Also, I pray tomorrow goes smoothly for me in the kitchen.*

After the prayer, I settled onto my pallet and curled up beside Julia, surrendering to the comforting embrace of unconsciousness.

Nine

Girl Talk

THE KITCHEN IN THE first few morning hours was a busy beehive. I met Gala, the chef—a short and stout man in his forties with a giant, red nose covered with acne scars.

Coincidentally, Julia also helped in the kitchen. The little episode from last night had naturally brought us closer. Without the cover of the night, I could now see her clearly, realizing she was a true beauty with a delicate frame, almond-shaped eyes, and long, dark hair tied up. We looked similar in many ways, but she was much daintier. In the midst of the relentless workload, I noticed that wherever Julia went, men's gazes always clung to her presence. I assumed that this was probably why those girls harbored such resentment toward her.

Seeing Julia occasionally wincing from the wounds of the whiplash, I offered to take part in her tasks. If I could help her a little, why would I not? She had a kind heart herself.

"You are far too kind. Do you know something? I've been in this house for a year, and you are the first person here who's really shown me kindness. Goddess Fortuna must surely have taken pity on me and sent you to save me," Julia said as her eyes glistened with a soft, radiant shimmer.

I gently put my arms around her. "I have always wanted a sister.

God must have heard my prayer."

Her eyes flickered.

Does she suspect that I am a Christian because I said "God" instead of "gods"?

Rufus had mentioned that in Rome, people shunned Christians because of various rumors. With this in mind, I decided not to talk too much about my faith and potentially scare my new friend. Luckily, Julia didn't press me on that topic.

Maybe she was just so grateful to have a friend, that even if her thoughts matched those of the majority of Rome, she would value the friendship over rumors, choosing to see with her own eyes and form her own opinions instead of taking on board stories whose veracity she couldn't confirm.

As summer rolled in, most Roman patricians were preparing to retreat to their suburban residences for some leisure time. However, our master was the type who never took time off in summer. Instead, he opted to host more feasts, extending invitations to the stewards responsible for overseeing the houses of absent patrician masters with the purpose of gleaning insights into the preferences and lifestyles of these patricians.

And that meant increased burdens for us kitchen slaves. Each day, we had to rise earlier than the day before, and toil ceaselessly until midnight, caught in an unending and exhausting cycle. Yet, whenever things seemed overwhelming, I would reflect on the time in the market when I could have easily been sold to the priest. Another source of hope for me was Nana's final words, firmly asserting that Rufus was still alive and located in a place with the seven hills, a detail I was certain I had seen when entering through the gates of Rome.

One humid afternoon, Gala sent the two of us to an open area of the garden to scrub some olive oil jars, which by the looks of them, hadn't been used for a long time. When I realized that we were alone, I kept scrubbing the jar in my hand, and quietly asked Julia, "Is there any chance for you to get out of this villa, I mean, like going to the streets or markets?"

"No, never. Gala only lets Antonia and Titus run errands in the market," she said. "And do you know why?"

"No, why?"

Julia turned her head left and right, ensuring we were still alone, and continued, "It's because Antonia sleeps with him, and Titus has a special talent which brings Gala money every time he goes to the market." Then she stuck out two fingers and made a "picking" gesture.

"You mean... Oh... I see." I quickly searched my mind for any talent I possessed to compete with the two.

I definitely can't do what Antonia does.

But if Gala loves money, maybe there is a way I can make him happy, I thought. *If I get to go to the market, I'll probably find a Christian gathering there. And if my Rufus is alive in Rome, maybe the Christians here can help me find him.*

Hope rose in my chest.

As I was lost in thoughts, my eyes fixed on the delicate jar in my hand.

"Beautiful work, isn't it?" Julia's voice brought me back to reality.

"Yes, it is," I murmured absentmindedly.

"This is the work of the potter Alexander. One of those is worth two gold coins," Julia said, beaming with pride.

"Two gold coins? That's enough to feed a family in our hometown for half a year." My eyes widened in disbelief.

"Talking about humble beginnings, you know..." Julia looked around again before she continued, "Well, our master was a cobbler's son. Although he has made lots of money in recent years, he still feels inadequate among the patricians. So, my guess is he likes to stuff the house with all kinds of luxurious items in the hope of impressing his patrician guests. But sadly, the true nobles still won't pay him any mind."

"What kind of lucrative business does the master do?"

"Don't you know? I thought everyone knew."

"Don't forget, I haven't been here long. This is all new to me."

"Sorry, I forgot. Well, Master Eubulus is the most famous fragrance supplier in Rome; half of the fragrances used for palace banquets are purchased from our family. Who wouldn't get rich with such royal orders?"

"Why do they need so many fragrances for their banquets?" I asked, genuinely curious.

"Aha, that's how people would know you are not a true Roman. In Rome, who's not aware of Emperor Nero's reputation for hosting extravagant banquets?"

Julia chuckled before continuing, "Since the emperor got rid of his own mother, Agrippina the Younger"—Julia moved her fingers across her neck as a sign of execution—"he expressed his true self without any holding back. There are banquets in the palace almost every night. Unlike other emperors who only invite a handful of important people, Nero isn't picky about his guests, so even famous gladiators and courtesans are also invited. It is inevitable that where there are so many people, especially in our oppressive heat, the smell soon grows unbearable. Thus, fragrances are in great demand. Does that answer your question?"

"I suppose so," I replied, taken aback. In my village, people didn't talk about things in the palace. The interest in gossip only went as far as Paphos.

Julia wore a triumphant expression and went on to say, "In the past, the emperor held banquets to win over the senate and the patricians, but Nero's banquets serve a single purpose—to showcase his 'remarkable' artistic talent. He plays and sings solos each time. There's a tale that a guest nodded off, I believe it was the previous year, and was promptly beheaded on the spot."

I took a deep breath, recovering from the shock of what I'd just heard. "It seems that the lives of the powerful and elite are not exactly easy either," I said after much thought.

Julia laughed. "You've got a point. Now, I feel so much better scrubbing those jugs. What a difference we've made, don't you agree?

I'm sure the master will appreciate all our hard work."

In the midst of our bustling slave lives, this unrestricted conversation brought me immense joy. Intrigued, I pressed on, posing more questions to Julia.

"Is our master always alone? I never see his wife and children."

Julia sighed. "Our mistress passed away long ago. She was said to be very kind to slaves. After her death, the master became consumed with grief and turned to his fortune for comfort. No one can get a smiling face from him in this house except for his daughter."

"His daughter?"

"Oh, I can't believe I haven't told you this. Our master has an only daughter named Cassia. She is currently living in the Temple of Juno, fasting and praying. She went there before you came, so you haven't seen her yet. But she'll return in a few days."

"Praying and fasting for so many days? For what?" I asked while dipping the brush into the bucket.

"For whom if it's not for Aurelius, her sweetheart?" Julia covered her mouth and giggled. "Our lady is so strange. She turned down so many rich young suitors, preferring a slave in the house. Well, I admit Aurelius is quite handsome and smart, but he is a slave regardless. And as you can imagine, the master has been furious about this for a while now. It certainly doesn't do anything for the reputation he craves among the patricians."

"That Aurelius must be a very unique man."

"Oh, yes," Julia went on. "Being a slave, Aurelius is a godsend. He came two years ago and quickly became the master's most trusted business helper. Now he is over the sea, importing valuable goods for an important order from the palace."

"That was a quick promotion," I exclaimed.

"Indeed. The master liked him so much that he even assigned a separate room to him. The one on the west corner of the atrium, with indigo linen curtains. Maybe you've seen it."

I did remember passing by a room with an indigo curtain when touring with Diana.

Julia continued, "Ever since he went out, the lady has been going to the Temple of Juno to make sacrifices, sometimes living there and praying day and night."

"The lady is so devoted!" I took the last jar and scrubbed heavily. "I respect her for that."

"She really is. While most Romans worship all kinds of gods and goddesses, our young lady stands out. Not only has she committed to Aurelius, but she's also devoted to the goddess Juno."

As I was about to pose my next question, a sudden, sharp pain jabbed at the back of my neck. Startled, I turned around to find Gala standing behind us, gripping a greasy spatula in his hand. "You wretched kids. You're just being lazy, standing around and chatting," Gala shouted.

"No! We've been washing all—" I replied, trying to plead our case.

"You two, go fetch some black walnut firewood and stack it in the kitchen. We need it for roasting a suckling pig for the master's dinner banquet tonight. Move quickly, and remember, no talking!"

Ten

Hit the Bottom

Spurred on by Gala's chastening, we hurried to the woodshed on the west side of the backyard. I bundled about twenty pieces of black walnut firewood and hoisted them onto my back. When I turned around, Julia was still standing by the bundle she had just made, looking worried.

"Your back must still be hurting," I said. "Give it to me. I can carry two at a time."

"But that's going to hurt *your* back."

"Stop babbling and hurry up. We'll both get in trouble if we're late," I urged, seizing her bundle and adding it atop mine. Despite the weight making me grit my teeth, I adjusted into a comfortable stance and started moving forward gradually.

"I'll carry some in my arms," Julia finally said, snapping out of watching me struggle with the load. She quickly gathered a smaller pile of wood and followed me.

We shuttled back and forth between the woodshed and the kitchen, making the trip about a dozen times before forming a substantial pile in the kitchen. The cooks promptly roasted the suckling pig using the firewood we had brought, serving it at the master's dinner banquet in no time.

Before I could catch my breath, Diana came into view, pointing at Gala and yelling, "What have you done? The pig had a bitter taste. I told you first thing this morning to use applewood. What did you use? Black walnut? It was terrible!"

Hearing this, Gala's expression twisted in horror.

He hovered behind Diana, massaging her shoulders in a tender and comforting manner. "Easy, my sweetest fig pie," he whispered. "I don't want to see a single hair on your head turn gray from anger, even though you'll still be beautiful with your hair as white as the master's toga." His lips were lightly parted, almost touching Diana's neck.

Diana's face softened immediately.

Gala suddenly jabbed his finger at us. "What did *you two* do? I specifically asked for applewood! Applewood! And yet you come back with black walnut? Explain yourselves!"

Julia and I exchanged astonished glances, our mouths agape and eyes wide. "But that's what you requested. I clearly heard you ask for black walnut," I exclaimed.

"Stop quibbling after you made such a mistake, you bloody idiot!" roared Diana again. "Do you know how much the master will deduct from my salary? By Jupiter's thunderbolt and scepter, you two won't have anything to eat until tomorrow night. Vita, wash all the dishes and pots and no one is allowed to help you. Do you hear me?"

Diana's screeching almost turned me deaf. Speechless, I just looked at Julia in disbelief. *So, this is how it works?*

Gala's suggestive grin and the way his fingers kneaded Diana's shoulders convinced me that accusing him of lying would be pointless.

"Yes, ma'am," I mumbled, eyes downcast.

After Diana and Gala left, I returned to the kitchen and found the towering stack of plates, piled up to my neck. As I carefully reached for the topmost one, Julia rushed in.

"Give it to me." She tried to take that plate from my hand. "Your fingers are blistered from working all day. How can you possibly wash so many plates?"

"No, Julia. I can't bear to let Diana see this and punish me even more," I insisted, holding on tightly.

Julia stood motionless, her voice strained. "This is all so unfair," she uttered, biting her lip. "Fine. I'll take care of your duties in the dorm, so you can rest when you get back."

As she stepped over the threshold, she turned to look back at me. "There is no hope in this house, Vita. We must find a way out."

But how?

I was too exhausted to ask it aloud, and even in my brief time here, I could tell Eubulus was not the kind of master who would grant us freedom someday.

In the middle of the night, I was still scrubbing plates, my hands now swollen, and the wounds numb from pain.

"Just ten more plates and I'm finished," I told myself, bracing against the edge of the sink and taking a deep breath. Suddenly, a pair of sweaty hands landed on my bare shoulders. Spinning around, I saw Gala standing there, his wine breath making me queasy. I managed to hide my disgust.

"Oh, Vita, my sweet marzipan," Gala cooed with a honeyed voice. "Forgive me. You know how crazy Diana can be. I felt bad about it all day. If I can't make it up to you, my tears will flood the River Tiber tonight."

He reached for my hip, causing me to pull away as if his touch were the venomous sting of a scorpion. "Please, Gala," I uttered before moving to the opposite side of the sink. My heart pounded in my chest. Desperation to escape this nasty man surged through me, yet I recognized he wielded the power to determine whether I could venture out and search for my Rufus.

Taking a deep breath to steady my racing heartbeat, I locked eyes with him and spoke firmly, "Please let me go to the market for you. I can get you whatever Titus does."

"You?" Gala scrutinized me from head to toe and sneered. "I don't see you having Titus' talent. You're just saying you can so I give you more time."

"It's not like that," I pushed back. "I have other ways of making money."

"I see." His small, shrewd eyes lit up. "No problem. I know some tavernkeepers who provide rooms for this kind of business. And the commission won't be too high."

A wave of nausea rushed up, as though I had just swallowed a dead fly. I wanted to slap him, but Rufus' face appeared in my mind. *No, calm down, Vita. You need a chance to get out of here, to look for Christian communities and to find Rufus.*

I tightened my fists and declared, "I know how to weave baskets, the kind that would sell. Just bring me some gladioli leaves from the garden and allow me to go to the market once a week. I promise I'll bring money back."

He looked at me, eyeballs rolling quickly. Finally, a grin spread across his face, and he pulled me into his arms, rubbing his chin against my collarbones.

"Selling baskets? That will take time. I'd rather you pay me the way Antonia does right now."

Something in me finally exploded. I forcefully pushed him away, and a pot crashed to the ground, shattering into pieces.

I picked up a shard and warned him, "Stop it! Or I'll tell Diana what you did. A wound on your arm will prove everything."

He stared at me, breathless. Regaining composure, he advanced toward the remaining pile, smashing all the plates to the ground with a single push.

"Looks like you must thank me instead. All the plates are as good as washed now. I'm confident Diana will give you plenty of praise tomorrow," he said with a smirk. "And oh, don't think about telling Diana anything. She comes to my bedroom three nights a week. If I tell her that you seduced me, imagine what punishment you will get." Then he spat in front of my feet and stormed off.

I sank to the ground, sitting there for a long time, wondering how on earth a terrible day had managed to get even worse.

As I stumbled back into the slave room, I found Julia fast asleep, much like everyone else. Collapsing onto my pallet, exhaustion enveloped me.

"Lord Jesus, God the Father," I started to pray. "I feel lost and like I'm drowning. Have you forgotten your daughter already? Help me! I don't ask for great miracles, just a little comfort tomorrow so I will feel there is still hope."

"Vita, I hear you," came a voice so quiet and gentle that I couldn't be certain whether it was real.

Is it you, God? Did you hear my prayer? This was my last thought before drifting off to sleep.

Eleven

A New Low

As expected, the broken plates earned me lashes, ten to be exact, one for each item *I* didn't smash. I couldn't tell Diana what had happened last night. Having already upset Gala, Diana was my only chance to get out of this place and find Rufus.

I couldn't afford to make her hate me.

Gala was standing by when I took the whipping, so I chinned up, refusing to let out any wail to give him satisfaction.

Gala's face was hard as stone when he summoned all the kitchen slaves. "Today is a busy day. Everyone needs to be quick, since Lady Cassia will be back at noon. The master has ordered us to prepare a spread of the lady's favorite dishes. Don't mess up again and make the master mad. And most importantly, listen carefully to what I say in the future."

This comment was obviously directed at me and Julia, even though we'd heard him clearly when he'd asked for black walnut firewood. Yet, being the lowest among house slaves, who would believe our account?

The throbbing pain from the wounds on my back caused me to wince from time to time. Throughout the morning, my hands, still swollen, never had a moment of rest. Whether I was cutting onions and cabbages, peeling beans and lentils, or adding firewood, they hurt each time I used them.

It was almost noon, and Gala asked me to bring a pot of piping hot lentil and barley soup to the dining room. Concerned that my numbed hands might falter, I searched for Julia to help me, but she was occupied elsewhere.

Gala ferociously urged, "Hurry up, the lady has arrived! We haven't got all day!" I grimaced as my fingers came into contact with the scalding pot. With considerable effort, I lifted the pot and made my way toward the dining room.

Walking in the portico along the backyard, a gust of breeze carried the enticing aroma of the soup to my nose, causing my empty stomach to grumble even louder. Before long, the pot became too hot to handle, prompting me to search for a spot to set it down and allow my hands to cool off. Failing to find a suitable place, I opted for the only available space—the floor.

However, my left hand released its grip on the pot sooner than intended. Fortunately, it was already near the floor, so the soup had only spilled a bit, with a small amount splashing onto my hands. I pulled them back swiftly, hissing from the burning pain.

It appeared that my streak of bad luck wasn't ending, as Diana happened to pass by at that very moment and witnessed the mess. She struck my head with the curtain rod she held and cursed, "Useless thing. This is the lady's favorite soup. How dare you spill it! Leave now! Go to the backyard and pull all the weeds. If there is one weed left, I'll have your skin."

I tried to retrieve the pot from the ground, but Diana struck me once more, hitting directly on the wounds on my back. "Go away, you've done enough damage!" Diana bellowed.

I quickly pulled back and hurried to the backyard, my hands contorted from the relentless toil and burning, to the point where I could barely recognize the mess before me. They were swollen and aching. Despite the pain, I had to use them to uproot all the weeds in the garden. Thorns pierced my fingers, and the wounds on my back hurt even more under the noon sun, but I didn't dare to stop for a moment.

Diana was someone who followed through on her words, and I was certain she would come to inspect whether the weeds had been pulled to her satisfaction. After a considerable amount of time spent clearing weeds under the sun, the day finally started to draw to a close.

At this point, I was growing more than a little dizzy, and my battered hands were starting to bleed. Unexpectedly, a drop of blood, freed from my torn palm, fell onto a gladiolus flower. The sight of the red blossom triggered a rush of childhood memories. As I pondered the near impossibility of escaping the house to find Rufus, a wave of heartache overwhelmed me.

I knelt down, leaning on a nearby marble bench, and poured out my bitterness to God. "Lord, did you not hear my pleas? How can you forsake me like this? Why won't you grant me even a glimmer of comfort and hope?" In frustration, I let all my feelings out to Him. "I truly cannot endure this kind of life. A life with no hope at all. It's unbearable, Lord. Please, release me from this turmoil, this torment."

As I murmured in prayer for an extended period, I felt a tap on my shoulder, causing me to whip around in shock. In front of me stood a young girl, her eyes deep, rich, and warm in color, framed by slightly curled, long lashes. Her clear, rosy complexion was accentuated by the radiant sapphire-blue silk dress she wore. Her luscious lips parted, and she started to speak, leaving me in complete surprise.

"Are you a Christian?"

Twelve

Lady Cassia

I stood there frozen, like a statue.

A multitude of thoughts raced through my mind before I mumbled, "Yes," for better or worse, not knowing who she might be or how the right answer would sound.

The girl smiled, a sight even more beautiful than the unfolding petals of a precious gladiolus blossom. "Don't be afraid!" she said. "You didn't pray in front of the house shrine, so I only guessed you might be. I don't hate Christians like the others. On the contrary, you remind me of someone. Come, sit here." She gracefully perched on the bench, patting the vacant spot beside her.

I gingerly settled into the seat, feeling a blend of nervousness and curiosity.

"What's your name?" she queried.

"Vita."

"The way you pray, it reminds me of a friend," the girl said with a pinkish hue on her cheeks.

I eased up slightly, but remained cautious as I asked, "Are you the master's daughter?"

"Yes, my name is Cassia. I just wanted to see how well my gladioli were doing while I was away." She gently caressed the petals, nodded approvingly, and added, "It seems that the gardeners are doing an excellent job. They look wonderfully healthy."

A mixture of longing and relief rose in my heart when I realized the lady also loved gladioli. If she shared my fondness for it, then she must be good.

Cassia smiled and asked, "Do you always come here to pray?"

"No, it's just that Diana asked me to pull the weeds today. I needed to unburden myself, so I knelt down and... Well, you know the rest."

Cassia nodded, and as her gaze shifted downward, she suddenly exclaimed, "What's wrong with your hands?" She gently picked them up, and I winced at the increasing pain.

"How could it come to this?" I sensed the concern in Cassia's voice, and my heart melted. Before I could answer, she frowned and said, "Oh. Well, of course. How could I be so ignorant? It must be Gala."

I gave a silent nod.

"I never really liked him, but Father can't live without the lamb stew he cooks. Don't worry, I'll give him a warning tonight, so he won't mistreat you any longer." Cassia's comforting words worked like a balm, easing the pain of my wounds.

"Vita, tell me your story. I want to know how you became a Christian, how you got here, and... I want to hear everything." Cassia looked at me with glistening eyes. "I'm not here to trick you into saying something you shouldn't. I just want to know more about you."

For a moment, I hesitated, unsure of where to begin. Since Nana fell ill, I hadn't opened up to anyone or shared my burdens, not even with Julia.

I sighed, and then slowly unfolded my narrative, painting a picture of my hometown—a quiet, small village. I talked about how Nana raised me and taught me the love of Christ. The words escaped my lips, recounting the cruel disease that had swept through our village and snatched away my beloved Nana. I shared the bitter twist of fate that led to my enslavement, a consequence of a debt I couldn't repay, and eventually brought me here.

At last, I told her about Rufus. The moment his name danced upon the air between us, I couldn't hold back my tears, breaking down completely. Cassia embraced me, and I wept bitterly, my body trembling with emotion.

All these years, I'd barely mentioned Rufus to anyone, but the great sadness never left. It weighed down my heart like a heavy stone. That day, with my tears gushing out, the stone cracked silently.

Cassia gently stroked my back without a word.

After some time, my tears finally ceased, and I told Cassia about the night that had changed my life.

Cassia embraced me once more, holding me tightly. "Don't worry. You are so devoted to your god. He will watch over your beloved. Besides, I'll plead with my father to help you find him with all available resources," she assured.

My eyes widened, my body trembling at her words. "You will?" I couldn't believe my ears.

Cassia stroked my head gently and said, "Dear one, our family has been in business for generations, with informants all over Rome and the surrounding towns. If he has been sold as a slave here, for sure we'll find some clues."

The sincerity in her warm brown eyes dissolved all my doubts. I clasped Cassia's hands firmly, expecting overwhelming joy that her sweet proclamation promised. And to some extent, I felt it. Yet, an unwelcome and terrifying thought emerged: *What if Rufus is no longer in this world? What if Nana's vision was merely an illusion?* I dared not dwell on these thoughts. As hope started to ascend, so did the fear.

She evidently sensed my unease and inner turmoil. Holding my fingertips, she spoke again, this time in a softer voice, "I understand your pain, Vita. Truly, I cannot imagine how you bear it all. If the man I love disappeared, I'd feel as if I were dying unless I found him."

Her voice quivered, even for this hypothetical situation she had sketched out with her words.

"You mean Aurelius?" I blurted out without thinking and quickly covered my mouth in embarrassment. "I'm sorry, my lady, I didn't mean to..."

"It's perfectly all right," Cassia said, her smile reassuring. "I suppose the whole household is chewing on the rumor of me and Aurelius."

"My... my lady, it is not... I... I didn't..."

"Vita, I don't blame you for being curious. I would be too if I were a slave girl and my master's only daughter favored a house slave over all rich suitors," Cassia said, a wry smile playing on her lips. Her cheeks blushed in unison.

"He must be a very special man," I said sincerely, looking at her.

"Yes, he's truly one of a kind." Cassia's face lit up as she spoke of her sweetheart.

"About two years ago, on my way back from the Temple of Juno, I stumbled upon a crowd of people gathered on the street. They were shouting that someone was dying. Normally, I would have quickly left the scene. However, that day, I felt a sudden urge that perhaps our divine goddess Juno would want me to save that person. Why that thought came to me, I did not know. So, I told my litter-bearer to carry me closer to check on him.

"It was then that I caught sight of a young man, bloodied and bruised from a beating. At first, I was frightened and wanted to leave immediately.

"But as the man opened his eyes, it felt as though he was looking directly at me. I couldn't explain why, but I felt compelled to stay and help him. So, I ordered my litter-bearer to help him into the litter beside me, and I brought him home. There was scarcely room for us both, Vita. It was awkward. But I swear his gentle eyes bored into my soul."

"Oh, my goodness! He was so fortunate to have met someone as kind as you!" I exclaimed.

Cassia smiled again and ventured, "You know, he believes in the same god as you. Maybe that's why I felt a connection with you when I saw you praying just now."

The thought of finding another Christian in the household filled me with hope. Maybe he would know of a local gathering spot or could provide information about Rufus.

My heart raced with excitement.

Cassia continued, "He recovered quickly in my house, and it was only then I discovered he was a slave owned by a tavernkeeper. He had been caught trying to escape and was beaten to near death and left on the street. Terrible, isn't it?"

"That *is* terrible," I agreed. But in that same moment, my inner voice was reminding me these things occurred to slaves all the time and the rich usually did not care. He was spared at the brink of death—all because of my lady's inner feeling, an intuition that sent her. Or perhaps he merely appeared too handsome to pass by.

I sought to swallow my cynicism, chastising myself silently, not liking my thoughts at all.

Cassia had more to say. "He was fortunate, though," she uttered. "If his master had wanted, he could have sent him to the arena to be fed to the lions."

I covered my mouth. I knew such atrocities happened, but to hear such a sweet person speak of it... It shocked me to my core, sending a shudder down my spine.

Cassia shook her head as she continued.

"When he recovered, I pleaded with my father to purchase him from his master. You see, according to the law, he still belonged to him at that point. That little businessman extorted a lot of money from my father, the coin value going up and up, such that we believed it might never stop until he could purchase the world with what father had offered him.

"But finally, a deal was struck, and I stopped crying. My father grumbled for a whole month," Cassia said, biting her lower lip to suppress a chuckle as she recalled the past. "It was a terrible case of extortion, Vita. The tavernkeeper was ruthless."

Then she leaned forward, emphasizing her next point. "However, a year later, my father realized it was his best investment ever. Can you imagine?" Cassia's eyes gleamed with pride. "Aurelius is extremely capable. By this time, he was an apprentice in my father's shop and was quickly promoted to shopkeeper. Within another year, my father entrusted him with the management of all thirteen shops on Bacchus Street and he excelled in the role."

"He must be an extraordinary man," I commented. "And extremely fortunate."

"Yes!" Cassia beamed. "Eventually, my father had so much faith in him that he put him in charge of the entire merchant fleet. This year, our family received a large order from the palace, so he traveled overseas to purchase the goods. And you know, he is incredibly humble. He credits his talents and wisdom to his god, even sharing a story with me about a Jewish man who was sold into Egypt and became a prime minister. His name was..." Cassia paused to think. "I cannot remember. But he impressed me with his storytelling skills, even if I cannot bring to mind the Jewish man's name."

"I can tell you the name. It was Joseph," I exclaimed, excited to hear a story I knew well from my childhood.

"Ah, yes, that's the name." Cassia clapped her hands, continuing to share anecdotes about Aurelius—his prowess, charm, and how much she missed him. While I listened, a deep longing welled up within me, wishing that Rufus could be standing before me so I could embrace him.

Meanwhile, as Cassia spoke, a slave came in with a message. "My lady," he said, bowing respectfully, "the master requests your presence."

"Of course, tell him I'll be there shortly," she replied, then shifted her attention to me. "Starting today, you will serve me. Gather your belongings now. You will be staying in my chamber tonight."

I couldn't believe what I was hearing. "Really? C-Can I?" I stammered, excitement making it difficult to form coherent words.

"Of course, you will live there, helping me style my hair and get dressed. I'll speak to my father right away; he rarely denies me anything," Cassia said with a playful wink.

"Thank you! Thank you, my lady," I exclaimed, ready to head to the slave quarters and gather my belongings. However, a concern crossed my mind as I thought of Julia. If I left, she might face bullying from the other girls. Meanwhile, Cassia's offer felt genuine, and I didn't want to let her down.

"What's with the gloomy look? Don't you want to serve me?" Cassia inquired with a worried expression. "Did I say something that bothered you?"

I had no choice but to be honest. "My lady, if it's possible, I would like to continue sleeping in the slave quarters. My best friend needs me there. But I give you my word to be in your bedchamber early every morning to serve you."

Cassia nodded. "You are a loyal friend who deserves my trust. Your wish is granted, but you mustn't be late in the morning. I usually start my day early with devotion to divine Juno."

She rose, took a few steps, then turned back, tilting her head with a gentle smile on her lips. "Remember to pick some gladioli tomorrow morning and put them in my vase."

"Not a chance of forgetting, my lady! I'll pick the loveliest ones for you!" I replied, brimming with joy. Standing up, my excitement overflowing, I twirled twice and stretched my arms to the sky, feeling as though I were about to soar.

"Heavenly Father and Lord Jesus," I whispered to the sky, "You truly didn't abandon me." Gratitude filled my heart as I exclaimed, "Thank you! Thank you! Thank you!"

I returned to the slave quarters and immediately sensed something was amiss. Several girls murmured among themselves and cast furtive glances in my direction. Antonia said with a sneer, "Oh, look who's back——the clever lady!" She then turned to Julia who was sitting on the edge of her pallet and snickered. "And *you,* what a fool. You deliberately sought out the master and got yourself beaten half to death, yet your friend captured the lady's heart just as soon as she returned."

I walked over to Julia, who kept her head lowered, and asked with concern, "Are you all right?"

"I'm fine," Julia said, but still didn't look up. She wiped the corners of her eyes with her hand, then pointed to the parcels on my pallet. "I've packed all your things for you. Go ahead, don't make the lady wait."

Amused by the tremor in her voice, I chuckled. "You silly girl, you think I would really abandon you?"

"But didn't the lady ask you to..." Julia looked confused.

I playfully pinched her nose, laughing. "Yes, the lady asked me to serve her, but I couldn't leave you behind. So, I asked her if I could still sleep here, and she agreed."

Julia's eyes widened, and she stammered, "Y-You would rather stay in this nasty place instead of the lady's chamber, just so you can be with me?"

Glancing around, I said, "This really is a nasty place." I locked eyes with Julia and continued, "But if I leave, who will protect you here?" Antonia snorted and left with a hard swipe on the curtain.

Julia sprang to her feet, embracing me tightly. "Vita. Why are you so kind to me? I'm afraid I will let you down one day..." Her voice wavered, and I could see the shimmer of unshed tears in her eyes.

I gently stroked her back and reassured her, "Don't be silly. We'll always be friends. I'm here, aren't I?"

As night descended and everyone succumbed to slumber, I lay on my pallet and prayed, "Lord, I have little faith and I blamed you this morning. But now I see that you have prepared everything for me. If I hadn't been punished by Diana, I might never have found favor in Cassia's eyes. Your ways are higher than mine. Please forgive me. Also, help me serve my lady well and honor your name."

With those words, I found solace in sleep, experiencing an unusual sense of happiness and contentment.

Thirteen

Birds Uncaged

The curtains of the bedchamber billowed as fresh air graced the room. Beams of sunlight bounced across all the shiny surfaces, giving a warm feeling like Lady Cassia's smile. She'd had that gentle, infectious grin since the break of dawn.

The morning bath was prepared, and Cassia hummed under her breath. I shared in her mirth with a quiet tune of my own.

Standing beside the wicker chair in which Cassia sat, I carefully applied jasmine oil on her tresses, then braided them into a new style I'd just learned.

Cassia, sitting in front of the dressing table, finally unable to hold back, clapped her hands and turned to me, disarranging her hair in the process.

"Do you know what day it is, Vita?"

"Let me take a wild guess." I squinted, faking the look of contemplation. "Is it the day my lady's beloved returns?" I said, gently correcting Cassia's head.

"Yes, it is! He sent a messenger home two days ago, telling me they were already unloading at the harbor. The goods should have reached the palace last night," Cassia said, clutching onto her necklace. She looked off dreamily as I continued working on her hair.

"No wonder someone is humming all morning," I said in a playful tone. The days of serving Cassia had forged a close bond between us. In moments when nobody was around, we often spoke like friends.

"What will you do after this?" Cassia asked suddenly.

"I will stay to help with anything you need, my lady."

"You are released from your duty today. Rome is beautiful in late summer. I'm sure you'll enjoy seeing the sights."

I was ecstatic at the offer. It had been three months since I began serving Cassia. I had considered requesting the opportunity to leave the house and look for clues to Rufus' whereabouts. However, tasks in Cassia's chamber were ever-present, and she mentioned that her father's informants were already on the search.

Guilt always overcame me when I even considered making such a request to my kind mistress.

However, despite my eagerness to accept the offer, I felt a sense of duty to finish my tasks before I could leave. Swiftly, I dipped a fine silver stick into an alabaster jar which contained a mixture of squid ink and olive oil. Meeting Cassia's gaze in the mirror, I suggested, "It's a special day. Surely, my lady would like me to enhance your eyes a little, right? After applying this to your lashes, they will appear twice as long."

"That won't be necessary," Cassia responded, a bashful grin lighting up her face. "Aurelius prefers natural beauty." Opening a drawer, she counted out ten silver coins and placed them in my hand. "Enjoy yourself," she added with a wink.

Overjoyed, I was on the verge of jumping to my feet. "Thanks, my lady. One little petition: May I bring Julia with me?" I looked at her with pleading eyes.

"Well, normally, kitchen slaves aren't allowed to go out, except during Saturnalia," Cassia said. "But I don't want to refuse you this small request to ruin your day. Moreover, having someone familiar with the city as your companion is safer. So, yes, she can go with you."

"You are too kind, my lady." I lifted her hand and planted a kiss on it.

"That's enough. Run along, so you can make the best of it. I will send someone to tell Diana and Gala that your friend is free for the day." Cassia grinned widely.

"I'll see you tonight, my lady. I really can't thank you enough," I exclaimed, dashing out of her chamber and into the colonnade surrounding the garden. The flowers smelled far more fragrant that day, and even the buzz of the greenhead flies hovering over the fish sauce pot outside the kitchen sounded like a sweet melody to my ears.

I found Julia in the kitchen, and she almost couldn't believe it when I told her the good news. "Let's hurry before the lady changes her mind. Plus, there are plenty of places to explore if we leave early," Julia urged, pulling me towards the gate.

When my feet planted on the ground outside, the sky above suddenly unfolded into an expansive canvas. Within the villa, the sky could only be glimpsed through the small square opening in the atrium roof and above the garden. I had nearly forgotten the sensation of seeing the entire sky without its familiar frame. A quick glance at Julia confirmed she was also in a daze. After a prolonged silence, she suggested, "Let's head down the famous Sacra Street to the Forum. It hosts the largest market and is the busiest place in the city."

The Forum.

How could I forget? It was the very place where I had been sold as a slave. The bustling activity was overwhelming; one could easily get lost in its chaotic energy. The thought that I might discover some Christian symbols there left by my people intrigued me.

I had little chance to think as Julia pulled me forward. Upon reaching Sacra Street, the air carried a peculiar blend—mingling the unpleasant odor of the public toilet with the rich aromas of spices, the smell of sweat from the gymnasiums, and the fragrant scent of ointments worn by affluent women in litters.

Taking a deep sniff, I grinned. "This is the smell of life, dear Julia.

An uncommon treat for us."

"Welcome to Sacra Street, the most famous street in Rome," said Julia. "It goes all the way through the Forum, connecting to Palatine Hill where the Royal Palace is."

"Land in this area is very expensive. Our house is only medium in price compared to many along this route; the most expensive ones are in the east of the Esquiline area."

We strolled on Sacra Street in the midst of a stream of people. Slaves dressed in fraying tunics walked in a steady stride, carrying pots or baskets on their heads or hips. Homeless people walked in groups, searching for handouts. Freeborn men were dressed in togas with elegant folds, while the womenfolk were adorned in colorful long dresses, sometimes tied twice around the waist and the chest. The hustle of the main street presented so much to see, making me a little dizzy.

Julia pointed to a man wearing a white toga with a purple border. "See that man there? The purple border means he is a senator."

I noticed some women with their hair dyed in shades of blue and yellow standing under the porch of a tavern, cheerfully waving to passersby. "Why are these women also wearing togas? Are they especially important ladies in high government positions? They look... well, they look quite different."

"Ha, no way!" Julia couldn't hide her amusement. "They are prostitutes! In Rome, only prostitutes ever wear togas like men. And you can tell them by the color of their hair; it's such an easy giveaway. There's so much to see and learn here, don't you think?"

"You bet there is! I've never seen such a mix of people. Why does this enormous house have so many windows?" I pointed to a giant building complex next to her.

"This is called an *insula*, a building complex with lots of units to be rented," Julia said. "Most people in Rome, except the very rich, live in buildings like these. They used to be very affordable, but with people rushing into the city, the rent rises every year. On Sacra Street, even the smallest unit in the worst insula building costs fifty silver coins a month. Yes, fifty whole coins. Every March, on the day when the tenants renew their contracts, homeless people will flood the streets."

"My goodness, fifty silver coins would be enough for a family in our village to live for a year. Living in Rome is really not easy," I complained.

"This is the heart of the empire, after all. It would be strange to have it any other way." Julia's eyes brimmed with pride as she continued, "Hundreds of thousands of people from other provinces come in every year, some doing business, some becoming hired hands for the rich. I've heard that many, who went bankrupt, would rather sell themselves into slavery than go back to their hometowns."

"Why? Who would want to be a slave by choice?" I questioned, feeling a bit perplexed. Despite the city's prosperity, it stirred up a mix of fear and loneliness within me.

"You don't understand the attractiveness of the city. Although the high class may get whatever they want, there is always hope for people of low status. If a slave is kissed by goddess Fortuna, he may be freed by his master on a whim. Then in a few more years, he can start his own business and get settled down in the city. His son will become a Roman citizen, who might one day seek a position in the Senate. Pretty enticing, isn't it?" Julia said with a longing look. "Living in the countryside, even as a free man, ties you to the land for a lifetime. What good is that?"

Fixing my gaze on Julia, I listened intently. Her eyes sparkled with enthusiasm as she continued, "There are many ways for men to change their lives in Rome, but there is only one way for women. I dare say it is an even better way. I'll show you something later."

After strolling a few blocks, Julia gestured toward one of the stunning villas. "I know the lady living here. She is a great example of a 'Roman dream' coming true for us slave girls."

"Tell me!" I couldn't help but become curious.

"It's a rather interesting story. She was born in the provincial rural area and used to be a slave just like us." Julia's eyes lit up with excitement as she carried on with the story. "She was favored by her master, a wealthy senator. Rumor has it that he fell in love with her voice while she sang, cleaning the garden floor. He made her sing him to sleep every night, and from there, she became his sweetheart." Julia winked at me before returning her gaze to the building.

"He eventually bought her this house, loaded with all sorts of luxuries," Julia added.

"So, did he end up marrying her?"

"Of course not!" Julia laughed, seemingly taken aback by my naivety. "Roman law outright forbids marriage between a senator and a slave, whether freed or not. Besides, the senator is already married to a well-born lady. There might be some kind of 'arrangement' between he and his wife, so she won't bother his mistress. But who cares? This girl is now a wealthy and free woman, living her blissful life with her lover. It's like a dream for all the slave girls in Rome."

Julia's voice was full of admiration. "Isn't it amazing? I mean, who wouldn't love to have a wealthy lover taking care of all your needs and treating you like a princess?"

"Well... I suppose it *is* nice." I looked away as thoughts of Rufus invaded my mind again. Up to this point, I hadn't noticed any Christian symbols along our way.

"You don't sound excited at all," Julia remarked, gently pulling me out of the path of a passing donkey. "Imagine it. Just imagine!"

"I guess the odds of such a thing happening are minimal anyway," I commented, hoping to steer the conversation elsewhere.

"Oh, don't be so pessimistic. Maybe goddess Fortuna will kiss us today, right in the Forum." Julia giggled and urged me to move faster. "Come on, let's pick up the pace."

Fourteen

The Fish!

THE FORUM WAS TRULY a bustling hub of activity, with a steady flow of people moving in and out of the square. Long colonnades, made up of rows of grand marble columns, surrounded the square, providing shade and shelter from the sun. Along the colonnade were busy shops, their awnings flapping in the breeze, selling everything from exotic spices and perfumes to fine textiles and jewelry. Traders were shouting out their wares, trying to attract more customers to stop and look at their goods. The air was filled with the sound of bargaining and haggling as shoppers moved from shop to shop, like fast currents of water.

Jumping and hopping along the way, with arms flailing, Julia enthusiastically introduced me to each of the buildings lining the road.

"Here is the temple of Saturn, the god of wealth," said Julia, gesturing toward the towering marble structure. "Every December, there is a huge celebration called the Saturnalia, when schools and courts are closed, and everybody is just feasting, gambling, and making merry in the streets all day. It's quite a sight to see people dressed in colorful clothes, singing, dancing, and giving gifts to each other —— even the slaves get a day off."

She gestured toward a golden temple perched on the hill to the west, overseeing the Forum. "That one over there, on Capitol Hill, is the temple of Juno, the goddess of marriage and childbirth—— the very sanctuary our lady often visits. It used to be the most worshiped temple among Roman women, but nowadays, the upper-class women are drawn to other goddesses, such as Isis and Mithra from Egypt and Persia. They find them more exotic and mysterious," Julia said with a grin. "Which I can totally understand."

Suddenly, a group of young men in white robes, adorned with fringes and golden bells, came into view, strutting in a procession with heads held high like a flock of roosters. Quickly, pedestrians stepped aside, many bowing respectfully as they passed. Julia pulled me to the side, out of their path. "These are the priests of goddess Isis," she said with a frown. "They are becoming increasingly powerful and wealthy these days. Better not mess with them."

I suddenly remembered the priest who had almost bought me when I was sold at the market. "I heard that even the empress is one of their followers. Is that true?" I asked.

"Yes, that's what a lot of people say. She desired a son, so it makes sense that she would worship a goddess of fertility. I also heard that their priestesses take a vow of chastity and consume a secret potion that renders them barren in this life and the next."

"That's a bit extreme," I said.

"Indeed," Julia commented thoughtfully. "But I think their power comes from the great sacrifices they make. You know, these gods and goddesses never give anything for free."

"But Jesus does," I replied almost too quickly, regretting it as soon as the words left my mouth. I sneaked a peek at Julia, and to my relief, her face didn't change.

Maybe she didn't hear me.

Moving on, we came to a large open space accommodating small vendors and jugglers. "As you may have guessed, this is an open market," Julia said. "These hawkers don't have fixed storefronts, so the prices are much cheaper. Sometimes, you can get a really good bargain. Come, take a look." She led me to some vendors, and I examined their wares one by one: cosmetics, pottery, clothes, shoes. The list was endless.

Everything looked amazing. Julia appeared to be an experienced shopper, knowing where to find the best deals and how to negotiate prices, enjoying the process of browsing and bargaining, which seemed to be all part of the added excitement.

But suddenly, she patted her head. "Oh, Venus!" she exclaimed. "I suddenly remember I have a friend who runs a barbershop near here, and I told her I'd stop by if I had a chance."

I saw her eyes darting around, avoiding mine as she shifted her weight from one foot to another. Understanding she didn't want me to follow her, I smiled. "Go ahead. Who knows when we'll go out next time? I'll be right here. Won't go very far. There's so much to see in just this one spot."

"Please, listen to me. You must be careful, Vita. This is Rome, and there are so many pickpockets. Don't let them steal your money," Julia said as she quickly walked away.

"It's truly fine; I'm not a three-year-old child. I know what is safe and what is not."

Julia looked back, blinking. "Losing money is a small matter. Just be cautious not to get yourself snatched. That's all I will say. The rest is up to you." With a mischievous twinkle in her eyes, she playfully added, "And be careful not to let anyone snatch your heart either."

She then disappeared into the crowd. I grinned, shaking my head at her usual wit.

After Julia left, I breathed a sigh of relief. Finally, I could have some time alone to look for Christian symbols. I continued wandering around the area, scanning every wall in passing, particularly focusing on the lower parts and where two walls met, because Rufus had mentioned that was where Christians left their symbols in cities and towns. Walking slowly, taking in the sights and sounds of the bustling city, I was disappointed to find only scribbles and graffiti about popular gladiators and charioteers.

As I made my way down a dimly lit corridor, the sound of a commotion caught my attention. Approaching, I saw a large crowd gathered around a small wooden stage. It looked like a storytelling stand, the seats filled with patrons, and a young man with a trident-shaped tattoo on his bare arm was standing on the stage telling a story.

"... then he had to flee the city to avoid being punished. He ran into the desert and sat by a well; there, he met the daughters of a priest..."

Murmurs began to rise from the back of the crowd. "Boring story, boring story!" shouted some.

"Give us something spicy. We want scandals and juicy tales," another chimed in. The murmurs grew louder until the entire crowd was in an uproar.

The man halted his story and chuckled in embarrassment. "Please, let me finish this one. Quiet, please! The next one will be different."

"No!" the crowd shouted in unison.

The storyteller raised his hands in surrender and the protest gradually subsided. "Calm down, brothers. Go grab some bread from the bakeries. We'll continue shortly," he announced, taking a seat on the edge of the stage.

Many in the audience left, still murmuring among themselves.

As the man removed his outer cloak, revealing a frayed tunic adorned with multiple patches, my attention was immediately captivated by the pendant hanging from his belt. The bronze fish pendant delivered a warm rich golden color in the light, and in that moment, my breath caught in my throat.

Fifteen

Get on the Stage

I MADE MY WAY to the storyteller.

He had his hands covering his face, and as he lowered them, he stared at the floor with a dejected look. I waited for him to speak, but he kept his head down.

I approached the stage and lightly tapped on its side, causing him to startle and glance up in my direction. I quickly drew a fish in the air, a symbol recognized by Christians, and his expression softened immediately.

"Peace to you, my sister," he said.

"My brother, do you know of any Christian gatherings nearby?" I asked, getting right to the point. He abruptly sat up straight and his eyes scanned me from head to toe.

"My name is Vita, and I grew up in Cyprus," I said, trying to convey my sincerity through my tone. "I was sold here as a slave four months ago. The reason I asked about the gathering place is because I am searching for someone very dear to me. He went missing from our home three years ago, but my Nana told me that she saw him in a vision, and it showed that he was still alive in Rome. If he truly is in Rome, he could have connections with other Christians, and I might uncover clues about his whereabouts in those gatherings."

He gazed at me, lost in words. Upon a closer look, I found he was a well-built man in his late twenties, with muscles too toned for such a profession. His round, soft eyes and flattened nose softened the sharp impression of his prominent cheekbones.

Despite only just meeting him, I felt at ease with this Christian brother, so I shared a brief version of my story. He listened quietly, and after a moment of silence, he embraced me in a comforting, brotherly hug.

"I'm sorry about your loss," he said, patting me on the back as he released the hug. "But our old gathering spot got ransacked by some thugs. The deacons are looking for a safer spot to meet up. I'll take your request to them, let them know what's up. When you come to see me next time, I'll take you to our new gathering place. And... and my name is Marcus, by the way. You can consider me a friend," Marcus said it all in a rush.

"Oh, Marcus, you don't know how much that means to me."

Thinking of meeting more Christians in this city, something deep in my heart began to come to life, and I found myself unconsciously holding onto his hands.

"Never mention it. I just... you know... want to help if I can," he responded, gently withdrawing his hands while a timid smile graced his face. Then he began sharing his faith journey with me.

"I used to be a gladiator, something I had done since I was thirteen. Five years ago, I injured my leg to protect the school master, so he freed me. To make a living after leaving my old profession, I became a storyteller. And here I am," Marcus said.

Now I understand why his physique doesn't seem to match his job. I chuckled inwardly.

"It's a struggle, believe me. People enjoy hearing dirty stories about fierce gladiators and wealthy Roman matrons, and I have plenty of tales to satisfy them," he continued. "But about two months ago, I was brought to a sermon given by Peter the Apostle, and it touched me deeply, so I became a believer. Since then, I have decided to use my talent to tell people stories about our God."

"Isn't that risky?" I lowered my voice unconsciously. "I've heard that our faith is not well accepted in Rome."

"You're right. But I've been very careful and haven't gotten myself into any trouble," Marcus explained. "The problem is people still expect me to tell them the same old stories. As a result, I've been losing my audience. If it were just about me, I wouldn't mind at all. However, my wife passed away two years ago, leaving me with a five-year-old son who suffers from seizures every now and then..." A shadow passed over Marcus' eyes as the furrow on his forehead deepened.

"I can only imagine how difficult that must be," I said. Suddenly, an idea struck me, causing my voice to rise a pitch higher than intended. "You see, Marcus? I have an idea. Would you mind letting me have a try?"

"Try what?" Marcus tilted his head, his eyes squinting in confusion. "You mean you want to—"

"Yes, I'd like to try telling a story in your place."

"Are you sure? Storytelling is not as easy as you might think. These folks, they're like sharks smelling blood at the slightest whiff of boredom. Perhaps you noticed it during my performance. These people are ruthless."

"Well, I am not short of stories, that's for sure. Nana always told me stories of Jesus and the Israelites when I grew up. I learned one thing or two from her about how to make a story captivating. I would listen to her for hours. She had this talent of immersing you into the scene."

"I think we can give it a try. They are leaving anyway. But please don't talk about Jesus' name too openly. The stories of the prophets and the ancient kings would be nice," Marcus said with a wry smile. "As you said, we'd better still be cautious."

"Got it. I won't get you into trouble, I promise." I grimaced. "Well, hopefully not."

As I climbed upon the stage, the crowd quieted and many stepped forward, squinting.

"Welcome one and all. Today, I bring you the tale of a young boy who defeated a GIANT!" I said, stretching my limbs to imitate a giant, trying to grasp the audience's attention.

"There was a twelve-year-old boy named David, still small in weight and stature. His job was tending his father's sheep. He took the sheep to green lands. There, he fed them, gave them water to drink, and protected them from beasts in the forest. Weeks went by without any issues until one day, a lion with a mighty roar—the biggest and most ferocious lion you could imagine—took one of the sheep as they grazed." I used my arms to mimic the wide-open mouth of the lion, and the audience gasped.

"What do you think David did?" I asked loudly.

"If he had any sense, he'd run in the other direction," someone shouted.

"You may think that, but you're wrong. No, David's tiny frame chased after it and eventually caught up with the lion." I did a running pose.

"Lies! Any twelve-year-old boy would run away from a lion," a man with a bulbous nose and a thick mustache exclaimed. "Get the other fellow back on stage! At least his stories are more believable."

"Ah, well, just wait and see. If he was just an ordinary boy, why would I bother telling the story?" I asked, shunning possible comments with a scowl. "After much pulling and groaning, young David snatched the sheep from the lion's mouth."

I demonstrated with the pulling of my hands, noticing several men smiling when I made the gesture.

"Tell us about the giant!" someone with bushy eyebrows demanded.

"Please hold your horses. I am getting there."

"Come on, we haven't got all day."

"Fine," I said. "Then came a time when his people went to war with a neighboring tribe."

"Who? The lion's people or this David boy?"

There was another outbreak of laughter. I ignored them and continued my story.

"The neighboring tribe had a powerful army with giants in its ranks. Their champion was a great hulk known as *Goliath of Gath*, a giant of giants, towering at over nine feet, standing above all men in his town. Six fingers on each hand and six toes on each foot." The audience looked on in consternation, some turning to each other with whispers of disbelief.

"He must be Argos in human form."

"No, he was Cacus, killed by Hercules," a double-chinned man yelled. The audience responded with approving murmurs.

"Blasphemy!" someone with a thick neck protested, tossing a grasp of fried beans over me. The crowd was getting out of hand, and I was at a loss for what to do. I scanned through the crowd for Marcus but couldn't see him.

"He is not a god!" I called out. Raising my hands to get their attention, the crowd gradually quieted down. "Although many who saw him trembled at his sight, and tales of him alone made soldiers shiver in their boots, he was still nothing but a human. For days, Goliath came out before the army of David's people and heaped insults at them. 'Weaklings! Tiny dogs! Pests on the surface of the earth!' he bellowed at them." I deepened my voice as I demonstrated the proud boasting of the giant, the crowd chuckling in response.

"He asked for any single soldier who dared to face him one on one, but no one stood up, not even the captains of the battalions. Now, all were afraid of this Goliath."

"They probably just peed in their pants." The comment came from a towering woman with ebony skin in the third row. "I know my husband would," the woman added, pointing to a petite man next to her.

"Who, me?" The man raised an eyebrow in mock defiance. "I'd never pee in my pants. Not even in front of this Goliath, and certainly not in front of you."

The couple's banter set off laughter in the crowd, briefly stealing everyone's attention.

"Anyway," I interjected, clearing my throat loudly to refocus the audience, "the men were so afraid that the king promised his daughter's hand in marriage to any man who could defeat Goliath, yet no one stepped up to the challenge."

"Maybe the king's daughter was ugly like Jyestha," a young man with a receding hairline well beyond his years shouted.

I almost cracked up with the rest of the crowd but managed to hold back.

"Now, David, being the youngest of eight brothers, had three older ones serving as soldiers in the battle camp. One day, his father told him to take some food to his brothers. As he arrived, he heard Goliath roaring his insults and taunts. Amidst the commotion, David was deeply angered by the giant's insults, which seemed like specks of dust on the face of his God. Furious, he asked one of the soldiers what he had to do to fight the giant."

"Fight the giant? Then he will die!" a young lad about my age exclaimed.

"He had fought the lion and won, so let us wait and see," another countered.

I smiled, happy at being able to create a picture in the minds of the audience so they could now argue based on the story.

"The soldiers and even his brothers mocked him. Word soon traveled to the king who immediately called for the brave young man. Like most of you standing here, the king tried to dissuade David by telling him he was only a boy and had little chance of survival. But still, David was not discouraged. He told the king about the lions and bears he had wrestled with while protecting his father's sheep.

"Finally, the king allowed David to go and offered him his powerful armor and weapons, but David refused, as they weighed him down.

"He took along only his staff and shepherd's sling and went to the riverbed. There, he picked five smooth stones and then returned to the battlefield."

"What was he going to do with the stones? Teach the giant to count?" Laughter erupted again, but I ignored them and kept on.

"When David stepped out before Goliath and challenged him, Goliath taunted him for being just a little boy, but David—yet again—was unfazed. He stepped forward, boldly holding his sling. Goliath could not believe that a boy had come to face him with only a sling. His rage grew, threatening to feed David to the wild birds and beasts.

"David replied to him saying these words, 'You come to me with a sword and a spear, but I come to you in the name of my God. Today, my God will deliver you into my hand. I will defeat you and claim your head. The corpses of your army will be left for the birds of the sky and the beasts of the earth to devour, so that all may know that the one true God is among us.'"

I delivered the words with such spirit that the audience was totally engrossed in the scene, seemingly hooked on each word and action, staring without blinking.

I took a moment to catch my breath and prayed silently, *Dear Lord, catch their hearts, and may the story pave a way for you to reach their souls.*

Then I continued with a steady tone.

"At David's words, Goliath was blinded with rage and took a menacing step toward him. Rather than flee from the giant, David ran toward him, swinging his sling. When the stone was spinning fast, he unleashed it with the force of a mighty arrow, sending it straight toward..." I intentionally slowed my pace, setting the stage for the most thrilling moment of the story. The audience was silent, their mouths wide open.

Suddenly, a loud and boisterous voice shattered the quietness.

"So, you left me to have fun by yourself, Theophilus!"

The voice boomed from behind the audience, and suddenly, all I saw were the backs of their heads as the crowd turned in unison. Gazing toward the source of the noise, I spotted a young man with raven black hair standing behind the last row of seats.

He had a lean, athletic build and a chiseled jawline, making him look handsome in a rugged way. Another man beside him, with wavy, chestnut brown hair, had his arm around the first man's shoulder, teasing him by tugging on his ear.

The second man had a more refined and polished look, with a sharp nose and piercing, amber-colored eyes that exuded confidence and charm.

"Don't you know we're about to be late!" the second man exclaimed, his voice growing louder. As he spoke, more people turned away from me, directing their attention toward them.

In an instant, all the blood rushed up to my head.

Sensing the epic ending to the story was going to be ruined by those strangers, I felt intense pressure building up in my temples, as if they were on the verge of bursting. And to make matters worse, my stomach made the loudest rumble of the day.

That was it—— Rufus was right; I really did have a short temper when I was hungry.

In a fit of impulsive rage, I stooped down to untie one of my sandals. "God, forgive me for what I'm about to do," I murmured. Taking aim, I hurled the sandal at the man with the chestnut brown hair.

"Shut. Your. Mouth. Up! I was telling a story!"

Sixteen

A Troublesome Pair

My aim was accurate, but my target was quick to react. Just as the sandal was about to hit his face, he reached out and caught it with ease, his expression remaining calm and composed. The other man, with ink black hair, suddenly stood up and bellowed, "How dare you!" His hand instinctively reached for the sheath on his belt, pulling out a dagger, the glint of the blade immediately snapping me back to reality.

Oh, God! Oh, God, what have I done? I screamed in my mind, staying rooted to the spot.

But the chestnut-haired man put his hand on his friend's dagger, pushing it back into the sheath. The audience gasped. Some even stood up quietly and slipped away.

Gaining some form of composure, I looked at the two men carefully; both were neatly dressed in charming togas, and the one who was holding my sandal even had a wide purple border on his.

A senator!

Julia had told me about this dress code of Rome.

Oh, Lord, look what I did, I cried in my heart. *I'm doomed. And no doubt this will get Marcus in trouble too.*

The black-haired man still stared at me, his eyes wild with rage. His lips parted, on the brink of saying something, but his friend signaled him to stop. Murmurs rippled through the crowd and more started to leave, but the chestnut-haired man spoke with a deep commanding voice, "Everyone stays."

There was something compelling about his voice, and I wasn't the only one who sensed it; instantly, the crowd stopped murmuring and held their positions.

Turning his gaze back to me, he said, "Go on, storyteller."

My heart hammered. *At least I get to finish my story before dying.* I smiled bitterly, taking a deep breath before continuing my story in front of the nervous crowd.

"The... The stone hurtled toward Goliath's forehead, lodging so deep into it that the giant immediately fell to the ground. Seeing his opportunity, David rushed forward to him, drew Goliath's mighty sword from his side, and... and with one deft motion, sliced off his head."

Several people prepared to clap, but their hands froze mid-air while their eyes focused on the chestnut-haired man. He stood with an unreadable expression, arms crossed.

I pushed aside my fears and carried on with my story.

"Those from Goliath's army who had just witnessed this event were shocked that their champion had been defeated; they turned tail and ran away. The army of David's people drew their swords and pursued them, killing many, and eventually winning the battle.

"And that was how David's God delivered his people from their enemies through David's hand. Now everyone knows David's God is God Almighty."

I completed my tale and gracefully dipped my head to the audience, feeling my entire back drenched in sweat. An uncomfortable silence ensued, but finally, one boy broke the ice with a clap. Slowly, others joined in, and soon the crowd gave me a standing ovation.

The tense atmosphere that had lingered earlier now gave way to cheers and applause. Copper coins were tossed onto the stage, like shimmering raindrops in a summer downpour.

If it had been in a different circumstance, I'd have picked them all up in no time, but I knew my trouble with the two men wasn't over. After the cheers had died down, I looked up and saw the crowd had dispersed, but the two men were still standing there. Summoning all my courage, I approached them with one foot bare.

"Forgive me, my lord. I... I never meant to be rude. I'm just glad you weren't hit," I stuttered. "If only I could turn back time. It was a stupid thing to do, and I'm truly sorry. I just hope you—"

"Nice story," the chestnut-haired man said, "and an even better face." Smirking, he handed me back my sandal. "But your feet smell."

My cheeks flushed with embarrassment, but I hoped this was his way of getting back at me and I'd be off the hook soon.

The black-haired man said sternly, "You are in the presence of the praetorian prefect..."

His friend stopped him with a wave of his hand. "I'm Caius and this is Theophilus, my friend. May I have your name please?" he asked in a rich, deep voice.

"Vita." I mustered the valor of a gladiator stepping into the arena. It was clear that these two lions could tear me into pieces if they wanted to. "My name is Vita."

Wait, have I seen him somewhere? I stared at Caius for a moment, and the sharp jawline looked familiar somehow. But I dismissed the thought right away; there was no way I could have encountered men of such status before.

"What house do you belong to?" Caius continued his investigation.

Oh, God, look what I have got myself into! I was worried to death that Master Eubulus would find out about my "little adventure".

"Am I so frightening?" Sensing my unease, Caius probed with a smile.

I had to admit that his smile was quite charming. Unlike Rufus' warm and genuine grin, Caius' was more like a subtle, confident smirk, one side of his lips slightly curving up, hinting at playfulness and a touch of mystery.

"My master is Eubulus. The villa isn't far from here," I answered, trying to be vague and hoping he wouldn't ask more questions.

"Eubulus the fragrance merchant? I didn't know he had such good taste in picking slaves," Caius said, looking at my earrings, a symbol of my slavery.

"You know him?" My heart dropped to my stomach.

"Don't worry, Vita. There's no chance I'll meet your master," Caius said, his amber-colored eyes seemingly seeing through my mind. "But I'm curious, how did this David manage to kill a giant with just a stone? It truly amazed me, the feat a man can achieve with so little. I find it extraordinary," he said it with a touch of wonder, as if genuinely intrigued.

"But this was no ordinary sling, my lord. The stone was slung with the help of God, and with Him, even ordinary men can do far more than you can imagine," I said, thanking God that the topic had changed.

"His god must be a warrior like Mars, but I still can't believe a sling on its own can possess such tremendous power with such precision."

"I've seen shepherds use them in my hometown. They can be extremely powerful in the right hands. I've seen it with my own eyes. The children there grow up learning how to use them, so over time, they become masters in the art."

"Maybe I'll try it someday," Caius said, a trace of amusement in his tone as he let out a smile that reached his eyes.

Theophilus discreetly pulled at Caius' sleeve, whispering, "We're running late for the Senate, Caius."

"As if you care." Caius turned to Theophilus, playfully ruffling his hair as if teasing a younger brother.

Then he turned back to me, a glimmer of wistfulness in his eyes. "Too bad we couldn't talk more, Vita. We have urgent business to attend to. It was an interesting story. If the gods permit, we may get the chance to meet again." As he said this, he placed a silk pouch into my hand and gave me a small smile before turning and walking away with Theophilus.

Taking a relieved breath, I muttered to myself, "Oh, God, please don't let us meet again."

As they walked away, Julia hurried over to me, her hair now intricately braided with beads tucked in between the strands.

"Who were those men?" she eagerly asked, unable to contain her curiosity while constantly glancing in the direction Caius and Theophilus had left.

"Welcome back. They were just two men from the audience. Come on. Help me with these coins!" I said, already busy picking up the copper coins from the stage and putting them in Marcus' small money chest.

"Audience? What audience?" Julia asked.

Before I could answer, she exclaimed, her eyes lighting up with excitement, "Did you see the toga one of them was wearing?"

"Yes, it looked good."

"Good? It's not *good;* it's exquisite! That's the work of Minerva Valerius, the best and most expensive tailor in all of Rome."

"How could you tell? That's impossible! You were so far off."

"The embroidery on the hem is unique; no one makes clothes like her. To top it off, Minerva met a tragic end, executed by the emperor five years ago. Before facing death, she ordered the burning of her entire shop. Amidst the ruined piles, five togas protected by a golden case were found intact, which were rendered almost priceless. Even wealthy lords and ladies are unable to get their hands on them. If I'm not mistaken, that toga was one of them."

I was amazed by Julia's knowledge of the noble lifestyle and opulent luxuries. "How did you come to know all these things?" I couldn't help but ask.

"You know, Vita, I wasn't always a slave."

Seventeen

A Resourceful Friend

Realizing that I had never bothered to ask Julia how she had become a slave in Eubulus' house, a deep sense of guilt washed over me. I gently took her hand, and we sat down at the edge of the stage.

"Forgive me for never asking. So... how did it happen?"

"It's not your fault. I'm the one who never bothered to mention it."

"I'm listening now."

She shifted her gaze on the flowing throng of people. With a deep breath, she began her story.

"Long ago, when things were all right, my father was a successful fabric merchant. And Minerva Valerius, the legendary tailor I just mentioned, only used silk my father provided."

I was so surprised that Julia had come from such a well-to-do family. "No wonder you had such knowledge about expensive clothes," I said.

"Yes." She smiled wryly and continued, "Our family acquired fabrics from the east and sold them to the prominent tailors in Rome. That's how I became familiar with each of their styles. Every tailor has their own distinguished marking or design. It may be ever so small, but once you know and understand, it's easy to recognize."

"And... what happened?" I asked carefully.

Julia let out another deep sigh and said, "One day, my father was caught by the Vigiles after they found one of our wagons contained a shipment of smuggled tubular tiles. My father did everything by the book. It was a set-up, of course. My family was stripped of our wealth and my father died of a stroke shortly after. The stress of losing everything and especially his good name ultimately put an end to his life. I was only five then."

I wrapped my arms around her scrawny trembling shoulders without saying a word.

"After my father's death, my mother was so heartbroken and constantly wondered why we were so unfortunate. She met an old lady on the street one day and was taken to a secret congregation. They called themselves Christians."

I gasped with shock.

"Julia, I didn't know you were a Christian. I should have told you that I am also—"

"No, I'm not a Christian," Julia interrupted me abruptly. "I know you are, Vita, and that's why I never talked about it in front of you. I utterly *hate* this god of yours, loathe him, and don't understand why you don't. To me, he is futile and meaningless. Among all the gods, he—"

She carried on speaking, but by now, my mind had disengaged and wandered off.

The words from her lips had been hideous. These, together with a gush of late afternoon breeze, sent chills down my back. I wanted to argue, but Julia's stern expression pinned me in silence.

I caught myself reminiscing. All these years, when things had gone so wrong one after another, I had blamed God. I had been angry at Him, but did I ever *hate* Him?

No, not even once.

Never for a single moment.

I suddenly realized that even though I never considered myself a strong believer, the seed of faith had been planted by Nana from my early childhood. And it had never died, even in the coldest of winters. A surge of gratitude filled my heart. To be a Christian meant to be filled with love, bravery, hope, and a sense of peace that no one could take away—all the good things.

I looked at Julia and asked softly, "May I know why?"

Julia closed her eyes briefly as if bracing for the onslaught of traumatic flashbacks.

"Ever since my mother became a Christian, she blamed our family's misfortunes on our sins. I mean, of course, we worshiped other gods, but who doesn't? Why are some of them living such good lives? It doesn't make any sense."

"I don't know, Julia... but God is—" I attempted to explain.

"I know your god is just. My mother told me that every day. Whenever the other kids bullied me, she asked me to kneel and confess my sins. Day after day, I repeated that. And I was sick of it. I still am." Julia's lips quivered, and her long eyelashes glistened with moisture.

"I'm sorry that you had to go through that." My words felt so powerless, but that was all I could manage.

Julia seemed deaf to my words and continued, "From the day I turned twelve, I started to rebel. I found a job as an apprentice at my father's friend's shop, crafting togas and tunics for men. So, I flirted with all the customers and even slept with the most handsome and rich ones. My mother found out, of course, since the men's tongues were wagging. She called me a harlot and almost beat me to death. That's when I decided to run away and live in the shop."

"I'm sorry you've suffered so much, Julia."

Julia kept on without looking at me. "Ever since then, my mom made a habit of showing up there every day, yelling all sorts of nasty stuff. It's crazy how someone who claims to love her enemies can be so cruel to her very own daughter."

"I can't imagine how painful you must feel," I said. "But how did you end up in Eubulus' house?"

"No matter what she told me, I just brushed it off. However, one day while I was fixing a customer's toga, she walked in, accompanied by Diana. I had no clue I was being sold until Diana called for two sturdy men from outside to bind my hands."

"How could your mother do that?" I exclaimed.

"'Only suffering can purge your sinful soul.' Those were her final words to me."

I didn't know what to say. All the words I had prepared seemed so feeble in front of such suffering. All I could do was hold her hands tightly.

"Vita, I must be honest with you. Before I met you, I hated all Christians. Really, I despised them and the ground they walked upon. But you made me realize that maybe not all Christians are like my mom. But please, don't try to convert me. Never will I allow myself to be controlled by anyone, divine or mortal." Julia looked me straight in the eye, her tone serious and final. A palpable rift seemed to be widening between us.

"But allow me to pray for you in my heart, will you?" I asked almost in a whisper.

"Well, if you have to." Julia smiled bitterly. "Not that it will do any good."

There was an uncomfortable silence, so I tried to change the topic.

"See how much money I made today." I showed Julia the money chest with a broad grin, but Julia's gaze was fixed on the silk pouch which I had placed beside me.

"What is that?"

"Oh, the man wearing the *priceless* tunic gave it to me."

"Let me see." Julia grabbed the pouch and opened it, her face immediately lit up with excitement. "Oh, divine Juno, are we in a dream?"

I leaned over and saw all the silver coins. "I... I can't believe it. I thought there were only copper coins in it when he handed it to me," I said, looking in the direction in which they had left. And meanwhile I was relieved that this newfound discovery successfully diverted us from our prior weighty conversations.

Julia chuckled and placed the pouch into the satchel I was wearing. "That rich man must have an eye on you. There's no other reason."

"You're talking nonsense."

Julia was still pressing on about the rich man when I saw Marcus running toward us carrying a wrapped package. He reached us panting and held up his hand, signifying we wait while he caught his breath.

"Marcus, are you all right?"

"Forgive me, Vita. While you were telling the story, a neighbor came to tell me that my son had another seizure. So, I rushed home to check on him. When I noticed the day getting dark, I hurried back. Was everything fine? How did it go?"

"Oh, no! Is your son any better now?" I asked in earnest.

"He is fine now. He's been having seizures since he was born, but thank God, they don't last as long as before," Marcus said and wiped his red eyes with his sleeves.

Then he quickly steered the conversation to another topic. "Hey, here is the food. I knew you must be hungry by now, so I bought some hot bread on the way back. Enjoy it; I've already eaten one."

He handed me the loaf of bread, carefully wrapped in a clean linen cloth.

My stomach growled as I opened the wrap. "I am really hungry. Thanks, Marcus, you are the best!" I mused, reflecting that if I had eaten earlier, I might not have been so reckless.

I broke the loaf in two, offering a piece to Julia, but she said she had eaten with her friend. So, I took a huge bite, and all of a sudden, the world brightened up. "Oh, this is so good," I said, still chewing the bread.

"Is this your friend?" he asked, his attention now on Julia.

I quickly swallowed the bread. "Sorry, my mind goes blank when it comes to food. Yes, this is Julia; Julia, this is Marcus. He owns the storytelling stand."

"A pleasure to meet you." Julia's eyes briefly scanned the tattoos adorning his arm.

"The pleasure is mine." Marcus nodded with a smile, and then looked toward the empty seats. "How did the story go? Before I left, I saw you managed to keep the audience amused."

"Well, it went surprisingly well. Here." I handed Marcus the money chest which was filled to the brim with copper coins. "See for yourself," I said. However, as I reached into my satchel for the silk pouch, I hesitated for a moment.

This money could bring me closer to my freedom, but the memory of Marcus wiping away his tears with his sleeve tugged at my heartstrings, so I took out the pouch and placed it in Marcus' hand.

Marcus' eyes brightened as he opened the pouch, his mouth dropping open as he looked at all the silver coins in it. "Wow, this is beyond my wildest dreams."

He held the pouch out to me, his hands trembling as he spoke. "No, I can't take them. You've earned it, Vita. You should keep them. Please, take them back."

"Your son needs it. Find a good physician to heal his seizures," I insisted as I pushed his hands back. After some hesitation, Marcus finally agreed to accept half of the money. He placed the pouch back in my hand with half of the coins inside.

I didn't argue any further. "Thank you," I said. Julia's eyes were wide, looking at me as if I was the biggest fool in the world.

"But how did this happen?" Marcus asked, still looking astonished. "How did you manage to collect so much? Really, this is unheard of."

"I only told a story. A story about David and Goliath."

"Vita, you truly have a gift. I should consider learning from you," Marcus said earnestly. "I am greatly indebted to you, Vita. On my way here, I was even considering selling myself to slavery to buy medicine for my son. But, thanks to you, I can erase that thought from my mind now. You can't believe how grateful I am."

"I'm so glad I could help."

I looked up. The sky was turning a deeper shade of blue, and the sun was setting, bathing the distant colonnades and roofs in a warm, orange glow. "We must leave, or we'll get in trouble. It's my first day out, and I don't want to spoil it or take advantage of Cassia's generosity."

"Vita, I'm not rich, but I have many friends in the city." Marcus said. "Should you ever find yourself needing help, do not hesitate to come to me. I live in the far-east unit on the top floor of Cupid Insula, located on Venus Street, near the gladiator school. It's the ugliest building in the neighborhood, so you can't miss it."

"Cupid Insula on Venus Street. I know that behemoth." Julia giggled behind her hand. "Truly, Marcus? You must live in such a monstrous ugly thing? I swear, if I lived there, I would never rise from my bed."

She giggled more and he joined in with a bashful grin.

"Regrettably, I do. You are right; it is indeed a grievous monster of a building. But at the same time, it is the only place in this area where you can secure a room for less than fifty silver coins a month," Marcus said with a bitter smile.

"Sounds good enough to me," I said, not wanting to cause further embarrassment to the good man. "I might hold you to your words someday. Have a good night." With that, I hurriedly made my way with Julia back to Eubulus' villa.

Eighteen

A Petrifying Glance

I took a deep sniff, cherishing the lingering smells of the streets, knowing full well that I wouldn't have the luxury of enjoying these wonderful aromas for a long time. The peculiar dust of freedom was like cool water to my parched throat. Observing the passing crowds, reminiscent of flowing streams, with each person engaged in self-determined activities, I felt a surge of longing. The thought echoed within me, "I wish I could be like them someday."

Julia was rambling all the way.

"... then he swooped her up in one arm and rescued her from the mob. So romantic, isn't it?" Julia sighed, seeing I was completely lost in thought. "So, you'd like that, wouldn't you?"

"Pardon? Like what? I do apologize; my mind had drifted somewhere else."

"Being the secret admiration of a handsome praetorian guard and then saved by him from troubles," Julia said. "You know, almost all the girls in Rome fancy those dazzling praetorian guards. They look awesome in their ceremonial uniforms."

"Hmm."

"Hmm? Come on, it's time to move on, Vita. I know you might have had someone in the past. But let the old things pass and embrace your new life. This is Rome. Anything can happen here. This place is magical—if you only allow it to be."

I had to admit that these were odd words from a girl who had been sold as a slave by her own mother.

Regardless, Julia offered me a comforting pat on the back as if she knew a secret I didn't.

I was struck by Julia's perception. "How did you know I had—" I could sense my cheeks getting hot.

"I grew up in a tailor's shop with customers coming and going. I know women. And men too." Julia beamed, her eyes twinkling with amusement. "Also, I happened to notice that storytelling ex-gladiator had a fondness for you. Maybe just a little bit."

"Marcus?" I brushed it off, but my blush deepened at the mere thought. "Wait, how did you know he used to be a gladiator?"

"The gladiator tattoo on his arm, of course," Julia said. "You noticed it, didn't you? All gladiators in Rome had tattoos with that kind of pattern. Well, my friend, you ought to learn more about the city. But yes. Marcus. I don't know how he ended up penniless, because wealthy matrons are so fond of this kind. But anyway, now he's broke and can't afford to redeem you. With your pretty face, you can do better than that."

Julia giggled as she playfully traced a soft finger along my pinked cheek, and I smacked her shoulder in return. "Oh, come on," I protested. "That's crazy."

This morning was overwhelming, and I felt a part of my world start to unravel.

Rufus had always been my world, and I'd never doubted that I would marry him someday. Even after he had disappeared, I never entertained any other thoughts except for finding him with my last shred of hope. If he did not return, I would never wed. But this morning, with so many new faces entering my life, something within me was stirring.

What if Nana's vision was just a hallucination? What if I can never find Rufus? Should I really move on as Julia suggested?

The idea intrigued me, but it also terrified me. *Oh Lord, please take away these unwanted thoughts. I don't need them.* I ruminated in my heart.

The atmosphere shifted as we entered Eubulus' villa through the backdoor, and even the leaves on the backyard trees appeared to stand still, resisting the playful melody carried by the night breeze.

A slave girl skittered as she walked out of the kitchen, carrying a dish. Obviously nervous, the dish soon clattered out of her shaky hands, and she quickly picked it up alongside the spilled content. Meanwhile, several other slaves lingered by a pillar of the colonnade, speaking in hushed voices and repeatedly glancing around to check if anyone would walk up to them.

"Something is wrong," Julia whispered. "Oh, no. It's Diana. Looks like she is ready to get someone in trouble."

"Quick! We better hide so she doesn't see us," I said, my palms sweaty.

Julia and I rushed to the kitchen as quickly as possible, searching for something to lay our hands on, and soon caught the muffled conversations of other slaves.

"... the empress broke the vials and cursed severely."

"Then if that is so, the master is going to chop his head off."

"But the lady won't let him, will she?"

"Did you see the master's face today? I doubt the lady can save him this time."

Upon hearing that Cassia was in trouble, I pushed my way through the crowd and urgently asked, "Where is the lady?"

"In the study with the master," one girl answered. "Don't go there; you really shouldn't be looking for trouble. Catena went to deliver a platter of fruits, and she was chased out by the master's angry yell."

"I must see her. She needs me," I said, dashing out of the kitchen and leaving Julia behind.

The curtains of the master's study hung motionless, mirroring the stillness of the air in the house. The heavy silk drapes were drawn closed, blocking any glimpse of what lay beyond. Suddenly, Eubulus' voice resonated from the other side of the curtains.

"Stupid! No other words for someone like you. Just stupid."

I carefully parted the curtains, creating a small opening through which I could catch a glimpse of the master's face. He was sitting behind a large marble desk, scattered with scrolls, quills, and an overturned inkwell. Adorning the wall behind him was a fresco depicting the scene of Apollo, the sun god, slaying Niobe's sons with his bow and arrows in a fit of fury.

Since entering this grand villa, I had closely adhered to Diana's warning and never dared to peek into the master's study before; it was a true eye-opener.

Cassia and a young man stood in front of his desk, their backs facing me.

"I am sorry, master." The young man's voice twisted with remorse.

"You keep saying 'sorry'. I have lost favor with the emperor; you think I will just walk up to the palace and tell him I'm sorry? Or when he sends the Praetorian Guard with my death warrant, will everything be suddenly fine with a 'sorry'?" Eubulus bellowed again. "Why does everyone keep giving me a 'sorry' after they mess up and expect me to accept it as a solution?"

"Father, this was a mistake. Please forgive him."

I could hear the emotion clogging my lady's voice even from afar.

"I called you back here, Cassia, to wake you from your childish sniveling, to let you understand how to deal with people who work for you, our slaves. No matter how much you trust them, like or *love* them, they are what they are, slaves! Slaves! Understand?"

From the small parting of the curtains, I could see Eubulus towering over Cassia who was flinching from the force of her father's proximity. The man beside her bowed his head, staring at the shiny floor as if probing there for the answers to his terrible predicament.

"Father, please don't say that," Cassia pleaded, placing her hands heavily on the desk.

"No, my lady. The master is right," the young man replied, his body trembling. In a fleeting moment, he lifted his head and turned his face slightly toward Cassia.

    Suddenly, the rest of the scene was obscured from my sight.

Nineteen

Secretly Kept Thoughts

Nothing mattered at that instant. I was rooted to the spot, eyes so wide that they could tear at the edges. All the blood rushed to my head and a faintness overcame me as if I would be sent tumbling to the floor. Not from the powerful boom of Eubulus' voice, not from Cassia's pleading, nor even from my own pounding heart.

No. It was all because of what I saw there.

Or not *what*.

More *who*.

In the room stood my Rufus, my beautiful, amazing beloved, his stance grown taller now than when I last set eyes on him, his strong jaw set tight with tension, his eyes moist but determined in the face of judgment.

But even with the changes time had brought, this was still the Rufus to whom I had clung in my childhood memories. This was the Rufus who used to call me "his little bride".

This was my Rufus, no shadow of a doubt.

Suddenly, a tap on my shoulder jolted me from my frozen state. I turned and met Diana's disapproving look. "What are you doing here?" Her voice was sharp and cold, like a whip crack.

"I... I am... The lady asked me to get something for her."

"And that thing is between these curtains through which you peeped?"

"I was just... it is..."

"Be gone, you sleazy girl. Thank your stars you are presently in the favor of her lady, or I'd have handed you over to the master's wrath and let him teach you some lessons about falling from grace. Now get out of here before I change my mind."

I scurried away as frenetic thoughts scattered sparks in the fireplace of my head.

How did this happen? Why is my Rufus called Aurelius now?

But when I thought about every detail lady Cassia had mentioned about Aurelius, everything started to make sense.

No wonder the lady loved gladioli! Now I blamed myself for my lack of perception.

I walked into the kitchen, my mind still preoccupied with my realization, when suddenly a sharp jolt ensued as I collided with Julia who was holding a soot-covered pot.

She quickly adjusted her grip on the pot to prevent it from dropping, but some of the used olive oil spilled out, creating a small mess on the floor.

"Did you see the lady? She didn't chastise you, did she?" Julia asked, wiping the mess with the hem of her tunic.

"She's fine; she said she'd send for me later," I said, trying to mask the wavering in my voice. Quickly, I joined the throng of workers, forcing my body to remain steady as I trembled from the recent revelation.

Rufus' dark cinnamon-colored hair and tender, warm eyes reappeared in my mind. Even in a grown man's frame, I could still discern those familiar features; the resemblance was striking.

I wanted so badly to reveal myself to him.

As the commotion in the house subsided later in the evening, Lady Cassia summoned me to her bath. Buzzing thoughts swarmed through my mind as I walked along the corridors.

"Oh, divine Juno." Cassia buried her head in her palms as she sat in the marble pool. "I've been waiting for this day for so long, and it turned out to be the worst day of my life," she lamented.

"What's the matter, my lady?" I said as I headed toward the dark wood wardrobe standing against the wall. On top was a small chest inlaid with a mosaic of colorful stones, portraying a scene of forest nymphs leisurely lounging in a river.

Taking the chest, I walked back to Cassia.

"I heard it from the other girls that Aurelius had an incident with the imperial order," I ventured, kneeling behind her, setting the chest by my side.

Now, I was taking slow deep breaths, trying to steady my racing heart.

"Oh, my poor Aurelius. Three months on the merchant fleet, and he's become as scrawny as a wood stick. It should be his triumphant day. But the palace chamberlain inspected the goods and said they were fake. Of course, my father blamed Aurelius for buying the fake goods. I don't believe it. He is such a prudent person. How could he have made such a mistake? The palace must have cheated us because they don't want to pay." Her words came out in a rush, tumbling over each other as her voice grew louder. "How could they do this to us?"

"That is terrible, my lady," I said, opening the chest and revealing a plush silken interior with three compartments and glass bottles of various shapes.

Carefully picking up an amber-colored bottle, I poured a few drops into my palm and applied the fragrant lavender oil to Cassia's back with a tender touch. "I hope the soothing scent of lavender brings you some comfort," I added, sincerely hoping to ease her troubled mind.

But Cassia raged on, "Nero holds banquets every night. I won't be surprised if the treasury is empty. It's a shame an emperor used such tactics to exploit our merchants. My poor Aurelius has been working so hard, only to endure such injustices. His god should have treated him better." As she finished speaking, tears cascaded down her cheeks.

"My lady, if you don't mind me asking, I remember you said that you brought Aurelius home from the side of the road. When did it happen?" I asked cautiously.

"Two years ago, on the fifteenth day of June, and I remember it very clearly. It was the last day of the temple fair of goddess Juno. I will never forget that day. He was beaten and bloodied by that nasty tavernkeeper. Fortunately for him, and for me, I brought him back here.

"Ever since he recovered from his injury, he has worked hard day and night. Oh, how much Father trusted him before…"

As Cassia rambled on, her words were falling on deaf ears. Relief found me, my mind preoccupied with its own thoughts, free from the need to engage in the conversation.

It makes sense. Rufus most likely spent about a year with the first master.

I aimlessly combed Cassia's hair. But in a sudden movement, she turned to face me, and the ivory comb snagged, pulling a few strands loose.

"Vita, I had it all figured out. I had thought that if things went well this time for Aurelius, I would have pleaded with my father to free him and buy him Roman citizenship. Maybe one day, he would agree to let me marry him. After all, my father does not have a son, and he needs someone to take care of the family business. Based on talent alone, Aurelius could not be more suitable. But that was all before this happened."

Cassia grabbed my hand and shook her head. "Now, my dream is gone. Father might even sell him, and I will never see him again. Oh, divine Juno, it breaks my heart to even imagine where this is heading." She sobbed bitterly.

Now that it looks impossible for the lady and Aurelius to be together in any way, if I tell her the truth, could it be possible that she will let Rufus leave with me? The thought suddenly filled me with so great a thrill.

But as I cast another glance at Cassia's swollen, red eyes and disheveled hair, I immediately dismissed the thought.

Oh, my Lord, what was I even thinking?

Cassia loves Rufus so deeply. How can she give him up to another woman, especially to her own slave? That's too much to bear. Even if she agrees, how could the master possibly agree to let both of us go, especially in such a situation?

Feeling the last shred of hope disappear completely, I sank heavily to the floor, burying my face between my knees.

Cassia, who'd stopped crying, beheld me in surprise, gently patting my back to console me.

"Vita, you are truly my dear sister. It's heartwarming to see you so concerned for me. Let us not dwell on this sad matter. Tell me, what exciting things did you do on your trip today? Did you treat yourself to something nice? There is so much to see and do in Rome, don't you agree?"

Hearing Cassia's kind words, I felt guilty for my hidden thoughts and realized that neither of us were in the mood for small talk. I briefly mentioned the weather and the bustling marketplace, also that Julia had been such a great help, explaining the general etiquette of life in Rome, which certainly made my first trip out so much easier.

Cassia smiled weakly, clearly exhausted.

I quickly said, "My lady, you must be tired. Let me help you to bed."

She nodded, and I helped her into her nightgown as she retired for the night.

Trudging back to the slave quarters later, my bones creaked in protest, my mind drained too from the day's events. The loud snores of the other girls only served to make me drowsier. I collapsed onto my pallet, and as I lay down, my heart grew so heavy that it almost pinned me to my bed.

I prayed in the darkness.

"Heavenly Father, is this a test? I thanked you for giving me such a good mistress. But how did things become so complicated in the blink of an eye? Father, your daughter has so little faith. Please don't put me on a trial I cannot handle. Have mercy and grant me wisdom, Lord."

Twenty
Reunion

Two hundred gold coins.

A ceramic chest filled with the choicest incense.

A string of pearls for meditation.

A small figurine of the goddess Juno.

These were a few things I placed in Cassia's leather trunk for her visit to the temple. I busied myself with packing things for my lady while sneaking occasional glances out of the opened window. Cassia's bedchamber was situated on the second floor on the west side of the backyard, providing a view that allowed me to catch glimpses of the stable on the opposite end of the yard.

"Move along, you slugs!" Eubulus' voice boomed as slaves piled the horses high with loads.

"I hope one day, he doesn't burst his lungs from all the shouting. An old man should cling to the sparse youthfulness in his blood as they last only a while," Cassia said, letting out a sigh. "He's going to do himself an injury if he carries on."

"Master is a resilient man. He will be fine," I replied absentmindedly, scanning carefully among the slaves who were bustling in the stable, hoping to see Rufus, but he was not there.

"I wonder how Aurelius is faring?" Cassia said as if reading my mind. "He's probably praying at this moment. Father ordered him to confine himself in his room to reflect on his terrible mistake, and I'm not allowed to see him today." Her voice rang heavy with sorrow.

"I'll pray to my God too." With a gentle touch, I placed my hand on Cassia's shoulder.

"Yes, by all means. I have prepared a heavy offering to divine Juno," Cassia said as she looked at the trunk. "But perhaps our divine mother is not powerful enough for a situation like this. I hope that you and Aurelius' god can help us too," she added.

Knowing Cassia's sole devotion to Juno, I was a little surprised.

"Is the master also going to the temple?" I asked.

Cassia laughed mirthlessly. "Father stopped praying after Mama succumbed to the grip of death. He renounced all the gods after weights of gold and flocks of sheep were sacrificed in temples. He only ever attends festivals to mingle with affluent patrons and secure more orders."

"What else could he do with all that cargo on horseback if not bring it to the temple?"

"Those are what he calls 'grease', bribes to the close kins, in-laws, and officials of the emperor. He will go on a courtesy visit and shower each of them with gifts. That keeps their opinion of him before the emperor always in good grace."

After carefully packing Cassia's belongings, I put my palm against my temple and said weakly, "I'm sorry, my lady, but I've had a bad headache since this morning..." I felt guilty for lying to Cassia, but knew I needed to speak with Rufus first.

Cassia placed her hand on my forehead, concern etched on her face.

"Oh, poor girl. You should've told me earlier. I must have scared you with my babbling last night. Stay home and rest, my girl," she said. The genuine concern in her tone only made me feel worse.

Oh, God. Breaking her heart is the last thing I want, I thought, forcing a smile and escorting Cassia to the carriage waiting outside the gate.

Eubulus had also left to deliver the "grease", taking Diana and several other chief slaves with him, leaving the household temporarily without any oversight.

Most slaves took this opportunity to slip out and enjoy themselves on the streets, while the remaining chose to rest in their quarters. Nobody seemed concerned about the impending danger facing the household; instead, they took the chance to indulge in a brief respite from their arduous lives.

Julia invited me to join her on another trip to the market, but I told her that I was not feeling well. "What a shame! I'll grab some fresh dates for you," she said before leaving. "They will help you recover."

As the villa quieted down, I grabbed a broom and pretended to sweep the floor, stealthily making my way toward the room with the indigo curtain on the southwest side of the atrium. It was a piece of information I received from Julia during our last chat.

Upon arriving, my heart pounded so fiercely that it almost jumped out of my throat. I leaned in close to the curtain and heard Rufus muttering a prayer.

"Save us, Oh Lord, from this storm, this pain. Save my soul from the depths of sorrow." His voice trembled with emotion, and I desperately wanted to go in and offer him a comforting embrace, but instead, I remained silent, listening until he finished with an "Amen."

I drew the curtain and spoke softly. "I'm sure the Lord heard it."

Startled, he jolted, and his head snapped back as a range of emotions played across his face. Fear was quickly replaced by consternation and utter bewilderment, leaving his mouth hanging open. He stared at me in disbelief, pinching his own arm fiercely.

"Vita!" he cried out. "Am I seeing a vision?"

He leapt to his feet, grabbing me and lifting me off the ground. After setting me back down, he reached out with a shaking hand and gently touched my hair and cheeks. In a trembling voice, he asked, "Vita. My Vita. How... How can this be happening? Is it really you?

Please, tell me it is you."

"Flesh and blood," I whispered, looking up at him.

He pulled me into his arms, embracing me tightly for a long time. He buried his face in my hair, taking in the familiar scent, inhaling deeply.

"What happened?" our voices echoed with each other's.

"Nana, where is Nana?" he suddenly asked, releasing me from his embrace and staring at me in fear. The sadness in my eyes gave him the answer he didn't want.

"Please don't tell me she's..." He sank to the ground, his shoulders trembling involuntarily. "No! No! No!" he cried bitterly.

I sat beside him, placing a comforting hand on his, holding back my tears so as not to add to his sadness.

"Rufus, the plague came like a nightmare, taking both the young and the old. Nana's frail body was not strong enough. Even after I got twenty gold coins from Drusus and bought medicines from the physician, her strength continued to fail. But thankfully, she died peacefully in her sleep. She's in a better place now, Rufus," I reassured him, even as my own tears fell in torrents down my face. "And the twenty gold coins I borrowed finally got me here."

Rufus ran a frustrated hand down his face.

"It was all my fault. Nana was quite healthy before I left. She could have survived the plague. And you wouldn't have ended up here. None of this would have happened if I hadn't gone on that fateful day," he said in a hoarse voice. "Why did I go? You told me not to, but... but I didn't listen."

"Don't blame yourself, Rufus. You were only trying to provide for the family and giving me the best gift."

"No, Vita. You deserve the best. I should have been more careful that day and not been tricked by evil men," he said with regret. "It was all my fault."

"Tell me, Rufus, what happened?"

Rufus rose and walked to the door. After making sure no one was listening in, he continued his story.

"As I descended from my donkey, I led it toward the harbor. The wind was strong, and the harbor was nearly empty, with only a few vendors and ships present. In the distance, a few fishermen were busy mending their nets. It didn't seem to be a good day for business.

"However, I noticed a ruggedly bearded man dressed in a hooded cloak, standing near the dock where several ships were moored. Our eyes met, and he beckoned me over. My pulse quickened with the hope of striking a deal, so I guided my donkey closer to him, and he asked, 'How much for your baskets?'

"I raised the prices a little, expecting the usual haggling. To my surprise, he simply said, 'Fair price. I want all of them,' without any further bargaining or inspection. Oh, Vita, I should have been more alert to this. It was a clear warning sign."

Rufus sighed and kept his story going. "But I was overexcited, thinking I could not only buy rouge and a scroll, but also some meat for your birthday dinner, so I brushed off any doubts that came to my mind.

"He said, 'Here are ten silver coins, which should be enough for all your baskets. Keep the change if you like,' and bounced a money pouch on his hand. 'All I need you to do is help me get these baskets onto that cargo ship over there, and then you can come back to me for your pay.' He pointed at a medium-sized ship with a single mast not far away.

"I tied my donkey and proceeded with my cart. My heart rang with joy, thinking of how God had graced me with such easy sales. When I arrived at the ship, two slaves were already waiting with a crane and a pulley. They attached all the baskets to the pulley, and someone on the deck pulled them up. I was about to leave, but one of them said, 'Sir, didn't our master tell you to help us load the baskets to the lower deck?'

"I was a little bewildered, not sure if he had said such things. But the payment was so close that I didn't want to risk losing the deal. So, I climbed up the rope ladder onto the upper deck, where a man with a scar running through his left cheek was standing beside my baskets. 'Follow the steps,' he commanded as he pointed to the gateway leading to the lower deck.

"His menacing tone made the hair on my neck stand on end. I tried to leave, but as I turned, a thud rammed into the back of my head. Then the world turned black."

Twenty-One

Promise Renewed

"And that was the beginning of the darkest time in my life. We traveled for days, living on stale bread and droplets of water. They shipped us down here to Rome and sold us off to all kinds of masters. I was sold to a tavernkeeper first. I tried to run away but was caught. He threw me into a pitch-black room for seven days straight, then beat me nearly to death before dumping me on the street," Rufus mumbled, his head buried in his hands.

I threw my arms around him. "Oh, Rufus. If you hadn't been out to cater for our home, for us, none of these things would have happened. If only I'd tried harder to keep you at home. I tried but it wasn't enough."

"Hey, don't say that! I'm the only man in the family; it's my duty to take care of you and Nana," he said, a bitter smile forming on his face as he gently stroked my cheek with his roughened fingertips. "But God has always been merciful. Lady Cassia saved my life and brought me here, so life wasn't so bad the last two years."

My heart felt a stab as Lady Cassia's name slipped from his lips.

"Rufus, do you remember the day before the tragedy happened? When I helped you load the baskets onto the donkey's back, you said…" I paused as I could feel my cheeks aflame, my heart beating wildly. I lowered my head, steeling myself for his response.

"I will never forget what I said, Vita." He gazed at me, his eyes brimming with emotions. "On the day I left, I told you that I wanted you to be my little bride."

"Yes, but perhaps we should forget it. Things have changed... Everything has changed. Maybe we can't go back to who we used to be." I took a deep sniff of the fragrance in the room. It emanated from a vase on the nightstand, boasting blooming red gladioli – the kind both Cassia and I loved. "I know the lady likes you and even wants to marry you."

"No, Vita. No matter what *other people* think, I'll never forget my promise," Rufus said as he gently lifted my chin. "I want you to be my little bride always, forever."

Torn between joy and worry, I hesitated before responding, "But the lady... You belong to her now. She even gave you a new name, Aurelius."

"Yes, I've been Aurelius for the past two years." Rufus sighed heavily. "But in my heart, I've never forgotten I'm Rufus. *Your* Rufus." Pulling me closer, he gazed into my eyes.

I smelled the lavender perfume on him, the kind I had put on Cassia's body yesterday.

"Do you really mean it?" I avoided his eyes. "If I hadn't found you—which I still cannot believe—then I'm sure you would have forgotten me and moved on, especially with someone as beautiful and caring as Cassia. And I totally understand that."

"I truly mean it. All these years, I've been trying to send letters home whenever I had the chance," Rufus said. "I've even bribed the courier responsible for delivering military documents to send a letter to you and Nana. But unfortunately, it looks like they didn't do their job faithfully. I tried and tried, but there was little else I could do."

Rufus' words filled my heart with sparks of hope.

"But the lady is so devoted to you." I was still worried, and who wouldn't be in my position? The scenario filled me with fear, not only due to the power and influence she wielded, but also because I was truly fond of her.

There was not a bone in me that wished to see such a kind person being hurt.

"She is a well-born lady with tons of suitors waiting out there. She'll find someone, no doubt. And I'm sure the master would be far happier if Cassia marries someone more... suitable." Rufus chuckled and gave me another affectionate squeeze before his eyes clouded over again. "But we've got a bigger issue on our hands. If we can't sort this out, I might end up being sold to a different master, and we might never see each other again. It's a miracle that we've found each other, and I don't want to be torn away from you once more."

"You've always been a prudent man, Rufus. I don't believe you bought the wrong goods. It's just not something you would do, and you know that too. Did you suspect anybody or anything through all this?"

"You're right. When I inspected the goods, I took a small amount from each jar and burnt them one by one; the saffron, sandalwood, frankincense... They were of the highest quality. If they had been inferior, I would never have accepted them. And they never left my eyes all the way back to Rome."

"Could it be the emperor himself? Maybe he just made up the fact that they were fake? The lady said the palace is short of money, after all."

"No. We've been fulfilling orders from the palace for years and they never argued about prices. Nero may be a nasty emperor, but he is certainly not a stingy one." Rufus shook his head.

"Has anyone else touched your goods? Even someone you hadn't suspected before?" Hearing my words, Rufus' body tensed up suddenly.

"What is it, Rufus? Do you know who it could be?"

"Yes! I should have suspected him earlier." He slapped his face forcefully. "Thinking about it now, it's so obvious. I knew it. It must be Tigellinus."

"Who's Tigellinus?"

"He's the praetorian prefect, I mean, one of them. He took the goods from our hands at the palace gate with an imperial token, saying he needed to inspect them first for safety concerns," Rufus continued with clenched fists. "Oh, God, I should have seen it coming. It used to be a different treasurer, not this Tigellinus. I should have been more careful. So stupid of me."

"Do you have witnesses? Surely there were people there who could vouch for you?"

"There were, but they were just my men and his soldiers. I doubt either could be a legitimate witness. Oh, God. I should have insisted on staying there when they inspected the goods. But you know, he came with his fully armed guards. I just got terrified and did whatever they asked." In a fit of desperation, Rufus violently struck the headboard of his bed. "I've ruined it all! I've ruined our lives!" he bellowed.

"Don't blame yourself too harshly, Rufus. Who wouldn't get scared in front of the armed praetorian guards? Julia told me the prefects are among the most powerful in Rome." I touched Rufus' arm gently. "Don't worry. We'll talk to the master about this when he comes back. Maybe he has resources to nail this man down. For the rest of the day, let's just pray. God will deliver us from such peril, just like He did in the time of Esther."

"Oh, Vita. Sometimes, I wish I had your faith," Rufus said with a hint of bitterness and admiration. "I suspect we are going to need every last drop of it to get through this."

"If you heard all my complaints and grumpy prayers at night, you probably wouldn't say that." I let out a soft giggle. "But God let us meet again, despite everything. It shouldn't end like this." I tugged at Rufus' sleeves, and we knelt down together to offer a brief prayer.

"I'd better go. The other slaves may come back soon," I said, getting to my feet. "But let's not stop praying, Rufus. Prayer is everything. It can move mountains." With that, I bent down to plant a swift kiss on Rufus' face before briskly leaving his room.

I was in a daze for the rest of the day, and knowing Rufus still remembered his promise gave me enough confidence and hope to face the trial tomorrow.

The lady came home after sunset, weariness evident in her drooping eyelids. After helping her with the bath and making sure she was comfortably settled in bed, I headed to the slave quarters for the night's rest.

It was almost midnight. The soft moonlight cast a silver glow over the dark path under the portico. The garden's tranquility was accentuated by the calming rustle of leaves and the sporadic hoots of an owl.

To my surprise, Julia was sitting on my pallet with her head bowed, engrossed in something held in her hand. The dim light filtering through the lone, small opening on the wall illuminated her delicate silhouette. I approached and gently patted her on the shoulder.

"Julia, what are you looking at?"

Her body jerked. The object in her hand dropped on the ground with a soft thud. "Hey, you shouldn't sneak up on me like that," she protested.

"I'm sorry. Here, let me get it." I picked it up. It felt like a ring, and its glimmer in the darkness hinted at its precious material. "Where did you get it, Julia?"

"I was going to ask you the same question."

"What do you mean, ask me?"

"It was in the pouch! You know, the pouch you got from the rich man at the market. Don't tell me you never noticed it," Julia said, dangling the pouch in front of my eyes.

"No, I didn't, really," I said, grabbing the pouch from her hand and holding the ring up to the moonlight for a better look. "How could I have never noticed it? I'm sure I emptied the entire contents."

"Yes, you did, but there's an inner pocket, and the ring was in it. The pouch feels heavy because of the extra layers of fabric and all the embroidery, and that's probably why you never suspected the extra weight."

Sticking a finger in the pouch, I felt the inner pocket. But my day had been so full of drama that I didn't even have time to question why I hadn't noticed it earlier. Taking another close look at the ring, I saw a flat image engraved on one side and letters on the other.

"Do you think the man left the ring here by mistake? He must be looking for it right now," I asked with concern. "How do you think I could return it?"

"He won't care. It's not a signet ring or anything important. Just a plain silver ring he has probably forgotten about," Julia said absentmindedly. "Rich men like him wouldn't even care about a gold ring, let alone this one."

"It has an engraving on it, but it's difficult to work out. What are these? I can't read much," I said. "Here, take a look to see if you can work it out."

Julia held the ring, turning it to better discern the wording. "I see what you mean. It's quite worn, but to me it looks like *Achillius* or *Aemilia*. Could be his family name," Julia said, her eyes sparkling with excitement. "I wonder what kind of person he is. He's probably from a renowned patrician family, especially considering the priceless tunic he was wearing. I also assume he is a military man, judging by the way he walked."

She paused and handed back the ring to me. "Do you think he's married?"

I covered my mouth as I let out a prolonged yawn, feeling as though my eyelids were glued shut. "Who knows? It's far too late, Julia, to talk about a man we'll probably never meet again. Let's get some sleep."

I crawled underneath my blanket and whispered, "Dear God, it's been such a long day. I can't thank you enough for finally being able to talk to Rufus and touch him after these three long years of separation. Please grant me the strength to face tomorrow's challenges." I murmured my gratitude, drifting into a deep sleep.

Twenty-Two

Hope Rekindled

MORNING SUNSHINE FILTERED THROUGH the translucent alabaster windowpanes, casting a gentle glow on Cassia's pale face when I arrived at her chamber. Her lips moved quietly, and I knew it was Mother Juno's sacred scripture she was reciting.

"Do you feel any better, Vita?" Cassia paused in her recitation, turning her attention toward me. "I'm sorry; I was exhausted from a full day of prayer, so I didn't check on you last night."

"Don't worry, my lady; I feel much better now." Cassia's kindness only deepened the guilt stemming from my secret encounter with Rufus.

"Pray for my father, Vita," Cassia said, her voice tinted with concern. "He spent the night out of town and is coming back around noon. I hope he will be in a good mood and not be too harsh with Aurelius."

I simply nodded, suppressing the urge to confess everything to her.

The morning hours slipped away unnoticed, and before long, a slave arrived, announcing that lunch was ready. Upon our arrival, Eubulus was already reclining on the couch with Rufus standing beside him, head bowed. The master dismissed our greetings with a perpetual frown. As he reached for a lidded bowl, Rufus rushed to help him.

"If only you were this useful when it mattered. I really don't understand how you could have made such a blunder. Your incompetence has doomed us all," Eubulus boomed.

"Father!" Cassia protested. "Please don't say things like that. Rufus had done his best!"

"You stay out of this. What was I even thinking, sending an idiot to handle such an important matter? Now it has backfired horribly. It is only a matter of time before the empress' wrath descends on us. Everyone I visited yesterday was telling me that there is no end to her anger."

Rufus stepped forward. "Forgive me, master; if I may, I have something to tell you."

"What more do you have to say?" Eubulus asked impatiently without even looking at him. "What crazy idea have you conjured up overnight? This had better be good. I am at the end of my tether with you already."

"Yes, master." Rufus nervously swallowed before continuing, "When I was at the palace gate, I was forced to leave the goods with Prefect Tigellinus for inspection. His men led us into a room for a weapon check. When I got back, I thought all was well and brought the goods into the palace storage."

"And? Come on, boy, spit it out."

"This was the only time the goods were out of my sight, master. And as I've always insisted, I thoroughly inspected all of them when I made the purchase."

"So? Are you suggesting the issue lies with Tigellinus?"

"I didn't suspect him at first, but now I realize it must have been Tigellinus who tampered with them, swapping the original good ones for poor copies."

"You know these are serious accusations." Eubulus breathed in deeply. "Are you certain of this?"

"Yes, master, I guarantee it with my life."

Eubulus maintained a prolonged silence, seemingly pondering the credibility of Rufus' account. When he realized that Cassia was still standing, he gestured for her to take a seat next to him, and I obediently positioned myself behind my mistress.

"Oh dear! What has happened? Let me think this over," Eubulus said, closing his eyes and rubbing his temples, weariness etched across his face. After a brief pause, he reopened his eyes and turned to Rufus. "Even if I am to believe what you have said, how do we prove to the empress that he was the thief?" With that said, his countenance softened a little.

"Maybe we can request an audience with her and explain the situation," Rufus suggested. "She has to believe us, quite simply because it is the truth."

"Idiot!"

"Father, please!" Cassia interjected.

"Quiet! I will not allow you to interrupt me again!" Eubulus bellowed, his expression hardened once more. "Do you think the empress is a pushover? Even if we were to secure an audience with her, which is highly unlikely, we would need solid proof to convince her!" Eubulus spat the word out. "So, if you can help supply that, I'm all for it."

"I understand, master. If only we knew someone who could get us back in the empress' favor long enough for us to find proof," Rufus moved on cautiously.

"You fool! You thought it was so easy to—"

"Father," Cassia interrupted again, ignoring Eubulus' angry outburst. "I know someone we can probably ask."

Eubulus looked at her and gestured for her to continue.

"Do you know Caius, one of the praetorian prefects who has great influence in the palace? He's a charming man, adored by all noble matrons; rumor has it that even the empress has a fondness for him. Perhaps he can save us from the empress' wrath temporarily and even use his power to help with a proper investigation. It's our only chance, don't you think? I would wager it is worth a try at least."

"Do you mean Caius Aemilia?" Eubulus' eyes narrowed.

"Yes, that is him."

"Caius indeed has great influence, but why would he ever help us? These snobbish patricians... They may attend your feasts, but they make fun of you behind your back," Eubulus said with a sigh.

"But Tigellinus is his political rival, and he may like the opportunity to bring him down before the emperor," Cassia suggested. "You never know, dear Father. It's worth trying. Think of it from Caius' perspective. It would make him look far superior if Tigellinus were found at fault."

"Hmm, that might be enough to persuade him." Eubulus straightened up. "But the challenge is that men of such importance receive hundreds of requests every day. It could take a month for his doorkeeper to even present our request to him, and by then, my head might already be separated from my shoulders, rolling in the gutters, and bathing in my own blood."

"Perhaps we could take lots of gifts and try to bribe our way in?" Rufus said.

Eubulus jeered bitterly. "You still have plenty to learn about how things work here in Rome. You must be as rich as Saturn to have enough money to bribe the Aemilias."

"Aemilia? Where have I heard that name before?" I murmured.

When I turned to Julia, who was also stationed in the dining room, I noticed her eyebrows furrowing as if lost in thought. Suddenly, she turned to face me and signaled by forming an O shape between her thumb and pointer finger.

"What?" I mouthed, unable to understand what she was indicating.

Quietly making her way over to me, she whispered, "Isn't that the name on the ring?"

"Yes... of course, it is," I whispered back. "And I think the rich man mentioned that his name was Caius too."

"Surely, he must be whom the master is talking about," Julia said.

As I grappled with the decision of whether to reveal

this information, Eubulus' thunderous voice interrupted our conversation. "You two, can't you see we are discussing serious matters here? Close those filthy mouths of yours!"

He turned back to Rufus. "There is nothing we can offer him that he doesn't already have. The Aemilia family is famous for its immense, unscalable wealth and standing in Rome. You may think *I* have wealth, but to them, I am but an ordinary tavern keeper."

Looking at Rufus' dejected expression, I realized that despite my reluctance to entangle myself in the peril of dealing with Caius again, I had no choice but to bring him into the discussion. "M-master, that Aemilia prefect, we've met him," I raised my voice, knowing there was limited time to get across my point.

"Who? You and her?" Eubulus stared at us. "Are you out of your mind?" He suddenly burst into hysterical laughter. "Mercury must be playing tricks on me today. First, it was him talking nonsense, and now you two. 'That Aemilia prefect'... Do you even know whom you were talking about? Were you all trying to take me for a fool?"

"Yes, master."

"What?" Eubulus roared. "You were taking me for a—"

"No, master. I mean we have met that prefect. The one of whom you talk so highly. We went to the Forum two days ago, and—"

"How dare you!" Eubulus snapped. "There is no way you could have gone."

"Lady Cassia gave us a day to explore the city."

"Is this true?" He turned to Cassia.

"Yes, Father, they have served me well, and I thought they deserved it."

"Fine, go on." Eubulus waved faintly.

"So, a wealthy-looking man at the Forum gave me a pouch as a gift. And we found a ring in it. And... And it has the name *Aemilia* engraved on it. Besides, he told me his name was Caius."

"Where is the ring?" he yelled, scanning me from head to toe as if he was seeing me for the first time.

"It's under my pillow, master."

"What are you waiting for? Bring it to me right now!"

Running quickly to the slave quarters, I collected the ring, and when I got back, I heard Julia describing Caius and Theophilus to the master.

"They were attired in opulent, lavish tunics and spoke of business in the senate."

Eubulus nodded. "It sounds like Caius Aemilia," he said. "Let me see it, girl!" he exclaimed as I approached.

I handed him the ring, and he examined it carefully. "I cannot believe it! It appears the gods have smiled upon us; this ring certainly does have the engraving of the Aemilia family." Clutching the ring in his hand, Eubulus then turned his gaze toward me. "Before I get too carried away by this extraordinary discovery, what exactly did you do for him to give you this ring? I hope there is no foul play involved."

"What do you mean, master?"

"What I mean is, are you sure he *gave* it to you? It didn't 'fall into' your pocket? We have not a little thief working in our midst, have we?"

"Father, how can you say such a thing?" The lady's voice was shrill.

"I'm only getting all the facts right before approaching Caius. The last thing this family needs right now is for me to show up with a stolen ring."

"No master, I promise you. I would never do such a thing. I only told a story at the Forum. There, I met a storyteller who was about to lose his audience, so I stepped in and told one on his behalf. Caius was among the audience and heard what I was saying. After I'd finished, he came up to me and gave me a pouch filled with coins. I didn't realize there was a ring in it until later." Deliberately, I omitted the part about throwing a sandal at Caius, silently grateful that the remaining account still sounded seamless.

"How dare you! Who permitted you to perform at the Forum? And you, Julia, have you forgotten the lashes you received last time?" Eubulus' face reddened with anger. "If people found out my slaves were telling stories in the marketplace to make money, what would they make of it?"

"Father, maybe this is our only chance to get acquainted with Caius." Cassia gently placed a hand on her father's shoulder. "I'll teach these girls a lesson so they won't do anything like that in the future. Yet think about the positives that could come from this. These girls may have done wrong, but they are offering you an opportunity to at least meet with Caius."

"Yes, master. It will never happen again, we promise." Before Eubulus could respond, I swiftly steered the conversation in line with Cassia's proposal. "Right now, Master, as our lady had suggested, perhaps you could visit him under the guise of returning the ring and use the opportunity to request his help."

"What if he doesn't care? It's just a plain silver ring after all," Eubulus expressed a hint of uncertainty.

"When you see the doorkeeper, just mention that you are returning something he lost. Out of curiosity, he might agree to meet you in person," Cassia said. "That's our only solution now. What have we got to lose?"

"Yes, master, please give it a try," I chimed in. "I believe you'll gain his trust once you get a chance to talk to him."

"Very well, I will try that. But be aware, I will hold you responsible if this fails." Giving me a menacing stare, he stood up and left the room.

Twenty-Three

Caius is Coming

The next morning, as soon as I arrived at Cassia's chamber, the first thing she did was explain the dream she'd had the night before. Without going into too much detail, during the dream, Mother Juno had told her to recite the sacred scriptures seventy times so that a wish of hers would be granted.

As Cassia intended to spend the entire morning in her chamber reciting the scriptures, I was released from my duties and free to do as I pleased. Therefore, I headed into the garden to water the gladioli, mostly to dispel any wandering thoughts.

Occasionally, I would spot Rufus passing by the garden and wish so badly that he could stop to give me some comfort. However, each time he passed, there were other slaves close by, so we didn't even make eye contact.

"What gorgeous flowers!" Cassia's voice startled me. I turned abruptly, still holding the watering can, and sparkling droplets cascaded onto her delicate light sapphire dress.

"Oh, my lady! I am so sorry. I-I didn't see you coming," I said, fussing over Cassia's slightly wet dress.

"Don't worry about my dress. It will soon dry in this beautiful weather," Cassia said, brushing her hand against the fabric. "So, I've finished my prayers, and guess what? I have great news, Vita."

Cassia's smile beamed as brilliantly as the glistening droplets on the gladioli leaves, taking my breath away. Amidst the enchanting scene, a subtle worry lingered within me—— a concern that, despite Rufus insisting I had always been his "little bride", Cassia's charm might still captivate him.

"Vita, are you all right?" Cassia reached out to touch my forehead. "You are not sick again, are you?"

"I'm very well, my lady. Did Caius agree to come?" I asked in haste, fearing she might glimpse into my inner thoughts.

"Yes! Yes, Vita! Father went to his villa yesterday afternoon, but Caius wasn't home. He waited outside the gate all night until he finally saw him returning this morning. His adjutant was about to dismiss my father, but Father caught his attention by showing him the ring. To our surprise, Father convinced him to stop by for a quick dinner before even mentioning Tigellinus. It feels like Mother Juno has fulfilled her promise to me, Vita. I can't explain it, but I have a good feeling about this Caius. I believe he's going to be our savior." Cassia's delicate hands gently cupped mine.

"That's fantastic news. Thank God. I'll pray more fervently today that this works out well for us all."

"Yes, Vita. Please pray to your god. Maybe it was also down to you and Aurelius asking him that we had our good luck today." Putting her hands gently on my shoulders, Cassia's voice trembled slightly with excitement. "And if this Caius really gets us out of trouble, our family will be indebted to you. I'll ask my father to grant you your freedom, to which I'm sure he'll agree."

With my throat suddenly dry, the words coming out of my mouth felt as though they weren't even mine. "Are you..." I tried clearing my throat. "I'm sorry, my lady, are you sure about this?"

"Absolutely. And even though he's known for being stingy, I doubt he will refuse." She let out a short laugh and added, "In fact, he can't refuse. I won't let him."

"Oh, my lady!" I threw my arms around Cassia, oblivious of

anyone watching. "I don't know what to say. You're so kind to me." My words were utterly genuine and sincere, but deep down, my heart knotted. *How am I going to reveal Rufus' identity to her? Will she also let Rufus go with me?* I tried pushing these thoughts away for the moment, but knew somewhere down the line, and soon, I'd have to deal with them.

Cassia graciously granted me the opportunity to spend the entire afternoon in prayer beside the gladioli patches. Despite my intention not to engage with Rufus during this time, I found myself instinctively scanning my surroundings for his presence. When I failed to find him, I couldn't help but wonder if he had been summoned by Cassia. The mere thought of Rufus providing comfort to Cassia in her bedchamber caused a pang in my heart.

"Lord, I beg you to free me from these distracting thoughts. Grant me the strength to depend on you completely," I whispered.

Suddenly, I was jolted from my prayers by a commotion emanating from the far side of the garden. "He's here! He's here," exclaimed one of the slave girls amidst a group hurrying toward the kitchen. "Oh, Venus, he is so handsome! Come! You must see him! I swear, he is built like a god. No, a posse of gods!"

Realizing it must be Caius' arrival, my heart raced with anticipation. *Please, God, let today bring good news for all our sakes.*

"Vita!" Diana's voice boomed, reminding me of the same shock I had suffered at the sound of the whip when the slave trader drove us to Rome.

"Vita!" Another lash.

"I am here," I replied shakily, running to stand before Diana, awaiting her orders.

Her nostrils widened, and I noticed a single hair hanging from her left nostril, like a rope clapper within a giant bell. This thought made my mouth curl upward.

Please don't laugh, I pleaded inwardly, struggling to divert my attention from the unsightly hair dangling so close to my face. But it was too late.

"What are you smiling about?" she asked, rubbing her nose.

"Nothing! I'm not smiling. It was a nervous twitch, ma'am."

"Let me tell you something. Don't for one moment think that just because you are *in* with the lady, you are untouchable. I would have no greater pleasure than wiping that smirk right off your face! To the dining room, now!" she yelled, placing a silver pitcher in my hands. "Join the girls there. Your job tonight is pouring this precious wine for our guests."

Several other girls were already lined up outside the entrance to the dining room, and I quickly moved to join them, still holding the pitcher tightly.

While I was standing there, Cassia's soft voice reached my ears, and the master muttered something in a flattering tone.

Soon, the other kitchen slaves arrived, each carrying a plate or jar.

"Now all of you, listen to me," Diana ordered, hands resting on her hips, scanning the group standing before her. "The fate of this household depends on the outcome of tonight. If you as much as set a plate down wrongly or spill a drop of wine, you'll find yourselves crucified in our backyard come tomorrow," she bellowed. "Do I make myself clear?"

"Yes!" we answered with shudders.

With my head bowed and my eyes fixed on the sleeping nymph engraved on the lid of the pitcher, I walked quietly forward, entering the dining space. "God, please let this night pass peacefully," I murmured as I stepped over the marble threshold.

"Ah, there she is," a mischievous voice entered my ears.

Looking up, I saw Caius, his amber-colored eyes sparkling along with a playful smile.

Twenty-Four

A Surprising Act

"Our magical little storyteller is here," Theophilus said, waving from beside Caius.

Eubulus turned to me at the same time, his glare made me shrink in my own skin. "Please, pay her no attention; she was spoiled because of my daughter's soft-heartedness," he said, wiping away the beads of sweat forming on his forehead.

"No need for apologies. I very much enjoyed the story. A dramatic storyteller, this one, even tossed a sandal at me when I caused a ruckus in her audience. A spirited one, that much is certain."

Oh, no! This is it! I lamented silently, shooting hateful glances at Caius. *Did he deliberately mention this to get me in trouble?*

"She did *what*?" All color drained from Eubulus' face in an instant, leaving it as white as his newly bleached toga. "By all the gods in Olympus, had I known the horrific offense she committed against you, believe me, I'd have had her whipped to death already!" Eubulus' tremble started from his lips and quickly spread throughout his whole body, his eyes darting between Caius and me like a terrified fawn. "I-I cannot apologize enough for her extraordinary behavior."

"Hold your peace, Eubulus; her anger was worth the story," Caius said. "With all the stress these days, her tale was like a soothing balm for the knots in my shoulders. Maybe you should listen to it at some point too. It will do you the world of good."

Upon hearing this, I let out a small breath of relief, but I still couldn't discern his true intentions toward me.

Looking around the room, I spotted Rufus standing in the corner, also wiping away sweat from his pale face.

"The workload must be enormous, sitting with the emperor," Cassia chipped in.

"It shouldn't be so, but the emperor's temper is as ever changing as the winds on the Tiber," Caius said.

"And may I ask, is the emperor in a favorable mood right now?" Eubulus looked at Caius, the little fawn's eyes now hinged with anticipation.

"It's difficult to tell, as sometimes he's hard to read. Like any true leader, he conceals his thoughts well."

"But he was most upset a few days ago, wasn't he, Caius?" Theophilus proclaimed.

"Oh, yes! How could I forget that?"

"What happened? If you don't mind me asking," Eubulus inquired carefully.

"It had more to do with the empress being upset about one of her indulgences. Apparently, someone had supplied her with fake fragrances, and she burst in, interrupting one of his meetings with the prefects, annoying him beyond all belief," Theophilus said, tossing a date into his mouth. "The emperor was quite displeased, and he remained irritable for the following few days."

"Indeed, he was very unhappy. Anyway, shall we change the subject now?" Caius said with an indifferent look.

"Well, I think we all know what triggered the whole ordeal." Eubulus clung to the subject desperately, determined to keep the conversation on its original course. "Unfortunately, Aurelius, my most trusted servant, failed——"

"What Father means is that someone swapped Aurelius' goods,

and we highly suspect that person is Prefect Tigellinus, your colleague," Cassia interjected, causing Eubulus' face to turn as red as the burning coal in the furnace. He cleared his throat loudly. "We would be very grateful if you could kindly—"

Cassia continued talking about Aurelius' misfortune, seemingly paying no attention to her father's hint.

"Cassia, could you do me a favor and check on the lamb stew in the kitchen, please?" Eubulus cut in, his thin lips stretched into a smile that didn't quite reach his eyes.

Cassia looked at all the slaves in the room and said, "Why not ask them?"

"If you lack the sense to see that your forwardness is inhibiting this very important conversation, then I ask that you shut your mouth," Eubulus whispered sternly through semi-closed lips.

"Father! I'm simply telling the truth."

"Enough, Cassia! Enough! You've done enough."

The discomfort chilled the room so quickly that we forgot it was a hot late summer's night. Eubulus ran a frustrated hand over his face, then gulped down the wine in his goblet.

"Most distinguished Prefect, please pardon my daughter's rudeness. Since she is my only jewel, I have pampered her too much, which may explain her audacity. Anyway, let me address a matter that troubles me, one for which I desperately need your help. As you mentioned, I have fallen out of favor with the empress. We suspect Tigellinus is behind it, but gathering enough evidence to incriminate him has proven challenging. Even if we could, the empress might have already sent soldiers to claim my head before——"

"And please tell me, Eubulus, what would you like me to do?" Caius interjected with a smirk, taking a sip from his golden goblet. "You have decent Setian wine in your house," he said with his eye half-closed. "My friends told me new money only drink Falernian wines because they are the priciest. Now, I consider it a prejudice."

Noticing his empty plate, a slave hurriedly whisked it away to refill it, but Caius raised a leisurely hand to stop him. "No more food, please. I have another banquet to attend later tonight."

"Could you plead my cause with the empress? If I can't give her a satisfactory explanation soon, I'm afraid my head will be chopped off, all my wealth will be gone, and my daughter will live on... well, I don't even want to imagine," Eubulus pleaded, beads of sweat trickling down his face with each anxious tremor. "You are our only chance of surviving, dear Prefect."

"I hear you, Eubulus. It will be thoroughly disheartening to lose one of the finest merchants the palace trusted for years over such a minor mistake. I see no justice in it. However, in return for my favors, what do I get?" Caius smiled impishly, holding his goblet as he watched Eubulus squirm. "If this is so important to you—which we all know is the case—then what's in it for me?"

"Anything within my power, most esteemed Prefect, anything I can afford. You have my word. You want the rarest of incense, spices, or fabrics, I-I will scour the corners of the earth for you. I've got properties in Rome, Campania, Etruria—take your pick, they're all yours," he said, his hands clasped in a plea.

"I'm impressed by your generosity, Eubulus," Caius chuckled, placing down his goblet. "Very well then. I'll take the storyteller."

"What?" The pitcher slipped from my hand, and all my muscles tensed up immediately. I glanced nervously at Eubulus, then turned to Cassia, whose widened eyes mirrored my own shock.

"The... The storyteller?" Eubulus asked, completely lost.

"Yes, you heard correctly." Caius pointed a heavily ringed finger at me. "That one."

"Oh, that is all?" Eubulus' face lit up with ecstasy. "I'll gladly hand her documents to you right away. And should you desire any other girls from my house, you can have them all."

"Drop it. Do you assert that my house lacks beautiful women—and can make use of your lowly ones? All I want is *this* girl, so that she may brighten my dreams by spinning her wondrous stories with her silken lips as I retire to bed by night."

Caius' teasing voice made my blood curdle in fear. "No, please don't!" I blurted out. "I... I can't go."

"Shut up! Remember where you came from. You should thank Fortuna that a great lord like Caius cast an eye on you," Eubulus bellowed. "Show your master the respect he deserves, especially within my home."

"Please master, she has served her lady well. Don't give her away." Rufus rushed forward from the back corner, his body trembling.

Suddenly, more than ten pairs of eyes turned toward him. Cassia's and Eubulus' faces went as pale as waxed parchment.

"By the gods, since when have slaves dared to talk to masters like this?" Eubulus thundered toward a slave standing behind him. "Tychicus, take this fool to the backyard and give him ten lashes."

Tychicus went to drag Rufus but couldn't move him, and as he did so, Cassia and I both cried out at the same time, trying to spare Rufus.

"And Vita, she is like my sister. Please have mercy," Cassia added amidst sobs.

"Have you blundering idiots been turned into stones by the Gorgons? Take that wretched fool to the backyard for whipping," Eubulus roared as he turned to the other slaves. "Then escort your lady to her bedchamber and *lock the door!*" At his words, several slaves hesitantly approached Cassia.

"Touch me and you'll see what you'll get," came Cassia's voice. She stared coldly at them, and to my surprise, none dared to make another move.

Rufus suddenly broke free from Tychicus' grasp and snatched a ceramic wine jug from a slave girl. He smashed it against a column and rushed to my side with a pointed shard in his right hand. Placing himself between me and the others, he held out the shard and roared, "No one can take her unless I die!"

"Rufus!" I wrapped my arms around his waist and cried. Seeing Rufus risk his life for me, I felt as if I could happily die right there with him. However, when I glanced at Cassia, I noticed she was also looking in our direction, tears glistening in her wide-open eyes.

"Well, do you always put on such a show for everyone? Or was this specially for me?" Caius clapped his hands slowly and smirked. "Looks like the storyteller has quite the network of connections here in the house. Very interesting. Pulled every which way, she is."

Eubulus' face turned as purple as a ripened fig. He gave Caius an uneasy smile. "I'm so sorry, my lord. I have been too busy recently to discipline this household. And today, you've seen the worst of it. Don't worry, I'll have this girl and her documents sent to your house early tomorrow morning."

"No need," Caius said. "I'm in the mood for carrying her home myself, right now. That way, she can relate a story to me as I drift into sweet slumber tonight."

Suddenly, the dining room fell so silent that even the rustling of leaves in the backyard became audible. I was unable to even make a sound when Caius easily grasped Rufus and tossed him to the side. "You see now? That's how you do it," he said to Tychicus.

Then he scooped me up onto his shoulder.

"Theophilus." Caius turned to his adjutant. "Get the girl's documents and tell Lady Sabina I'll miss her banquet tonight." With that, he strode toward the gate. "Hold on tight, sweetheart."

Twenty-Five

A Secret Plan

My mind was a void until Caius' foot crossed the threshold of the front gate, the setting sun's beams jolting me from my stupor. I yelled, cried, and kicked, but Caius' grip was so strong that I couldn't break it. "Rufus, help!" My plea echoed, mingling with his muffled cries from within the villa.

"Put me down!" I continued kicking and fighting. "Put me down right now!"

"I like fierce women, so keep kicking as much as you want," Caius said in a mischievous voice as he continued without breaking his stride. "The more you struggle and holler, the more I do like you. So please, carry on."

He strode briskly, and soon Eubulus' villa vanished from view. Before I realized it, we had passed the Forum, bustling with the market's activity and surrounded by busy streets. I felt so embarrassed as passersby strained their necks to watch us, some even colliding in their surprise at the sight before them, while whispers of gossip spread from mouth to ear.

Soon, we reached a tranquil, narrow lane lined with imposing villas, each one distanced from its neighbor by expansive grounds. Caius stopped in front of a towering gate beside a pink myrtle tree, which was blooming vibrantly. I stared at the tree and felt every flower on it was laughing at me. By now, my futile struggles had ceased, and I had resigned myself to the reality that this time, Rufus would not come to rescue his "little bride".

"M-my lord..." The doorkeeper's voice trembled with surprise as he swung open the gate.

Caius carried me into his house with lengthy strides. As he walked past the atrium, the hushed gasps and whispers of slaves trailed behind him.

Suddenly, a calm and warm voice, seemingly belonging to a middle-aged woman, reached my ears. "My lord, you're home early. Is there anything I can do for you?"

"Go heat the bath. Someone—and it's not me—needs a good wash tonight."

"Yes, master." Her voice remained as composed as before.

As we passed by her, I noticed she wore a turquoise silk dress, her hair neatly tied back. With a smirk playing on her lips, her eyes locked onto mine. Heat flooded my cheeks, and I wished the ground would open up and swallow me whole.

Finally, after passing through two panes of heavy curtains adorned with golden fringes, we entered an enormous chamber. Caius tossed me onto a canopy bed adorned with a variety of embroidered cushions and began to loosen his belt.

"No, please. Please don't..." I begged, my voice growing weaker with each desperate plea. I knew I was doomed and had already lost my edge as tears fell onto the silky cushions. "Please, have mercy. Please don't..."

"Don't what? Don't sleep with you? Is that what you mean?" Caius grinned mischievously, placing the belt on the nightstand. "My, my, what a perverted little mind you have. I just needed to loosen my tunic a little to let some air in. I've been sweating a lot carrying you all the way here. Guess what? You are much heavier than the heaviest sandbag we use in our barracks. And that's quite a weight, I tell you."

I had ceased sobbing, utterly bewildered by his unexpected demeanor.

"Look at you. You are sweating too, and you didn't even do any of the hard work. I would even call that an affront if I did not find you so charming."

Bending down, he retrieved a handkerchief from among the scattered cushions, gently blotting the moisture from my forehead with the care of a nursemaid tending to a child. The lilac pink fabric carried the scent of roses, undoubtedly belonging to a woman. I frowned and turned my head away.

"You don't need to be afraid. I would never sleep with a woman with calluses on her hands, especially ones as prominent as those," he said, casting an amused glance at my hands. Unconsciously, I buried my hands under the cushions and asked, "Then why did you bring me in here? Surely you don't really want to hear another story, do you?"

"Well, not quite. Perhaps some other time, but not now."

"So, what is it you want from me?"

Caius seated himself across from me. He looked me straight in the eyes, saying, "I want you to put on a show with me."

"A show? What do you mean? I'm sorry, but you'll have to explain."

"And I certainly will explain." Leaning in closer, Caius continued, "Starting today, and even with your callused hands, I want you to *pretend* to be my new passion. We'll spread the rumors that you're a banquet lover. And the precious fragrances you so dearly love will be used lavishly when we attend banquets together, especially the kinds presumably stolen by Tigellinus. As all the matrons in Rome imitate your taste and rush to buy the fragrances you wear, the prices will soar. Are you seeing where I'm taking this?"

"We'll lure him into selling the stolen goods?"

"Exactly! I'm impressed."

"But won't he easily see through our plot? He is said to be a cunning man."

"You're right. He is indeed cunning, but also terribly greedy. Sometimes, greediness can blind even the most cunning. In fact, Tigellinus is a blacksmith's son, what we would call lowborn. It was his ambition for wealth that drove him to rise to his current position."

Lowborn. Caius' words and sneering tone made my stomach drop.

Apparently, he didn't notice my change of expression and continued, "Take it from me, Tigellinus won't pass up an opportunity to make gains on a tempting deal, no matter how risky it seems to be." Caius then folded his hands and smiled. "So, it all depends on how tempting we can make the deal. That's why I need you to put on a great show with me. This show will push the prices of the stolen goods through the roof."

I looked at him, yet to fully recover from the shock, trying to take in all the information and find the catch in it. "Since you've said you have many women, why don't you just pick one and put on a show with her?"

"Good point. The reason I've chosen you is because I need a new face," Caius said. "In the past, every woman I've favored quickly gained renown in our circle. Matrons would emulate their tastes, and vendors would stock their preferred styles. It is hard to convince people they have changed their tastes."

I scrutinized his explanation, searching for any flaws, but none surfaced in my mind. "Wait, if people find out I used to be in Eubulus' house, wouldn't they suspect something?"

"Again, I'm one step ahead. I asked Eubulus when he visited me, and he said you hadn't been in his house for long and that you were never allowed out."

"Except on that day."

"Yes, and on that day, you made a big show, but judging by your attitude when we had our chat, I believe you never told anyone to which house you belonged. Again, well done."

All my doubts were temporarily cast away by his reasoning. He'd certainly thought things through in little time.

"Plus, I need someone who won't demand my attention after the show is over," Caius said. "And I think you can manage that."

"By all means I won't!" I exclaimed.

"That Rufus guy, your master's daughter is also in love with him, right?"

My face blushed instantly. "How did you—"

"It was obvious. Part of my job as the praetorian prefect is to observe people," Caius said with a smirk. "So, when this is all settled, I promise I'll grant you freedom and even pay the ransom for your sweetheart so he can leave with you. Even if your master's daughter were to object, I doubt she could do anything about it. Does that sound like a plan to you?"

Free. With Rufus.

These notions ignited my dwindling hope, setting my heart ablaze with anticipation. But Caius' offer—could it truly be this good?

Bowing my head, I thought through everything Caius had offered.

This sounds too good to be true, I mused silently. *Maybe, but it's the best deal I can possibly get in such a situation. I'm already his slave, so things can't be any worse.*

"Just one thing. Where is my room? I hope this is not it." I gestured to the chamber we were in. "Surely you can't expect me to sleep in here... with you?"

"Look, we must do this correctly if we want the plan to work. As my pampered mistress, you'll need to reside in my private bedchamber—a privilege never before granted to any other women. And don't give me that look. I have no intention of sharing my bed. You'll sleep on this lovely couch." He pointed to a couch with a curved backrest on the left side of his bed.

Thinking about sleeping so close to a man, my heart set off beating wildly. But if Caius really wanted me in that manner, there was no reason he couldn't have what he wanted right now. In a roundabout way, I found myself trusting him.

Oh, Lord, please give me courage and wisdom. This might be my only chance to receive my freedom and reunite with my Rufus.

Summoning my courage, I met Caius' gaze head-on. "Right, I understand you. But for this to work, I have two conditions. Send a message to my Rufus telling him what is really happening, or *not* happening between us, explaining in detail the whole plan. And bring my friend Julia here. She won't survive there without me.

"If you don't agree, I won't play this game with you, even if you threaten to kill me. So how does that sound to you?" After uttering those words, my body involuntarily quivered, fearing that my boldness might provoke his ire.

Caius looked shocked, but after a while, he shook his head and chuckled. "Oh, gods. You shifted into negotiations so swiftly, spinning me around your fingertips. You are cunning, you know? Cunning, ruthless, and manipulative. Some may even say devious and scheming. If you were a man, you'd make a fine senator."

"So... I take it you agree, then?" I giggled aloud at what he had said, though I had tried hard not to laugh.

"Deal," Caius said as he bent down and stroked my face gently. "You are a very smart girl, and I think I've made a good decision."

I shoved his hand away vigorously. "Hey, I only act when there are people around! It's a show, don't forget. A show to put on like a garment we don in public."

Before he could react, a young slave's voice sounded from the other side of the curtains. "M-Master, there's a message from the palace."

"What's the matter again?" Caius said impatiently.

"The empress got word of some suspicious activity tonight. She wanted you to go there right now."

"By the gods!" Caius raised his voice. "Does she have to call me at a moment like this? She spoiled my night with my newfound pearl." Then he pinched my face. "You little charmer. We will continue this when I'm back."

With a sly grin, Caius fastened his belt and draped a shawl over his shoulders before heading toward the door. "Enjoy your bath, my dear," he purred, "and make yourself smell like a goddess before I come back." He winked playfully before leaving the room.

I immediately knew the show was already on, and there was no turning back. With what I hoped was a flirtatious tone, I teased, "Don't make me wait too long, or I might have to punish you, my naughty prefect."

A broad smile lit up Caius' face as he mouthed the words, "You're quite good." With that, he strode out of the room.

Twenty-Six

The First Night

As Caius departed, a wave of relief washed over me, but it left my mind swirling with disorienting thoughts. *Oh, God. What have I just got myself into? Am I a fool agreeing to be his fake mistress? Just a few hours ago, I was at Eubulus' house, worrying about my future with Rufus. Now I'm in the bedchamber of another man.*

"Oh, God. Guide my way. This is beyond what I can handle," I cried out in prayer.

After a while, my racing heart gradually calmed, and my surroundings came into focus. The bedchamber stretched out before me, vast and expansive, easily twice the size of Cassia's. However, unlike her bedroom with its delicate flower frescoes, these walls were lined with imposing figures of fully armored soldiers.

In fact, upon closer inspection, each depiction portrayed the same soldier. On one side of the wall, he was riding a shining chariot pulled by four magnificent horses. On the other side, he was towering over a young half-naked woman. As I observed the scene, I could feel my cheeks flush with heat. Judging by Caius' position, I guessed the soldier must have been the war god Mars and the lady, his scandalous mistress, Venus. Nana had told the story before, warning me of dangerous men.

While I was still lost in thoughts, a voice from behind the curtains caught me off-guard. "My lady, the hot bath is ready. May I come in to serve you?"

"Y-yes, please come in," I stuttered.

The curtains parted, revealing a woman whom I recognized from our earlier encounter in the corridor. Her turquoise dress with its white carnation patterns stood out, but her face remained impassive.

"Why are you calling me 'my lady'?" I asked, taken aback. I had never been addressed in such a manner before.

"This is how we address any woman the master brings home. By the way, you may call me Decima," the woman answered politely.

"But I'm..." I hesitated, resisting the urge to divulge the truth. "All right. So where is the bath?"

"Follow me," Decima said, gesturing toward a tapestry hanging beside Caius' bed. It was a magnificent piece, depicting an image of Venus bathing in the river with intricately woven golden and silver threads. The scene was so vivid that when Decima parted it to reveal a space behind, I was startled.

"This is the master's private bath. Used only by himself and the one that's closest to him. He said he won't be here until midnight, so my lady has enough time to enjoy herself."

Wave-patterned mosaics in varying shades of blue covered every inch of the floor. A shell-shaped pool took up the center of the room, also inlaid with mosaics of all kinds of water nymphs and mermen chasing each other. Glittering gems crowned the heads of the nymphs, adding a touch of radiant splendor to the scene.

Steam billowed from the water's surface, obscuring the frescoes on the walls. In one corner of the room stood a majestic marble statue of Neptune, the sea god, gripping his trident, partially shrouded in the mist.

"Welcome to the hot bath," Decima said, gesturing toward the steaming pool. "And over there," she pointed to a beaded curtain on the room's west side, "is the cold bath. Though, I must warn you, my lady, the water is quite chilly, and not many find it enjoyable.

However, you're more than welcome to give it a try. Just be prepared for the temperature difference."

She then called out toward a pale purple double door on the room's east side, "Please enter, girls."

Two slender young girls came in, their heads bowed respectfully, their hands outstretched, holding golden trays upon which were neatly folded silk gowns, linen cloth, and a pair of new sandals. "Livia and Tullia will help you get undressed," Decima said.

"No, I-I think I'll do it myself," I stuttered again. "Really, I-I'll be fine."

"We serve the master and any guests in this room," Decima said with a smile. "But the master informed me that you can do as you wish."

"Thank you, but I prefer to take care of myself," I insisted. "I wouldn't want to burden you with extra tasks."

"As you wish, my lady." The two girls placed the golden trays on the floor near the pool and retreated with Decima through the pale purple door.

I stretched my body and let out a yawn, realizing my toes had been curled up all the time because of the nervousness. "Well, like it or not, I'm trapped here. Might as well make the most of it."

Glancing around to ensure I was alone, I shed my clothes and slipped into the pool, settling on the first step beneath the water's surface. The warmth enveloped my body, and I reached for a linen cloth from the tray, bringing it to my nose.

It carried the delightful scent of jasmine and rose, further enhancing the soothing atmosphere.

After wiping my face with the cloth, my gaze was drawn to the frescos on the wall. The one directly in front of me portrayed a scene where a group of soldiers were capturing half-naked, young women in a field.

Could it be Romulus, the legendary founder of Rome, and his warriors abducting the Sabine women? Studying it further, the scene suddenly brought me back to my childhood memories and to the second time Rufus took me to Paphos. I was ten then, old enough to be left alone at a storyteller's stand when Rufus went to the toilet. That day, the storyteller was telling that very story. At the time, I couldn't quite grasp the meaning of the tale, but those names—Romulus, Sabine women—and the raucous laughter emanating from the largely male audience remained etched in my memory. When Rufus came back shortly afterwards, he quickly covered my ears before whisking me away.

My eyes cast on the leading warrior who was carrying a girl over his shoulder. The arrogance in his demeanor and the cocky smirk he wore mirrored those of Caius.

"Nana was right. The things you see every day finally become part of you." Thinking of having to share a room with a man like that for who knows how long, I slid deeper into the bath, submerging my head under the water.

Resurfacing, I ran my hands over my wet hair.

"Dear Lord, please protect my heart from all the bad influences of this man and this household..." I said aloud in the empty room. "And please be gracious in sparing me from temptations, perhaps," I added in a low voice.

Because, amidst all the feelings of contempt and disgust, I felt deep in my heart that somewhere in the mix was a longing and secret lust aroused by the luxurious lifestyle surrounding me.

Stepping out of the pool, I dried myself with another piece of soft linen cloth from the tray and put on the gown and sandals. The fabric of the gown felt as delicate as a baby's skin—smooth, utterly sumptuous, exuding opulence in every thread.

I carefully navigated my way back to Caius' bedchamber, mindful not to knock over anything valuable. The room was filled with a soothing balsamic fragrance, emanating from the incense burner in the shape of Bacchus the wine god.

My eyelids grew heavier with exhaustion. It had been a long and overly dramatic day. Despite the warnings from my mind to remain cautious in this unfamiliar environment, my body succumbed to the allure of the plush couch and silk pillows. With a yawn, I eased onto the couch, drawing the silky blanket over me.

In my subconscious, a peculiar dream invaded. Again, it involved Rufus, and this time, we strolled hand in hand along a bridge. Enjoying the serene moment, we paused to gaze into the calm waters below, only to be startled as they transformed into raging waves.

The sudden deluge caught us off guard, leaving us no time to seek refuge before the third colossal wave engulfed us both. Fighting to stay afloat, I grasped onto a log, frantically searching for Rufus amidst the chaos. "Rufus! Rufus!" I cried out, but to no avail. I remained adrift for what felt like days and nights until a loud voice jolted me awake.

"Get up, lazy girl!"

Twenty-Seven

Are You a Christian?

Feeling a sudden jolt in my ear, I couldn't help but cry out. Gradually, I blinked open my eyes, only to notice a strong hand with long fingers gently tugging at my ear. As the figure seated before me sharpened into focus, I realized it was Caius.

"Wake up, lazy girl!" Caius scowled, letting go of my ear.

It was then that I noticed his attire—a scarlet linen tunic paired with black, form-fitting pants that reached above his knees, giving him a rugged and practical appearance, quite distinct from the dandy boy I saw yesterday.

"What time is it? I'm sorry. Have I overslept?" I sat up immediately, fumbling for words.

"The rooster in my backyard has crowed three times already. By Mercury, old Eubulus has surely spoiled his household slaves," he said. "I didn't expect him to be so accommodating. Maybe it's just the image he tries to project, but deep down, he's quite lenient."

"No, I usually get up before sunrise. It's just… this couch is so comfortable," I said, quickly hiding the silk pillow with my saliva stain behind my back.

"Seems you've made yourself quite at home. Had a refreshing bath?" He took a strand of my hair and brought it close to his nose.

"I'm glad you don't smell like a kitchen slave anymore."

"You don't have to sniff my hair to know that." I grabbed my hair back and gave him a protesting look.

"How are your hands? Did the girls treat them with beeswax and honey? Give it ten days, and they'll be as smooth as silk."

"I didn't let them help me bathe last night," I confessed. "It... It would have felt strange."

"You didn't?" His eyebrows raised slightly. "Well... that's fine. Even if we can soften your calloused hands, there are still other things that won't change in ten days, like the way you talk and walk. There's no way you'll transform into a well-born matron. Let's just make people think I've had a sudden change of taste," he said with a smirk.

"Hey, I'm not ashamed of my calloused hands at all. They prove I'm a hard-working girl," I protested.

"Stop whining! Help me with my armor. I need to reach the barracks in time." Caius rose from the chair and gestured toward the armor rack. "Since we need to keep our *secret*, I dismissed the girls who used to help me get dressed. Now, it's your job. Hurry up. We have much to do today."

It felt strange having to dress a man, but I couldn't find any excuse to refuse.

Reluctantly, I rose from the couch and walked barefoot to the rack. I grabbed the leather vest and the belt with dangling straps before fitting them onto Caius. Moving to his back, I secured the vest's threads together, and as I attempted to adjust the leather belt, my fingers brushed against the firmness of his waist. Suddenly, a tingling sensation spread throughout my body. A momentary dizziness took hold of me as the patterns on the marble floor seemed to swirl before my eyes.

"Oh, Lord," I muttered, taking a deep breath to steady myself. "It must be the hot bath yesterday that's making me feel so lightheaded."

"A little tighter with the belt, please," Caius said. "Livia used to help me with the undergarments too, but I knew you would object, so I did it myself. It's a shame for a patrician to dress himself, so don't ever tell anybody, understand?"

"Why would I do that?" I exclaimed, louder than intended. "You patricians are just big babies. You really can't take care of yourselves, can you? What would you do on the battlefield? Bring your slave girls to help you with your undergarments? Have them feed you wine and grapes?"

My outburst was followed with a muted *oops*. Realizing I'd gone too far, I lowered my head and stole quick glances at Caius, fearing he would be livid at my insolence.

But to my relief, Caius didn't seem angry. Instead, he said calmly, "I have different rules in my home compared to those on the battlefield. Regardless of my rank, I consider myself a soldier." A sense of boyish pride shone through in his demeanor.

I looked at him in his armor and suddenly, some old memories came to me. The bustling slave market, the robber, the chaos, and then the striking figure on horseback with sunlight framing him from behind... Yes, the slave trader had addressed him as "the prefect".

No wonder he looked familiar. And in a strange twist of fate, he had unknowingly saved me that day.

"I know what you're thinking," Caius suddenly disrupted my thoughts. "This is the training armor," he said with a beaming smile, seemingly confident he could read my mind. "The ceremonial one is kept in my barracks. Every girl I've brought home has asked to see it, and today you'll be the only fortunate one not just to see it, but to touch it as well."

"That's not what I was..." I was about to argue when suddenly, something struck me as odd about what Caius had just mentioned. "What do you mean I'll see it today?"

"We need to spread the rumor that you are my new mistress, a spoiled one. What is a better way than showing up in front of three hundred solid men in my barracks, which I never allowed any of my women to enter?"

"But won't that tarnish your perfect image as a good prefect?" I asked carefully, feeling a little uneasy about staging our performance in front of such a large audience.

"Maybe a little. But my soldiers trust me. They see how hard I work and how disciplined I am in the barracks. It's harmless to give them something to tease me about occasionally. Besides, if we want Tigellinus to believe us, we need to put on a bit of a show." Caius smiled and gently patted my shoulder. "You'd better act well. If my soldiers suspect us, word will reach Tigellinus' barracks, and our plan will be ruined. So, are you up to it?"

The idea of pretending to be Caius' mistress in public gave me goosebumps. "I can't object, can I?" I said with a sigh and added, "But promise me you're going to send a message to Rufus today."

"No, not today! It's too risky if we contact your lover at this moment."

"But what if he thinks we are really…" My voice became pitchy.

"Young lady," Caius laughed. "Is there such a lack of faith in your man? If he truly loves you, which I'm sure he does, he'll trust you regardless. Can't you see that?"

"Trust me?" A sizzling anger rose from deep within. "I was carried home like a bag of goods by a man who can determine my fate in a snap of a finger. And you think he'd be wrong to assume the worst? You are asking too much of a human, a helpless slave, you arrogant patrician!" I roared, tears welling up and my breath coming in gasps.

"Calm down now! Don't be so emotional. If there is one thing I can't stand, it's… it's—" Caius fumbled for a handkerchief. Unable to find one, he tried to wipe my tears with his sleeves.

"What… what can't you tolerate? Weakness? Tears from a woman, all caused by you? Well, that's tough for you, isn't it? Anyway, stop it," I said, pushing his hand away. "Send a message to Rufus now, or I'll never have a part in your plan, no matter what you do to me! And… and…" I searched for reasons to convince him that the loss would be his. "And you'll miss this great opportunity to eliminate your political opponent because by the time you find another actress for your show, he will have already sold the goods on the black ma rket."

Then I turned away and prayed silently. *Oh, Lord. The king's heart is in your hand, as the rivers of water, so as this man's heart. Please make him agree with me.*

A long, horrible silence.

"Fine," Caius finally said with a blank look. "I'll ask Theophilus to send a message secretly *tomorrow*. This is the best I can do; don't push me any further. You must know that I'm taking great risks for your stupid worries. And if you threaten me one more time..." He tipped my chin and stared at me, his eyes burning with anger.

I never expected Caius to compromise so quickly, and my temper had dissipated by now, leaving only regret in its wake. Realizing that even though he needed me for his plan, it didn't cancel out the fact that he owned me and could legally kill me on a whim. I decided not to push him too far.

But I had another request, so I found myself asking in a soft, pleading voice, "Please also bring my friend Julia here. The other girls will bully her when I'm not around to protect her."

"I'll make sure you can meet her by dinner today," Caius assured me. "It's good to have someone you can trust to attend to your needs. The girls in my house, they are sweet, but they surely don't know how to keep secrets."

"Oh, thank God," I said with much relief.

"Hey, when did the gods get involved? You should thank me, girl," Caius said in a playful voice, then suddenly frowned, scrutinizing me suspiciously. "Wait a minute. Did you just say 'thank God' instead of 'the gods'?"

I was speechless as he continued, "Judging by your accent, you're not a Jew, so you must be one of the donkey head worshipers!"

"No, we don't do that," I blurted out.

"So, you admit you're a Christian then," Caius said, staring at me sternly.

There was no use denying it at this moment, and my faith wouldn't allow me to. So I said in the calmest tone I could manage,

"Yes, I am a Christian. I know you've probably heard those rumors about us, but we are not like that, I promise."

"Your honesty is appreciated." Caius' eyes softened a little. "I don't mind your little unique sect actually."

"You... You don't mind?"

"I know your cult may not be widely accepted, and sometimes people are suspicious of those who are different," he answered, smirking, "but I believe a true Roman should always remain open to new things. As long as you are loyal to the emperor, I have no issue with whatever gods or god you worship."

I was so surprised and relieved to hear this from someone with so much power. If Caius was all right with it, then why couldn't others follow his lead?

"I need to go to the barracks now. The slaves already know you're my new mistress, so they'll see to your needs. Just remember to tidy up the blanket on the couch. Don't let them find out you spent the night there." He approached the door and added, "By the way, there are plenty of nice clothes in the guest bedchamber, left by my previous lovers, so have a look and choose whatever you like."

As he parted the curtain, he turned and gave me a wink. "Enjoy your morning in my villa. I'll be expecting Your Highness at the barracks after lunchtime."

Twenty-Eight
A Tour of the Villa

Decima came in carrying a silver tray right after I tidied up my couch.

"Morning, my lady." Her voice was gentle and soothing. "Your breakfast is here. The master wanted to make sure you have something nourishing after a long night."

I tried to maintain a languid smile while my cheeks grew hot. "Thank you." I pointed to the table and said, "Please leave it there."

When she saw I was tidying up Caius' bed, she said, "My lady, why toil yourself over these matters? Livia will take care of that."

"I don't want other girls to touch his bed. And I enjoy doing everything I can for him. He is so wonderful, isn't he?" With that, I turned away from Decima, trying to hide the redness on my face, unable to believe what I had just said.

Decima gave me a knowing smile. "As you wish, my lady," she said. "Please allow me to give you a tour of the villa after you finish breakfast. The garden flowers are still blooming; it would be an auspicious time to see them."

She concluded with a bow before retreating to the hallway.

I glanced at the tray before me where a plate held a delicacy—a poached egg infused with the aroma of honeyed wine, adorned with a generous sprinkling of crushed pine nuts. The creamy color of the oozing yolk made my stomach growl.

I settled in and ate quickly.

After finishing breakfast, I stepped out of the chamber to find Decima waiting for me. "My lady, let me show you around the villa," she said, beckoning me to follow. As we made our way to the atrium, I was struck by its enormity. Though I had been here when Caius carried me to his bedchamber yesterday, I hadn't the composure to truly observe it then. It surpassed Eubulus' in size, boasting higher ceilings and thicker columns. Beneath the opening in the ceiling, instead of a mere pool as in Eubulus', there lay a miniature indoor garden, featuring a small crescent-shaped pond embellished with floating water lilies and lily pads covering almost half of the water surface.

As a gentle breeze drifted in through the roof opening, reflections of ripples gracefully danced along the walls, swaying to the rhythm of the wind. Surrounding the pond, ferns, arrowheads, and reeds thrived, while small critter statues lay nestled among them. A bronze deer leaned toward the water, as if taking a refreshing drink.

As I was marveling at the tranquility of the scene, Decima said, "Most villas in Rome have pools in the atriums to collect rainwater for household use. But this house has water directly coming from the aqueduct, so we can dedicate this area solely to landscaping."

"That must have cost a fortune," I exclaimed.

"No money can buy it." Decima beamed with pride. "The master's father sponsored the Aqueduct Claudia, one of the greatest in Rome."

As I stood in the atrium, my attention was drawn to a series of elegant marble busts arranged in a line parallel to the walls. "These are the ancestors of the Aemilia family," Decima said proudly. "Our family has 102 senators, 514 tribunes since Emperor Augustus' time."

"See this?" She walked toward a marble bust of a middle-aged man with an aura of regal sophistication, whose right hand clasped a scroll. "This was the master's late father. He passed away five years ago; the face was cast on his death bed at the age of forty-five." Decima reached out and touched the face of the statue gently. And when my eyes met hers, I saw a trace of wistfulness which she quickly sought to hide from me.

Noticing her discomfort, I swiftly changed the subject. "Does your master have any siblings?"

"No, the master is the sole heir of the Aemilia family. The old master and mistress passed away five years ago, and they didn't have any other children."

Suddenly, I felt a pang of sympathy for Caius. He owned such a grand villa but no family to share it with. The familiar ache of loneliness resonated within me, but thoughts of Rufus came rushing back, filling my heart with warmth.

"Allow me to show you the master's study, my lady." Decima gestured toward the screens depicting goddess Athena wearing a long robe with an owl perched on her shoulder. Pushing them open, she led me into a spacious room. My eyes were immediately drawn to the tall bookshelves lining the walls, filled with leather-bound scrolls and manuscripts. The sweet, subtle scent of aged parchment permeated the air, triggering memories of childhood longing.

For a moment, I stood there speechless, transported back to a time when I had yearned to learn to read and write but life had made it impossible.

With an unexpected gust, the strong breeze entering from the open side of the study caused the purple, silky, translucent curtains to sway and dance, while the bells attached to them tinkled in a harmonious rhythm. As the sweet fragrance of flowers wafted in from the backyard garden, it filled my nostrils and made me feel refreshed and rejuvenated from head to toe.

"In my opinion, the garden is most enchanting this time of year," Decima said, deftly securing the curtains with the large bronze rings attached to the columns, before gesturing for me to join her outside.

As I stepped into the garden, I found myself surrounded by

myrtles, roses, violets, and lilies, all organized in neat, gridded flower beds. Although it was toward the end of summer, the late bloomers mixed beautifully with the others that had already withered, creating a unique tapestry of colors and textures. Buzzing bees and fluttering butterflies darted among the flowers, collecting the last bits of nectar before the cooler weather arrived.

Two peacocks wandered gracefully beneath the canopy of pine trees, their vibrant feathers sweeping elegantly on the ground.

I had anticipated the garden to be magnificent, but never in my wildest dreams did I imagine encountering five tranquil ponds scattered throughout. The sight of a semicircular pond, encompassed by an arc-shaped mosaic wall and a lush grape arbor, stole my breath.

"These ponds are all connected to the aqueducts in the city," Decima explained with a proud smile. "Our men work hard to keep the water clean and as clear as crystal. See those two over there? They are currently changing the filters at the water inlet. It's a lot of work and needs to be done once a month."

She gestured toward the two strong slaves, who diligently bent over the largest pond at the center.

Feeling uneasy about being idle, I feigned a languid voice and said, "I'm bored." Glancing around, I noticed some iris patches near the grape arbor. "May I pick some iris leaves and make something for fun?" I asked.

"Sure. I'll ask one of the gardeners to pick them for you."

"Thanks, but I'd rather do it myself."

"As you wish, my lady. However, I must excuse myself right now. There's much to attend to, but should you need anything, just ask Paulinus or Lucius to find me." Decima pointed to the gardeners standing a couple of arm lengths apart, each tending to their own section of the iris patches.

I nodded and made my way to the taller gardener, Lucius, who greeted me with a bow. "How may I be of your service, my lady?"

"Would you mind me picking some iris leaves?" I asked and

noticed his eyes widen in surprise.

"Please allow me to pick them for you. The leaves can be quite sharp for your delicate fingers," Lucius offered, his eyes resting on my calloused hands. Suddenly, embarrassment crossed his rugged face.

"Oh, um, I mean, let us help you," another gardener, Paulinus, chimed in, his chest heaving as he approached us.

"All right, thanks," I yielded to their insistence. "I prefer the slightly browned ones."

"Here, my lady." Paulinus quickly gathered a handful of leaves into a basket and handed them to me with a bow. Meanwhile, Lucius maintained a respectful distance with his hands straightened by his sides, avoiding eye contact.

"Thank you," I replied graciously, accepting the basket and offering them a warm smile. "I'm Vita, and as you can see," I gestured toward my calloused hands, "I'm no stranger to hard work."

As their shocked gazes bore into me, I realized I had ruined my act as a spoiled mistress. But I decided to forgive myself, as it was too difficult to keep up the charade all day. Trying to change the subject, I asked, "How long have you two been working in this house?"

"We are brothers born and raised here," Paulinus said. "Our family has been serving as gardeners here for three generations, ever since our great-grandfather was brought to work in this house." His tone resonated with a deep sense of belonging, a sentiment I had never perceived from any of Eubulus' slaves.

"Is your master treating you well?" I asked.

"Yes." He nodded heavily. "He's always been kind to us all. But the girls he brought home... Well, not all of them are nice." Realizing he had talked too much, he lowered his voice.

Somehow, his eyes reminded me of those of Rufus, especially on the night I caught him in Eubulus' room, being scolded by his master. The memory of his wary eyes, like those of a timid deer, triggered a dull but piercing pain in my heart, like a blunt needle's jab.

When everything has settled, I'll leave Rome with Rufus, and no one can keep us down anymore. Lord, will you help me? I prayed in my heart.

I nestled into a cozy spot on the bench below the grape arbor and started to weave, while the two gardeners continued their tasks nearby. Soon enough, I had six small, woven objects around me.

A slave girl, no older than twelve, carrying a water jar on her head, stopped to admire the woven objects. "How adorable!" she exclaimed.

"Would you like to choose one for yourself?" I offered.

She hesitated before approaching me, pointing to a little fan. "Can I have that?" she asked.

"Sure." I handed it to her.

"Thank you, this is amazing," she said, marveling as she turned it over in her hands. Soon, several other girls, including Livia and Tullia, came along.

"May I have the basket?"

"I want the little star."

"That bunny is so playful."

They giggled and happily selected their favorite pieces.

The youngest girl, who had come first, examined me curiously from head to toe. "Are you Vita? Everyone in the house knows the master carried you home on his shoulder last night. You must be the master's special friend," she said with candid innocence. "I never thought you'd be so kind. When Sabina was here, she made us all crawl—"

"Marcia!" Livia shushed her gently.

"Does your master often carry girls home on his shoulder?" My curiosity got the best of me; the question slipped out before I could stop it.

"No, the girls always arrived in carriages with him," Tullia said. "He had always brought girls home from banquets and let them stay here for a month or so. But he never let anyone live in his bedchamber."

"You must be so special to the master, my lady. And you are so kind too. Which house are you from?" Marcia asked.

"I'm a tavern keeper's daughter." I came up with the idea on the spot. "Caius and I met in the Forum, when he was on the way to Lady Sabina's banquet last night," I explained, feeling regretful that I had to lie to such a sweet girl.

"Wow, love at first sight!" Her eyes sparkled with mischief. "Lady Sabina must be livid about it."

As they surrounded me, their curious eyes palpably scanned me, questioning how I'd managed to ensnare their master's attention. Realizing that lying was not my strong point, I deftly shifted the conversation to Caius. To my surprise, each one of them had a handful of funny anecdotes to share about him.

Engrossed in their stories, I lost all sense of time. As Livia shared a tale of Theophilus' prank on Caius, where he'd made him eat garum, something he despised, I suddenly noticed the sun had moved above the arbor, its rays filtering through the grape leaves, leaving flickering light spots on her face.

Dear Lord, it is time to face my arena, my mind said to me.

Twenty-Nine

Visiting the Barracks

THE SUN WAS HIGH atop the watchtower as the carriage pulled up to the barracks of the Praetorian Guard.

"My lady, have you thought this through?" Felix the coachman asked with a worried look. "None of his women were ever allowed to enter. Last month, Lady Antonia insisted I bring her here, but the master refused to let her in. She felt so humiliated and cried all the way home."

The genuine concern from this hunchbacked old man warmed my heart.

"You haven't known the master for long, my lady," Felix continued. "At first, he can be very charming and passionate with a woman, but over time, you may see a colder side."

A flicker of sympathy crossed his face, and for a moment, I wasn't sure if it was for me or for Caius.

"We'll see. But for now, please don't trouble yourself with worries over me," I said, not wanting to burden the old man unnecessarily.

Quickly, I tidied my piled-up hair with the golden pins and clips. It was more challenging to style my own hair compared to Cassia's. I could never seem to achieve the same elegance. As expected, wispy strands escaped and fluttered around my cheeks.

Jumping out of the carriage, I almost tripped on the trailing fabric of my extravagant pomegranate-colored long dress.

Should've chosen a simpler one, I thought.

Murmuring a prayer, I rushed to the door of the barracks, which were guarded by two praetorian guards.

"Lady, kindly state your business here," the taller one said, towering over me.

"Caius left this at home." I dangled a golden armband in front of him. "So, I thought I'd stop by to hand it to him."

"I'm pretty sure the prefect doesn't need it on a training day," he said with a smirk. "But I'll report it anyway. Please wait here." He then glanced at the other guard and said, "Hey, Petronius! Don't stare at her. It's impolite." Petronius averted his gaze, slightly embarrassed.

The taller guard disappeared down the short corridor, through which I caught a glimpse of the exercising field and the archery targets at the far end. Several pairs of soldiers were sparring, their movements calculated and precise.

"It's a tough job being a praetorian guard, isn't it?" I asked Petronius, trying to break the awkward silence.

"Yes, lots of training. But the pay is good. And the honor. We guard the palace and the city," he said with boyish pride, something I had also witnessed on Caius' face.

As we were talking, the taller guard came back.

"The prefect said you can enter," he said with a surprised look. "Good for you, lady. This is the first time he's allowed a woman into the barracks. He's training new recruits in the northeast section. But please be careful; our men are so focused on their drills that they might accidentally bump into you."

"Thank you for your warning," I said with a nod. "I see that *my* Caius is correct when he says his men are the best. You show me great care. I will take the utmost caution."

Then I scuttled off toward the exercising field. The smell of sweat and sand flooded my nostrils as I went, cautiously picking my way through the sparring soldiers.

As I walked, a familiar figure caught my eye. It was Caius, standing with his side facing me. His posture was straight, and his shoulders squared as he held a wooden rod.

"Figure Four Striking Drill!" he bellowed at a soldier beside him, knocking the stake with his rod. The soldier quickly obliged, stabbing the stake with a wooden sword.

"Good stance, but no stamina," Caius remarked as he took the sword from the soldier. With a swift and impactful motion, he demonstrated the stabbing action in front of him, leaving a deep etch on the stake.

The midday sun beat down, causing droplets of sweat to glisten on Caius' forehead and trickle down his chiseled jawline. Suddenly, he turned and caught sight of me, a bright smile spreading across his face. With swift strides, he approached me, gently lifting me to sit on his arm.

"Missing me so much, you little nymph?" he teased.

"Hey, put me down and don't get your sweat on my new dress. It will stain all the fabric," I scolded, holding the armband to his eye level. "Anyway, you forgot this."

"We both know I don't need it, you cunning little beauty," he said, gently setting me on the ground. "But since you brought it here, help me put it on." I did as he asked, but when my fingertips briefly touched his sweat-covered arm, a rush of dizziness spread over me, just like the sensation I had yesterday when I helped him with the belt.

What's wrong with me? It must be the strong sunshine, I thought, trying to refocus.

My thoughts were abruptly interrupted by a man's voice cutting in. "Sir, no more training today. Don't keep your lovely companion waiting," a soldier shouted as others crowded around us.

"Sir, it's time to give your guest a tour of your study," another added, inciting a bout of roaring, raucous laughter from the group.

Their brazenness made me frown, yet I secretly rejoiced in the success of our plan. "Oh, hush," I said, with an expression of both genuine and feigned embarrassment, my gaze directed downward and away.

"But Theophilus is there, working on some paperwork," an olive-skinned soldier pointed out.

"Then let's drag him out. Time to make room for the prefect and his girl," another rallied.

"No need! I'm done," Theophilus said, suddenly appearing in the crowd. "Hold your horses, boys!" He patted Caius' shoulder. "Prefect, your study is ready to use now. The scrolls are safely tucked away, and I have even dusted the bed. You can thank me later."

"All right, all right. As you wish. You have a half-hour's rest, then resume your training."

"Prefect, how about…" a skinny soldier called out something with a thick accent, followed by more raucous laughter from the group.

Intense heat surged to the base of my ears. *Oh, Lord. What am I doing? Help me.*

Seemingly sensing my embarrassment, Caius announced, "The jesting time is over. Now, take the rest you requested and be quiet." Then, he grew serious once more and gestured to his men to clear a path for him.

"Come on, let me give you a tour of my study," Caius said, grabbing my hand. I followed him with my head bowed, not daring to meet his men's lascivious and suggestive gazes.

Oh, God. Help me get through this quickly.

Finally reaching Caius' study—tucked at the very northwest end of the barracks—he shut the door immediately as we stepped in, latching it from the inside.

"You made it!" he said loudly, attempting to pull me into a hug. "You are the finest mistress of acting and ridicule, sustaining even the worst of taunts. If only they knew—"

"Hey, be careful! They might hear us," I cautioned, stepping back from him and rushing to the window to check for any potential eavesdroppers.

"My men may occasionally have their quirks, but they wouldn't dare to eavesdrop outside my study," Caius said. As he settled onto the bench, he gently filled the water clock on the desk with a pitcher, watching droplets trickle into the tray below. "They are aware of the consequences should any be caught eavesdropping. A flogging... that's how it would go. Besides, Theophilus will make sure everything is fine."

Upon hearing Theophilus' name, I couldn't help but ask, "Have you sent him to deliver the message?"

"Yes, I have," Caius said. "He will go to Eubulus' house this afternoon to fetch Julia and find a chance to talk to your lover in person, telling him that you are safe and sound with me. Please stop fretting about him."

If I wasn't mistaken, he seemed just a slight tad irritated at my constant worry over Rufus. Well, I didn't care. With the assurance that Rufus would receive the message soon, relief poured through me, into my veins, making my heart swell.

"Oh, thank God," I cried out. "Well, I mean, thank *you* as well, before you correct me. I do appreciate what you will tell me."

"And what might that be?"

"That God is not the one who informed Theophilus. I'm right, am I not?" I chuckled. It was good that in his presence, I was at least permitted to speak of my God.

Caius smirked but didn't object or argue against my supposition.

"Is this the place you work every day?" I asked, looking around the room.

"Yes. Is it different from what you expected?"

Caius' study presented a stark contrast to his opulent bedchamber. The desk bore signs of wear, its paint chipped in places, while the bench beside it was strikingly plain. No marble or mosaic floors, no frescoes on the wall, only stucco with wooden columns half exposed, and a humble bed covered with white linen tucked on the wall opposite the window side.

"I mostly work in the training field as you just saw. That's the best part of this job. But as a prefect, there's a ton of paperwork to get through each day." Caius pointed to an opened scroll on the desk, a long parchment bearing all kinds of lines and dots.

"What is that?" My curiosity was aroused, and I sat on the bench beside him.

"This is the map of Rome," Caius said. "I'm working on the fire prevention system of the city. We need to make sure every community has enough water reserved for emergencies. I've completed over half of them, but it's so time-consuming."

"Oh, I didn't know a praetorian prefect would also take responsibility for that."

"Understandable. Many people assume that we're just palace guards, and while that's a significant part of our job, we're also responsible for maintaining the security of the entire city."

"So, you are familiar with all the streets and lanes in Rome?"

"Of course!" Caius said, beaming with pride. "Every summer, there are lots of fire reports. I'm writing a letter to the emperor, asking for more tents this year in case of emergencies." The seriousness in his eyes made me secretly amused. I never expected this man to have such a different side than the banquet boy I knew.

I opened a smaller scroll in front of me, and although the written words were incomprehensible to me, their calligraphy was stunning.

Suddenly, an idea struck me. "Perhaps you could teach me to read and write when you have time?" I turned to Caius with a hopeful gaze.

"Why do you want to learn that? A lot of patrician women don't even know how to spell."

"Because... I just thought it would be nice if I could read the scrolls. This was what I always dreamed since I was little, you know, to learn stuff... to possess knowledge."

I caressed the scroll tenderly, but then met his gaze and noticed a hint of an enigmatic smile on his lips. *Perhaps he thinks it foolish for a slave girl to harbor such aspirations.*

Shaking off the self-doubt, I continued, "Additionally, Rufus and

I have always dreamed of returning to Cyprus, where we plan to start a small basket shop. Proper bookkeeping skills would definitely come in handy for that."

"Believe me, your Rufus is a lucky fellow." A hint of sadness flickered within his smiling eyes but disappeared immediately. "Sure, I'll teach you some basics when I have time. But right now, if I go into a room with a beautiful girl and leave smelling of ink, my reputation would be ruined." Caius laughed loudly.

The implication of Caius' words made my cheeks burn, so I tried to switch to another topic. "Where is your shiny ceremonial armor? You said you left it in the barracks."

"Ha, it's in this room, but you'll never find it unless I tell you," Caius said with a mischievous smile.

I looked around. The room wasn't that big, and I could see no chests or wardrobes. It was hard to imagine he could hide the bulky armor anywhere in this place. As my eyes wandered the nooks and crannies of the study, looking for any indication of the armor's whereabouts, Caius turned a vase on his desk. A door slowly creaked open on the wall opposite the entrance of the room, revealing a large inner space. Dominating its center stood the ceremonial armor, meticulously displayed on a rack, complete with the helmet, body armor, sword, dagger, and shield.

"Genius design, isn't it?" Caius said. "We invited Heron of Alexandria to build this door for us. He was the greatest mathematician in Egypt, the most esteemed scholar at the Library of Alexandria."

Mathematician. Library. Scholar. These words fascinated me to no end.

Stepping closer, Caius pointed at each part of his armor, explaining the meanings of the decorations.

"That's Mars on the left side and Athena on the right. You know, they both symbolize the strategic and peace-seeking side of the military leader. And see the little Medusa head here? It's meant to intimidate our enemies, like a warning sign."

I reached out, touching these decorative figures, amazed at how intricate they were.

"You know, every one of my mistresses wanted to see these, but you are the only one I have ever allowed to touch them."

"If I might remind you, Caius, just so you know, I'm not your real mistress." I fixed him with a pointed stare.

He gave a careless shrug. "Anyway, it doesn't matter. You're doing an excellent job, so take it as a reward."

Glancing over at the water clock on his desk, Caius said, "It's time for us to go back. Let's not keep my men waiting too long." With that, he took my hand and led me toward the door.

As we stepped outside, hundreds of eyes locked onto us. However, in an instant, the soldiers resumed their disciplined drills, pretending to train diligently.

Caius shook his head with a grin and said, "I'm willing to bet the tavernkeepers near the barracks will soon know your name. Well, maybe not your name, but they'll undoubtedly refer to you as the prefect's latest paramour."

·•·♥·♥·♥·•·

I arrived at Caius' villa just as the sun was hanging heavily on the west side of the sky. After a tall Numidian slave had washed my feet, Livia hurriedly approached me with the news.

"There is a guest waiting for you in the atrium."

"It must be Julia," I murmured as I made my way there. However, to my surprise, the atrium was empty. As I searched around, my eyes were suddenly covered by a pair of bony hands. Instinctively, I spun around to face the person behind me.

"Julia!" I cried out, embracing my dear friend. "Oh, how I've missed you!"

Julia's eyes widened in amazement as she took in the opulent surroundings of Caius' villa. "Venus! This place is remarkable," she exclaimed, unable to contain her excitement. "It's even more splendid than the palace. Not that I've ever been to the palace, but I doubt there is a place better than this!"

I giggled at Julia's enthusiastic reaction. "Yes, I know, it's an amazing house. But let's find a safe place to talk." I lowered my voice and led Julia to Caius' bedchamber, but the journey was slower than anticipated as she kept stopping at different points, appreciating the grandeur of the house and its impressive decorations.

"You live here? In his bedchamber? Oh, goddess Fortuna, what have you done to this girl, kissed her a million times?" Julia gawked at a double-handed glass vase and exclaimed, "Oh, gods. This vase must be more valuable than the one I broke in Eubulus' study."

Realizing Julia was talking about the tragic event when I had first met her, I placed a hand on her shoulder and said tenderly, "Don't worry, Julia. We don't have to live like that anymore."

"Of course, we don't. Now you're the mistress of the praetorian prefect, the sole heir of the Aemilia family. Who dares to put a finger on us?"

Unable to lie to her, I knew there was only one way I could handle the guilt, even if it meant dampening Julia's good mood.

"Julia, I have to tell you something."

"What?" she said, then a look of shock appeared on her face. "Don't tell me you're with his child now. It would be too early to tell."

"No way. You silly girl!" I pinched Julia's arm, and after checking we were alone, I told her about the fake mistress plan between me and Caius.

Julia's face scrunched up in disbelief. "Wow. That's a lot to take in." She rubbed her temple. "I need time to piece it all together. But I can't believe you never told me about your past with Aurelius."

"I'm sorry, Julia. Too many things happened in the past few days. It's been a dramatic period for us all. I didn't even get a chance to explain our plan to Rufus. I just hope Theophilus—"

"Ah, I got it," Julia said, looking lost in thought. "No wonder Theophilus required only Aurelius to accompany us to the gate.

They let me get into the carriage first, and later, I heard them talking. And I heard Aurelius, I mean your Rufus, repeating 'thank God' so many times. I was so curious about their discussion. Now I understand Theophilus must have been briefing him about the plan."

"Oh, thank God!" I also blurted out.

"Yes, the same phrase! Looks like you two are in sync."

"Listen to me, Julia. Please keep this secret. The fate of Rufus and me depends on Caius' plan coming off. If we fail, I'll probably never see Rufus again," I said, holding her hands tightly.

"You can trust me," Julia said firmly. "And I'm here to help you with your plan."

As we talked, a voice boomed from behind us. "Hey, are you girls gossiping about me already?"

Thirty
Sabina's Banquet

Julia and I looked up and saw Caius leaning on the door frame. "So, I guess you have told your friend everything, Vita?"

"Yes, and she has promised to keep it all a secret."

"Excellent. Since I have dismissed the slaves assigned to serve in my chamber, we need someone to do the cleaning and tidying. She can also help you dress and do your hair. I have assigned a separate room for her at the end of the hallway." Then he turned to Julia and said, "Now you may go there and settle in."

Julia curtsied and left, leaving me a little uneasy at being alone with Caius again. "Um... did our show succeed today?" I stumbled to determine a topic.

"They're probably chattering about it in taverns right now." Caius chuckled. "Now, hurry up and get dressed. We're attending Lady Sabina's banquet tonight, with Julia as your fan bearer. I'll meet you in the carriage," he said, before making his exit.

"There's no end to this, is there?" I sighed.

When Julia came back to the bedchamber, I explained to her the plan for the night. "Sorry, Julia. I never intended that you should hold the fan for me."

"Don't be silly. Isn't it one hundred times better than scrubbing the pots and dishes at Eubulus' house?" Julia giggled. "I am having so much fun here. And I can't wait to see those grand banquets. When Eubulus held feasts, I almost never got to serve in the dining room."

Time passed quickly as we chatted and helped each other to dress up.

The evening sky was like a fresco, dripping with crimson and golden paint as our carriage approached Lady Sabina's immense and resplendent villa, perched halfway up the Esquiline Hill. Caius took out a blue sachet and deftly tied it to my belt.

"What is this?" I asked.

"We don't have the time to infuse your clothes with saffron over several days, so you need to wear this today. It holds a mixture called the Kiss of Persephone, created from the finest saffron and a blend of other aromatic spices. You understand the purpose, don't you?"

I nodded as my stomach growled at the same time.

"Are you hungry?" Caius said, visibly amused.

"No... I mean, yes, a little." I felt embarrassed. "When I was at Eubulus' house, we usually had dinner before the sun started going down. The master and the lady dined later, but not this late."

"We patricians are known for our lengthy dinner banquets that can last from sunset until midnight. Come with me and let's indulge in some flamingo tongues to fill your belly." The carriage came to a stop and Caius assisted me in getting out, Julia following us.

"Didn't I tell you to wear something more extravagant? You chose a modest dress amongst all the expensive ones," Caius teased. Then he turned to Julia and added, "Look, even your maid is dressed better than you."

Julia's face suddenly lit up as she avoided Caius' gaze.

"We can still make the change," I said, secretly hoping that Caius would agree to let Julia take my part. "Maybe she'd play the role better than me."

"Too late. The show must go on," Caius said, winking at Julia. "But I will definitely consider you the next time I am in need of an actress."

"I am at your disposal, my lord," Julia replied with a graceful bow.

Arriving at the dining room, we were greeted by an extravagantly dressed woman, her scarlet hair piled up like a mound and free strands falling loosely on her shoulders.

"I like the color of your new wig, Sabina. Very exotic," Caius commented.

"Yes, indeed. It is made from the hair of a Germanic tribal princess, and every strand is worth thirty gold coins," she said and planted a fervent kiss on Caius' cheek.

Then, she turned her gaze toward me, assessing me from head to toe for a long moment without saying a word. Finally, she called out to a handsome slave boy with copper-colored skin to guide us to our seats before turning to greet the other guests.

"Is that Lady Sabina?" I asked.

"Yes, she is the most famous widow in Rome, and perhaps the richest too," Caius murmured in my ear. "But she seems to be jealous of you."

"Of course she is. It's like Juno's jealousy against Latona," Julia interjected.

"No way!" I exclaimed.

"I can see you beaming with pride." Caius chuckled.

As we chattered, most couches in the room were already becoming occupied by well-dressed women and men. Almost all women's stares were directed toward me, and I could feel the heat rising in the room. The boy guided us toward a wide couch at the room's east end and said, "As always, the lady has reserved the best seat for you, my lord."

"Come on, let's lie down," Caius said to me.

My palms were moist. Throughout my life, I had never eaten meals while reclining on a couch. Slaves and plebeians in poverty typically ate while sitting or even standing. I carefully lay down on the silk-covered couch beside Caius and leaned my body on an embroidered cushion.

"Please relax, girl." Caius laughed. "You look like a wooden stick."

"Don't be nervous, Vita. You're doing great," Julia whispered, gently fanning the peacock-feathered fan behind me.

As all the guests had settled onto their couches, a lively melody filled the air, announcing the entrance of a troupe of flute players. The cheerful tune was soon joined by the graceful movements of dancers, their lithe bodies weaving in a hypnotic rhythm.

The music and dance continued as the kitchen slaves brought in dishes, and Caius nudged me slightly, explaining the fine foods being set in front of us.

"This is roasted dormouse dipped in honey." He pointed to the closest dish. "These are sea urchins boiled in olive oil and..." Caius grabbed a tidbit and tasted it. "Um... lemon juice. That's a smart combination. Oh, and the dish to the left is skate braised in... Setian wine. You should try some." Caius took a piece and brought it to my mouth as a lover might.

I hesitated, more than a little uneasy about eating from a man's hand, but remembering my role, I took the skate and gave him a grateful smile.

Suddenly, my forced smile turned into a genuine one. The skate was tender and flavorful, unlike anything I'd tasted before. Now, I was eager to try the other dishes.

While I was savoring the flavors of each dish in front of us, Sabina glided over and settled onto our couch, an emerald goblet in her hand. Her lashes were now lined with more kohl than when we first met. She cast a cursory glance my way before turning to Caius.

"Word has it that you missed my banquet last night for a girl you just met. I assume this is her?"

Sitting up straight, I met Sabina's gaze with confidence.

"You guessed correctly," I replied with a smile.

No doubt surprised by my reaction, Caius also straightened, placing his arm around my shoulders. "Yes, she's most certainly the one," he affirmed. "And I am sorry for missing your banquet, Sabina. But I am sure you know how it is when Cupid strikes; someone irresistible comes along and..." Caius looked at me as though he really was infatuated. "But we are here today to make amends for it. Again, my humblest apologies."

Sabina's face darkened. "Your taste has taken a turn for the worse, Caius. I never thought you would have an eye for women with such rough, callused hands. A girl who has clearly had to work hard for her living, no less, doing manual labor. And the strong saffron smell... only lowborn people use this in a desperate bid to impress. And *that* dress."

That was a low blow.

I wished I could disappear, but Caius' arm only held onto me tighter with every hurled insult, as if he would allow nothing to cleave us apart.

"Well, beauty is in the eye of the beholder, and to your and my own surprise, I now find these traits attractive, because they are so unusual in our circle. It's such a welcome change."

"Suit yourself," Sabina said, her smile still poised. With a gulp, she drained the liquid in her goblet and stood to leave.

Two skilled acrobats entered the room, drawing the attention of the guests by balancing one atop the other, contorting their bodies into impossible shapes.

The night stretched on and on; guests were eating, drinking, and having a swell time. Several girls came to talk to Caius without even glancing at me. Some even gave random sniffs with disgusted looks before passing comments on the smell of my sachet.

Caius responded to them calmly, constantly indicating how much he was attracted to me. I found myself growing accustomed to these remarks, no longer feeling as hurt as I did during the encounter with Sabina.

After the acrobats finished their performance and cartwheeled out to applause, I overheard some chatter from a couch behind me.

"I heard Sabina's new memoir was a hit. Scribes were competing to produce copies, causing the price of blank scrolls to soar."

"Yes, I heard that too. She wrote in detail about her traumatic marriage with her first husband. It was arranged by her family, of course. She had hope for the first couple of months, but eventually realized they weren't a good match in bed. Imagine that."

"And she felt so much relief when he met his end in a chariot race, leaving her with a considerable fortune."

"According to her, now is the best time in her life when she can choose whoever to sleep with, not for money or responsibility, but solely for pleasure. She even mentioned that a girl should never marry without trying it out first. Quite innovative, don't you think? I suppose it makes complete sense, though I can barely imagine it coming to pass."

"Indeed, it does make some sense, and that's why I hear lots of patrician girls bought her memoir. Even the empress patronized a hundred copies, people said."

These unsettling conversations appalled me deeply. To avoid saying anything rash, I shifted my focus to the spread of food laid out before me. And as if on cue, a slave girl approached, placing a beautiful ceramic plate of marzipans in front of me. Without hesitation, I reached for one and popped it into my mouth.

The sweet almond fragrance was bold and the texture so chewy and soft that I couldn't resist taking one after another. The banquet continued toward midnight when I finished the whole plate of marzipans.

"What did you think of tonight?" Caius asked me in the carriage on our way home.

"Well, the evening was fantastic. The food and entertainment were out of this world, but I'm not sure if our plan worked." I sighed. "Sabina plainly believed I was a girl of low taste, and she absolutely despised the smell of my sachet. And the other girls who came to speak to you did the same. This plan might not even work. How did *you* see it?"

"You don't know these women, Vita," Julia commented. "These women are like no other. They're shallow, and no matter their pretense, tomorrow they will rush to the fragrance stores and clear their storage."

"So, your friend is right." Caius chuckled. "You may be a smart girl, Vita, but you really don't know a lot about women... or men for that matter."

"Very well. I honestly don't care either way! Sometimes, I find you too confident about yourself," I said in a bland tone. "It is far from becoming in a man. So, you see, we are ill-matched as a couple. You do not rate me, and I find you conceited."

"Ah well, we'll see, we'll see... I mean *you'll* see." Caius smirked. "I think you and Julia were both superb tonight, and thanks to that, the wheels are now in motion."

Arriving back at the villa, we took baths separately, and I lay on the couch facing the wall, staring at the obscure patterns, trying to push away the strange feeling of sharing a room with a man I barely had begun to know. I listened intently for any signs of movement, and to my relief, there was no sound coming from Caius' bed.

Perhaps he's already fallen asleep, I thought.

I focused on taking slow, deep breaths, hoping to ease into slumber. Unfortunately, the marzipans in which I had indulged earlier did not sit well with me. I felt terrible, and with no other option, a solitary burp escaped. It happened again, and the noise only grew louder. Despite covering my mouth with my hands, I couldn't seem to stop. Just as I was thanking God for Caius' sound sleep, his groggy voice broke the silence.

"What's that noise?"

I tried my best to suppress my burps, hoping he would ignore them and fall back to sleep, but the more I tried to hold them in, the louder my burps became.

"What is going on here?" Caius' footsteps approached the couch.

"Hey, you woke me up with all your noise, girl," he scolded, his hand tugging at my shoulder. Then he let out a muffled chuckle. "Oh, dear gods, are you burping?"

"No, I'm certainly not..." I tried to deny, only to be interrupted by another.

"Oh, gods! Those are the loudest burps I've ever heard!" he said and went into fits of laughter. "It must be those marzipans. Didn't I tell you to go easy with them?"

"No, you didn't tell me. And they were so good." I was just thankful the room was dark, and he couldn't see the intense flush burning across my face. "I just can't stop."

"I can see that! You must have eaten... well, you ate my quota and most of Julia's."

"Leave me alone. I feel terrible."

"You are killing me, girl." Caius still couldn't hold back his laughter. "Let me use my magic hands. Trust me, it works. I learned it from a military physician."

Grabbing me before I could protest, he tossed me onto his spacious canopy bed which was tucked into an arched niche in the wall.

"What are you doing? Leave me alone! I told you I was feeling awful."

"A larger space to stretch your body will do you good. Tonight, we switch beds," he said in a commanding tone and reached for my wrist.

"No, stop it. We had a deal. Don't touch me," I cried out, sitting up and holding the blanket tighter. "Besides, I don't like being carried and tossed around like a sandbag."

"Fair complaint." He looked amused. "I guess that's part of my military habit as I carry and toss sandbags every day. Come on, I'll just give your arm a quick massage. I promise it'll help."

Realizing the burping still hadn't stopped, I reluctantly held out my arm. Holding it, Caius pressed his thumb in a spot about one finger's width above the palm.

"Ouch! You'll break my wrist!" I screamed, trying to pull my arm away.

"Shut up and hold still," he commanded, his grip unyielding.

Despite my efforts, I couldn't break free. His touch was warm and sent shivers down my spine. The light from the lamp above the niche illuminated his profile, making his features even more striking.

Suddenly, I understood why so many girls were enamored with him. *Would I fall for him if I didn't have Rufus?* I was amused when the thought suddenly came into my mind. *No way.* I shook it away. *What am I even thinking about?*

"See? It works." He let go of my arm and smiled like a young boy. "Hey, why are you not talking? Did I hurt you?"

"Oh, no, no, you didn't." I retrieved my wandering thoughts and suddenly realized the burping was gone. "Well, thank you. How did this work? It's amazing. What did you do?"

"My military physician has traveled a lot. He mentioned learning this technique from a silk vendor from the East. But I never had the chance to try it on any of my girls, because, you know..."

He burst into another hysterical laugh.

"Because you've never met a girl who went crazy with food at a banquet the way I did?"

This was mortifying!

"Yes, exactly." He couldn't even hold back his tears.

"Shut up!" I tossed a pillow at him and tried to go back to my couch.

"I said tonight, we switch beds," he asserted firmly, his hands pressing me down.

"Fine." I gave up arguing. "Just stay away from me. I'm tired."

"All right." He went back to the couch and lay down, but after a few seconds, he burst into laughter again, rolling about on the couch. "I still can't believe you stuffed yourself with so many marzipans as to get such terrible burps. What were you thinking?"

"You've never been poor. How could you understand? I've never been offered so much lavish food. That is why I ate so much. So there!"

An awkward silence followed.

"Vita, can you tell me something about your past?" he suddenly asked, breaking the silence. "I mean, in your hometown when you were little."

"There's nothing to say really. Nothing exciting anyway. The boring life of a poor village girl will put you to sleep right away."

"But I would like to know, even if it does." His voice was sincere.

"Fine. But I'll stop if I hear you laugh again, or if you start snoring, do you understand?"

"I won't, I promise. I'm genuinely interested."

"All right then, I'll give you a summary," I continued. "It started in a small village in Cyprus."

"Oh..." His voice sounded a little surprised.

"What's wrong?"

"Nothing. Keep going. I'm listening."

"I was abandoned by my parents when I was born; they left me at the gate of an old villa on a cold winter's night. It was Rufus who heard me crying and brought Nana to find me. He pleaded with her to take me home..."

As I continued, I divulged more and more details about my childhood, about the bond I shared with Rufus, and about the challenges we had faced together. It was as though a dam had been opened and all my pent-up emotions and memories came flooding out.

It was a good feeling, and in releasing them, I must have had some trust in Caius.

"We barely had enough to eat, and one day, he went to help at the wedding of a rich man's daughter in town, while I stayed at home with Nana. He worked all day, and they gave him a leftover marzipan and some coins. He wrapped the marzipan with his clothes and walked all the way home with an empty stomach. Then he gave the marzipan to me.

"It tasted so good, and I still remember the chewy texture of it. I was too young to realize he was lying when he told me he didn't like it. He just gave it to me because..."

No more needed saying. I sensed that Caius understood.

He was listening quietly. It was impossible to make out his face in the dim light, but he never teased like he usually did, so I even suspected he might be asleep after all.

Between us was just the black stillness of the nighttime.

But then I heard his voice. "Vita, believe it or not, I'm jealous of you. You might lead a hard life, but you are so loved, and it makes you such a loving girl."

"When it comes to being loved, who is more loved than you, Caius?" I blurted out. However, I soon regretted the lightheartedness in my tone, as Caius didn't laugh or tease as usual, his expression unreadable from a distance.

"I don't know," he finally said. "All I can say is that the love that has come to me is not the kind of love I was looking for. It might feel good at first, but in the end, my heart is still left empty."

A tingle of compassion rose from my heart.

"You know, Caius, there is a hole in everyone's heart that no human love can fill." I wanted to delve deeper, to talk about my beliefs about God and His divine love that can fill the void in all human hearts, but he had already turned his face to the wall.

"It's late. We should sleep. Thanks, Vita. Your stories never fail to touch me," he murmured.

"All right then; goodnight," I said, feeling a little disappointed. "I hope we'll put on a better show tomorrow."

After that, I uttered a silent prayer in my heart before falling asleep.

Dear God. Thanks for protecting me in all these difficult situations. I thank you that Caius is not such a terrible person as I thought. I don't know him well, but I can feel the loss and pain in his heart. Please fill the hole in his heart with your holy love, in your way and in your time. Please help us get the thief as quickly as possible so I can reunite with my Rufus.

Amen.

Thirty-One

A Statue with Memories

AFTER THAT MEMORABLE NIGHT, a succession of banquets ensued, graced by the presence of senators, patricians, and Rome's most affluent merchants. With the transition from autumn to winter came a chill in the air, prompting us to wrap ourselves in woolen cloaks for warmth as we frequented these grand festivities, often returning well past midnight. During occasions when we played host, Caius would generously employ saffron in the banquets, at times even adorning the entire floor of the dining room with its precious threads.

After the night when we switched beds, Caius never allowed me to switch them back.

Caius and Julia were right. Wherever we went, I could smell the scent of saffron emanating from the attire of patrician women. Our plan had worked remarkably well.

Caius also sent slaves to the most prestigious fragrance store in Rome to buy jars of saffron. And the next day, the slaves would return them all to the store and complain about the quality of the products. "If you have the real good stuff, price is not an issue. Our master only wants the best for his new mistress," was what they said to the shop owner.

Three days later, the shop owner came in a carriage with a golden jar of saffron which he claimed he had been saving for his only son's wedding day.

Caius bought it at double the price he had promised.

Two days later, he sent a different group of slaves to discretely inquire about the price of saffron at every fragrance vendor in the Forum. As predicted, the price had shot through the roof. And again, Caius bought them all. Days went by, and we received word there was no longer saffron in stock. At this point, we knew the plan was coming together; we just had to wait for the fish to take the bait.

During the day, Caius was busy training new recruits in his barracks. On those nights when we didn't have banquets to attend, we retreated to his study, where Caius patiently tutored me in reading Vigil's *Georgics*, encouraging me to write down each new word I encountered on a wax tablet.

In the beginning, he constantly teased me about my writing, but as time went on, these remarks became compliments when I managed to write a few complete sentences.

"You are a quick learner, Vita," Caius said with a proud smile. "I think what you have learnt is enough for bookkeeping in your future basket store. Shall we stop here?"

"No. I hope I can learn more. I hope someday I can read verses, poems, and stories all by myself."

"But what for?"

"I don't know. I just thought it would be a fun thing to do. And maybe someday… don't laugh at me, all right?" I looked at him, struggling to know if I should tell him about my little ambition. "Someday, I'll write my own story," I said.

"Your story? Then tell me."

"Yes, my story. I'm a poor slave girl raised in a small village, but I believe my God has a unique plan for everyone, even me. I would like to write down how He led me through all kinds of ups and downs in my life—— how He steered me, anchored me, buoyed me, and surrounded me with love."

"That sounds fascinating," he replied, genuine curiosity gleaming in his eyes. "I'd love to hear more about your story and your god, if you're willing to share."

"Really? You don't find my ambition foolish?" I asked, touched by his interest.

"Not at all," he reassured me. "I know that some patrician women are writing memoirs, like Sabina. However, most of them tend to focus on their love affairs. It's uncommon to find a young woman writing about the spiritual journey with her god."

His sincere gaze warmed my heart. Even Rufus had never displayed such genuine interest in my future writing.

"How do you find out the kind of plan your god has for you?" Caius continued with his questions. "It seems you don't visit any temples or consult any priests."

"I don't need to. My God hears my prayer whenever I call unto Him."

"Does he always answer your prayer? Those I consulted never did." Caius smiled wryly.

"Yes, but not always the way I expect or hope for. It is not for me to dictate to God. He has a plan for everyone, and He's determined to carry it out."

"It appears your god is very powerful and omniscient. However, if he knows everything, why do you find it necessary to pray?"

I was amused by the boyish curiosity in his eyes.

"Because it's the relationship that matters, like father and child. When we pray, we call on the name of our Father in heaven. No matter if He answers our prayers with 'yes' or 'no', He will let us experience Him and grow closer to him."

"Father?" An ambiguous look appeared on Caius' face, but he immediately resumed his usual playful expression and said, "Well... will you give me a special chapter in your story?"

"Sure. I'll dedicate an entire chapter to the most conceited people I've ever met, just to entertain my readers, you know."

Giving me a gentle knuckle knock on my head, he stormed out

of the chamber. "I need to inspect the palace security tonight. Keep practicing, and I'll review everything when I come back."

※ ※ ※ ※ ※

The next day, he brought home a leather satchel engraved with an Egyptian building.

"The Library of Alexandria in Egypt, the greatest library in the empire. I had the best leather smith in Rome design this school bag for you." He beamed.

I opened it carefully and saw there were ten pieces of parchment paper, a small alabaster bottle of ink and a quill pen inside.

"You can start writing your story now," Caius said, his smile warm and encouraging. "Though, may I request a mention beyond the 'most conceited' chapter?"

※ ※ ※ ※ ※

Life in the villa was serene and enjoyable.

Julia and I spent much of our daylight hours in the garden, where the gardeners guided us in plant care while I taught Julia and the other girls the art of weaving using iris leaves. However, as winter progressed, the plants withered, and we soon found ourselves running out of foliage. Julia grew restless, and one day, before Caius headed to the barracks, she implored him to allow us to visit the market once more.

"Can we go, please?"

"Hmm. I suppose you've both been doing your parts well in our plan, and that should be rewarded accordingly," Caius said. "Go buy whatever you want and have the shops send the bills to me later. Oh, and the ordered goods too, assuming you will leave nothing on the shelves and cannot possibly be expected to port it all homeward." He chuckled, a sweet, warm laugh that brightened the room.

"Thank you, my lord!" Julia exclaimed with a twirl. "What are you waiting for?" she asked eagerly, tugging at my hand. "Let's go!"

Before long, we arrived at the market, our pace quickened by the chill of the winter air. Compared to the last time I had gone with Julia, the market was far less crowded. Julia kept complaining that we hadn't traveled here in a litter or carriage.

"It's fun to walk. By the way, shall we go to the open market we went to last time?" I asked. "I've been craving those candied dates."

"Vita, are you crazy?" Julia scoffed, rolling her eyes. "We have an unlimited coin purse, and you want to waste it on candied dates from those cheap open stalls where the wind will freeze us to death?"

"But they're so delicious!"

"Come on. Let's head to the most upscale street, the fanciest jewelry store, and adorn ourselves with jewels. Then to the milliner, where we'll buy dresses studded with gold—" Julia said, her eyes twinkled with excitement.

"But that's Caius' money," I said hesitantly. "We can't take advantage of his generosity. I'm sorry, but I really don't agree with that."

"Don't be naive, Vita. He won't even care," Julia urged. "He was so frivolous, mentioning how much we would buy. Think about it. When this is over, you and Rufus will need money to start your new life. Why not buy something that can easily be traded for money later, like jewelry and expensive clothes? We can't pass up this opportunity."

The thought of starting a basket boutique with the extra money pushed my legs to follow Julia's hurried steps. My head tried to convince me Julia was right. But in my heart, a part of me hated taking advantage of Caius' kindness. Despite my inner conflict, Julia steered us both toward the east corner of the market.

"This is where rich people come to shop," said Julia suddenly, absolutely beaming as she pointed to a shopfront flanked by two intricately carved columns. "Let's go to Lucan's. The shop owned by his family has been here since the times of Julius Caesar."

As we entered the shop, Lucan, a robust, middle-aged man with an elegantly curved mustache, was busy attending to a lady donning an opulent fur cloak. The head of the slain small beast dangled around her collar.

Two beautiful boys stood dutifully by Lucan's side, each holding trays brimming with jewelry, as Lucan meticulously presented piece after piece to the lady.

Julia and I relished the warmth emanating from the sizable charcoal basin resting on a wooden stand at the center of the room. Lucan turned to us with a polite smile and gestured toward the west corner. "Ladies, are you finding everything all right? We have some fantastic sale items if you would like to have a look."

However, as his attention was drawn to my armband bearing the Aemilia family emblem, his face suddenly changed. In a hushed tone, he addressed the other guest, "I apologize, Lady Claudia. We will be closing the store shortly."

"What? But I haven't had time to decide what I want," the lady grumbled, tossing the necklace back at Lucan with a huff. "The quality is below what I am used to anyway." With a flounce, she left the shop.

Lucan then approached me, with more graciousness than before.

"Please accept my sincerest apologies, my lady. I didn't know who you were. Please allow me to assist with whatever you require. I have heard much about you, and it is a great honor to have you in our shop today."

Before I had a chance to open my mouth, Julia said, "Then bring us your choicest jewelry."

Lucan gestured to the boy standing to his left, who promptly made his way to the rear of the store. Soon, the footsteps sounded again, and he returned, bearing a chest gleaming with inlaid gold and precious stones. With a flourish, Lucan unlatched the chest, revealing a dazzling array of jewels that nearly blinded me with their brilliance.

"These are our finest wares. We bring them out only for our most esteemed clientele," he said, laying on the flattery thickly.

My gaze alighted on a beaded wristband in a rich shade of red.

Lucan noted my interest and exclaimed, "My lady has exquisite taste! My grandfather made a pair of them. The other one was gifted by Augustus to Lady Livia on their wedding day."

"We'll take it," declared Julia, snatching up the wristband and putting it on me. "It looks so good on her, doesn't it?" She directed her question to Lucan.

"Well, I'm sure everything will look so good—"

"No, I can't!" I said, attempting to remove the wristband. "I'm sorry, but I just can't do it. This piece must be quite expensive."

"Worry not, my lady," Lucan interjected. "The prefect will settle the bill. Who doesn't know he would buy the moon for you if you so desired?"

Before I could protest, Julia had piled three more ornate cuffs and five rings onto my hands.

"They're all top-of-the-line pieces," Lucan assured us.

I dragged Julia toward the door before she could load me like a donkey.

"No, no, no. We still haven't got enough," Julia said firmly. "Think about the future and imagine how much money you'll have when you sell them in a few months."

"No, Julia. I don't want to owe Caius too much," I said, regretting ever entering this place. "Besides, Rufus and I will work hard and make money on our own."

"Oh, Vita. Sometimes, I don't know if you are too stubborn or just naïve." Julia shook her head.

"Maybe both." I laughed and poked her pouted cheeks before stepping away from the shop. "It's getting late. Let's go home."

Why did I call it home? As soon as the word leapt out of my lips, my heart shuddered a beat.

Julia was silent for a while too. Then she held my hands and said, "Vita, you are my friend; I want good things for you. I've been here for a while now, and as someone who knows men well, I'm pretty sure that Caius has feelings for you. Do you really want to leave him if, someday, the plan is accomplished?"

"I highly doubt he has any 'feelings' in that regard, Julia. But let us say you're correct; in that case, I suspect it's because of my being lowborn, which sets me apart from his previous paramours. Besides, I've been dreaming marrying Rufus since I was six years old."

"But look at what kind of life you have right now. You are living most women's dreams. And I can see you feel more at home every day in that grand villa."

"Maybe you are right, Julia. Life in that grand villa is far better than I thought at first. And I do feel *at home* sometimes. But in my heart, Rufus *is* home."

"Oh, Vita. Life is hard for us women, and it's better to grab onto something practical while you can."

I smiled without saying anything. *Something practical? What about true love?*

The once overcast sky now became veiled by a denser, slate-gray blanket of clouds, accompanied by the distant rumble of thunder. We slipped into a hired carriage on the side of the street and headed home.

When Caius saw the jewelry on my arms and hands, he laughed. "Only nine pieces? Are you girls trying to keep my purse strings tight?"

"See? Remember what I told you," Julia said, then turned to Caius. "This silly girl said she didn't want to take advantage of your generosity. I tried my best to get her to buy more, but she refused."

"That's why I always said I should've let Julia play your part. She fits more like a pampered mistress." Caius laughed louder and Julia's face reddened once again.

"I won't object if you wish to swap out the actress right now." I shrugged.

"Pity it's too late. People already know *you* are my mistress. You'd better act well."

"I hope this show ends soon so I can finally be myself," I said disinterestedly, noticing what seemed to be a flicker of sadness in Caius' eyes.

Or am I just reading too much into it?

At that moment, a slave rushed in. "Master," he panted, "the sculpture has been found."

Caius' expression suddenly turned grave. "Bring it to me," he ordered. "You two"—he gestured to us—"go to the bedchamber, and don't come back until I call for you."

I felt a pang of curiosity, but as I caught a glimpse of Caius' expression, I knew better than to press the issue. Julia and I quickly exited the study and made our way toward Caius' bedchamber. As we were walking along the corridor, four brawny slaves rushed past, carrying a large, intricately carved marble statue depicting a beautiful woman cradling a baby.

"Have I seen her somewhere?" I murmured.

"Who?" Julia asked.

"Nothing. Just thinking aloud."

But when we'd almost got to Caius' bedchamber, I suddenly paused my steps.

"What?" Julia looked at me, perplexed.

I quickly took off all the jewelry and dumped them into Julia's hands. "Put them in my trunk and I'll explain later." I ran toward Caius' study with Julia yelling behind me.

When I arrived at the screens outside the study, I was out of breath. Peering through a gap between the screens, I saw the sculpture standing next to the window, with two slaves positioned beside it. Caius' back was facing me as he reached out, gently caressing the woman's face.

But all of a sudden, his hand dropped. "Smash her," he commanded, his voice cold and unfamiliar to me. One slave turned, lifting a hammer toward the sculpture.

"Stop!" I shouted, and the hammer stopped mid-air, the momentum almost causing the slave to fall to the ground.

Caius turned around and glared at me. "Didn't I tell you girls to leave?" he asked angrily.

"Caius, we need to talk before you do this."

Rushing to him, I tugged his sleeve, looking deep into his eyes.

He looked at me tensely, still with a frown. But after a few moments of silence, he ordered the slaves to leave us.

"Now speak," he said coldly.

"Caius, may I know who that woman is?"

Another silence descended, this time longer than the last. He then turned to the sculpture and touched the baby in the woman's arms.

"She is my mother."

I was speechless, memories flooding back. *The House of Darkness, the wooden rabbit, Gato, Rufus, and the marble sculpture of the Roman matron.*

"Did you find the sculpture in a small village in the south of Paphos? I mean, in a grand villa that has been deserted for many years?" I said, trembling, unable to believe the coincidence.

Caius looked at me, also in disbelief. "Yes, a small village close to Paphos. My men retrieved her from a deserted villa, the place where I was born. I didn't know where it was until they told me today. How did you even know?"

"Do you remember the 'House of Darkness' I told you about, the night we came back from Sabina's banquet? The sculpture was there, in the atrium. I remember it clearly. The face, the look, I can't be mistaken."

He seemed to be lost in thought for a long time. "So, I guess we've met long before?" he finally said with a smile, his anger all but subsided.

"Yes, you can say that." I smiled back, relieved he'd calmed down. "I've told you my story; now I'd like to hear yours." Glancing at the sculpture, I noticed the woman's emotionless eyes. Suddenly, pieces started to fall into place, and I began to peek through the sorrow he showed every now and then, although my understanding was still v ague.

He walked to the sculpture, gently stroking the face of the woman, and said, "My mother was born in a patrician family, renowned for her breathtaking beauty and free-spirited nature. At the tender age of twelve, she was promised in marriage to the eldest son of the Aemilia family. However, just before their wedding, my grandfather, Sergius Paulus, was appointed as the proconsul of Cyprus.

"Although my mother was expected to stay in Rome and prepare for her wedding, she felt it was her last chance to savor the freedom of her youth. Thus, she pleaded with her father to allow her to spend the summer in Cyprus. And during that time, my mother met a dashing young merchant at a lavish banquet and fell passionately in love with him.

"She threatened her parents that she would starve herself to death if she couldn't marry the merchant. My poor grandparents finally gave in and built a beautiful villa on the outskirts of Paphos for her. She and my father moved into the villa and had a son the next year. You already know who he is.

"They lived there happily for a few more years, but gradually, the passion wore off. My mother began to regret leaving behind the luxurious life in Rome. My early childhood memory was filled with their quarrelsome noises. The fights were bitter, vicious, and sometimes turned physical. I'd learned to live like that.

"Well, on a rainy day… the rain poured heavily, and I can still recall the sound of it drumming against the atrium's roof and cascading down through the ceiling opening into the pool below. That morning, Mother received a letter from her ex-betrothed from the Aemilia family. Can you believe it? He still held a torch for her, even though she had made him look like a joke in front of all the high and mighty patricians. Anyway, later that same day, her carriage just vanished into the rain, and my father and I were left standing there getting drenched. I was only five years old, but let me tell you, I've hated rain ever since."

Seeing the sadness in Caius' eyes, I put my hand on his arm as he continued his story.

"My father was devastated. He left behind all his possessions and decided to flee; the memories were too unkind. He took me with him to Hispania, where his childhood friend Galba served as governor.

My father joined Galba's ranks as a simple centurion, and I lived with him in the barracks for seven years. During that time, my father trained me to be a warrior. Life was difficult, but it also grew into the happiest time of my life," he said, his eyes sparkling with the same boyish smile when he talked about how he had loved his life in the praetorian barracks.

"However, one day, everything changed. My father received a letter from the emperor, ordering him to send me back to Rome. That day, I cried so much that my father held me tightly in his arms, shedding tears like a little boy himself. I was only twelve years old, and little did I know it would be the last time I ever saw my father."

"Oh..." I didn't know what to say. "Oh my! Oh... Lord."

Caius suggested we sit on a bench next to the window.

"When I arrived in Rome, I was taken to a grand villa—the very one you're in now. It was right here that I met my stepfather and the woman who had abandoned me. Later, I found out from the slaves why my mother suddenly wanted me back."

"Was it because she missed you and wanted to make amends?" I asked cautiously.

"That was what I thought at first," Caius said with a deep sigh. "But the truth proved my naivety. Actually, right after my mother left us, she married my stepfather and gave birth to a son the following year.

"Unfortunately, the birth was difficult, and the physician duly declared that she would be unable to bear children again.

"My mother devoted all her love to my half-brother, but he tragically passed away at the age of three. To ensure the Aemilia family's title and wealth would be passed down in the future, she now had to secure an heir. Knowing my father would never relinquish me, she used her family connections to sway the royal court and obtain an order from the emperor, compelling my father to give me up.

"I missed my father, but my mother always told me he was too busy to visit or even write to me. And because of this, I resented him for many long years. It wasn't until later that I discovered she had convinced the emperor to issue another order to prevent my father from ever entering Rome, and she had hidden every letter he'd sent me," he said, turning his gaze on me. "Now, do you understand why I hate her so much?"

I nodded, feeling deeply touched by his suffering.

"In order to please my mother, I worked very hard in the praetorian barracks and received promotions every year.

"I tried to imitate the ways patricians lived and courted women, and I soon became quite popular. My mother said she was proud of me, yet she never touched or kissed me. The way she looked at me was always so cold and distant. It was as if she had no heart in her ribcage.

"Last year, my mother passed. When I was cleaning up her stuff, I found the letters my father had written to me. He had missed me so much. And the last letter was from his friend Otho, who penned that my father had died murmuring my name."

"I'm so sorry, Caius," I said softly. "I really am sorry. That's terrible."

"You don't have to be sorry. I don't know why I told you this. But it feels good... strangely good," he said with a bitter smile.

"No, I'm sorry because I had judged you in my heart. I thought you were just a pampered dandy boy who knew nothing about suffering. Now I know I was wrong. We all have our own struggles to bear." I looked at him sincerely. "Caius, can you do me a favor by allowing me to pray for you?"

"Pray to your carpenter god?" he said cynically. "I doubt he even cares about someone like me, since I've never made any offerings to him. Besides, the past has... well, it's passed. There is nothing we can do."

"Caius, trust me. Jesus knew you long before you knew him."

"Fine. Do as you wish."

"Come on. Let's hold our hands." I reached out. His hands were cold. Without acting, it was the first time we'd held hands of our own accord.

"Dear God, I know there is a reason behind everything that has happened in our lives. I thank you for revealing to me Caius' sadness and struggles. I believe you loved him long before he knew you. I know you've also experienced a broken heart, so you understand how he feels. Therefore, I plead with you to heal him, to make peace in places where there was no peace, to release him from all the bitterness of the past.

"Because in you, Lord, everything can be renewed."

I opened my eyes to find Caius' still closed, and as he opened them, he said softly, "Thank you, Vita. This is the most beautiful prayer I have ever heard. I don't believe a prayer could help, but even if your god never heard it, I feel lifted by it. I can't forgive my mother yet, but I think you are right. Perhaps all things happen for a divine purpose. I will keep this statue. A hammer can shatter marble, but it can't shatter memories."

I clasped his hands tightly, deeply moved by his heartfelt words.

At that moment, a slave's voice sounded from outside, "Master, Claudius has a report."

"Wait for me here, Vita," Caius' said, his face lit up. "The fish has taken the bait." With that, he strode out of the study.

After a while, he returned, announcing with excitement, "Claudius, the fragrance shop owner, is my informant, who has been told to offer a ridiculously high price to attract our target. He just sent a message reporting that a freed slave named Quintus arrived this afternoon with two jars of premium saffron. If we're correct, he should be the one Tigellinus hired to manage his products. Claudius requested that he bring twenty more jars back and sent two slaves to follow him. The slaves saw him go into a deserted bath house and never come out. The goods must be stored there."

"Thank God, that's such good news!" I exclaimed, too thrilled to say much else. "You must catch him quickly. Don't let him slip away."

"No worries. Claudius' men have hemmed in the place. He can't escape, Vita, not even if Mercury lends him his winged sandals," Caius replied, his confidence overflowing. We both chuckled and held onto each other tightly, and for one moment at least, I quite forgot I was supposed to be only feigning a fondness for this man.

Thirty-Two

The Interrogation

WHEN I WOKE UP the next morning, Caius was still not home.

Julia wanted me to go to the market with her, but I was not in the mood, so she went alone. I stayed in Caius' study reading *Georgics*, but my attempt to use reading as an escape failed hopelessly when I realized that I had stared at the first line for almost an hour.

"Oh Lord, please help Caius gather enough evidence to prove Tigellinus guilty," I murmured hundreds of times.

Noon finally came, and Decima appeared too, bringing me some cheese and fruits.

I ate them absentmindedly, unable to think of anything other than the outcome of the stolen goods. Suddenly, the sound of hooves pounding outside jolted me from my reverie, prompting me to rush to the atrium, where I caught sight of Theophilus entering through the front door.

His eyebrows were furrowed, and his tunic was covered with bloodstains.

"What happened? Are you all right?"

"I'm fine. The blood is not mine," he reassured me. "Caius and I didn't find the stolen goods in the bathhouse. That cunning fox had already sensed he was being followed, so he deliberately led Claudius' slaves there to deceive them," Theophilus said with a sigh. "But don't worry, Vita. We got him and took him to the barracks. Caius is now interrogating him. We'll make him talk, one way or another."

The determination in his eyes and the bloodstains on his clothes made me worry about the man who had been caught.

"I need to see Caius," I said firmly.

"No, that is not a place for ladies. Besides, we need to hurry. If we can't get anything from the fox, we'll have to release him before sunset. I'm here to collect some documents for the interrogation."

"Please, take me with you. I must see Caius." I grabbed Theophilus' sleeve. "Take me to him. We'll figure out a way together."

Theophilus stared at me as if it was the first time we'd met. But after a long moment, he sighed. "Fine, I'll take you to him. But be prepared for what you'll see."

After Theophilus got the documents he needed, we boarded his carriage. I prayed fervently on the way to the barracks. "Dear God, please give me wisdom to save that man. And give me even more wisdom to crack this case."

Upon arrival, Theophilus led me into the barracks through the back door. We made a right turn and walked toward a small cottage tucked at the northwest end of the compound. Even from a distance, I could hear the swishing of the scourge and the suppressed moan of a man, causing the hair on my neck to stand on end.

When we entered the interrogation room, I shuddered at the scene before me. A middle-aged man was bound to a wooden stake in the center of the room. His rough tunic was torn and soaked in so much blood that I couldn't even make out the color it was supposed to be. The young soldier standing by him raised a scourge above his head and was about to give him another whip.

"Stop it!" I instinctively rushed toward the soldier, grasping his arm to stop the impending blow. The whip halted mid-air, but its momentum carried it dangerously close to my shoulder, narrowly missing me.

Caius, who had been watching from a distance, dashed to my side, his expression etched with concern. He loosened my grip on the soldier's arm and demanded, "What are you doing here, Vita? Are you out of your mind?"

His eyes searched me for any signs of injury, and then settled on Theophilus as he bellowed, "Who told you to bring her here? You've been too bold lately! I swear, you will end up flogged if this continues."

"It's not Theophilus' fault. I begged him to bring me," I said. "You are going to kill this man. And that won't make him talk. A dead man cannot speak."

"You don't understand, Vita. Tigellinus' men are on the way here. If we can't get any solid proof from this man, we'll be forced to release him, and our plan will fail completely," Caius said, his voice filled with frustration.

"Caius, you've been beating him for so long and you are getting nowhere." I gently placed my hand on his arm. "We have to think of another way."

"There is no other way. The only way is to beat him harder and make him talk."

"Give this man a break and I'll talk to you alone," I urged, tugging his hand and leading him toward the door.

"Theophilus, go prepare the Devil's Ivy!" Caius snapped an order before we left the room. When we got outside, he pressed his hands on my shoulders and said, "Vita, I know you are a soft-hearted girl, but there is no room for mercy in this."

"No, Caius, listen to me. You told me you have the entire map of Rome in your head, right?"

"Yes, why? And what's that got to do with anything?"

"Do you remember the night I was telling you things about my childhood? That gave me an idea."

"What is it?" Caius asked, his expression perplexed, but his grip on my shoulder loosened.

"I told you I used to play a game with kids in my village. A game where we hid and sought the rabbit."

"Hide and seek the rabbit? Yes, all the kids were looking for the wooden rabbit hidden by the village chief's son, and you found it quickly," he recounted, growing impatient. "Vita, we can talk about your childhood stories at home tonight. We really don't have time for this right now. This is our only opportunity to bring down Tigellinus."

"Yes, I know that, and there's nothing I want more than to see that happen. Now calm down and listen to me," I continued. "The thing I didn't tell you is *how* I did it. Other kids just looked everywhere for it. But I got the answer from Gato, the boy who hid the rabbit."

"You charmed him with your beauty?"

"Stop it! I'm talking seriously!" I gave him a warning stare, and he responded with a surrendering gesture before telling me to continue.

"I had come up with this sneaky idea. I asked him a string of questions quickly, such as, 'Is it in the atrium?' or 'Is it in the backyard?' Of course, he wouldn't say a thing, but I asked him so fast that there was no time for him to hide his emotions."

"So, you could tell by his emotions? What you're saying is, you found the rabbit by analyzing the boy's reaction to each question?"

"Correct. When I mentioned the place where he'd hidden the rabbit, he twitched."

Caius gaped at me, silent for a long moment. "So, you want me to do the same thing with that man?" he finally said.

"Yes. The trick is you must toss all the questions at him faster than lightning, leaving him no time to fake anything. Rome is huge, so it may take several rounds of narrowing down the range. But if you have the whole map in your mind—"

"Then it shouldn't be a problem." Caius' face lit up. "I'll do it, Vita."

We went back in, and the man stared at us, his eyes bloodshot.

"So, you're back. What will it be now, more whips? Time is running out, Prefect, and it looks like you lost this one!" he said with a sneer. "Bring it on, if you have more ways to torture me!"

Caius smirked and brought a wine goblet to the man's lips, saying, "No hurries, loyal servant. It's been a long day; let's take a break. After that, we will have a little chat."

"What's in there? The magic water from the goddess of hallucinations' temple? I'm telling you, no matter what method you use, you won't get anything from me!"

"Don't be so suspicious. I'll drink it myself." Caius took a sip from the goblet and set it down on the table beside the man, amidst various torture tools. "Fine, since you are not thirsty, let's begin our chat."

The man spat again and turned his head away.

"Rome has fourteen districts, and the goods have to be in one of them."

"Come on, give me more lashes!" he snarled. "I'm in the mood now. You coward! Scared to finish me off, huh?"

"No, your death means nothing to me. I'd much rather enjoy a little chat with you, my friend. So, I guess it's in Region One, Porta Capena," Caius said, fixing his gaze on the man's face.

The man's expression remained defiant. "Probably not the right answer." Caius smiled and then, with lightning speed, he called out the names of the rest of the thirteen regions:

"Caelian Hill.

Sanctuary of Jupiter.

Temple of Peace.

Esquiline Hill.

High Path.

Central Region.

Palatine Hill.

Circus Maximus..."

Hearing the name of Circus Maximus, the man's mouth twitched, his eyes flitting away sharply. "Thanks!" Caius patted his left cheek. The sneer in the man's eyes turned to fear.

"North of Bellona Street.

South of Bellona Street.

East of the Gladiator School
West of the Gladiator School..."

Caius tossed the names of different areas at him at an increasing speed, causing beads of sweat to trickle down the man's face. Despite his attempts to bury his head lower and lower, I could still see his body quiver slightly when certain areas were mentioned.

I breathed a sigh of relief when Caius finally finished.

The man's face had turned as white as bleached linen. Caius patted him on the shoulder and smirked. "Thanks, brother. You've been a big help today. Now you can enjoy the wine with peace of mind." He cupped the man's trembling hand and placed the wine goblet in it. "This is on me. In fact, have the flask too."

He shoved the flask across the table toward the captive.

At this moment, Theophilus came in from outside, holding a jade jar. "I've soaked Devil's Ivy in wine for a while. It should be strong enough for him to talk," he said.

"No need. Thanks to Vita's brilliant idea, we've already got the answer," Caius said with a triumphant smile. "Let's go to Luna Tavern and get the things we've been looking for all these days."

With his mouth agape, Theophilus looked at me disbelievingly when he followed Caius out of the room.

At that moment, a clanking sound resonated as the goblet slipped from the man's grasp, its spilled wine intermingling with the crimson hue of blood on the ground, enveloping the air with an unsettling scent.

I walked up to the man, his body now shaking violently.

"I'm a finished man. Tigellinus is going to kill me, for sure, and might even kill my wife and children," he groaned, before his sobbing developed into a loud hysterical weep. I picked up a linen towel from the table, wiped away the blood from his face and said tenderly, "I'll release you. Go home, take your family and leave Rome, right now."

"What? You'll let me go?" His eyes filled with half disbelief and half ecstasy. But soon, his face clouded again. "No, Tigellinus will find us. He's got the best spies."

"Don't be afraid. Tigellinus will be busy for a few days. Go to the mountains and hide there. He'll forget about you when things have settled," I reassured him, supporting him out of the interrogation room and leading him straight ahead toward the back door of the barracks.

The door guard scrutinized us with hesitation. "My lady, without the prefect's order, this man has to stay here," he finally said.

I mustered my sternest look and locked eyes with him. "The prefect left specific orders for me to bring this man for a private interrogation. We have no time to waste before Tigellinus' men arrive. Now please move aside. Or do you refuse to obey?"

The guard scratched his head nervously, and with an even more demanding tone, I continued, "Do you want to ruin the prefect's plan? This is a critical case, and if we fail, the consequences will be dire. So, do your duty and let us pass. We don't have time for all your nonsense."

Those words sufficed.

The fear in the guard's eyes was palpable, and he sheepishly stepped aside, allowing us to leave the barracks. I helped the man to a carriage rental shop across the street.

"Take this man according to his order," I said to the shop's owner. Then I took off my golden wristband and placed it in the man's hand, closing his fingers around it as if to convey he must keep it safe.

"This should be enough to pay for the trip," I said. The man looked at me, his swollen lips quivering. "Why are you doing this for me? You don't even know me."

"I wish we could talk more, sir. But there is no time to lose." I sighed, holding his other hand in mine, and then very gently, I drew a fish sign on his palm. "Remember, Jesus of Nazareth loves you and He died on the cross for you," I whispered to him.

He widened his eyes as he got into the carriage in such a daze.

I looked at the carriage as it disappeared at the end of the lane and felt all strength evaporate from my body as I collapsed to the ground.

Thank you, God, for granting me wisdom to save this man. May you bless his trip and give him a chance to know you in the future.

Thirty-Three
The Last Night

Caius burst into his study as the sun dipped below the horizon, his fist colliding with a marble column. I stood up from the desk, where I had been diligently writing on a piece of parchment paper, and approached him.

"What's wrong? Did you find the goods?"

"We did," he said with a hardened face.

"Then why are you still—"

"He only got forfeited two months' salary. Can you believe that?"

"Who? The slave?"

"No, Tigellinus, of course!" Caius bellowed, but he quickly softened his tone and apologized. "Sorry, I shouldn't have yelled."

"Please, have a seat," I said, gesturing for him to settle onto the couch against the wall. As he sat down, I reached for a wine goblet from the table beside the couch and handed it to him. "Now, tell me what has happened."

He downed the goblet in a gulp before managing to speak.

"We went to Luna Tavern according to the information we had squeezed out of that man, and we found all the goods there. The tavernkeeper was also a freed slave of Tigellinus, and we brought him to the palace. Tigellinus was called in. The tavernkeeper accused him in front of everyone."

"Wasn't everything going according to our plan?"

Caius poured more wine into his goblet and said, "But Nero was traveling in the eastern provinces, leaving only the empress to deal with the case."

"Oh..."

"Poppaea, that nasty woman, only forfeited Tigellinus two months' salary. And then there's the provocative smile she gave me. If you witnessed it, you would have wanted to throw up. She even had the nerve to flirt with Tigellinus in front of me. What a disgusting woman!"

"I guess she just wanted you to be jealous," I said, but immediately regretted it when I realized Caius had never mentioned the empress having feelings for him. "I'm sorry, I didn't mean to gossip," I added quickly.

"That's fine. Many people believe that I was promoted to prefect because of her. In fact, instead of helping me, she only hindered me when she realized she couldn't manipulate me into her bed. And I know many think I hate Tigellinus because we are political rivals. That's true to a point, but it is mostly because his vices have hurt the praetorian morality."

"I believe you, Caius," I said sincerely, meeting his gaze. Though we had only spent a few months together, I could already attest to his unmistakable soldier's pride.

He looked at me, smiling wryly. "Well, maybe it's not bad news that the empress got herself a new toy. At least I hope she'll give me a break. And I'm glad old Eubulus is cleared of the guilt of cheating the emperor."

"Yes, and I'm glad I can finally go home now," I said joyfully.

Caius' expression momentarily faltered, but he quickly regained his composure, offering a reassuring smile. "There's no rush. You've helped me a lot, Vita. I haven't properly thanked you yet. Please, stay one more day, and let me prepare a farewell gift for you."

"No, you don't have to, Caius. It is you I must thank. You've saved me and Rufus."

"Just stay one more day," he pleaded. "I need to attend some business in the barracks right now. Please don't leave until I come back to bid you farewell."

"But I just..." As I was trying to explain that Rufus might be worried about me, Julia hurried in and clasped my hand.

"Please, let's stay one more night. We'll have no other chance to enjoy such a beautiful villa." Then she asked Caius in a purring voice, "Can we use your bath tonight, please?"

Caius laughed heartily. "Sure, enjoy yourself. I'll be using the one in my barracks with hundreds of sweating men." Then he left the room.

When we retreated to Caius' bedchamber, Decima had already brought plates of food. Julia urged me to enter the bath, and we found that the water had just been heated.

"Let's bring the food to the bath and eat in the pool. It'll be such a treat," Julia suggested eagerly.

Julia's excitement eased my worry about Rufus. "Yes, let's do that. It's our last night here, so we'd better make the most of it," I said.

Very quickly, the warm water relaxed our bodies while we ate the mussels from the plates.

"What a life!" Julia exclaimed. "Do you really want to leave all of this, Vita? Please think carefully! You are not Penelope and Rufus is not Odysseus. Think about it long and hard before deciding anything."

"Yes, I told you in the market before," I said, unable to believe she was still trying to persuade me. "Rufus is the only man in this world I want to spend my life with. Simple as that."

"Fine, Vita, but let me ask you a question. You really don't want Caius, do you?"

"Of course not, and he is not for me to have anyway. He is such a sought-after man. He once said he didn't like women with calluses on their hands. And just look at mine." I held out my hands. "Look at them."

"So, you wouldn't mind *me* having him then?"

I almost choked on a piece of mussel I was eating. "Julia, what are you talking about? You are... I mean, Caius is... he is not... Well, I mean, he's a patrician, so he can't marry a slave, freed or not. That's what you told me," I exclaimed.

"Vita, the life you so carelessly discard is all I've ever yearned for. A handsome patrician lover, a grand villa, an unlimited purse to buy anything I desire. And I'm confident enough to acquire it all once you leave," she said with a smile that flushed her cheeks. "Perhaps for a few months if I'm fortunate enough."

"But how? We're leaving tomorrow."

"No, *you* are leaving tomorrow. I'm not. I'm going to tell him that I bruised my ankle and need to stay a few weeks. I doubt he'll object," Julia said seriously. "Vita, you're my best friend. I won't steal the man if you like him. But if you decide to leave, I know how to get him into my bed. I know men. He likes you, but he also doesn't dislike me."

"But why? You know it won't last for long." I was surprised at the volume of my voice. "Don't worry about life in Eubulus' house; I'll plead with Caius to buy your freedom as well. You can have a new life and go wherever you wish. Julia, you don't have to stay here!"

"Don't have to stay? I *yearn* to stay! Vita, are you so blind that you don't even realize how charming Caius is? I'd feel so complete if I could have him. Besides, even if he were to leave me in a few months, or maybe a few weeks, I'd still be the girl who once had Caius. That's a title even the empress would envy." She looked into my eyes and added, "And do not judge me with your god's commandments. I had enough of that from my mother."

Seeing the determination in Julia's eyes, I knew it was no use pressing the matter any further.

"If you don't leave tomorrow, this might be the last night we are under the same roof. I'll be on the way to Cyprus with Rufus soon. And I'll miss you," I murmured, gently embracing my friend.

"I'll miss you too." She wrapped her arms around me tightly.

That night, Julia and I talked until midnight, and after she retired to her room, I tiptoed into the atrium. It was quiet and eerie there, with only the moonlight casting a soft glow on the pond.

I whispered a prayer to God, thanking Him for making the day go so well.

"Dear God, thank you for making everything go so smoothly. Tomorrow I'll finally be able to reunite with my beloved Rufus. This place has been more like home every day, and everyone—Decima, Livia, Tullia, Felix—they are like my family now. I'll miss them when I'm gone, so I pray that you watch over them every day," I said, sweetness mixed with a hint of sorrow filled my heart.

"Lord, I'm worried about dear Julia, however. I can't change her mind, but I put her in your hands. Please protect her. And for Caius…"

Thinking of him, a subtle smile tugged at the corners of my mouth unconsciously.

"I never expected we'd become… friends, good ones even. Please guide his way, and I sincerely hope one day, he will get to know you, and we may see each other again."

Thirty-Four

Two Surprises in a Day

As I awoke to the sound of the winter wind whistling outside, I noticed that Caius was not in the chamber. After getting dressed, I sat down to enjoy the food that Decima had brought me earlier. It was then I heard Theophilus' voice from the other side of the curtains.

"My lady, can you please come with me? Caius has a surprise for you."

What could the surprise be? I thought.

Regardless, I needed to show the first paragraph of my story to Caius before I left. So, I took the leather satchel with me and hurried out.

"Come on, let's go," I urged Theophilus.

"There's no hurry," Theophilus said with a smile and took out a silk scarf from his sleeve. "Caius said I need to cover your eyes."

"But what for? You are not going to prank me, are you?" I asked, feeling a bit nervous, recalling stories the slave girls had once talked about, in which Theophilus had tricked Caius into eating something he didn't like.

"You'll know the reason very soon," he said, tying the scarf around my eyes. "Is that acceptable? It's not too tight, is it?"

"No, it's fine."

"And you can't see through it?"

"No, I can't see a thing."

"Very good. Let's go!" He grabbed my hand, leading me slowly, alerting me to potential obstacles along the way. With each step, my curiosity grew.

Theophilus finally stopped. "There is a bench here; sit down please, my lady," he said. "Just turn around, and I will guide you. The master said he didn't want you to trip yourself from being too excited about the surprise."

"Oh, come on. Just let me see it. The suspense is killing me." I giggled. "And it's cold out here," I added, touching my bare arms.

"I will leave you here, and please only remove the scarf when you can no longer hear my footsteps."

"All right. I promise," I said, then heard Theophilus' steps gradually fade away.

When I could no longer hear his movements, I removed the scarf and couldn't believe what lay before me.

Gladioli.

I found myself surrounded by a sea of gladioli, with patches of flowers stretching out in front of me and to my sides. They came in an array of colors—red, yellow, pink, orange, blue—every hue and shade imaginable. At a loss for words, I could only stare in a daze.

"Am I in a dream? How can this be? It is winter," I murmured, the chilly wind reminding me of the season.

"Do you like them?" A deep brooding voice startled me. I turned and found Caius standing behind the bench. He quickly untied his fur cloak and placed it over me.

"Thanks. I... I adore them, but how did you... in this season?" I stuttered.

"I had my servants transport these flowers here while you were sleeping last night," Caius explained, gesturing toward the lush gladioli patches. "They were cultivated in another villa under a roof made of mica plates, allowing only sunshine to reach them. The late

Emperor Tiberius had a penchant for eating cucumbers year-round, so he tasked his gardener with this endeavor. I managed to locate the retired gardener in Brundisium and brought him all the way back to Rome. Looks like he's done a fine job."

"Caius"—I covered my mouth with my hands—"I don't know what to say."

He walked out from behind the bench and sat next to me.

"It is a pity we can't plant the fragrant kind. They don't do well in cold weather. But I'll grow more in the summer."

"Summer?" I suddenly grew alert. "But Caius, our show is over, and I won't even be here for summer." I turned my head and met Caius' hot gaze. "I'll be long gone."

There followed an awkward silence, interrupted only by the sound of my pounding heart.

"Stay with me, Vita," he finally said, not breaking his gaze. "This villa will be lifeless without you." He reached out and took my hand.

"But you said you didn't want that when you got me into this," I exclaimed, attempting to withdraw my hand, yet his grip was too firm to break. My voice trembled as I continued, "You know I long to return home and be with Rufus."

Caius scoffed slightly, his gaze still unyielding. I started to wonder if he had not heard me or simply couldn't accept being rejected. Knowing people like Caius were not used to rejection, I prayed fiercely in my heart. *Oh, God, please help me.*

Another unsettling quiet ensued, during which I stared at my feet and caught a glimpse of the gladioli. *Nana was right. I've always been like the gladioli; they too survive in all circumstances.* With that thought, I suddenly felt stronger.

"Well, if you *command* me, I'll stay, *master*."

His hand quivered for a fleeting moment, but immediately his grip became even tighter.

Towering over me, he placed one hand on the edge of the backrest of the bench, his face barely inches from mine. I could feel his warm breath, carrying the scent of fresh mint. His expression was unreadable, but his proximity made my face flush.

"What do you want?" I asked, avoiding his gaze.

"Look at me," Caius said, gently tipping my chin up. "Do you truly wish to know what I want at this moment?"

"Not... not really," I replied, immediately regretting the dangerous question. But he ignored me and continued, "I want to lock you up in my villa, just as Hades held Persephone in the underworld. And as your master, I have every right to do so."

My face flushed with heat, and my entire body trembled as fears welled up within.

"But you promised..."

"Yes, I promised. Besides, I, Caius Aemilia, have never forced any woman and won't start now." Caius gently squeezed my chin and released me. "Go back to your lover, and never show your face in front of me again," he said with a glint of pain in his voice.

He retrieved a small silk pouch hanging from his belt and placed it on my lap. "Your document of slavery is here. Now, you are free. Free from me. Theophilus will prepare a carriage to send you and Julia back. As for your lover, just tell Eubulus to release him; I'll settle the payment after you both leave." He walked away without glancing back. "Leave and never come back to Rome!"

I stood there, rendered speechless for a long moment, watching as Caius' tall and slender figure disappeared at the far end of the portico. A profound ache gnawed at my heart. Reflecting on the past three months we had shared, my memories were filled with moments of joy and laughter. Hurting him was never my intention. However, as I glanced down at the document in my hand, a sudden realization engulfed my thoughts.

I'm free... free!

After being a slave for almost fourteen months, freedom seemed so foreign to me. I couldn't even believe it had really happened.

Taking hold of the pouch, I ran to Julia's room and shouted with joy, "Julia, I'm free! Quick, let's leave before he changes his mind."

Julia sat on the bed, looking confused and staring back blankly.

"What do you mean? Who's going to change their mind?"

"Caius. He just granted me freedom, and I'm free to go home," I replied, waving my document. A flicker of excitement showed up in Julia's eyes, but soon, it turned into blankness. "What's going on, Julia? What's bothering you?" I asked. "Aren't you excited?"

"I guess you forgot what we talked about last night." Julia frowned. "I just sprained my ankle this morning." She exposed her ankle, which was really swollen and red, and then my mind drifted to our conversation from the prior evening.

"You did this to yourself?" I exclaimed. "Why? You could have just pretended."

"I must make it believable," she said firmly.

Knowing how determined Julia was, I sighed and embraced her gently. "Take care of yourself, my sister. You'll always be in my heart," I said wistfully, then left the room.

Thinking about returning to Caius' bedchamber to gather my belongings, I hesitated. His final warning echoed in my mind: *Never show your face in front of me.*

Besides, most of my belongings here had been gifts from Caius, and I didn't want to take them, especially after I had found out what he really wanted from me.

I put the document into my leather satchel, and my fingers felt the parchment paper and the ink bottle. "Lord, please allow me to keep these," I whispered.

Theophilus, with a darkened face, stood waiting outside the gate with a carriage by his side. "I'm sorry," he said with a sigh. "To be honest, I really don't know if I should be happy or sad for him, Vita. He has never treated any woman like this before... but maybe it's for the best."

"Yes, it is. He will forget about me in no time and get back to women worthy of his status," I said, giving Theophilus a gentle hug. "And thank you for everything you've done for me."

Theophilus sighed again and gestured for me to get into the carriage.

"I'd rather take a walk today," I said, taking off Caius' cloak and handing it over to Theophilus.

"You really don't want to have anything to do with him, do you?" Theophilus smiled bitterly. "As you wish, my lady. Farewell."

So, I stepped over the grand threshold, empty-handed and alone. The winter air was chilly as I gazed at the myrtle tree in front of the villa, still remembering the beautiful flowers from the day when Caius had carried me through the gate.

Now the flowers were gone, leaving only bare branches.

"When Rufus and I arrive in Cyprus, it will probably be early spring," I whispered to myself. "And soon, we'll have a yard full of blooming trees."

Picking up my pace, alternating between speedwalking and sprinting, I made my way through the streets, only stopping a few times to ask for directions.

As I turned into a narrow lane, I noticed dark clouds gathering above, with women's heads popping out from the small window openings of a shabby insula, calling out to their children. Traders chased after items lifted from their shops by the strong wind. A few steps more, and a fat raindrop landed on my neck. Moments later, the heavens opened, the rain falling in full effect.

Seeking shelter from the rain, I hurriedly ducked under the protective overhang of a nearby tavern, grateful for the refuge it offered. As I checked to ensure my parchment remained dry, I felt a gentle brush against my leg. Peering down, I discovered the tiny hands of a little girl, who was no more than two or three years old.

"Mama. Mama," she repeated softly.

Watching her innocent smile, I couldn't help but wonder if my own future child would possess such a carefree and endearing grin—a simple, one-toothed smile unaffected by the chaos of the world.

How many children will Rufus want? A large family, perhaps. Our sons will take after their father, playful yet responsible and protective of their sisters.

I will work hard with Rufus, providing our children with the best, everything we struggled to have while growing up. They will even learn to read and write better than me.

Most of all, we will teach them about God's love and faithfulness, just as Nana did.

"There you are, you little rascal! Come over here," the tavernkeeper's wife called out. The girl saw her mom and ran toward her, giggling.

Soon, the rain subsided and people trooped out of the tavern, thanking the tavernkeeper for his kind heart. I continued on my walk, clutching the leather satchel against my chest. Giddy with baby fever, I couldn't wait to see the future father of my dream children.

The sun peeked shyly from the clouds when I arrived at Eubulus' villa. My legs were tired from the long walk, my damp clothes clinging to my body uncomfortably, but none of the discomforts could even begin to cloud my happiness.

As I approached, the front door stood out with its fresh coat of scarlet paint and a laurel leaf wreath adorning it. *Is this the same house?* I pondered, questioning myself. *Perhaps Eubulus is celebrating the exoneration of this household.*

Raising the ring on the knocker, which was shaped like a bronze lion's mouth, I struck it against the metal plate. No response. *That's odd.* I knocked again, growing increasingly puzzled.

Suddenly, and to my surprise, a wide-eyed Antonia opened the door, holding a basket filled with rose petals. "You are back? We were not expecting you," she said. "We heard..." she murmured, but the usual haughty look was no longer in her eyes.

"Long story," I said, not intending to explain anything further. "Why are you here today? Where is Publius? It used to be his job to greet people."

"We are running out of hands for the wedding banquet, so he's assigned to help in the kitchen. I was in the atrium, spreading rose petals in the pool when I heard someone knocking."

"Wedding? Whose wedding?"

"Who else but our lady and Aurelius?"

"Wait, you mean *Aurelius?* The same man living in this house?"

"Of course. How many Aurelius do you know?"

I couldn't believe my ears. My heart sank, my fingers trembled, and a tingling sensation in my limbs mirrored my state of panic.

"Antonia! You haven't finished your job yet!" someone called out from the atrium.

"I must go. You might want to join us tonight. The lady must be so happy that you could attend the wedding," Atonia said and hurried away.

The dog mosaic under my feet started to spin and blur as I staggered toward the indigo curtains down the hallway. I parted the curtains forcefully but saw no one. Taking a deep breath, I hurried further into the villa.

"Where is Ru... Aurelius?" I asked, grasping the arm of a girl carrying a wine jug in the corridor.

"Vita! You are back?"

"Please, where is Aurelius?" I demanded, shaking her shoulders, causing drops of wine to spill onto the ground.

"In the old master's bedchamber," she said, looking at me, perplexed, and pointing to the southeastern corner of the atrium.

I stormed toward the door and flung it open. Before me, Rufus sat on a chair, his toga draped in elegant folds, while a slave girl attended to his hair. With a crack, the ceramic comb in her hand dropped to the floor, shattering into pieces.

"How dare..." The words died on Rufus' lips as he saw my face.

"Leave, everybody," he ordered sternly.

As all the slaves retreated from the chamber, he approached me, his voice trembling. "Vita——"

"You betrayer! You liar!" I picked up a pillow from the couch and hurled it at him.

"I'm sorry, Vita," Rufus muttered, his face flushed and veins bulging in his temples. His hands reached out hesitantly towards mine but retreated before making contact. Silence enveloped the room.

"Why?" My face was drenched with tears.

"It's not important now." Rufus sighed, shaking his head. "I don't deserve you, Vita."

Suddenly, a chilling thought seized my mind. "Caius! It must be Caius. He didn't tell you the truth about us, did he?" I shook Rufus' shoulders violently, searching for confirmation in his eyes.

"It was not Caius' fault, Vita," Cassia interjected from the doorway, her bridal jewels gleaming. "Caius did tell Aurelius about your plan. And Aurelius waited and prayed for you for many days."

Then she paused, sighing deeply before continuing, "My father was deeply disturbed by the loss of imperial favor; he suffered a stroke and fell into a coma. He only woke for a few hours before passing. Before he passed, my father made Aurelius swear an oath to take care of me and preserve our family's wealth. Please forgive us, Vita."

Can it get any worse? Trying to gather my senses, my gaze landed on Rufus at last. "So, is it the oath or wealth that made you break your promise to me?"

"Vita, it's not what you think."

"No need to explain," I said coldly, shaking my head. Taking a deep breath, I dragged myself out of the chamber and trudged toward the front gate.

Emerging from the gate, I erupted into a furious sprint, darting through the bustling streets, narrowly avoiding collisions with pedestrians and carriages, as if an invisible barrier clouded my vision. The rain intensified, pouring down with greater intensity than before, yet I persisted in my relentless pace, tears streaming down my face, blending seamlessly with the downpour.

I had no sense of direction, just running and running without a care in the world. Suddenly, I spotted it—the familiar tavern where I had sought shelter before, and there was the same little girl waving at me. Her innocent smile felt like a stab to my heart. *Vita, you were such a fool to believe you could have children with Rufus.* I laughed bitterly. "Liars, all liars."

Unknowingly, I entered the Forum, which lay empty as people had sought shelter from the rain. I wandered aimlessly under the heavy downpour, soon stumbling upon the part of the market where I had once stood on the stage and told that story.

The stage was empty too, and the benches for the audience had been removed. I sat down heavily on the edge of the stage. Rain poured down and continued to drench my body, yet the coldness seemed to escape my senses.

I stared at a dirt mound by my feet, observing as it rapidly dissolved under the relentless rain.

"Lord, why are you doing this to me?" I raged. "Rufus is the only reason I have been able to endure all trials. Why are you making me look like a fool? If you hate me so much, let me be like this mound—let the rain dissolve my body, my soul, so I can no longer feel any pain."

Sitting lost in thought, time seemed to stealthily slip away.

My mind spun through a whirlwind of memories and scenarios, while my body grew numb and my vision blurred. During my subconsciousness, I still held the leather satchel close to my chest, which was now totally drenched.

Just as darkness threatened to envelop me entirely, a familiar figure emerged from the deluge.

Thirty-Five
A Pool with Ice

"It's been three days! And none of you idiots could reduce her fever? She was as strong as a lioness before she left me. Don't tell me just sitting in the rain for a couple of hours will make her sick like this!" Caius roared. The five Greek physicians, whom he had summoned, stood before him, trembling with their heads bowed in trepidation.

"My lord, we have done our best. If the patient has no intent to live, that's not something any physician can influence. The lady has given up; it is plain to see."

"What will happen if the fever won't stop?" Caius asked with his brow furrowed.

There was a pause, each of the physicians waiting for one of the others to talk.

"Well?" Caius roared.

"Hard to say, my lord. I had a patient last month who died in a similar condition," the plump physician with long white beard said, constantly shooting glances at Caius.

"There has to be a way!"

"My lord, there is a way we haven't tried, but..." He rubbed his hands nervously.

Caius grabbed his shoulder and shook it vigorously.

"Tell me. No matter how much it will cost, I'll save her."

"My father was Emperor Tiberius' royal physician. He told me that he once let the emperor get into a pool filled with ice to reduce the fever. And the emperor recovered the next day."

"Shut up! Everybody knows how strong Emperor Tiberius was. How is a delicate girl like her going to survive such harsh treatment? How many other patients have you tried it on? I won't let you test your absurd method on her," Caius bellowed.

The physician took a few steps away from Caius, evidently terrified.

From a safer distance, he murmured, "Of course, not many patients have tried this method. There aren't many people in Rome who can afford a pool full of ice anyway."

Theophilus patted his friend's back.

"Look, maybe we should give it a try. She is a strong girl; I think she'll survive it."

Caius was silent for a long time.

"Very well, I'll do it," he finally said to Theophilus. "Go tell Alexander to fetch the ice from the ice pit in the villa and fill the pool of the cold bathroom. Do not add water. Now everyone must leave."

Theophilus' lips moved, but no words were uttered. Finally, he shook his head and said, "As you wish, my lord." He departed the room.

The hurried footsteps and the sound of ice pouring into the pool persisted for some time. Once the clamor subsided, Caius removed his cloak, clad only in his thin tunic, and cautiously stepped into the cold bath. With a measured resolve, he stretched out facedown upon the ice.

The biting cold made his teeth clench unconsciously. After enduring the numbing chill for a moment longer, he stood up slowly from the ice bath and dashed toward his bed. There, he cradled Vita in his arms, the warmth of her back seeping into his skin, causing his heart to twinge with a mixture of concern and tenderness.

"We must get the fever down," he whispered, feeling the feverish heat of Vita's body gradually warming his chilled bones. Once the piercing cold had abated, he carefully laid Vita back onto the bed before returning to the pool.

He had lost count of how many times he lay on the ice pile until moonlight cast a soft glow on the curtain of his bed. Vita was still in a coma in his arms, burning like a furnace and every time her temperature subsided, it would soon creep back up.

Holding her tightly, Caius whispered, "Don't die. You're not allowed to die without my permission. Do you hear me?"

The physician's words sounded again, filling his heart with rage.

"Losing hope of life for a man who doesn't even cherish you? Vita, you can do better than this. Didn't you tell me that Christians should be strong in their god?

"If you die like this, you're a coward, do you hear me?"

The word 'die' made his spine tingle, a kind of fear he had never experienced before filling his heart. Since his father had trained him as a fighter, he'd never feared death.

He'd caught a glimpse of Hades' smile several times during his career as a praetorian stopping assassins, but he had never been shaken like this.

He hadn't prayed to any gods since coming to Rome, except for public appearances, but at this moment, he felt a strong urge to pray.

"Mighty Mars, Venus, Hercules, all the Olympian gods, whoever can save her, I will clad your temple with gold. And Vita's carpenter god, Jesus, you don't know me. Vita said you don't love gold, so you must tell me what it is I must give to you. If you desire any sacrifice, I will gladly provide it if such is within my power, even it's worth my life."

A tear rolled freely down his face. Weird.

He hadn't cried since that pouring day when his mother's carriage had vanished in the rain. Now, following his prayer, a wave of fatigue mixed in with a strange surge of peace overwhelmed him, and soon he surrendered to the comforting embrace of sleep.

The rays of sunlight streaked through the windows and the shade on his bed, as Caius woke from the same position in which he had dozed off, and Vita was still in his arms.

Her body was cool to the touch.

A peculiar sensation washed over him, the belief that his final, fervent prayer to Vita's carpenter god had somehow spared her.

"Thank you, Jesus. Whatever god you may be, I owe you," he murmured.

He stared at her sleeping face and felt very strange. He'd been longing to hold her for some time, and it made his blood boil every time he thought of it. But now she was in his arms and her fragrance was in his nose, all he could feel was... peace, the peace he had never felt with other women. He continued to stare as she slept like a baby in his arms and for a moment, he just wanted time to stop.

Just then, the curtain parted and Theophilus barged in.

Caius shushed him. "Don't make a noise. Her fever just calmed, and she needs some rest." Theophilus looked at Caius and stared at the watery footprints on the marble floor.

Almost yelling, he replied, "Caius, don't tell me you jumped in that icy..."

Caius hushed him again with a warning frown, and Theophilus left, quietly shaking his head in disbelief.

In the afternoon, Theophilus was called in again.

"That Rufus... he can read, can't he?"

"Yes, he does business on his own, so he must know some basics," Theophilus said.

Caius handed him a tablet and said, "Give this to him, secretly."

Theophilus saw the scribble on the tablet, his eyes filled with shock. "You want to meet him? Are you sure about this?"

"Yes, I need to talk to him about Vita."

"Prefect..." Theophilus hesitated a little, and continued, "I feel you have changed... a little. Being at your side for ten years, I consider myself your friend. And as a friend, I warn you; don't get lost in all this. I can't tell you why, but I have a feeling that this girl will bring you trouble."

"Are you worried about her little cult?"

Theophilus nodded.

"Their little cult may sound absurd, but I've made sure it's harmless. The nasty things you've heard about are just some urban rumors."

"I guess you can call it a 'little cult' if you only look at their number. But let me tell you something." Theophilus sat down on the couch where Vita used to sleep and continued. "Last winter, there were some minor riots between this cult's followers and the Jewish community they originated from. You were too busy with your work at the palace, so I didn't report it to you. When the riots finally died down, I received a letter from a Greek physician. His name was Luke, an important figure in this cult."

"What did this Luke write?" Caius inquired, his curiosity piqued.

"He claimed their god was a man called Jesus, from a poor Jewish family. He performed lots of miracles but was finally crucified by the prefect of Judea about thirty years ago."

"I can't believe they worship a criminal who died on the cross. No god who possesses any level of power would ever allow himself to associate with such a shameful thing," Caius exclaimed.

"I know. And this is the strangest part. He claimed their god came to life again after being laid in a tomb for three days. And after that, he appeared before many witnesses."

"Such nonsense!" Caius exclaimed again. "No one can survive the Roman cross!"

"Not survive. Luke said he rose from death," Theophilus explained. "I thought it was absurd, so I ignored that letter. But after a few months, he wrote me another. And this letter was about Jesus' followers."

"What did they do?"

"After they saw Jesus was resurrected, they were going crazy sharing this 'good news' with others. I don't believe those exaggerated miracles in his letters."

"I guess you shouldn't."

"No, but I've interrogated many criminals alongside you, Caius. I've seen more than my fair share of liars. Yet, there was something in this letter, a fearful earnestness, that sent a shiver down my spine. I believe this Luke was sincere in what he wrote."

"Maybe he was a gullible person who believed whatever others told him."

"Not really. He was the one who went on many trips with one of Jesus' chief disciples to share the 'good news'."

"What is your worry, Theophilus?" Caius asked. "I'm a military man. I won't be easily deceived. So, what are you saying, exactly?"

"I hope you're right. Yet, I can't shake the feeling that there's a certain peril associated with these individuals," Theophilus said. "Maybe I shouldn't have told you I found out about Rufus and Cassia's wedding that day. I really shouldn't. But I was too soft-hearted to see you suffer so much."

Theophilus left the room, leaving Caius drifting off in thought.

· ♥ · ♥ · ♥ · ♥ · ♥ ·

The sun dipped low in the sky as Rufus arrived at the modest inn nestled on the eastern end of Cupid Street. Caius was already waiting at a table close to the road, and the innkeeper had already emptied the room after receiving a pouch of silver coins from this generous guest.

"My lord, you sent for me?" Rufus inquired with a respectful dip of his head.

Caius rose, his gaze fixed on Rufus for a moment in silent scrutiny, then delivered a forceful punch to his face. Rufus wasn't prepared and stumbled to the ground, his face immediately covered with blood.

The innkeeper looked on, but Caius indicated all was well.

"That was a good one. Deserved too." Rufus smiled bitterly. "You are right to punch me. I broke her heart, her trust, and her sacrifice."

Caius' anger was still seething. He grabbed Rufus by the collar and pressed him to the wall. "Why did you do this to her?" he bellowed. "Do you know how much she suffered from your betrayal? She had a fever for three days and almost lost her life. But what do you care?"

Rufus' eyes reddened. "How is she right now?"

"She's fine now. Only because *I* won't let her die," Caius said, releasing his grip.

"Oh, thank God." Rufus dropped to the ground with his hands covering his face. "I'm so sorry."

"Why?" Caius sat on a bench near him. "Why have you done this to her? Is it all about money? Which slave can resist the temptation of marrying the only daughter of a wealthy merchant? Is that what this is about?"

"It is not what you think," Rufus tried to explain, but Caius continued.

"I asked her to stay with me. But she said that *you* are the only man in the world she wants to be with. She chose you over all the wealth I could give her." Caius smiled dejectedly. "You broke the heart of the girl who broke mine."

Hearing Caius' words, Rufus covered his face and sobbed.

"I've failed her. I promised to marry her when she was just six years old." He wiped his eyes with his right sleeve. "But Eubulus begged me to take care of his daughter on his deathbed. And Cassia, she was so broken after her father's sudden death, so I had to be by her side day and night. I can't say no to a woman who saved my life."

"So, you offered comfort by sharing her bed, I take it?" Caius said sarcastically. "How magnanimous of you. Oh, gods, sometimes, I wish Vita were so easy to tempt."

"I didn't mean to. But the other day, I was fetching dresses for her from a tailor's shop and saw Vita and Julia coming out of a jewelry store, covered with dazzling bracelets and necklaces. You don't know how my heart ached at that moment. I could never give her the life she was enjoying. I felt so powerless, and I thought from all the lavish gifts she was wearing that you had become her suitor. From then on,

I tried to turn my mind from Vita.

"That night when Cassia asked me to drink wine with her, I agreed, for the first time. We both got drunk. And... things happened."

"You idiot!" Caius snapped, rubbing his temples. "Vita never cared about anything I gave her. All she cared about was you. You were an idiot by leaving her for some stupid rogue three years ago, and you are still just as stupid today. Well, even more so!"

"I know. But it's too late." Rufus grabbed a goblet and gulped its contents. "She is a very good girl. Please take good care of her."

"As if she would let me." Caius laughed bitterly. "Now go back to your new wife and your big villa. My advice is to be vigilant when you deal with people in the palace. Don't get Vita worried when you get into trouble next time."

Thirty-Six

Stay

Flames engulfed the river, and a similar fire of fever consumed my body. Rufus and I tread cautiously across a narrow plank bridge, the fire teasing the edges of my dress. Terror gripped me; I clung to Rufus for safety. Abruptly, the plank beneath us fractured. I plummeted into the fiery abyss, my scream piercing the chaos, "Rufus, help!" He glanced over his shoulder, his expression as impassive as marble, then proceeded to walk away, never looking back again.

I cried, drifting in and out of consciousness, feeling sweat and tears drench my tunic. A warm hand comforted me, caressing my face with a tender touch. "It's all right. You're going to be fine," soothed a voice, quenching the fires around me like a gentle rain.

Bit by bit, awareness crept back into my consciousness, and with it came the recognizable aroma of frankincense. It filled my nostrils with its soothing presence. Beneath me, the silkiness of the blanket and pillow lent a tender comfort, while a delicate daylight seeped through the lavender-tinted curtains, casting a tranquil glow around the bed.

It was Caius' bedchamber in which I reposed.

I almost jumped up at this realization, if not held back by the dizziness.

"Don't get up. You're still weak," came his voice, rough and weary with fatigue yet tinged with an undercurrent of elation. His hand was gentle as it brushed my forehead, checking for signs of fever. "Good, your fever has broken."

"Did you...? I mean, did I...?" I looked down at my new robe and couldn't form a complete sentence.

"And that's what you think of me?" Caius sighed. "Livia changed your clothes."

Relieved and embarrassed at the same time, my fingers grazed my waist, seeking the familiar presence of my leather satchel, but met with nothing. "Where is my..."

Before the sentence could be completed, Caius placed his fingers gently upon my lips, cutting off my words with a tender yet silencing gesture.

"No worries. The satchel was made with a beeswax coating, so the rain didn't damage it or anything inside it. I know it's important to you, so I sent it to the leathersmith to be refurbished. It will look like new when it's returned to you."

"But—"

"No more talking. You need only rest."

His smile retained its beauty, undiminished despite the pallor and fatigue etching his features. As another wave of dizziness overtook me, I turned, succumbing to the embrace of a profound slumber.

When awareness next graced me, the dizziness had dissipated, replaced by the gnawing pangs of hunger. Yet, it was the aroma of food that nudged me back to the waking world, encouraging my eyes to flutter open. There, a silver tray awaited, adorned with a steaming bowl of soup and a side of bread.

Lifting my gaze, I found Julia, the tray balanced in her hands.

"Thank the gods you're awake. I've been so worried about you."

I looked around the room and couldn't see Caius.

"He's in the barracks now. He didn't leave your side for a moment until you woke up," Julia said with a hint of pain in her voice. "Vita,

I'm so glad you've recovered. But you shouldn't have lied to me."

"But I never——"

"Enough!" Julia cut in sharply. "If you really wanted to leave, how on earth did he find you and make such a show by carrying you home in the pouring rain?" Tears welled in her eyes. "Oh, how stupid I was to think I had a chance!"

"No, Julia. It's not as you think. I don't even know how it happened. I'm a Christian, so I won't swear. But believe me, I don't even know how I got here."

Memories of pain flooded my mind, reigniting the all-too-familiar ache of a broken heart. I found myself taking short, shallow breaths.

"Rome is so big, and you just end up in the place in which you first met him," Julia said sarcastically. "Coincidence?"

Julia's question stirred a disquiet within me, leaving me grappling for an answer—or perhaps unwilling to confront one. "That's the place where I had some great victories. I won a large audience with a story representing God's name," I murmured, more to convince myself than to inform her.

Caius' voice sliced through my muddled thoughts as he swept aside the curtains and entered the room. "Don't sit up for too long. The physician said you need more rest," he admonished gently.

He hurried to my side and eased me back down with a careful hand, drawing the blanket over my shoulder with a protective fold.

Julia's face turned a shade lighter. Without a word, she slipped quietly out of the room.

Caius settled beside me, his fingers lightly tousling my hair. "You're looking better now. Little fool, you nearly scared me to death," he chided with a weary smile.

My instinct was to swat his hand away, but the sight of his red-rimmed eyes thawed my resolve. My heart softened, and my hand, once poised for dismissal, fell back to my side, still.

"Thanks, Caius, but how did you come to know I was there?" I asked, my voice still weak.

Caius sighed, a hint of frustration in his tone. "Theophilus actually caught wind of Rufus and Cassia's wedding days ago, but he chose not to tell me," he said. "However, when you left, I was so heartbroken that I sought solace in wine. He felt bad for me then and let the whole thing slip."

Reflecting on Theophilus' expression and his words as I departed the house, I softened. "I can't hold it against him," I conceded. "He was just trying to have your back."

"Look, I was really worried about you. I went over to Eubulus' place first, but you'd already gone. The market was the next place I thought of. You have no idea how much I was hoping inside, praying to your god, that I'd find you there."

"Thank you." My voice came out faint, barely a whisper.

"You were burning up with fever and slipped into a coma for three days," Caius said, his gaze shifting away as he gripped my hands more firmly. "Scared me half to death. One physician even said you'd given up on living, that there was no use trying to save you if you didn't have the will to fight."

A surge of deep sadness mixed with anger welled up inside me, sending tremors through my body. "How could Rufus do this to me? He's been promising since I was six to marry me in the future." I let out a hysterical cry. "He swore it again just months ago. Why has he torn my heart out?"

"Perhaps he had his reasons," Caius ventured.

"Impossible! He made his choice. Men are all liars!" My voice escalated to a roar. Tears streamed down my cheeks as I twisted away, facing the wall, and buried my face in the plush silk of the cushion.

A lengthy silence fell over the room.

Then, I sensed the pressure of Caius' hand resting upon the blanket over my shoulder.

"Do you want to get back at him?" he asked, his voice carrying a weight of earnestness.

"Revenge?" The concept felt alien upon my tongue, yet it resonated with an unexpected allure. Propping myself up, I met Caius' gaze.

"He's a scoundrel, no doubt about it. He ought to be taught a lesson," Caius said, his lips curving into a smirk.

"Yes, he is a scoundrel. And he surely needs to learn his lesson," I echoed, the words bringing a covert thrill as they tumbled out. The sensation was empowering; I no longer felt so powerless.

"But how?" I asked.

"He is the owner of Eubulus' business now. Let's destroy his business and make him a beggar. I've got connections with other spice suppliers in Rome. I can pay them to undercut his prices. Rufus won't last more than a month before his business crumbles."

"Sounds great!"

The memory of his stern visage from my dream, as I was consumed by the flames, flooded my thoughts. My anger burned hot, and the idea of him losing the riches he had gained through his union with Cassia filled me with zeal. "Yes, he betrayed me, and he'll pay for it. And Cassia too! Let's make them both beggars on the street," I declared, clenching my fist.

Caius raised an eyebrow. "Wow. I'm surprised you agreed with my plan. Are you sure about this?"

"Yes, I've never been surer of a thing ever."

"You sure you don't still have a fever, affecting your mind?" He laughed.

"No fever, thanks to you. I have never felt more alert. Really, your plan—it's good."

"So, let's do it," Caius suggested with a mischievous grin.

I turned and caught a glimpse of my reflection in a bronze mirror on the table.

In that moment, all the satisfaction that had welled up from envisioning a grand act of vengeance dissipated. "Oh, no. Look what an ugly person I have become." I covered my face in shame. "No. I don't want revenge. Nana said that hatred would consume a person's soul."

Caius chuckled. "That's my Vita. So, it was a test. You really are back."

I looked at him and smiled bitterly. "Now you've seen the worst of me."

He leaned over and stroked my hair. "And I'm still obsessed," he whispered.

I bowed my head to avoid his burning gaze.

"So, what is your plan now?" He turned away, giving a seemingly careless shrug.

"I want to return to Cyprus, my hometown, and start a basket workshop, but not in Paphos. There are too many memories there," I confessed.

I didn't raise my eyes to meet his, but I sensed a subtle tremor in his frame as I spoke. "The problem is, I don't have enough money to cover the trip."

"You can keep the pieces of jewelry you purchased from Lucan's shop," he offered, his expression void of emotion. "The proceeds should provide for you for a while."

It was a tempting offer, but I couldn't bring myself to accept such generosity from a man I had just rejected, not once, but twice—especially after he had already given me the priceless gift of saving my life.

"No, I can't accept that," I replied firmly. "I've earned my freedom by playing a role in your performance. Anything more than that, I'll earn with my own hands. Can I work in your household, even if it's for the lowest pay? Pay me the wage you would pay your freed slaves. I've heard that the next ship to Cyprus won't depart for another two months. I'll work to earn enough for my ticket."

"As you wish," he replied with a bitter smile, then stood and departed from the room.

I watched his retreating back, my heart heavy with remorse. "Oh, God," I whispered, near tears. "I never meant to hurt him. But what choice did I have? I can't become his mistress. Please, God, grant him the strength to move on swiftly, and guide me to live out the rest of my days in this villa with peace and safety."

Thirty-Seven

An Invitation to the Palace

"Vita, what happened?" Livia asked, her eyes widened like two copper coins. "The day we heard you had left the master, we were so disappointed," she continued. "I wished you could have stayed, so we could be sure no mean girls would be brought into this house."

"I heard the master carried you home on that rainy afternoon," Tullia chimed in. "And he took care of you for five days straight, barely closing his eyes." However, they were considerate enough not to ask how I had ended up here despite all the commotion.

Calina and Octavia approached me, patting me gently on the shoulder and offering a comforting hug. "We're so sorry, Vita. Please don't worry. We'll do everything to make your life easier here."

"That's right. You don't have to do anything. Just rest and wait for the master to change his mind and take you back," one of the girls reassured me.

"Thank you, but I'm able to work and I'd like to help in the kitchen," I replied, my heart warmed by the sincere kindness of these girls.

After several days of orientation, it became apparent that my cooking skills were not up to par for the fine cuisine in this household. As a result, I found myself assigned to the task of carrying garbage away to the midden, the waste pile discreetly nestled at the back of the stable. They hesitated at first, but I insisted. It was a dirty job, but I was determined to demonstrate that I deserved the wages Caius was providing.

Every day before sunset, I would meet Felix at the waste pile and help him load the garbage onto his cart, destined for disposal in the valley outside the city. "You really don't have to do this, my lady. I can handle it myself," Felix would say to me.

"It's part of my job."

"I've seen many ladies come and go from this villa, but you're the most peculiar one," he remarked, shaking his gray head.

Each evening, once my daily tasks were completed, I would retire to the slave quarters and engage in weaving. On the day of my departure, Caius had uprooted all the gladioli from the garden. Despite this setback, I managed to gather enough fallen leaves from the ground, using them as weaving material. With an abundance of time at my disposal, I crafted gifts for all those I encountered.

Caius sent a slave to bring the satchel to me. It did look like new and even the ink on the parchment was not smeared. But I didn't feel like writing anything at that moment.

Since my duties didn't require me to work around the front part of the villa, I rarely saw Caius these days. However, Felix saw him every night as he led his horse away to the stable. "He's gotten more tanned. Too much time in the barracks, I think," Felix commented, his tone full of fatherly concern.

Hearing Felix's words about Caius, a sharp pang of pain struck my heart, catching me off-guard. "He'll soon find someone else. And as his friend, I will be happy for him," I whispered to myself.

Adding to my sense of loneliness, Julia rarely visited me these days, continuing to live in her own separate quarters.

One afternoon, as I sat weaving alone in the unit while the other girls gathered around a campfire in the garden, Octavia returned to retrieve a cape. Noticing I was by myself, she chose to sit down beside me

"Vita, I probably shouldn't tell you this, but I couldn't hold it in any longer."

"What's happened?" I stopped weaving.

"Your maid, Julia..." She hesitated before continuing, "Last night, Decima had me polish the floor in the atrium. I was there when the master came home, drunk, at midnight. I saw Julia rush forward to help him to his bedchamber, but the master rebuked her."

I couldn't explain it, but a strange sense of satisfaction crept through me as I listened to the turn of events. Octavia, her voice tinged with indignation, said, "That girl was so shameless. She was your maid, and when she saw that you were no longer in favor, she tried to step in. Don't worry, Vita. Girls like her never get their way!"

I mustered a weak smile, countering gently, "Perhaps she was just trying to be kind." Yet inwardly, I wrestled with my own emotions. *Oh, why Lord, why this secret happiness when I see my friend being rejected?*

"Vita, your problem is your naivety." Octavia shook her head, oblivious to my shifting expression, and left the room.

Gently tapping my cheeks, I murmured under my breath, "What are you thinking, Vita? Hasn't he told you himself that he's never been serious with any girls? Pull yourself together, save up, and when the time comes, leave!"

As days turned into weeks, fresh leaves unfurled on the sweet bay trees in the garden, and pairs of wrens came back, busily preparing their nests for new life. I tallied my earnings, fingers crossed that it would suffice. Claudius had updated me——the next ship was scheduled for departure in a fortnight, precisely on the eighteenth. Yet, I was still short by two gold coins for the ship's boarding and meal expenses.

One day when dinner was over, the girls all drifted back to our quarters to chat and relax. Suddenly, Octavia charged in, her eyes sparkling with excitement. "Guess what? The master is in the garden practicing his archery skills! Who wants to come and watch?" Her enthusiasm was contagious, and one by one, the girls scurried out after her.

As they left, Marcia, the youngest among us, turned to me with a puzzled look. "Aren't you coming, Vita? He looks absolutely stunning when he's out there, focused and moving with such grace," she urged, her voice bubbling with eagerness.

I hesitated, feeling a twist of unease. "I-I'm not feeling too great today," I managed to say, my voice faltering slightly.

Memories from my last trip to the barracks surged through my thoughts. I could vividly remember Caius, clad in his training armor, masterfully handling a sword. As the echoes of the girls' excited yells and shouts from the garden reached my ears, curiosity got the better of me. Before I knew it, I was heading toward the door.

Stepping into the corridor, I couldn't help but glance toward the garden. At that moment, a flaming arrow zipped across the air, soaring over the arched passageway. The air was filled with the excited shrieks of the girls, gushing, "He's so handsome!"

I shut my eyes for a moment, yet the afterimage of the glowing arrow lingered. "Pull yourself together, Vita," I told myself firmly. Quickly changing my plan, I veered off course, darted into the kitchen, grabbed a pot filled with chicken bones, and made a beeline for the back door.

Felix was already in the kitchen. "Let me take that to the midden," he offered, reaching for the pot.

"No, let me do it this time, please!" I found myself almost pleading with him.

"It's cold out there," he called after me as I hurried out the back door.

"The cold is exactly what I need right now," I whispered to myself.

I wandered down the shadowy street, the brisk winds of early spring nipping at my shoulders. Strangely, their chill soothed me, calming the turmoil inside. I skipped the first cesspit and kept walking to a farther one, all the way to the end of the long street. Taking a deep breath, I closed my eyes and dumped the chicken bones into the pit. For a moment, the stink of old trash pushed away thoughts of that fiery arrow.

"Oh, Lord. What is wrong with me?" I whispered into the night, letting the cool air gently quell the unwanted flames of desire within me.

I prayed mindlessly and carried the pot back slowly.

The moment I crossed the threshold of the back door, Decima was there. "The master requests your presence in his chamber," she said, her voice a gentle melody. "Please, follow me."

My heart skipped a beat.

"Isn't he in the garden practicing archery?" I inquired, trailing her before she could respond.

"A slave came in and delivered a message to him, and he retreated to his bedchamber," Decima explained, her steps graceful and measured.

"But why does he wish to see me?" The question escaped my lips, tinged with a mix of curiosity and anticipation.

"I am not privy to his reasons, my lady," Decima replied tenderly. "I am merely the bearer of his summons."

Knowing Caius well enough, I could trust he wouldn't do anything against my will. And subconsciously, I sniffed my hand, making sure it bore no smell of the midden.

As Decima swept aside the familiar embroidered curtain, a flutter of excitement raced through my heart. Stepping into the room, my eyes immediately found Caius. He was seated, a tablet in hand, bathed in the soft glow of moonlight that accentuated his chiseled jawline and the broad shoulders. My gaze lingered on him, a warm flush spreading across my cheeks.

"You look well," I said, striving for a calm tone.

"I get by." The old mischievous smile appeared. "How is the work here treating you?"

"It's been very good. Thank you again for this opportunity."

"Don't mention it, Vita. It's the least I can do, as a friend."

I thought of the harshness of my first few months at Eubulus' villa, so being a servant here was really not a terrible thing. "This has been much more than the least, thank you," I said sincerely.

"Careful now, your appreciation might go to my head." He had another playful smile, and I suddenly realized I'd always enjoyed talking to this man.

This realization sent a pleasant shiver all the way down to the soles of my feet.

"So, why did you call me? Pleasantries can't be why you ordered me here," I said, trying to stop my mind from wandering too far.

"Now I need an excuse to call you?" he asked with a sly look.

"You know what I mean, Caius."

"You are right; I do have a reason. Nero has invited me to one of his banquets, and as is customary, I'm expected to bring a date."

"That shouldn't be a problem for the great Caius Aemilia. I'm sure the many ladies of Rome would jump at the opportunity."

"Not after I've offended them because of taking you."

"You jest with me."

"Why don't you come with me? It will be just like the past days."

"That time of our lives is over. I'm only your servant now to earn money for my trip."

"Your ship departs on the eighteenth, am I correct? Only one day after the banquet. If I haven't miscalculated, you still haven't saved enough for it."

I looked at him, surprised at how much he knew.

"Accompany me to the banquet, and I'll pay you extra for this special service. After the banquet, I'll ride with you to the harbor. Then you'll start your new life without owing me anything."

Vita, you need to pray about this decision.

I could hear that cautioning voice in my head, but I pushed it aside. No time for prayers now, I told myself. He's right. If I miss this ship, it'll be another month or two before the next chance.

"Okay, I'll go with you one last time," I said decisively. "You're covering my ticket and meals for the trip. And you must promise: no intimate stuff, not in public, not in private. We attend, and then we're out of there."

"Deal!" he agreed, his grin spreading as wide and innocent as that of a shepherd boy from my village.

Thirty-Eight

An Audacious Answer

The day of the royal banquet arrived swiftly, and that evening, Decima summoned me into the dressing room where Julia, to my surprise, was already waiting. "We should begin," she announced, piercing the uneasy silence.

Seeing Julia for the first time in two months, my words stumbled out, "Julia, how... how've you been?"

"I'm good. Come on. It's a royal banquet and we can't afford to be late," Julia replied, a hint of urgency in her voice, perhaps masking deeper emotions.

I agreed and removed my servant's attire as she adorned me in a lustrous ginger yellow gown gathered both under the bust and around the waist. Though the slaves in Caius' household wore finer garments than many free plebeians in Rome, the delightful feeling of this exquisite silk caressing my skin still filled me with joy.

Sitting at the dressing table while Julia began styling my hair, an unexpected thought drifted through my mind.

This might be the last time you wear such a wonderful dress. Won't you regret it?

How come I never thought of it when I played Caius' fake mistress? Maybe it's because I was so preoccupied by the hope of reuniting with

Rufus.

Then another question followed as I picked up an ivory hairpin from the dressing table.

Now, everything has changed. Will it make a difference?

No, it doesn't matter. No matter what, I can't accept an intimate relationship outside marriage, not to say with a man who doesn't even understand my faith.

That's not going to happen.

The hairpin snapped in two as my grip involuntarily tightened.

Julia expertly braided silk laces into my hair and sprinkled gold dust over it. Then, she carefully selected a pair of delicate light-blue topaz earrings and a stunning pear-shaped amber necklace from among the jewelry pieces. "You look like all the goddesses combined, Vita; I'm sure Caius will lose his mind when he sees you," Julia said with a hint of jealousy mixed with sincerity. I was heartened to know she seemed to want the best for me now and had put her own wishes to be with Caius out of her mind. Until I departed, anyway.

I gently grasped Julia's hand and looked her in the eyes. "The ship is departing tomorrow at noon, I'll leave when I get back from the palace," I reassured her. "I'll be out of your way."

There was a time when such news might have pleased her. But now, her expression held a trace of uncertainty.

"And what if he won't let you go tomorrow?"

I smiled and gave her hand a comforting pat. "Don't worry, Julia. Caius may be a dandy, but he's a man of his word."

"I hope you won't let me down this time." Julia smiled bitterly.

Just as she had predicted, Caius' face lit up like a torch when he saw me. I felt his glance slip from my face to my amber-adorned neck, down to my feet which were elegantly adorned by a pair of gem-encrusted sandals. When the length of the stare became inappropriately long, he shut his eyelids briefly before finally finding the words, "Surely, I must be staring at a goddess living among men."

"We should head out now or we'll be late," I said, glancing downward to conceal the blush on my cheeks.

We climbed into Caius' carriage, setting off toward Palatine Hill.

Upon arriving at the palace, the banquet was still in the setup phase, with slaves bustling around in preparation. A handful of other guests had already arrived, each garbed in stunning and undoubtedly costly attire.

"Shall we stay here and mingle with these patricians or go explore the royal garden?" Caius asked me.

The idea of socializing with the haughty patrician women, likely among Caius' admirers, was far from appealing to me.

"I thought you might pick the garden. Follow me, you'll love it." He reached for my hand to lead me, but I quickly withdrew.

"No handholding," I protested.

"All right, as you wish." He released my hand and shrugged nonchalantly.

As we walked past a line of tall pines and fancy marble statues, the royal garden spread out before us like a scene from a dream. Bright colors and sweet scents from early blossoms of daffodils, roses and crocuses signaled the arrival of spring. Among the plants, three leopards roamed, held by a trainer's chains, their eyes shining with wild fierceness.

The vastness of the garden was impressive, yet it lacked the cozy, inviting charm that I so admired in Caius' own garden.

As we ambled along the arcade and rounded the corner, I spotted a cute little girl wearing a delicate white silk dress under a bay tree. She was jumping up and down, trying her best to reach a kite entangled in the branches overhead.

Her tiny arms reached out eagerly, beads of sweat glistening on her brow. With a warm smile, I gently handed the kite to her. "Here you go, you little cutie."

The girl grinned back and handed me some of the flowers she had been holding. "You are so beautiful, lady. Even more beautiful than my mom." Her dimpled beam was like that of an angel, melting my heart, and I thought of the little girl I had met on that rainy day at the tavern when I'd dreamed of having children with Rufus. I thought my heart would ache unbearably at the reminiscence, but to my surprise, it didn't hurt so much.

God, have you healed me before I even realized it?

"Can you play with me?" the little girl said, pulling at my sleeve. "Mom never plays with me. She's always busy. You seem really fun!"

"We'd better hurry, Vita. The banquet is about to begin," Caius urged.

"Just a little while. Please," I pleaded. Caius shook his head with an indulgent smile.

Crouching down to pick some flowers, I matched them together, weaving them into a small wreath and placing it on her little head.

"Thank you," she giggled, her eyes sparkling with delight. Reaching into a small, gem-studded pouch, she pulled out a miniature wooden horse and handed it to me. "This is for you, a gift."

"So sweet of you," I chirped back and put the wooden horse into my leather satchel.

"You like children?" Caius had sat down on a nearby bench and watched us having fun.

"Yes, they have pure and kind hearts."

"Well, if you ever think about having one, I'm more than willing to help," he said, wiggling his brows. "The emperor complains about how hard it is to improve the national birth rate. As good citizens, I think we need to contribute our share."

"I'm not even a citizen!" I tossed a flower at his head.

"I've found her!" a rough voice boomed from behind.

I turned and saw a dark-skinned woman with a full figure rushing toward the girl, quickly scooping her up. "You've scared me to death, my little lady."

In tow was a woman in splendid clothing flanked by two young slave boys who were holding peacock fans behind her. "Olivia, take the princess to her chamber. The banquet is about to start," she ordered angrily.

The nanny scooped up the little girl, who kicked and screamed as they left.

As the woman approached us, I couldn't help but notice her striking, large eyes and refined features. Her blonde hair, styled in an elaborate fashion reminiscent of Sabina's, was arranged even more intricately and was lavishly embellished with an array of jewelry.

"Caius, it is always a pleasure to see you." She smiled, revealing some fine wrinkles at the corners of her eyes.

"The pleasure is mine, my lady," Caius replied courteously.

It must be Poppaea, the empress. My body suddenly tensed up. "It's an honor to meet you, my lady," I said with a bow.

"I'm sure it is," she replied, giving me a brief, indifferent look.

Before Caius could say anything to ease the embarrassment, the sound of a flute began to drift from within the palace.

"We should all head inside to enjoy the banquet," Poppaea announced, then confidently walked off with her slave boys trailing behind. "Enjoy yourselves. I'll see you inside."

"The empress is surely not in a good mood today," I said when I was sure they were out of earshot.

Caius responded with a sly smirk, "Can't really blame her, can we? Especially when she's faced with someone ten times more beautiful than herself."

"She was angry because of you. Maybe I shouldn't have come. I can't afford to be making enemies the night before I leave Rome."

"Don't worry, Vita. I won't let anything happen to you."

The grand hall hosting the banquet was a dazzling sight, each of its twenty-four columns sheathed in shimmering gold foil. A semi-circle of twelve luxurious couches, their cushions intricately stitched with golden threads, encircled the central stage. Across the room, a magnificent fresco, its colors mixed with fine gold powder, spanned the wall, accentuating an extravagant double door. This doorway, framed in lustrous gold and embellished with detailed friezes, completed the room's aura of grandeur and opulence.

The fresco looked fantastic, depicting Olympian gods encircling a round-faced Pluto, the god of the underworld, with his large eyes, prominent chin, and curly, reddish hair.

"My stepfather mentioned that during Claudius' reign, the fresco featured Jupiter at its center. But Nero preferred Pluto, so he had artisans redo it," Caius remarked.

The floor was ankle-deep in rose petals and saffron, muffling the sound of our sandals. The pungent aroma of incense combined with the guests' perfumes made my nose tingle.

Even though it had only started a little while ago, the banquet was already in full swing. Musicians with all kinds of instruments performed, giving one thrill after another, and the guests were already dining on several delicacies I had never seen before.

Each table was filled with an array of dishes.

There were also two standby slaves, a boy holding an emerald tray with a golden bowl and a pinkish feather upon it and to his right, a girl with hair falling below her hips.

A man to the left of our table stirred his throat with the feather and vomited into the golden bowl, spilling some on the slave boy.

The girl quickly came and wiped his mouth and hands with her silky hair.

"Some guests want to taste all the dishes which are more than their stomach can hold, so they have to release themselves every now and then," Caius said. "And Nero prefers to offer silky hair as hand towels rather than Egyptian linens."

"You high-society folks are weird," I said, rolling my eyes in disgust as we settle down on a couch facing steps that led to a stage covered in rose petals.

The music abruptly shifted to a much livelier tune, prompting a burst of cheers from the crowd. Curious, I turned to see what was going on. A group of half-naked girls and boys dressed as nymphs and satyrs came into the hall, dancing provocatively in pairs to the rhythm.

As their performance got steamier, the cheers grew louder.

Why did I even agree to come here?

I sighed, remembering how quickly I'd made the decision.

Oh, Lord, I should've prayed to you before saying yes. Please have mercy and let this night pass quickly.

As the evening deepened, the sound of trumpets echoed from every corner of the room, prompting everyone to abruptly set down their wine goblets and rise to their feet. Caius tugged at my sleeve, urging me to stand alongside him. "Nero is arriving," he whispered. Alerted by his words, my focus sharpened, and I turned my gaze in the same direction as the others, anticipating Nero's entrance.

Nero and Poppaea made a grand entrance through the double doors, emerging amidst the effigies of all the Olympian gods. Nero strode confidently to the center stage, while Poppaea gracefully seated herself on a couch near us. The guests erupted into cheers on their arrival.

In that moment, I was struck by how Nero bore a striking resemblance to Zeus, depicted in the fresco behind him. He stood there for a moment with a grave expression, then raised his hand, signaling for silence. The audience immediately responded, falling into a hushed silence.

Gesturing to the musicians, they started playing a melody as Nero timed his words to match the tune, launching into a song about the story of Remus and Romulus, the founders of Rome. As he sang, his eyes sparkled and his lips curled into a poised smile, fully immersed in his performance.

The song wasn't bad, but I couldn't quite call it beautiful either.

As Nero's performance came to an end, the guests burst into cheers and applause, throwing flowers and exquisite jewelry onto the stage amid shouts and tears, with some nearly fainting from excitement. Nero soaked up all the compliments, his arms wide open and his face beaming with pride, grinning from ear to ear.

"My lord." Poppaea's voice was alluring. "You should give your subjects a chance to appreciate your talent personally."

"Excellent idea. Who should start first? How about you Seneca, my dear teacher?"

An old man with neatly groomed, gray hair and well-trimmed

beard stood up and said it was the most beautiful song he'd ever heard. Then several others joined him one by one in flattery, Nero's face glowing more at every praise.

Suddenly the empress said, "My lord, we have a new face here. Why don't you ask her opinion?" She pointed her jewelry-laden finger at me. "It seems to me that she didn't quite approve of your performance."

Nero's face darkened like a storm cloud, casting a shadow over the once jubilant atmosphere. He descended from the stage and loomed over me.

"So, what did you think of my performance?" he asked with a piercing tone.

"Of course, she relished it, my lord!" Caius jumped in before I could respond.

But Poppaea cut him off, her voice sharp as a sword. "Let her speak for herself, Caius. Remember, deceiving the emperor means immediate death."

My heart almost leapt into the golden cup in front of me, and my body trembled slightly under the weight of his gaze. I closed my eyes briefly, offering a fervent prayer for wisdom. *Lord, I know I probably shouldn't have come to this banquet, but please, have mercy on me.*

After a moment of reflection, I rose to my feet slowly and spoke with as much calm as I could muster. "Forgive me, my lord, but I must express that it was not good enough." A hush descended upon the room, and in that stillness, I was sure I heard Caius swallow.

"What did you say?" Nero barked as he drew a sword from one of his guards. "Did I hear you right?"

Despite the fear gripping me, I noticed a spark of opportunity in Nero's gaze, a man ever-thirsty for praise and admiration. Summoning all my courage, I addressed him, "My lord, if the gods have truly blessed you with greater gifts than any mere mortal, then surely your talent surpasses that of all the artists in Rome combined."

Slowly, Nero nodded in agreement, and I could feel the tension in the room dissipating.

"Therefore, I dare you to push yourself even harder and create a masterpiece that truly reflects your magnificent gifts."

Nero's eyes moistened as he listened intently to my words.

"You're absolutely right," he replied, and turned to address the room. "You have not seen the best of me yet. Just wait, and one day, you'll hear something so remarkable that you'll never forget it. It will go down in history."

The crowd erupted into a greater wave of applause and cheers.

Nero walked toward Poppaea's couch, giving me and Caius a wink.

"You have a sharp eye, girl. And so do you, my prefect." Caius tightened his grip on my wrist, but I didn't draw back.

Looking toward the empress, I saw she was casting lustful glances at Caius, seeming to not care about Nero at all. *The woman appears quite insane.*

Thirty-Nine

Orpheus and Eurydice

THE LAVISH BANQUET EXTENDED late into the night, with many guests drinking themselves into a stupor. The performances had long ended but the food and drinks still flowed in abundance.

Nero rose to his feet, gesturing for silence, and immediately, all eyes were upon him.

"I extend my deepest gratitude to each of you for joining this splendid evening," he announced. "It's been a night of joy for us all. Please continue to enjoy the generous offerings of food and wine." With these words, he withdrew through the golden door, tenderly holding the empress' hand.

After their departure, the guests kept on drinking and chatting with each other. As the night went on, their rowdy behavior got even worse because of the wine. A few revelers tumbled to the floor in laughter, while others engaged in wild and unrestrained dancing. One particularly daring guest impulsively kissed the toes of a nearby statue of goddess Diana, while another stumbled into a large pot of soup, soaking himself and those nearby.

"Let's leave," Caius whispered urgently, his grip firm on my hand as he quickly led me toward the guest passageway. Suddenly, our way was blocked by a slave woman who shared a notable similarity with Poppaea in appearance, but her eyes were softer, revealing a touch of underlying sorrow.

"Wait, Prefect," she implored, reaching out to gently grasp his arm, her voice trembling slightly. "The empress requests your presence at her private gathering."

"Step aside, Acte. I cannot leave Vita unattended," he asserted, attempting to ease Acte's hand off his arm. "Acte, everyone's talking about your health, saying you're too frail to even hold a cup of wine. Shouldn't you be resting in your quarters?" Caius added, impatiently.

"I am simply fulfilling my duties, Prefect," Acte responded with polite composure, her face betraying no emotion.

Before Caius could protest further, a muscular slave approached from behind. "Prefect! The empress insists on your immediate attendance."

"I can't leave her!" Caius snapped at the slave.

Acte leaned closer, her voice a hushed murmur, "The empress is not in good spirits today. We don't want to irritate her even more, or the situation will become dire. But rest assured, Prefect, I'll take good care of Vita in your absence."

I gave Caius' hand a gentle, reassuring squeeze and said, "You must go. Defying the empress in public would be a grave mistake. Trust me. I'll be fine."

Caius looked at me, his grip on my hands tightening even further.

"You have to go," I told him firmly, pushing his hand away. "Don't hesitate and get both of us killed." Understanding the seriousness of the situation, Caius reluctantly let go of my hand and began to follow the slave down the corridor. After a few paces, he paused and looked back at Acte. "Please, take good care of her!" he implored.

As Caius disappeared down the corridor, Acte turned to me with an apologetic expression. "There is something more," she said hesitantly. "The emperor has also summoned you. He wishes to see you in his private library."

I felt a momentary surge of apprehension at her words. The thought of a private audience with the emperor was daunting, yet I knew resistance could prove more dangerous.

Acte continued, her voice laced with regret. "I apologize for not revealing this earlier. I feared the prefect's reaction had he known. He might have refused to leave your side, causing more trouble for both of you."

I nodded, understanding her predicament. "It's all right, Acte. You did what you thought best in a difficult situation," I replied, trying to mask my own nervousness.

With a deep breath, I prepared myself for the encounter. Acte led the way to the emperor's library, her steps measured and solemn. As we walked, my mind raced with thoughts of what lay ahead, and I silently prayed for strength and wisdom to navigate the upcoming meeting.

Dear Lord, I'm sorry I didn't ask your opinion before I agreed to come here.

Forgive me and don't withdraw your grace from me. Please protect me and give me the wisdom to say things wisely when I meet the emperor.

We quickly reached a set of open double doors, flanked by two towering slaves. Acte departed in silence, leaving me to step forward alone. As I peered into the room, my attention was immediately drawn to the bookshelves lining the walls. Their elaborate carvings lent an air of majesty to the space. Above these shelves, an enchanting fresco depicting the three Muse goddesses took on a lifelike quality, illuminated by the soft glow from four swan-shaped lamps suspended from the ceiling.

Meanwhile, Nero was deeply engrossed in the shelves, fervently seeking out something.

Suddenly, he turned and caught sight of me. "Why don't you come in?" he said, gesturing for me to take a seat nearby as he held up a scroll. "This is my latest poem. Would you like to hear it?" His eyes conveyed a sense of longing.

I nodded and stepped onto the plush Persian rugs, feeling a knot form in my stomach as the door closed behind me. Taking a deep breath, I sat down beside him, now able to take a closer look at the most powerful man in the empire. It was clear he must have been quite handsome in his youth, but his fair complexion and protruding belly betrayed a lack of physical exercise. As he gazed at me, his eyes seemed slightly unfocused.

And so, the emperor began reciting his poem, painting a vivid picture of the glorious Roman city. As he concluded with a dramatic flourish, he fixed his gaze on me.

I felt my nerves mounting, not sure what to say to appease him when a soft whisper, barely audible, reached my ears. "Just speak the truth, my daughter."

A sense of calm washed over me. Silently, I replied to the voice in my heart, *Lord, I'll trust you this time. Please don't let me die.*

Thus, I respectfully requested that he recite each verse and line again, allowing us to meticulously examine them together. I pointed out the strengths in his work and offered suggestions for enhancement where needed.

As he listened, his eyes shone with an attentive gleam. It occurred to me that perhaps I was the first to provide him with such candid feedback.

Upon concluding our review, he burst out with enthusiasm, "Your insights are exceptional!" With newfound eagerness, he then retrieved another scroll and began to read aloud.

By the time he had finished reading from the scrolls, a look of weariness crossed his face. His gaze, distant and thoughtful, alternated between the Muses in the fresco and me. Then, unexpectedly, he leaned closer, gently taking my hands in his, and whispered softly, "You must be a messenger of the Muses."

"My lord, I'm just an ordinary person," I replied, my heart racing from his intense stare.

"No, you are more. Does your goddess know the sacrifices I made for her?" His voice cracked with emotion. "My mother, wife, brother. I killed them all and offered them to her."

His face lowered into my hands, his breath quivering. "Do you think the gods will forgive me? They must know I didn't do this for myself. I did it so mankind could be blessed with something incredible, a masterpiece, something that history will remember. They will, won't they?"

I was at a loss for words. I had heard rumors from Julia back at Eubulus' house but hearing it straight from the emperor left me utterly stunned.

Suddenly, Nero pulled me into his arms. "I won't let you go, Vita. I'll build a shrine for you in my palace, and you'll intercede for me with your goddess, day and night."

"No, I'm not a messenger of the Muses," I mumbled, trying to break free from his embrace. "Oh, Jesus, Son of God, help me!" I cried out in desperation.

Suddenly, the door burst open with a resounding bang. Caius stumbled into the library's entrance, his eyes visibly red. His hands clenched into unsteady fists as he swayed, struggling to maintain his balance.

"My lord, it's getting late. Please allow me to take my girl home. She becomes irritable when she's tired, and I fear she might start saying things that could displease you."

A vein throbbed at the side of Nero's head. "Guards! Remove this fool!" he roared. "How dare you barge in?"

The guards rushed in, seizing Caius. As I witnessed this, a chill ran through me, and I felt my blood turn ice-cold with fear.

Lord, please help me! I prayed desperately in my heart before I chose my words, "My lord, does this scene remind you of anything?"

"What do you mean?" Nero looked at me, anger blazing in his eyes.

"Orpheus," I said. "How he journeyed into the depths of the underworld to save his beloved wife."

"Are you comparing me to Hades, lord of the underworld?" His eyes narrowed.

"Yes, my lord. Just as the mighty Hades ruled the underworld without question, you rule our magnificent empire."

To my immense relief, Nero's expression softened.

"I appreciate this comparison." Nero laughed, his demeanor resembling that of a little boy being playfully teased.

"You are full of surprises, Vita. I shall compose a song about this."

"I'd be delighted to hear it when it's finished." I stood and bowed. "I am honored."

"I have greatly enjoyed your company, Vita," he told me, then turned back to Caius with a grin. "Take her and leave quickly. But remember, don't look back, or she forever belongs to me."

Understanding the urgency, I swiftly winked at Nero, acknowledging the clever reference, and immediately grabbed Caius' hand, hurrying him out of the room. We dashed down the corridor, racing against time for our lives.

Forty

Temptation Draws Near

I sank my body into the soft cushion piles in the carriage, secretly thanking the pounding hoofs of the carriage horses for drowning my wild heartbeat. The smell of the cinnamon and jasmine which Caius' slaves sprayed filled my nostrils. My hands had already let go of his when we were out of the palace, but he grabbed mine when he helped me into the carriage. He still held onto them, and I felt I should break them free, but since we'd just been through such a great threat of death, I felt no grounds to do so.

"That Orpheus and Eurydice story was a marvelous idea," Caius said, seemingly sobered up by the late-night chill. "You are such a quick-witted girl."

"I'm just grateful we had enough time to cover the fourth book in Vigil's *Georgics*. That one was my favorite story in the fourth book," I replied.

"The story is indeed beautiful. When a man truly loves a woman, he fears nothing, not even death itself."

"You're right. It is a very touching story," I said. As I spoke, a sudden inspiration washed over me, a feeling almost like a divine whisper guiding my thoughts. "Caius, a man may have the courage to face death when he is in love; however, finally, death swallows him as well as his beloved. There is one person whose love can conquer death."

"Who is that person?" Caius asked.

"Jesus," I replied, the darkness masking the excitement on my face.

Caius put his arms around me and pressed his face toward mine. "You're always talking about this Jesus. I'm a little jealous."

"Ew, back off, your breath is terrible!" I exclaimed, playfully pushing him away.

"Yours isn't any better! And your hair looks like a wild bird's nest," he retorted.

"And your beard stubble is as patchy as a poorly plucked chicken," I shot back.

Our teasing abruptly ceased as the mood turned solemn.

Caius sighed, his expression somber. "I'm sorry. I shouldn't have barged into Nero's library like that. It was reckless and could have endangered us both," he admitted. "But hearing that he'd summoned you alone... I just lost it. The thought of him possibly taking advantage of you... I couldn't stand it."

Hearing his words, a surge of warmth grew from the bottom of my heart. "Don't feel sorry, Caius. I couldn't believe you would risk your life to come to my side. It... it really means a lot to me," I said softly, thanking the darkness which hid my blushed face.

"You don't know how much you mean to *me*, Vita." He looked at me, his gaze so intense, and his grip tightened on my wrist. "If Nero dared to touch you, I'd kill him even if it means I end up in the arena."

"Nero is a strange man. If you hadn't told me he had murdered his mother and wife, I'd almost believe he is just a crazy person too much devoted to art."

"He can be quite unpredictable and dangerous. It must be your god who is protecting us," he said seriously. I knew he didn't believe in my god, but I was still happy to hear him say things like that. *Oh, God. Have you planted seeds of faith in his heart?*

When I noticed his persistent gaze, I felt the need to shift the topic. Gently nudging him, I said, "Hey, enough about me. What happened in the empress' chamber?"

Caius chuckled. "Is someone feeling jealous?"

"Absolutely not. Merely curious, that is all."

"Well, she and her patrician matron companions kept offering me wine, trying to get me drunk, while the guards blocked the door. However, my concern for you overshadowed everything, so I didn't even take a single sip."

"I thought she would have eaten you with the way she kept looking at you."

"So, you noticed her looking at me?"

"I was only worried about you."

"Oh, such concern from a disinterested person."

"You flatter yourself."

We both shared a laugh, but my heart suddenly grew heavy at the thought of the approaching ship I would soon board to take me to Cyprus. In that instant, I was certain of my feelings. I had become deeply drawn to this man and didn't want to leave him.

Oh, God, no. Don't tempt me like this. I want so badly to believe it is your will. But how could you want me to stay with a man who only wants me as his concubine?

The light-hearted banter of our conversation gradually faded into an uneasy silence as we journeyed back home. Upon our arrival, we were met at the villa's gate by a gathering of our servants and slaves, Theophilus among them. When they saw our carriage, their worried looks changed into ones of joy and relief. "Oh, master. We have been deeply concerned," Decima said with a choked throat. "We feared the worst and prayed to all the gods of Rome—"

"What happened, Caius?" Theophilus asked. "I was waiting here at the palace gate when I overheard some slaves coming out gossiping that Vita had offended Nero by critiquing his song. I cannot believe it. If that were true, I doubt you would have returned unscathed."

"You'll be surprised in that case. And yes, the story is true. I'll share the details later. We are really tired now, so please prepare the baths for us," Caius said.

"I have no time for the bath. The ship for Cyprus should depart this afternoon, and I must get ready for it." I rushed off to my quarters to collect my belongings before I lost all courage to do so.

In my room, I tried to concentrate on gathering my things, but every item seemed to bring back a memory of being with Caius. The silk pouch he had gifted me at the market, the parchments on which he had patiently taught me to write and the saffron sachet he had given me to adorn myself with at the banquet.

My heart continued to ache as a knock on the door interrupted my thoughts.

It was Julia. Glancing around and noticing no other girls around, she took a seat on a stool opposite me. "There's no need to rush," she said. "The ship left earlier this morning."

"What?" I gasped in disbelief.

"Theophilus went to the harbor and discovered that the ship had set sail half a day early," she explained, her voice icy. "Are you satisfied now?"

I was irritated by the swift return of her unpleasant attitude and said, "Julia, it is not my fault. I didn't expect it either."

"Oh, really? Then why did you go to the banquet with him? If you had stayed home, you would have been on the ship miles away from Rome right now," she pressed harshly.

"Because I needed the money to pay for the ticket. I haven't saved enough in a few days."

"Or because you never wanted to leave." She gave a mocking smile and left the room.

"There's no way it's true…" I was on the verge of tears, partly due to my best friend's attitude, and partly because I harbored a nagging suspicion that she might be right.

At that precise moment, Caius entered the room, donning a pristine tunic adorned with intricate silver-thread embroidery and infused with the alluring aroma of sandalwood.

His hair, still damp from the bath, framed his face.

Caius approached and settled down beside me, his presence

enveloping me.

He extended his hand to grasp mine, and though I longed to pull away, I was unable to resist. The warmth of his body and the intoxicating scent he bore slowly eroded my defenses. My weapon, it seemed, was lost.

"Vita," he whispered tenderly, "the ship has already departed. I'm truly sorry. Yet, I must confess that a part of me is glad, for it means you cannot leave me now."

"I'll wait for the next available ship," I replied, avoiding his gaze.

"Vita, must it be this way between us?" He tightened his grip on my hand and placed his other hand on my shoulder. "I can sense you have feelings for me, and you'd be a fool not to recognize my sincerity."

Seeing my silence, he continued, "After you left me last time, I realized I might be wrong. Perhaps I seemed like a predatory master, causing you pain. I apologize, Vita, and I'm also sorry for bringing you here against your will. You deserve to be treated with respect."

The earnestness in his eyes further softened my resolve, and I nearly surrendered to the urge to embrace him.

Before I could say anything, he continued, "I have changed, Vita. This time, I decided to ask you to stay with me, not as your master, but as your lover. I have thought about this carefully. You are the girl I want to spend my life with. You, and only you."

"No, please stop," I cried out. *Oh, Lord Jesus. Don't test me like this. I don't want to break your law, but this temptation is overwhelming for me.*

"Vita, please allow me to finish," he implored. "I understand your concerns. I've led a reckless life, with numerous mistresses. However, I've made a decision to change, for you, eternally. You will be the sole woman in my life, the keeper of my heart. May all the Olympian gods and your God punish me if I ever break this vow." He punctuated his words with a raised hand, a solemn gesture of commitment.

"I... I can't," I choked out between sobs. "I'm sorry, Caius, I just can't."

"What can't you do, Vita?"

"I cannot be your mistress."

"Are you worried about no security for your future? Sorry, I should have thought about that, Vita. Although I vowed, it is not enough for you to trust a man like me will be faithful to you. Don't worry, Vita, I'll give you added assurance."

"That's not what I meant."

I felt the strength of resisting him evaporate every time I heard his words.

"We'll go to the council tomorrow and transfer half of my property under your name. If I leave you, you will end up the wealthiest woman in Rome, except the empress, maybe. But you know I'll never do that."

To say I was not tempted by this offer would be a lie. His sincerity really touched me. I felt guilty for even contemplating asking for more or something different.

But I had no choice.

"Caius, wealth security is not something I worry about." I gathered up my courage and said, "I can't be your mistress because my faith forbids it."

Caius' eyes sparked with anger and confusion.

"He forbids what? Man and woman having the pleasure they both crave? Oh, I heard a rumor that he never had any women, so he probably never tasted the pleasure before. But why did he create it in the first place if your god is really the creator of mankind he claims to be?"

"Don't you dare talk about my God like this!" I felt anger rising like steam. "He is kind and just and he has good reasons for all his laws."

"Vita, you are a fake. Do you dare to look into my eyes and tell me you never had that kind of desire toward me?" he sneered.

The anger grew stronger, not only toward him, but also toward myself as I'd almost lost my ground. I locked eyes with him, my tone unwavering. "No, I can't do that, and I won't pretend I've never felt such desires. That would be ridiculous. Yes, I feel them, every inch of my skin tingles with it, day and night, even in my dreams. And I've never claimed otherwise."

Shock briefly crossed his eyes, mingled with a hint of elation.

I pressed on, resolute, "I'm not going to deny those desires, but I won't let them control me. Jesus has set me free, and I won't be a slave to anything, not even my own desires. I'll never be intimate with anyone who isn't my husband."

"Marriage?" he bellowed. "And you're just going to throw away what we have for some stupid certificate? You're an idiot, Vita. If a man and a woman are in love, it makes no difference if they are married or not."

"If it matters to my God, then it matters to me." I stepped closer to him and stared into his eyes. "If you claim you love me, try to understand it or respect my belief at least!"

He paused for a long time and sighed. "Vita, I don't really understand your faith though I do respect it; I am disappointed if you think I do not as I believe I've shown otherwise. But making future plans is important, so I'll wait for you until midnight. Let me know what your final decision is," he said before he walked out of the room, closing the door slowly behind him.

I looked toward the door as he left, and tears streamed down my cheeks. I buried my face in my pillow and wept loudly. With my eyes glassy, I prayed again.

"Oh, Heavenly Father, you know my heart. You know I've come to love Caius deeply. I admit I've wanted badly to be his mistress, even if it's only for a day. He's broken down my defenses, making me feel as I have never felt before, like no man has made me feel before... I'm afraid I'll never fall in love again if I leave him."

I wept for an extended period before a thought began to take shape.

"If I remain here as his mistress, it could grant me more time to share Your word, God. He might even embrace our faith." The idea didn't bring me peace as I expected, but it was too alluring to give up, so I continued, "Lord, I don't know what to do; I need your guidance; if this is a bad idea, show me a clear sign and I will turn away completely. Please be quick, Lord. If you don't show me a sign, I might have no other option."

As soon as I concluded my prayer, a commotion erupted from the atrium, the sound of slaves scampering and exclaiming, "Oh, Juno! That monstrous Tigellinus has arrived!"

Moments later, Caius' voice rang out, strained and furious.

"Tigellinus, you have no right to do this! If you seek vengeance, direct it at me. It's disgraceful for you to target a woman."

Tigellinus! The name sent shivers down my spine. Had he come to cause trouble? I pondered on it as I hurried toward the atrium.

Upon arriving, I saw Caius standing defiantly before a group of soldiers, their leader donning praetorian armor. He was roughly half a head shorter than Caius, but significantly more robust. His eyes, with their sharp, triangular slant, gave him a calculating and sinister look.

Extending his arm, he unfurled a scroll and declared in an authoritative tone, "I am here to execute the empress' command. Vita stands accused of witchcraft and must be escorted to the palace without delay. Anyone who dares obstruct this order shall be met with immediate execution."

Forty-One

A Plan to Escape

Caius' face darkened when he saw me. "Go to your room, Vita. This matter does not concern you," he thundered as he tried to push me away. But Tigellinus interrupted him.

"There is no use for that. This is the empress' order. We must take her today."

"Take me? What did I do that you have to take me?" I asked incredulously.

"This is ridiculous. A charge for placing a curse on the princess? How is this possible? Wasn't she under the protection of the divine power of the emperor?" Caius bellowed.

"You dare call the empress a fool?" Tigellinus snapped back. "I will advise you to take good rein on your words; they could ride you to the dungeon on the empress' command. And I will only be carrying out my duty."

"The emperor should be able to prove her innocence. He only made the acquaintance of Vita just last night," Caius said, tightening his grip on my hand.

"The emperor is on his way to the temple of Salus for the sake of his daughter. And he left his royal signet ring to the empress so she could assign orders when he is absent." Tigellinus' slanted eyes flickered with wicked glee.

"This is a trap! We all know that woman detests Vita," Caius said as he plunged himself between me and Tigellinus. "Nobody can take her away except over my dead body!"

"How dare you, Caius!" Tigellinus shouted, taking a menacing step toward us; multiple swords were pulled from their sheaths with metallic clanks.

"If it weren't for the fact that you are a prefect, I would have had you in captivity and bound to the dungeon. Make one more foolish statement about the empress, and I will surely have you thrown in there with the rats, and once again, will only be carrying out my duty. You understand me? Do you heed what I say?"

I looked at Caius; his eyes were red, the veins on his temple protruding. Quietly, he nodded but his look was that of a man affording deep thought to the quandary.

A sudden sadness arose in my heart. *Oh Lord, I know it is your will that I leave him. I just never expected it would be in such a dramatic way.*

"Prefect Tigellinus." I stepped out from behind Caius' back and engaged in a direct, unblinking stare with Tigellinus. "I will go with you. However, could you please grant me a moment to speak with Caius?"

"Nonsense! Who do you think you are to bargain with me?"

"Tigellinus, you know Caius' capabilities and what he would do in a rage. I don't want any of your soldiers to be injured today."

"No, Vita. You can't." Caius tried to stop me, but I spoke with my sternest voice.

"Enough! If you want to die, that's your choice. *I* don't want to die before my trial."

"This young lady seems to have more sense than you," Tigellinus chuckled darkly. "If either of you attempts anything, I've been instructed to execute you both on the spot."

Taking that as permission, I cast a look at Caius. To my astonishment, he didn't voice any objection this time; instead, he nodded and took my hand, leading me toward his bedchamber.

"No, let's go to my room," I said, leading him to the slave quarters.

Once inside my room, Caius asserted, "You're right, Vita. We need a place to strategize. I have thirty sturdy slaves in my villa who could buy us some time against Tigellinus.

"I'll send Theophilus to the barracks to fetch my most trusted men. There are fifteen elite fighters who swore to give their lives for me whenever the need arises. If we can buy enough time before Nero returns, he will declare you innocent."

"No, Caius. Defying the royal order with force is treason. It could mean destruction for your whole household and men in your barracks. Who knows what they'll do to them?"

He fell silent.

"But I can't just stand back and let them take you," he said, holding onto my hands tightly. "I promised to protect you before we went to that banquet."

"Caius, please, hear me out! Trust what I'm about to say," I pleaded, looking straight into his eyes. "I won't let them take me to the palace. I had a dream, and in my dream my God showed me an escape plan. Once I'm safe, I'll send you a message. But don't even think about looking for me until I give you the signal. You have to trust me on this, or it's all going to fall apart."

A prolonged hush settled over the room, during which I could hear his heartbeat. "I suppose I have to trust you and your god," he finally conceded.

"Yes, because you don't have any other choice."

"What's the plan?"

"Our people, the Christians, have a unique signal. When we're in danger, we release the signal, and angels will come to our aid."

"A signal?" He looked at me, disbelief in his eyes.

"Yes. That's why I need your help. Go to a nearby high place, kneel, say the prayer three times, 'Holy Jesus, Lamb of God, save your daughter Vita,' and shoot an arrow into the sky. My guardian angels will come to my aid." I knew lies like this wouldn't usually deceive

Caius. I just hoped that his desperation would cloud his judgment.

"Don't fool me, Vita." He stared at me intensely. "If you die, I'll take revenge on anyone who I deem to have hurt you, no matter what it costs me."

"No, I won't die." I pulled out one hand from his grip and stroked his face gently. His body quivered at my touch. "I know you are a man of your word. Wait a moment, I have something for you." I retrieved a leaf-woven belt from under my pillow. "I've been working on this for weeks," I confessed, a sad smile on my face as I watched him examine the belt closely. "I realize it might be embarrassing for a man of your stature to be seen wearing this around town, but if you promise to keep it and not do anything reckless, I'll return after six months. My god revealed to me that this is the duration of my exile."

Six months should be long enough for him to move on.

"I'll wear this for the rest of my life," Caius declared. "Life is unbearable without you by my side. At least I have something to hold onto. Besides, if you never come back, I'll have the dogs in my barracks sniff it and track you down to the ends of the Earth."

His teasing tone wavered beneath a trembling voice.

"I bet you will." I forced a smile and guided him toward the back door. "Now go, as fast as you can. My life depends on it."

He looked at me, hesitated, then released my hand and left the room.

As I watched him disappear, tears welled up. "I'm sorry, Caius. I lied to you. This is the last time we'll see each other. May my God be with you and protect you in the future." I wiped away my tears and headed to Julia's room down the hallway.

Julia was pacing anxiously when I arrived.

"Vita, what happened? I heard the slaves talking, but no one told me what's going on."

"There's no time to explain, Julia. Do you remember Marcus, the storyteller we met at the market? He told us where he lived, and you said you knew the place."

"Yes, the insulae at the corner of Cupid and Venus Street. Top floor, far right. I remember that part," Julia replied, looking puzzled.

"Great! Go to his place. Tell him Vita, the 'fish girl', needs his help. I will be held captive by a praetorian squad en route to the palace."

"But—"

"No buts. Go! Have Felix at the stables give you one of Caius' fastest horses, and make sure to tell him to keep this a secret. He will do it, because he's my friend."

"Go!" I urged Julia once more, her bewilderment evident as I directed her toward the door.

Julia turned, grasping my hand, tears choking her voice. "Vita, I blamed you for not leaving Caius, but please don't hate me. I'm still your friend. Stay safe, all right?"

"I will." I embraced her tightly. "Farewell, my sister. And this time, I won't come back." I emphasized the last words. Perhaps she could provide some solace to Caius during the difficult time after I left.

With those parting words, I made my way toward the atrium where Tigellinus and his guards awaited.

Forty-Two
To the Rescue

Shrouded in complete darkness, the carriage crept forward, much like the previous night. However, gone were the soothing scents of cinnamon and jasmine, as well as the comforting touch of the silky cushions. Instead, there was only a hard wooden bench and the musty odor of despair. The rhythmic clatter of hooves and the sound of foot soldiers' boots striking the ground served as a relentless reminder that this was not a dream.

To my surprise, they hadn't even bothered to bind my hands. Perhaps they were overly confident in their numbers, dismissing any concern about my odds of escape. Truth be told, I wasn't particularly confident in my chances either.

However, I held onto faith that Julia would successfully deliver my message. After all, even in death, I would forever occupy a cherished place in Caius' heart, unmatched by any other woman. But if I were to escape, he might feel betrayed and eventually move on, leaving an opportunity for Julia to win his heart.

But could Marcus truly find a way to rescue me from the clutches of so many praetorian guards? The more I contemplated it, the more fear began to creep in.

My hands unconsciously held tightly onto the satchel on my waist, the one Caius had given to me to hold my parchments, pen and ink, and the only thing I'd brought out from his villa.

For the second time.

"Oh, Lord. I'm worried. I wish I could be calmer in the face of the turmoil, but I can't. I want to live, not die. If I perish, I can't imagine what crazy things Caius will do. His entire household could be destroyed, including Julia. Please give Marcus and his friends wisdom to figure out a way. And please protect them from any harm," I prayed fervently in the darkness.

The iron-barred carriage had no openings on its walls, leaving me unable to discern our location. However, after a while, the surface beneath us grew rougher, and the pungent odor of urine permeated the air. I could tell we were in an impoverished neighborhood.

Suddenly, a deafening commotion erupted, and something slammed onto the carriage roof with tremendous force, causing the vehicle to shake violently. Simultaneously, the clamor of heavy objects crashing to the ground mixed with the frantic shouts of the guards and the distressed neighs of the horses.

"Bees! Bees!" The voices were contorted with pain.

"Hold on!" Tigellinus yelled, his words abruptly cut short by his own agonized cry.

Soon, amidst the chaos, the carriage toppled over, its door swinging open. I tumbled out, landing on the ground with a resounding thud. A sharp, intense pain shot through my side. My head spun and rang as I struggled to stay upright, and the scene before me left me speechless.

Swarms of bees descended upon both the men and the horses. Crushed bee nests were strewn across the ground, some trampled under the hooves of the horses.

"It must be Marcus." I leaped to my feet and, scanning my surroundings, spotted a shadowy silhouette gesturing from around the corner. I bolted toward him, and he grabbed my hand in the thick of the commotion. "There is no time to talk, Vita," he said in haste. "Let's get out of here."

Even in the darkness, Marcus' voice resonated with my memories.

We sprinted through the winding lanes, summoning every bit of strength we possessed. Even though we had put considerable distance between us and the soldiers, our breaths still came in ragged gasps. We couldn't afford to halt or slow down.

Rome at night was a world apart from the village of my upbringing. I stumbled upon drunkards three times along our path, while malevolent eyes followed our steps from the shadows of the dimly lit lanes.

Soon, we reached the bank of the Tiber River, where the water shimmered under the moonlight, casting a tranquil glow, and an enormous bridge stretched before us. On the bridge stood a shadowy figure, a soldier clad in full armor.

"What are we going to do? He is going to question us. How can we explain our presence at this hour?" I asked, feeling sweat on my palms.

"Don't worry, Vita. He is one of us," Marcus said, beaming with pride.

Taking my hand, he led me toward the bridge, and as we passed the soldier, Marcus drew a cross in the air. The soldier's eyes widened as he recognized Marcus.

"Peace be with you, dear brother Marcus," he said, waving to us. "I really enjoyed your stories, by the way."

"Thanks. Peace be with you too." Marcus waved back and guided me across the bridge.

The other side of the river was quite different. Vast, undeveloped land stretched out, only a few residential areas dotting the landscape. We walked across the open terrain for about half an hour before arriving at a small hut. "Thank God. We're safe now," Marcus finally announced. In the darkness, I could still see his broad smile. It had been a long journey, and nerves kept us mostly silent along the way.

Marcus knocked on the door—three times forcefully followed by three gentler ones. Soon, an elderly woman, holding a lamp, opened the door. Her hair was half gray, her face deeply etched with wrinkles, but her smile was the most comforting sight I had ever seen.

Forty-Three

The Fisherman's Wife

"Come on in, my dear children," the woman said, shielding the lamp with her hand to protect it from the wind. "I was about to go to bed tonight and the Lord showed me in a vision that there would be guests today. So, I stayed up and waited. Well, let's say my wait was not in vain. Oh, how pleasant it is to have company!"

"Vita, this is Elaina, Peter's wife," said Marcus. "And this is Vita, whom I just saved from the praetorians. I don't even know the full story yet. But you have enough time to tell Elaina in the following days."

"Thanks, dear Marcus. And there is no need to rush, Vita. We can hear your story later. I'll go get you something to drink," Elaina said in a maternal manner, leading us into the room before she disappeared through another door.

"Sorry, Vita, I must leave now," Marcus said with a worried look. "I've left my son with my neighbor. Can't be away for too long."

Recalling that Marcus had mentioned his son's seizures, I was deeply moved by the fact that he had come to my rescue late at night, leaving his son behind.

"Oh, Marcus. How can I ever thank you?"

"No, don't say that, Vita. I'm only glad you remembered me in times of trouble. The money you gave me helped me greatly. I even used it to pay a physician who helped immensely in keeping my son's seizures under control. Because of that, I felt comfortable leaving him with a neighbor and coming to help you tonight. Otherwise, I wouldn't have been able to take the risk."

Elaina returned and joined our conversation. "That's why we say, 'In all things, God is at work for the good of those who love Him'," she said with a loaf of bread and a rough pottery cup in her hands. "Come here, Vita. Sit down and eat something."

Breaking off a piece of bread, she handed half to me and another half to Marcus. "I know you are eager to go home. Take this with you for your son."

Marcus thanked her and put the bread inside his cloak before walking toward the door. With one foot stepping out, he turned, and his gaze lingered on me. "Have a good night, Vita. It is so good to see you again." With that, he vanished into the darkness.

I sat down at a table and savored the bread, each bite tasting heavenly. I was ravenous, having had no time to eat since returning from Nero's palace, so the food was a warmly welcomed respite, along with Elaina's companionship.

Elaina sat next to me, watching me devouring the bread. "You are really hungry, child," she said with a smile.

The tone, the gesture, and even the wrinkles on her face, everything reminded me of dear Nana. When I was a little girl, every time I came back home after playing with other kids, Nana would bring me a piece of bread and watch me eat it with a smile on her face as if she was deeply delighted and content to have me around to feed.

I had never met this elderly lady before, but her resemblance to Nana had a soothing effect on my frayed nerves. I could feel every muscle in my body gradually relaxing as a surge of warmth washed over me, reminiscent of sitting by the charcoal basin on a winter night in our hut in Cyprus.

"Home" was the foremost word that sprang to mind, even more

so than the time it had occurred to me when I considered returning to Caius' villa, the time when Julia had interrogated me. Yes, now I found myself in the middle of nowhere with a stranger, and yet, I'd never felt more at home since leaving Cyprus.

It was a peculiar sensation after so many months of wandering.

"Poor child. You must have been through a lot," Elaina said, gently stroking my hair, just as Nana used to do when she was alive.

All the emotional turmoil suddenly surged within me, and I threw myself into her arms, sobbing uncontrollably.

"There, there," she murmured, tenderly massaging my back. "It's all good. You are God's beloved daughter, so he brought you to me. You can stay here for as long as you wish; this is your home."

Her words melted me, affirming what I had already sensed. I rested my head on her lap and cried tears of joy while she continued to stroke my hair. I felt truly blessed.

Lord, I thank you for keeping me safe, for giving me refuge and safe harbor, and for sending me to Elaina. You are gracious and merciful, my ever-loving God.

Much later, I retired to the small room kindly provided by Elaina and settled onto a humble bed. It was nothing like Caius' magnificent bedchamber, of course, with an interior even simpler than the slave quarters in his villa. However, everything about it felt so comforting—the scent of the straw woven pillow, the rough yet clean wool sheets, the semicircular table strategically placed against the wall to save space, and the small wooden cross hanging on the wall. They all brought peace to my heart. Being in the company of people who shared my faith filled me with joy, as if I had discovered a sense of belonging and comfort with a family I never knew existed.

Family. My thoughts went to Rufus.

The feeling of bitterness threatened to overwhelm me again. How naive I was to think I'd already got over this!

"God, please teach me how to forgive. I once judged Caius for not forgiving his mother. How simple-minded I was! Naive, a word even Julia uses to describe me.

"Now I have tasted the pain of betrayal from someone so dear to me. Please help me, Lord. Don't let bitterness take hold of my heart. Please show me your light and your way."

As I considered how Caius would react upon learning of my escape, his amber-colored eyes, chestnut-colored hair, and well-defined jawline all filled my thoughts.

What is he doing right now? Tigellinus is probably searching for me in Caius' villa, going stir-crazy. I hope he will be wise enough not to defy the imperial order.

"God, I thought leaving Caius would be difficult, but now I'm fine. I miss him, but I know my decision is right. Thank you, once again, for showing me your way," I prayed softly. "Also, please grant healing to the little princess and help her recover from her illness."

I soon dozed off. In my subconsciousness, a beautiful little girl appeared before me, adorned in a radiant, white tunic. She was jumping and giggling in a garden with flowers of such beauty and fragrance that I struggled to recall ever encountering such a captivating spectacle.

"Who is this little girl?" I pondered.

Suddenly, the girl's face became clear, revealing her as Nero's daughter. Upon spotting me, she waved, filling the air with her cheerful giggles.

I approached and embraced her happily. "Are you feeling better, little princess? I was concerned about you."

"I feel no pain anymore." She smiled.

Suddenly, I noticed a glow beneath her white tunic. Peering closer, I discerned a diamond-shaped mark on her back, visible through the semi-transparent fabric. *Is that a birthmark? Where do these bright beams come from?* I pondered as I slipped into a deep and restful sleep.

Forty-Four
Little Achilles

As I lay half-dozing, my senses gradually awakening, I felt a delicate, feathery hand brush against my cheek.

Little princess?

I opened my eyes, only to be surprised by the sight of a young boy standing beside my bed. He appeared to be about five or six years old, with rosy cheeks, tousled hair, and dimples deepening as he grinned at me.

"You are so beautiful, Miss Vita, just as my father told me," he said in a sweet, innocent voice, with a touch of childlike wonder.

Before I could respond, Marcus burst into the room, his tone stern. "Get out of there, you silly head. Who told you to bother Miss Vita?" He rushed over to the boy, grabbing his cloak from behind.

Upon seeing me awake, Marcus lowered his gaze to the ground. "I'm sorry, Vita. My son snuck in when I wasn't looking. Let me take him out of here." He started to drag the boy toward the door.

But the little boy protested, tears welling up. "No, leave me alone! I want to stay with Miss Vita!" Breaking free, he cried and ran to the other side of the room.

"It is all well, Marcus. He can stay. I was about to get up anyway," I interjected, stopping Marcus in his tracks. With a shrug, Marcus raised his hands in surrender, grinned, and left the room.

The boy rushed back to me, a smile spreading across his face, making him snort with joy. "Miss Vita, you're the best!" he exclaimed, reaching out his little hands to hug me.

"What's your name?" I asked.

"Achilles! My mom gave me that name, hoping I'd be a great warrior someday," he declared proudly. "But I no longer remember what she looks like," he added, lowering his head.

My heart ached as I gazed upon the boy's sorrowful visage. Rising from the bed, I draped a shawl around my shoulders and gently grasped Achilles' hand before leading him to the living room. Elaina and Marcus were sitting at the table, eating porridge and bread. Marcus' face brightened when he saw me and his son.

"I hope this little rascal didn't bother you too much, Vita," he said.

"No, don't say that. He's a sweet boy. I enjoy his company." I sat beside Elaina, and Achilles swiftly climbed onto my lap, leaning his little head against my chest.

"Miss Vita is my best friend in the whole wide world!" he proclaimed.

Laughter filled the room as Elaina playfully clapped her hands and exclaimed, "Oh dear! What about me? Silly me. I thought *I* would be your best friend."

The boy just stared at her with wondrous eyes as if deeply thinking through how to extricate himself from this awkwardness. As only a young child could reason, he came up with a swift answer. "Don't worry. You're *both* my best friends." Then suddenly, he yelled as if by way of a distraction, "Look what I found in your parcel, Miss Vita!"

"Achilles! Who told you to rummage through other people's belongings without permission?" Marcus roared at his son. "Put it back right now!"

"I'm sorry," Achilles said, placing a wooden horse in my hand. "Sorry, Miss Vita, here! You keep it." Then I realized it was the gift I had received from the little princess.

"Well, you can play with it for a while. But it was a gift from a friend. So, you must take care of it and give it back later," I said ruffling his soft curly hair. "Now go play outside."

"Thanks, Miss Vita." Achilles planted a kiss on my hand before slipping down from my lap and rushing out of the door.

Elaina filled a bowl with hot porridge and handed it to me. "Last night had too much going on. I guess you and Marcus must have a lot to catch up on. I need to take some bread to the widows we took in a few days ago, so please make yourselves at home." Picking up the basket of bread on the table, she left the room.

"I'd love to hear about the bees' nests, Marcus. How did you do that? That was genius. Never in a million years could I have imagined you'd be able to summon a bee swarm."

"Ah, you see, *I* didn't. It was all God's providence. When your friend came to tell me that you had been arrested, I was devastated. But there was a brother living on Vulcan Street." Marcus took a bite of the bread and continued, "He always mentioned that soldiers made use of that path to the palace every time as it was faster than most routes."

Marcus smiled broadly. "And would you believe it? He happens to be a beekeeper. So, you can guess the rest."

I was taken aback by the coincidence. Filled with curiosity, I asked, "I had no idea one could keep bees in such a small place."

"Yes, it's extremely hard, but he designed a kind of beehive that could be hung on the walls. Somehow, it worked, which brought him a good extra income. At the same time, it helped keep robbers away."

Marcus and I both laughed.

Then he said, "Most interestingly, the bees he keeps are a unique nocturnal species, because living in such places, you don't want to scare your neighbors with all the buzzing creatures during the day."

He paused to eat a spoonful of porridge and continued, "I went there and told him everything. He agreed to help immediately. So, we knelt on the balcony; it was a perfect spot, so we prayed briefly and waited patiently. When we heard the hooves of the Praetorian

Guard, our hearts pounded, and we almost lost our nerve. I mean, what if it failed, and we got caught or killed? But then, as the noise grew louder, a surge of determination overcame our fear, and on the count of three, we hurled the beehives down onto the street below."

"Wow. Thank you for going to such lengths for me," I said, overwhelmed with emotion. "And I owe your friend my life too. Those beehives must have cost him a fortune, and after last night, he may not be able to stay at his old place anymore. I want to thank him in person and compensate him."

"No worries, Vita. He was glad that he could help a Christian sister in danger. Although I have to say that you are right. He left his place last night and might now be looking for a new place to live. He is a cautious person, so he said he would not like you to meet him because after all, you are..." Marcus seemed embarrassed to say the remaining words.

"I understand. I'm a fugitive wanted by the palace." I smiled bitterly. "You are right. If I meet him, it may bring danger to him. But I must pay for his beehives and the deposit he lost because of his sudden leaving." I hurried to my room, retrieved the pouch from under my pillow, and handed it to Marcus.

"This is the money I earned at my master's house," I said. "I planned to use it to pay for my ticket to Cyprus. Please take it to your friend."

"But what about your ticket?" Marcus asked.

"Don't worry about me. I'll figure out a way to make some more. There is still a month before the next ship to Cyprus departs." I smiled. "So, there's plenty of time."

"You could work with us," Elaina suggested.

She had come back with the empty basket in her hand. "Since winter, we've been bringing in more homeless women and children who needed shelter and care. We raised some funds from the kind innkeeper Cornelius to build shelters for them. If you want, you can stay here and help to accommodate those people. I'll pay you one denarius a day."

"Thank you so much, Elaina. I'll do my best," I said, thanking God in my heart for such timely provision.

"I'm glad you can stay with us for a while," she said.

Elaina then turned to Marcus and said, "Marcus, I've... I've heard your storytelling business isn't doing well. If you want, you can also stay here and help us build the shelters. We have a spare room for you, and you can save on the ludicrously expensive rent."

Marcus cast a quick glance at me, and his face turned red again. "Yes, I would love that if it's not too much trouble. And I guess my son would not object to it either," he said, glancing at Achilles who was playing with another boy in the courtyard.

"Wonderful. God has not only provided money for our shelters, but He also sent two able helpers and a little scamp who will amuse us all. Praise His name!" Elaina exclaimed, raising her hands to the air. "By the way, my husband, Peter, is on the way back to Rome. You two probably want to meet him." Elaina's eyes glistened with a girlish glow.

"Of course," Marcus exclaimed. "Who wouldn't want to meet Jesus' first disciples? I have many questions to ask him."

I almost jumped to my feet. "What did you just say? You mean, *that* Peter? Jesus' first disciple? You're telling me he's your husband?"

"Yes, that Peter." Elaina laughed.

"I've heard a lot about him from Nana many times, but never thought I'd meet him in person." I really couldn't believe what I was hearing. *Surely, it cannot be true.*

"He will live with us for a few months before he sets off on another mission trip. So, you'll have plenty of time to talk with him." Elaina grinned and beckoned Marcus. "Marcus, now follow me. I'll show you where you'll be living."

Forty-Five

A Sudden Accusation

At Elaina's house, I felt an unparalleled sense of peace. Being among like-minded people who shared the same beliefs put me at ease. Prayer and worship were regular practices, and we often gathered on the outskirts of the city to make sure our voices wouldn't be heard by others. There were moments when I couldn't contain my joy and would burst into loud praise, only to catch myself and continue without fear, knowing that I had nothing to hide.

Elaina brought back memories of Nana in many ways. Most of all, she always engaged me in the word of God and shared with me stories of Jesus and his disciples. I was amazed by the simple life they had led, even though they had received so much power from God. If Nero had just half of their power, nobody, not even the praetorian guards or his manipulative wife, would have been spared from his drunken abuse. He might have even built his palace upon the waters, placing his throne high in the skies, far above the reach of mere mortals.

Marcus came every day, bringing wood boards from a forest nearby and helping us build the shelters, which started from an open area behind our complex.

Most of the time, Elaina's house bustled with activity as people in need sought refuge, especially women. We welcomed weary souls from all walks of life—wives fleeing abusive husbands who viewed their newfound faith as madness, young maidens facing arranged marriages to wealthy yet cruel suitors known for discarding their wives like used linens, and elderly, disabled widows with no means of support. They arrived seeking solace and a chance for a better life. Elaina and I were ever ready to lend a helping hand, tending to the sick and the wounded, offering a comforting presence, and doing our best to provide a haven.

On certain days, when the pace slowed, only one or two visitors would stop by, seeking nothing more than a friendly chat. Elaina would always accompany them while I prepared food. One of the frequent "chat-seeking" guests was Bellona, a loud-speaking woman with a tiny mole near the corner of her mouth. She always came a little early before lunchtime, usually on the last day of the month when she had a day off from work. Each time, she would sit with Elaina, lamenting her unpleasant job at the tavern and sharing some recent news she had just heard.

"Catena was in a fight with her husband yesterday, you know, such a shameful affair. Their children and neighbors watched as they threw words of insult that no believers should say to each other." Bellona punctuated her words with vivid gestures, as if relishing the tale's juicy details.

"Hmm," Elaina grunted disinterestedly.

"And what was it all about? Food! Can you believe it? Her husband was not pleased with the lamb stew she served him. Instead of doing what a submissive wife should do, as the Lord has told us, she went on hurling insults about how he had drunk all the money away in the taverns. Such a shame!"

"But did you pray for her? You do realize she is a new believer, don't you?"

"Well, I meant to, but you know, work at the tavern can be really tough," Bellona explained with a sheepish chuckle. "If I had more free time, I would've prayed for her. But sometimes, prayer has to wait its turn."

"Even those standing long in the faith will be faced with temptations to resort to our base instincts from time to time. After all, we are sinners and only set apart by grace," Elaina said in a gentle, motherly tone of admonishment.

"Yes. And oh, did you hear about the—"

"Vita, please come and serve our guest some food," Elaina called out to me.

"No, please Elaina, I do not intend to burden you," Bellona exclaimed.

"Who said you were burdening me?" Elaina said, rising to lead her to the dining table.

It was evident that Elaina did carry burdens, but they weren't related to extending hospitality; rather, they were the constant weight of Bellona's relentless gossip. She appeared visibly relieved when I entered, carrying the meal for our guest. However, when Bellona saw me, the woman emitted a gasp that soon turned into a fit of body-wracking coughs.

"Are you not feeling well? Would you like some water?" I swiftly placed the food plate on the table and moved to get a cup of water.

"I... I shall not have anything delivered by your hands," struggling to breathe, she choked out a few words.

"What do you mean, Bellona?" Elaina asked as she placed a comforting hand on her back.

"Do you not know who you harbor in your house?" The woman looked at Elaina in disbelief.

"A Christian sister to whom I offered solace, not harbored. She is not an abomination."

"She is a cheap prostitute"—Bellona coughed once again—"gracing the bed of the praetorian prefect. She is no Christian sister. You should not allow her to corrupt the young women in your house. I-I can't believe—"

"Corrupt? What in the world are you talking about?"

"You should ask her. Are you not the mistress of Caius Aemilia, the praetorian prefect who stands at the side of the emperor? You and your servant girl went on a lavish shopping spree at the most exclusive jewelry store just a couple of months ago. Am I wrong?" she asked with her two sparse eyebrows erected.

Then she looked at Elaina and confirmed, "I saw her with my own eyes, because the tavern I work in is right next door to that jewelry shop. Later, a slave boy in the shop told me who she was. And here she is, standing right before me."

I stood shaking, my face drained of color, and my tongue felt tied in knots in the wake of the sudden accusations. "No, it's not... not as you think," I stammered, glancing anxiously at Elaina, fearing that she might believe what Bellona had said.

"Think?" Bellona probed further with a sneer. "It's not what I *think*! It's what I *saw* and *heard*! Are you saying that I'm lying?" Then she turned to Elaina again. "She cannot talk for herself. Let me tell you, for months, she was parading among Rome's nobilities, who are known for their dirty ways. And I've heard that she had even attended one of Nero's shameless banquets. We all know that no one who claims to have the spirit of the Holy God should do such things," Bellona erupted, pointing an accusatory finger at me with disdain, her words tumbling like a torrent.

Anger and guilt rushed over me at the same time.

"Calm down, Bellona. And Vita, please go into your room; I will call for you later," Elaina said calmly as Bellona eyed me with disgust from head to toe.

I retreated to my room, tears welling in my eyes. From beyond the door, I could hear Elaina's voice, likely addressing Bellona's brash behavior. But that didn't provide me with much comfort, as there were grains of truth in the accusations against me. My relationship with Caius had always been shrouded in secrecy because nobody knew the full story. But even if they did, could I honestly claim that I'd never entertained impure thoughts about Caius?

No, I couldn't. There were moments when I had come dangerously close to becoming his real mistress.

"Jesus knows our weaknesses because he went through it all too.

So, whenever we're struggling, we should just go straight to His throne," Nana's wise words echoed in my mind, compelling me to seek refuge from my own inner turmoil before God.

I knelt beside my bed with rage toward Bellona, who might just have made me lose another family with her open accusations. *It won't take long before people know my past and demand my exit from what they consider a holy sanctuary,* I thought painfully.

Meanwhile, I seethed with anger over my own role in the predicament I found myself in, chastising myself for failing to recall that I was supposed to set an example for my fellow Christians. I should never have allowed myself to become entangled in the ambiguous role of a fake mistress. But had I really been given much of a choice?

All I had attempted was to rescue the house of Eubulus from impending ruin, as well as to save Rufus. The memory of the betrayal that ensued left my heart feeling icy cold. The pain became so overwhelming that I couldn't contain it, and I broke down in a torrent of fresh, salty tears that soaked my bed sheets.

Amidst my sorrow, a hand gently rubbed my back in soothing circles.

"Vita, it is all right. Bellona's accusation is not God's verdict on you," Elaina said, pulling me into an embrace. "God knows the real you and won't be swayed by her gossip."

My body shook with sobs, inhaling Elaina's flowery scent.

"Elaina, I'm sorry. I-I should have told you about my past. But I'm struggling to find the right words to explain everything so that you can truly understand and believe me."

"I *will* believe you, my daughter," Elaina said as she wiped away my tears.

I took a deep breath and continued, "Bellona was right. I was Caius' mistress. But it was all an act, a deal to help bring a criminal to justice. He had stolen from my master Eubulus and put his favorite slave, who happens to be my... my brother, in harm's way."

As I spoke, Elaina's eyes widened with a mixture of surprise and concern. Her hands gently reached out to grasp mine.

"My master sought Caius' help, and he demanded me as the payment," I explained, my voice cracking. "In the end, I was to play the role of his mistress, but it was only in name. I-I never slept with him. I pretended to be an extravagant woman who had a taste for a specific fragrance. You know, the kind that was made from the spices that were stolen. Because the taste of Caius' mistress was always sought after by Rome's noble matrons, demand for the stolen goods rose. Driven by greed, the thief gave up the stolen items to be sold. That's how he was caught."

My words were interrupted by occasional sobs, and Elaina held my hands gently throughout my narrative.

"You did just by bringing a thief to book and saving your master's house." Elaina dried my wet cheeks with her sleeves. "There is nothing to be ashamed of. Nothing to cry for."

"No, Elaina," I said with a heavy heart, my gaze dropping to the ground. "You don't understand. I'm not totally innocent. Nana had told me that Jesus said when a man looks at a woman lustfully, he has already committed adultery in his heart. When I was with Caius, I was so drawn to him that I almost decided to become his real mistress. I felt so unworthy to be called a Christian." With all that said, I buried my head in Elaina's bosom.

"There, there, my daughter. I'm glad you told me how you feel. It must have been a heavy burden, wasn't it?" Elaina's voice was gentle and warm as usual.

"Yes. It tortures me day and night."

"My poor girl," Elaina whispered. "And I'm so proud of you because you resisted such a great temptation. Not every girl would reject such a handsome and rich man. I couldn't confidently say *I* could do that if I were twenty years younger." She paused a little and laughed. "Well, I wouldn't confidently say I'd even pass the test right now. I'm just grateful that my old age has spared me from such tests altogether."

I burst into laughter amidst my tears, surprised by Elaina's candidness about our shared vulnerability. She joined in, and soon the room was filled with infectious mirth.

"Oh, my dear," she said. "Your smile is truly beautiful. Let it stay there."

"Elaina, I didn't pass the test myself." I lowered my head. "That day, I told God if He didn't show me a sign, I would agree to become Caius' real mistress. And I meant it."

"Then what happened?" Elaina asked curiously.

"Well, then God showed me a sign——an imperial order to arrest me. The empress accused me of bewitching her little daughter." I sighed. "That woman always has a fondness for Caius, so she undoubtedly hates me."

"See, that's what I said," Elaina remarked. "God never lets you fight your battle alone if you connect with Him in prayer. When the temptation is too great, He opens a door so you can endure it."

"I guess He does." I nodded in agreement.

"Sometimes, He does it in the most unexpected way." Elaina paused and then continued in a tender tone, "But as you can see, people are watching us closely because we represent Jesus wherever we go. That's why we need to pray for wisdom in everything, so we won't cause our brothers and sisters to stumble. We don't do this to please people. We do this out of love."

In Elaina's softly spoken words, there was a quiet authority. I listened attentively, allowing everything to sink in.

"I see a bright future for you, a beautiful ending, but also great torrents," Elaina declared, her tone a mix of anticipation and concern, as she clasped my hands firmly. "Pray, without ceasing, every time you are in joy or deep sorrow. Keep praying for God's guidance in all you do."

"Thank you, Elaina. I'll pack my bags soon. I can't let anyone else accuse you of harboring someone with a questionable past. Who knows where that might lead?"

"Oh, nonsense! You'll remain here, child. Christ never turned away those in need, and I'm not about to start it either. What kind of Christian would I be if I allowed a gossipmonger to take my girl away? Besides, you wouldn't want to miss Peter's sermon, would you?" she said with a warm grin, then pulled me into a comforting embrace, holding me closely for a long while.

I couldn't help but ask, "Oh, Elaina, why has God been so gracious in bringing you into my life?"

"Because you are His beloved daughter," she said firmly.

Forty-Six

Her Hidden Purpose

Light poured in from the windows under the high ceiling of the gymnasium, casting long shadows of Caius and Theophilus as they fiercely tangled together in sword-fighting practice. Caius' face was contorted with anger and frustration, his movements aggressive and unyielding. Sweat poured down his face and chest, soaking his clothes.

"Can you believe it?" he grumbled. "It's been a month since Nero announced her innocence, and she's never shown up."

"Agreed." Theophilus smirked. "Right after the unfortunate passing of our beloved princess, the emperor decided the cause was some kind of contagious disease starting from a servant in the palace, clearing Vita of her guilt of witchcraft. In other words, she's safe and free now."

"Maybe she didn't get the news," Caius murmured, seemingly trying to convince himself. "There's a chance of that."

"Unless she's not in Rome, which is quite unlikely since you've sent slaves to every city gate and none of them saw her leaving," Theophilus said, dodging a routine attack from Caius. "If her friends were resourceful enough to save her from Tigellinus' men, they would have received the news and informed her. So, the only reason she didn't come back is..."

"She never intended to!" Caius' sword clashed with Theophilus', the latter's dropping onto the marble ground, making a loud crash. Following suit, Caius tossed his own sword aside and removed his training armor, revealing his casual tunic and belt—the one Vita had given to him the night before she was taken away.

Memories flooded back hopelessly. He closed his eyes.

"That girl had me fooled from the beginning." He sat down on a bench heavily.

"Ha! She did! And you still can't give up on her." Theophilus laughed. "I'd have believed she does practice witchcraft if she were not a Christian."

"Maybe she does, who knows?" Caius smiled wryly. "I don't understand anything these days, even though I've tried my hardest. Perhaps she was only pretending to be a Christian."

Theophilus continued to tease, saying, "I now know the reason for your misfortune. Remember two years ago when we passed by the Venus temple on Capitoline Hill and made an offering to the goddess? Then I suggested we pay some homage to the altar of Cupid. Do you recall what you said?"

Caius shook his head.

"You said, 'Why pay homage to a five-year-old boy?' No matter how I urged you, you refused to yield. It seems you are now receiving your retribution from him."

"Cupid or witch, either one, I'm not letting her go. Will you help me, Theophilus?" Caius said resolutely.

"I wish I could. But I don't know how to locate these Christians, since they are known for their discretion. Even the letters from that Luke physician didn't provide any clues," Theophilus replied, picking up Caius' and his own swords and dropping them into the weapon bucket.

At that moment, hesitant steps announced someone's presence behind the curtains. Caius wondered who it could be as he had not called for any servant.

"Come in," he ordered. Julia entered the room bearing a plate of fruits, which he couldn't remember requesting.

"Maybe she could give you some clues?" Theophilus said with a smirk, leaving the gymnasium.

Caius' face lit up. "Julia, you come at a good time. I have things to ask you," he said, gesturing for her to sit beside him.

"What is it, my lord?" She sat down, setting the plate on a small table and lifting her head to meet his gaze.

"You are Vita's best friend. Did she ever tell you about any resourceful friend?"

"No, my lord. As I've told you before, she never told me anything about her escape. But..."

"But what?" Caius grabbed her shoulders and unconsciously tightened his grip.

"My lord, you are hurting me," Julia said, casting down her lashes which were rimmed with kohl and golden glitter.

"Sorry." Caius quickly withdrew his hands. "Go ahead."

"Vita and I spent lots of time together at our old master's house. I can tell you all the details and maybe you'll find some clues," she said in a cat-like voice with a languid drawl in the last syllable of each sentence, reminiscent of those high-born girls at banquets.

Caius was amazed at how fast she had learned the way they talked.

"Yes, that's exactly what I need. Go ahead, Julia. If you help me find any clues, I'll reward you beyond your wildest dreams."

"No, my lord. To be of any worth to you is the greatest reward I can imagine."

Caius looked at her for a moment and let out a sigh. He used to relish the fact that all women put his needs first, trying to please him. He used to dream that Vita could be like this, but not anymore. Vita was Vita. She had escaped from him, and he still loved her to the core.

"Your devotion is greatly appreciated," he said wistfully.

Julia blushed and started talking about their life in Eubulus' house. Caius listened carefully, not wanting to leave out any valuable information. Although he didn't find any clues in Julia's narrative, the vivid stories about Vita delighted him. Some parts even forced out a few laughs from him.

After some time, Julia said, "I apologize, my lord, but I'm feeling quite dizzy. I've been consumed with worry for Vita all these days and haven't had a proper night's sleep."

Caius wanted to urge her to share more, but he was afraid her condition could get worse, and she wouldn't be able to recall anything further. "Please, go to your room and get some rest. When you're feeling better, do return to see me," he said.

Julia curtsied and left. The next day, she returned. And the day after that. For several consecutive days, Julia visited Caius' study, sharing anecdotes about Vita.

Naturally, the servants began to gossip.

One sunny afternoon, Julia suggested they take a walk in the garden because the breeze and sunshine might jog her memory further. She had recounted everything to him, from the moment Vita had been brought into Eubulus' house, all the way up to when the fragrance issue had surfaced.

As they wandered through the garden, they came upon the deserted flower patches, where Caius had proudly showcased all the gladioli he had painstakingly cultivated during the winter. Julia settled on the bench where Vita had seated herself on the day Caius had revealed the "gift" for her. Then, she recounted, "One day, I witnessed Vita and Rufus embracing for quite a while near the gladioli patches in Eubulus' garden. They were both in tears, and Vita was passionately kissing Rufus."

Caius felt blood surge into his head. "We can skip that part," he snapped.

Julia seemed to be ignorant to his order. "No, my lord. I shouldn't miss any details because there may be clues in it. You must learn to be less sensitive, my lord. I am sorry for saying so; it is not my place." And she continued, "That night, Vita came back to our quarters and told me how much she loved Rufus and how he was the only man she'd ever loved in her life. She would die if she couldn't marry him for no other man could ever be of interest."

"Stop it!" Caius felt a burning fire explode in his chest. "That's enough."

But Julia sported a mischievous grin and seemingly paid no heed to Caius' command as she continued, "Can you believe it? She even told me she has already thought about their children's names. The first girl shall be called Ruth or Rebecca and the first boy, David or Jonathan. She said she dreamed of having many children with him, praying they all resembled Rufus."

"Shut——" Caius paused mid-sentence, returning to his observant self as he took a closer look at Julia. It was then he noticed the clothes she was wearing resembled the ones he had purchased for Vita during her time of masquerading as his mistress. She had also dusted powders onto her face, and the sweet scents of cinnamon and jasmine captivated his senses as she drew nearer.

He was, without any doubt, under the attack of feminine powers. He smirked; this was not new to him.

"Too bad I have been so fooled by a girl who never loved me in the first place," Caius said with an exaggerated sigh and settled beside Julia. "Maybe it is the time to stop all the stupidness. I shouldn't let the girl who never cared about me ruin my life, should I?"

He was amused to see sparks in Julia's eyes.

"My lord, I have been so worried about you after Vita left. You have lost your color and joy, and it is weighing on your shoulders so heavily that your eyes have lost their shine," she said with a gentle and caring tone.

"Have they now?" he asked, giving her a flirty look as he gently removed a fringe of hair from her forehead.

A blush crept into Julia's cheeks.

"I understand Vita is a very sweet girl." A petite hand gently landed on Caius' shoulder. As he glared down at her, he couldn't help but notice that her delicate face had a childlike appearance. This only served to heighten the contrast between her innocent visage and her devious intention, which filled him with disdain.

"But if she had any love for you, she would have found a way to let you out of this misery. She has robbed you of your joy." Julia laid her other hand on Caius' thigh and looked into his eyes boldly. "That is why I am here for your welfare. The light in your eyes is very important to me," she said in an alluring voice.

"Traitor!" Caius' eyes turned murderous as he yanked her hands off, causing her to almost fall from the bench. "You shameless urchin, knowing your friend's place in my heart, yet you intend to weasel your way into her space," he said, rising to leave.

"That is not true, Master." Julia's face alternated between shades of red and white. "I have never betrayed her. I asked her if I should approach you after her departure, and she told me she's totally fine with it."

A great pang spread in Caius' chest that he almost lost his balance. He knew Julia was probably telling the truth, but he turned all the bitterness and anger to the girl in front of him.

Now, his insides spilled over with wrath.

"If you wish to live beyond tomorrow, you shall leave my house this very moment, and never let me see you again."

"My lord—"

"Leave!" he growled, his eyes cold and ferocious, making her scamper out of the garden.

Caius exhaled heavily. He collapsed back onto the bench, a sense of hopelessness shrouding him as he looked at the flower patches, now filled with weeds. With a weary heart, he prayed, "I hope you can hear me like last time, dear god of Vita. I owe you a lot for saving her life. If truly this is orchestrated by you as she said, then I beg you, let me see her again."

Forty-Seven

The Symbol

It was quite hot for a late spring afternoon, not even a trace of wind reaching the longest arcade in the Forum. Caius and Theophilus walked side by side, the hem of their bright togas gently brushing against each other's as they strolled under the arcade.

As they rounded the next corner, Caius' gaze caught on four men huddled around a gambling table. Clad in tattered tunics, the men were engrossed in rowdy banter, their voices carrying amidst the clatter of dice hitting the wooden surface.

Caius' eyebrows furrowed. Quickly approaching, he tipped up their table, sending all the stacks jingling on the ground. "You scoundrels, hasn't the council announced that no one should block this arcade? Last year, a fire broke out and praetorians couldn't get access to the Senate House because of all the clutter here."

Without uttering a word in response, the four men swiftly turned and fled in terror.

"That nasty Tigellinus secured authority over Region VIII by sleeping with Poppaea, but he never took the job seriously! This is the most crowded area, and he should be paying more attention…"

Theophilus patted him on the back and said, "Easy. You can't purge all the corruption from Rome by yourself. You've done your best, so let it go. Besides, you've been quite aggressive lately. Look at how you debated with those old fellows at the Senate today. They must be cursing you at the public bath right now."

"It irked me to see those old-timers playing it safe with bureaucratic responses. I prefer drilling with my soldiers over debating with them."

"Yes, someone always needs violence to quench his lovesick desire," Theophilus said with a smirk. "You need to get jilted more often. It really fires you up."

Caius gestured toward the crowds bustling about on the street, deliberately brushing aside Theophilus' teasing remarks as if they had missed their mark entirely.

"There must be Christians among these people," Caius said. "I just wish they would wear a symbol so we could identify them. You would imagine they would use such… I mean, surely, they would find it easier to recognize one another too."

"It's a pity we didn't get that storyteller who owns the stand where Vita told the story. It's highly likely he was either a Christian or closely associated with them," Theophilus commented.

"That scoundrel disappeared, and I managed to locate the place he had rented, but the neighbors mentioned that he moved out suddenly, right after the day Vita had left. There must be something fishy about it." Caius punched his fist onto a column. "Now, we've lost all clues."

"I heard they worship donkey heads. Maybe we could look for symbols like that," Theophilus said.

"That's just a myth, proven by Vita," Caius said. "I wish it held truth though. At least we'd have a clue."

Suddenly, Theophilus came to a sudden stop, his eyes widening as he thumped Caius on the shoulder.

"Ouch, what's the matter with you?" Caius roared. "And you say *I'm* aggressive."

"You idiot. If there is a symbol among them, Vita might have used it on her belongings. She still has a lot of possessions left at your house. Have you checked?" Theophilus asked.

"You really think I've been made an idiot because of love? Of course I did! Right after she left. There was nothing."

"What about this?" Theophilus pointed at Caius' belt. Caius looked down and untied it, bringing it near Theophilus' face. It had five Greek words woven into the belt with darker leaves. "These are the only patterns on this belt. I've told you; I've checked it a hundred times," Caius said impatiently.

"Jesus Christ God's Son Savior. Greek words of the god she worshiped," Theophilus murmured.

"Yes. She asked me to teach her these words," Caius said wistfully as another wave of memories choked him.

"Do you think these words could be some kind of a symbol?" Theophilus said.

"No way. I've looked everywhere and never spotted any written words like those. And that just makes sense because their cult is hated by most Romans, and it would be stupid to show those words so openly."

"But I still think if Vita put them on your belt, they must carry some level of importance." Theophilus tossed the belt in his hands back and forth. "You know, I used to work as a military spy, and sometimes, we had to deal with codes."

Caius was suddenly alert. He clutched Theophilus' shoulders and snapped, "Military codes? How are they usually encoded?"

"Hey, get your claws away! You don't know how strong your hands are." Theophilus shoved his hands away and said, "I don't think Vita is professionally trained to create sophisticated ones. How about we try some simple forms, like taking the first letter of each word and putting them together?"

"I-Χ-Θ-Υ-Σ, ichthus... a fish." Caius stared at the letters, his brow furrowed in confusion at first, but then his eyes widened as recognition dawned.

"Theophilus, I remember seeing it somewhere."

·▾·♥·♥·♥·▾·

Ever since Caius and Theophilus began searching for the fish symbol, they started noticing it everywhere. On the corner of an apartment building, under the windowsill of some shabby tavern, and even on one of the columns of the Senate House.

"Dear Mars, there are so many Christians in Rome?" Caius exclaimed.

"Looks like it," Theophilus said with a wry smile. "The Romans are known for their tolerance toward all kinds of gods or goddesses, yet those people are still hated. There must be something really disturbing about their teachings."

"What can be more disturbing than teaching a young girl to run away from a man whom she is clearly attracted to?" Caius said bitterly. "It is unnatural. Someday, I'll uncover the root of this cult and prove their vanity so no more beautiful girls will be fooled by it."

Noticing Theophilus' shocked expression, a broad grin spread across Caius' face. "But now, let's head to the tavern for a drink and discuss our plan," he said, wrapping his arm around Theophilus' shoulder. "I remember you haven't taken a vacation in quite a while. Perhaps it's time to use it before it expires."

※ ※ ※

About two weeks later, Theophilus sent him a letter.

Dear Caius, ever since we discovered the fish symbol, everything has become more straightforward. It didn't take much effort to locate an elderly Christian woman selling fig wines on the street I live on.

She's always been fond of me because last year, when she waited the whole day without getting any customers, I bought all her wines. I did this out of sheer kindness, but it turned out to be the turning point of our relationship.

I pretended I was interested in their faith and wanted to know more. She told me there would be a great congregation at the end of this month because their god's first disciple Peter would visit Rome on that day. I think if your Vita is such a passionate believer, she would not want to miss this great event. But before you jump at the opportunity of going there, please stop by my apartment early that day; we have some preparations to make.

Forty-Eight

A Secret Gathering

When Caius arrived, wearing a hooded cloak and carrying a lantern, he saw Theophilus talking to the man running a bakery shop along the street, right next to the entrance of his apartment building.

"Your rent is due, Gallus," Theophilus said to the petite man in his fifties, whose mustache was dusted with flour.

The baker hastily made his way to the back of the shop, returning shortly with a pouch of coins, which he then pressed into Theophilus' hand.

"I didn't know you had become a landlord," Caius said with amusement as they walked down the corridor beyond the vestibule. "How did you manage to save so much from your praetorian salary?"

"Well, I never waste funds on women, banquets, or chariot races. And all my fine clothes come from you." Theophilus laughed and opened a door with chipped paint. "I save every coin and I'm an avid investor, with the aim of owning the entire floor before I turn thirty-five."

"Good for you!" Caius patted his shoulder and followed him into his unit. "Maybe I'll hire you to manage my properties someday. Besides, I don't understand why a reliable man like you hasn't got married yet. You should find a wife, Theophilus. A business-savvy woman who can take care of your investments."

"It's none of your business." Theophilus smirked, taking out a bundle of clothes from a plain wooden chest and tossing it onto the bed. He loosened the rope and unfolded the tunics which were made with coarse wool. "I'm telling you. You've asked me to do way too many things beyond my job duty. You need to pay me extra this month."

"Before anything else, repay me for all those tickets to the gladiator shows," Caius said, grabbing a piece of clothing and bringing it to his nose. "Good Mercury, these clothes stink."

"Come on. Poor people can't afford to get their clothes washed frequently like us. Just go with it," Theophilus said. "It's all part of the plan."

Caius put on the clothes, and shortly after, there came a gentle knock on the door. Theophilus opened it and a tiny old man with a hunched back came in, slightly bowing his head.

"This is Lucas the mute. He works in the Theater of Pompey, doing make-up for the actors. You don't know how much effort it took me to find a mute man who knows this craft. So, once again, you owe me."

"See, that's why I say you're not totally useless." Caius gave Theophilus a punch on the side. "If I find Vita, you can have all the girls in my house."

"As if I care." Theophilus shrugged.

Lucas was as talented as suggested, his hands moving swiftly over his client's face. In about an hour, when Caius looked in the bronze mirror, he took a deep gasp.

"How do you like it?" Theophilus moved closer with two cloves of garlic in his hands. "If you need more disguise, I can stick these two in your nostrils to make them look wider."

"Don't even think about it." Caius shot him a warning look. "I think not even the slaves in my household would recognize me," he said. "Now give me the map of their gathering."

Theophilus took a piece of parchment from under his pillow and handed it to Caius. "Are you sure you don't want me to go with you?" he asked, his voice infused with concern. "If they catch you spying on them, what might they do to you? You might be a good fighter, but you are obviously outnumbered tonight."

"Judging by what I saw of Vita, their kind are harmless people. They may be foolish enough to worship a dead carpenter, but I trust they won't do anything crazy to me." Caius smirked. "Besides, I need you to take my place in the barracks."

Theophilus sighed as he placed a terracotta tablet engraved with a delicate fish pattern into Caius' hand. "Here, you'll need this," he said. "And don't forget to double my pay when you come back with the girl."

Caius' eyes brightened. "Is it the pass to the secret gathering?"

"Yes, indeed." Theophilus beamed. "Nobody can get in without a fish symbol. I made this one myself."

"The next year's chariot race tickets are all on me for sure." Caius laughed, took the lantern, and walked toward the door.

"Did you bring any weapons?" Theophilus called out from behind.

Caius lifted one of his feet and pointed to the side of his boot. He didn't consider this trip dangerous, but as a military man, he always carried weapons wherever he went. Tonight, he aimed to avoid drawing attention from the crowd, so he had chosen a pair of boots unsuitable for the season, allowing him to hide a tiny dagger within them.

He left Theophilus' apartment building and strode toward the Nomentan Gate. Seeing it was getting dark, he stopped at a local grocery shop and replaced the half-burnt tallow candle in his lantern, then resumed his journey. He followed Street Patricius, traversing the valley nestled between Mount Verminal and Mount Cespian. As he passed through the Gate, the sky began to darken. After approximately half an hour of walking, Caius entered a hilly area adorned with ancient burial sites, sand dunes, and gravel pits.

"By the gods, what a desolate area. It hasn't changed a bit all these years," Caius murmured as he remembered patrolling this area when he was first appointed as praetorian prefect.

As he was feeling disoriented in the dim surroundings, shadowy figures began to emerge from behind the sand dunes and gravel pits. Soon, he found himself surrounded by several torchbearers all moving in the same direction. They traveled silently and with haste, some softly humming tunes in the background.

"They must be Christians heading to hear the sermon of the carpenter god's first disciple," he whispered, his heart quickening its pace. He followed these people until the road in front of him dipped, and he took the ramp down toward an underground cave. He noticed the place was surrounded by a wall of shrubs, concealing the cavern entrance from outside views.

The massive throng of people slowed down here and formed a line.

Caius noticed someone standing at the entrance, and all those passing by paused in front of him. He assumed this person must be responsible for checking the passes.

Up ahead, the torches led the way into the cave and disappeared inside.

Caius followed suit and soon arrived at the entrance. He presented his fish tablet to the sentry, who nodded and greeted him with, "Peace be with you," before granting him passage inside.

A few steps into the dim lit, cave-like room, he arrived at a stairway.

Torches illuminated the space, casting solemn shadows as people hummed softly. At the foot of the staircase, an extended corridor stretched before him, lined with recessed compartments holding coffins.

"I've heard of poor people in Rome burying their dead in catacombs, but never seen one," Caius couldn't help but reflect. He stuck his lantern into one of the concaves, and the wall on the other end showed illuminated paintings with two fish and an anchor.

"I guess this is the place where the Christians bury their dead," he murmured.

As the corridor widened to accommodate five to six people walking side by side, Caius scanned ahead and behind, but there seemed to be no end to the passage. He marveled at the size of the congregation in this clandestine location. Without wasting any time, he began searching for the person he had come for, squinting to catch a glimpse of Vita as he moved in sync with the crowd.

Moments later, Caius arrived at a spacious semicircular area. He looked up at the lofty, rough, stony ceiling with a hole in the middle through which he could see the starry sky. At the sides of the area, he noticed two more openings, from which different groups of people were pouring in.

His heart pounded as he scanned the crowd for Vita's slender figure. In the midst of the throng, on a slightly elevated platform, an elderly man with a thick white beard and curly hair addressed the gathering. In front of him, a pit held several logs ablaze, their flames crackling and dancing while casting a warm, inviting glow.

"Is this Peter?" Caius scrutinized the elderly man, who wore a linen tunic beneath a brown wool cloak. Although his face appeared fatigued, his engaging manner of addressing the audience was captivating. Considering his esteemed position as a leader among Christians, Caius had anticipated a more formal attire.

At the very least, he believed a person of his stature should have been adorned in an embroidered robe, crowned with headgear resembling their god's symbol, and clutching either palm leaves or a staff.

But this Peter seemed quite ordinary for a religious leader. Nevertheless, Caius couldn't help but be struck by the profound respect and awe in people's eyes as they gazed upon him.

"This old man must have something truly outstanding," he pondered.

"Brothers and sisters," Peter said, staring at the firepit in front of him before taking a long pause. "I'm sixty-seven years old now. One sign of getting old is that everything around you brings back memories." His stance was a bit shaky, probably due to fatigue from the journey.

He pointed to the firepit in front of him. "In my life, there were two moments associated with fire pits that I will never forget."

"This is an unusual way to start a priestly talk," Caius mused, recalling the sermons he had listened to in the various temples he'd visited. None of the priests or priestesses ever talked about such mundane things as fire pits.

Peter continued, "The first one was the night our Lord was arrested and taken to the high priest's house. I followed them but was stopped outside the courtyard. John was known to the high priest, so he went in with Jesus to the courtyard. Later, he came back, talked to the servant girl on duty there and managed to get me in.

"Suddenly, the servant girl stared at me and asked, 'Aren't you also one of this man's disciples?' I was terrified, so I blurted out, 'No, of course I'm not!'

"She gave me a skeptical look and I couldn't bring myself to meet her gaze. Once I entered the courtyard, I found a fire pit with several people gathered around it. I felt cold, both inside and out, so I moved a little closer to the fire to warm myself. Just at that moment, some other men came up and challenged me, saying, 'Didn't I see you in the garden with that man?'

"And I... I denied my Lord once more. And not long after, it happened again." Peter closed his eyes, and his lips trembled as he continued, "In that moment, a rooster crowed, and I remembered the Lord's words to me: Peter, before the rooster crows, you will disown me three times."

The crowd was so silent that even the faintest cracks in the fire pit were clear to hear.

Caius was appalled at Peter's words.

All his life, he had witnessed countless political, religious, and military leaders deliver stirring speeches, but none had ever revealed such humbling experiences to their audience.

After a brief pause, Peter opened his eyes and continued his story. "That was the first memory with the fire pit. The second one happened about two weeks later. As some of you might already know, our Lord was crucified, and then, on the third day, he rose from the dead and appeared to many of us. But there was still a heavy burden on my mind. I denied our Lord three times, feeling like I didn't deserve to follow him anymore. So, I went back to my old job as a fisherman, and a few other disciples did the same.

"We toiled all night but didn't catch anything. Early the next morning, we saw someone standing on the shore, calling out to us, 'Friends, haven't you caught any fish?' We answered, 'No.' Then he told us to throw the net over the right side. We didn't believe his words. We had been fishermen all our lives, and any decent fisherman knew better than to cast his net during the day. But I said to the others, 'what can we lose? Let's give it a try.' So we did as he said, and a miracle happened. Suddenly, we felt the net become so heavy that it almost broke loose from our hands. We hauled it up and there were more fish than we usually caught in a week."

Caius found himself involuntarily drawn into the story, holding his breath without even realizing it.

"Right then," Peter went on, "John leaned over and said to me, 'That's the Lord.' My eyes lit up with recognition. I quickly threw on some clothes and jumped into the sea. As I made it to the shore, there was our Lord, sitting by a fire, cooking some fish and bread. The rest of the crew had also hurried ashore in our boat. He just asked us to bring over some of the fish we'd just caught.

"So, I climbed back into the boat and dragged the net to shore. It was incredibly heavy, like I'd never dealt with such a cumbersome and unwieldy net before. I couldn't believe it didn't rip."

Strange, Caius mused.

Throughout his career, he had interrogated countless criminals. Usually, when they started providing excessive detail like this old man, he could discern numerous inconsistencies in their narratives. However, Peter's tale held up remarkably well and appeared entirely credible. Moreover, the sincerity etched on his face was unmistakable—the authenticity was palpable. Caius had never encountered anyone he'd questioned who could maintain such a convincing facade.

Peter continued, "We all sat down and ate with him. It was quiet, and I just kept my head down, staring at his feet, secretly hoping he'd suddenly disappear from my sight, just as he did after he revealed himself to the two disciples on the road to Emmaus. But he didn't. He turned to me and asked, 'Simon, son of John, do you love me more than these?' I said, 'Yes, my Lord. You know that I love you.' Oh, how I hoped our conversation would come to an end at that moment!"

"Our Lord, however, wouldn't let me off the hook," Peter said with a chuckle, though tears still glistened in his eyes. "He asked me the same question three times. I was deeply troubled and almost cried. I said to him, 'Lord, you know all things. You know I love you.' However, after many years, I finally realized that since I had denied our Lord three times, He had to restore me three times."

As Peter finished his story and gave his blessings to the audience, Caius found himself lost in thought. He had braced himself for well-dressed priests chanting spells, performing mysterious rituals, or peddling miraculous relics. An ill-attired old man with a simple, straightforward tale about his own failure was the last thing he expected. Still, his soldierly integrity wouldn't allow him to deny the sincerity of Peter's story. And the idea of forgiveness that Peter talked about was testing his Roman pride to its limits.

What kind of god is this?

How can he sustain his honor without vengeance on people who betray him?

Caius carried on pondering on all these questions as the crowds dispersed. He realized there was something very strong in these people's faith, and that these strong beliefs could rip a chasm between him and Vita. As he was thinking how to get out of this unwelcoming situation, a girl's voice caught his attention from behind.

"Marcus! Good to see you here."

Caius felt a jolt of excitement surge through his body. Without needing to turn around, he recognized the voice and sensed that she was standing incredibly close, practically within a few paces.

Caius swiftly ducked behind a column. From his hiding spot, he peered cautiously and laid eyes on sweet Vita, the same Vita he had envisioned countless times in his dreams.

She was thinner than when she'd been living in his villa, yet in other ways, she was still the same, wearing her blonde locks braided along the sides of her ears as usual. Her lips curved into a bright smile, the brightest he had ever seen, and her eyes sparkled as she talked to… a man. A man who was already setting him on edge.

Every noise surrounding him was muted.

He watched their jolly faces and their mouths moving, but he couldn't hear what they were saying. When Caius saw the man reaching out to touch Vita's hair, as if brushing off some dust, he felt the urge to lunge at him and land a punch squarely on his face.

But he held himself back.

"No wonder she never came back to me," Caius murmured, clenching his fists. But he remained hidden until Vita and the man bid one another farewell and headed in separate directions. Caius put out the candle in the lantern and followed Vita from a distance.

He saw her joining an elderly woman and continued to follow them quietly.

They left the catacomb via another exit, fewer people heading in their direction. Caius continued to tail them as they ventured into the narrower lanes, wrestling with a decision—— should he reveal himself right now, or follow her all the way to where she lived?

Maybe right now I should merely find out where she lives and come back again tomorrow so I won't look so peculiar. As his thoughts raced, a black shadow emerged from the corner ahead of Vita, brandishing a gleaming knife. Before Caius had time to ponder the sudden situation, he dropped his lantern, launching himself in front of Vita.

"Vita!" Caius cried out, but the attack happened too swiftly, leaving him no time to dodge. The knife plunged deep into his left shoulder, blood swiftly gushing forth.

Gripping the man's arm, Caius spun around and yelled, "Run!" However, his lack of focus allowed the man to break free from his grasp and engage in a fight with him.

Seeing that Vita was still standing there, mouth agape in shock, he shouted once more, "Run, get some help!"

"Caius?" Vita's voice trembled as if she had just snapped out of a dream.

He heard the old woman say, "Hurry, Vita. If we stay, it's only going to be worse. Let's go get more people." Then she pulled Vita along and departed swiftly from the scene.

Caius grappled with the man, and now that Vita was out of immediate danger, he could concentrate on his opponent. The man was stocky yet powerfully built, vast sinews of muscle bulging at every visible part of his skin. He moved with an eerie and deliberate precision, a hood pulled low over his head and a mask concealing his face, leaving his identity shrouded in mystery.

Caius smartly dodged a flurry of jabs as the attacker furiously swung a dagger at him. His injured shoulder made it difficult, and he knew it was only a matter of time before exhaustion set in. The attacker speeded his attacks, focusing on the weakened shoulder. With time running short, Caius crouched down to avoid a jab, simultaneously retrieving a small dagger from his right boot.

Jumping forward with his left arm raised, Caius narrowly avoided the knife, which passed just a few inches below his ribs. He then clamped down on the outstretched arm of the attacker, disarming him quickly, before delivering a furious knee kick into the attacker's groin.

The attacker groaned in pain as he staggered to the ground.

Instantly reacting, Caius pressed his foot on the man's broad chest and stooped down to inspect his face. Bright moonlight shone on the man's chest and revealed some tattoos beneath his garment. Caius' eyes narrowed. Ripping open the garment, he clearly saw the pattern of a bear.

"Who are you? Who sent you here?" Caius bellowed as he pressed his dagger against the man's throat.

The man stared with bloodshot eyes; his lips moved but nothing came out.

About to press harder with the blade, Caius heard footsteps coming from a distance, then his ears attuned to the sweetest voice in the world. "He's right there! Hurry or he will die!"

Vita's voice was teary, and Caius felt his heart start to melt.

Lowering the dagger, he warned the assassinator, "Go, and tell whoever sent you: if they dare to take another step, I'll send them to meet Hades!" The man got up and limped away, disappearing into the dark alley without a word.

As the approaching footsteps grew louder, Caius tossed the dagger, then lay on the ground, closing his eyes.

Forty-Nine

The Christian Community

With his eyes tightly shut, his senses remained sharp. The sound of a group of people approaching reached his ears. He felt Vita's hurried steps as she rushed to his side and called out his name. Though he longed to jump to his feet and embrace her, he resisted the temptation.

If Vita made up her mind to leave him, he would have to have a solid reason to convince her otherwise. His sole chance rested on the sight of his injured shoulder and the spilled blood, hoping they'd soften Vita's heart.

To his relief, he heard Vita sobbing, "He's lost too much blood; we must take him home! Quick, I need something to tie around the wound." Someone tore a strip from his clothing, wrapping it tightly around Caius' wound to staunch the bleeding. Another group approached with a stretcher. "Hang in there, Caius. Don't give up," Vita implored.

And when he sensed hot tears falling on his face, a profound joy and relief washed over him. The loss of blood finally took its toll, and he fell into a deep slumber.

After an indeterminate amount of time, he felt the dull thud resonating in his head. He stretched his hand up but hit a post.

Have I grown taller overnight, or has my bed shrunk?

He had stretched the same way for years without ever bumping into anything. The sheets felt scratchy, a far cry from the silk he was accustomed to. As he extended himself a bit further, an intense pain shot through his shoulder, forcing a groan to escape his lips.

Before Caius' eyes fully adjusted to the light, he discerned a blurred yet familiar figure by his side. Then a soft hand gently descended onto his chest.

"Don't get up, or your wound will start bleeding again," came the most soothing voice in the world, even though it sounded a little stuffy.

As his vision cleared, he saw Vita's swollen eyes, and a surge of warmth spread through his body. "Oh, gods. If I die right now, I'll die with a smile," he thought. Reaching out his hand, he tried to wipe away the tear on her cheek, but she caught his hand mid-air. He reverted to his usual teasing tone, "Someone's eyes feel as heavy as potato sacks!"

"Stop it!" Vita chuckled through the streaks of tears on her face. "You don't know how worried I was about you." Her voice trailed off to a whisper as she lowered her head, and a blush painted her cheeks with red clouds. Her caring words and the beauty of her shyness stirred something within Caius, causing his heart to pound wildly in his chest.

He couldn't even utter a word.

"How do you feel?" Vita placed her hand on his forehead. "It's good there's no fever. Do you feel any pain?"

"I feel pain everywhere." Caius made an exaggerated groan and took hold of her hand. "I guess I won't recover for months. You won't cast me out, will you?"

"You'd better behave, or you'll never heal." Vita drew back her hand and adopted a stern face. "Now close your eyes and rest. Don't talk anymore."

As Caius gazed into Vita's concerned eyes, he knew she wouldn't send him away for now. Knowing he could stay close to her brought enough satisfaction to him. However, he suddenly realized that Theophilus must be worried about him right now. If he failed to come back, his loyal friend might send soldiers to turn the meeting place upside down. That was the last thing he wanted.

"Vita, could you find someone trustworthy to deliver a message to Theophilus? Let him know I'm here and safe. He needs to oversee the barracks for a few days," Caius said.

"Don't worry," Vita reassured with a smile. "Everyone here can be trusted."

· ▼ · ♥ · ♥ · ▼ · ▼ ·

Theophilus arrived at Caius' side before the backyard roosters crowed for the first time in the morning.

"The attacker's fighting skills were typical of a well-trained soldier. Do you recall anyone in Tigellinus' barracks with a bear tattoo on his chest?" Caius asked after he had assured Theophilus many times that he was fine.

"No. I don't recall any. But speaking of the bear tattoo, it did remind me of someone," Theophilus replied.

"Who?"

"Do you remember two years ago at the emperor's birthday banquet? A gladiator was invited, and his name was—"

"Glaucus!" Caius filled in before Theophilus could finish. "Yes, I remember. He does have such a bear tattoo on his chest. And the man's eyes were just like his. It's him."

"Rumor has it that after the banquet, he became one of Poppaea's lovers," Theophilus continued. "I had my doubts at that time because, clearly, this boy doesn't have a handsome face like her other lovers."

"That she-cat enjoys eating rotten fish once in a while," Caius sneered. "Surely, Poppaea is the one who sent him!" His face contorted with anger.

"Yes, it is our best bet."

"But how could she have gotten the news before us? Who reported to her?" A face appeared in his mind. "Julia…"

"Do you mean Vita's girlfriend? I doubt a slave like her could find ways to talk to the empress—"

"You are probably right. Or it could be some girl in my household with whom Vita shared a room. I used to bring some patrician girls to my house. Maybe their slave girls communicate with mine."

"Maybe. But what shall we do then?" Theophilus asked.

"I'll find out who gave away Vita's whereabouts when I get back. For now, I need you to deliver a message to the empress," Caius said sternly. "You will tell her I have seen her handiwork, and that if anything happens to Vita, she will have to answer to Nero about how the messenger of a goddess, precious to Nero, was accused of witchcraft and banished from town."

"You are not thinking this through, Caius. You might as well declare war."

"Are you listening at all? If she wants a fight, I will give her one. I know secrets of hers that could make Nero order her to be buried alive. Nero may not care about her affairs; he surely cares about her financial corruption. Now go, and do not question me. Use my seal in the letter and ensure you deliver it to her personally," Caius said with a tone of finality.

"Yes. Very well, master," Theophilus replied. But before he stepped out of the room, he turned to look at Caius and said, "My lord, I say this as your devoted adjutant and friend, don't delve too deep into this. I sense something dangerous in front of you."

Gazing into Theophilus' sincere eyes, Caius sank into deep thought.

Theophilus always had a knack for detecting danger and even rescued Caius from an assassin's ambush early in his career. Perhaps Theophilus was right again this time. Ever since Vita entered his life, Caius had sensed his world gradually shifting away from its old track.

The change was subtle yet unmistakable, and he felt powerless to stop it. As a patrician and military leader, Caius was not accustomed to feeling out of control.

But when Vita came into the room and brought dinner for him, all the dark thoughts vanished. His mind filled with her sweet presence. It was so sweet that when he woke up the next morning, his mouth was spasming from a night of unrestrained smiling.

And he could carry that smile all day until the next night.

Dinner time was Caius' favorite, because it was the only time he could see Vita. Throughout the day, Vita helped Elaina attend to the needs of the poor widows, but every dinner time, she would come with a bowl of soup to feed him.

At first, Elaina arranged for another widow to care for him, but he adamantly refused to eat anything from anyone else. Finally, Vita pleaded with Elaina to let her take care of Caius, and after some hesitation, Elaina reluctantly agreed.

"You have to pray for God's protection every time you enter his room, Vita," she'd said.

"I couldn't even get off my bed. What could I do to her?" Caius objected.

"It is not you I need to be careful of," Vita whispered with a light blush. "It is my own heart."

The answer pleased Caius tremendously, so he didn't ask for more.

Every night, Peter would return, and he and Elaina would stay in the living room, welcoming visitors. Caius' bedroom was situated right next to that room, with a small rectangular opening high on the wall, allowing him to hear everything while lying in bed.

The visitors were usually widows with young children and occasionally, young couples.

One day, they even held a simple wedding ceremony with a room full of people. Peter asked them to pledge their love and devotion to each other and to promise to stay one in Christ forever.

The bride officially expressed her consent in a voice tinkling with joy. "Wherever you go, there also go I, your wife." The room erupted in applause and cheers.

After the cheers had died down, Peter said, "Today, I speak to you not as a preacher, but as someone who has been married for forty years. There are two things I learned about marriage after I became a follower of Jesus. The first thing is always to remember you have married a sinner. And the second thing is you are a sinner yourself. Both of you are corrupt enough that only the death and sacrifice of the Son of God could save you."

"That's a pretty depressing speech for a wedding." Caius smirked, again believing Christianity to be an odd cult with a set of even more bizarre ideas.

"I'm not telling you this to make you lose hope in your marriage. Trust me, there will be moments in your married life in which you will find your spouse unbelievably selfish or ungrateful, and you'll regret marrying them. It's in those moments you should recall what I've just said. By doing so, you'll find it easier to extend extra grace to your spouse.

"Am I saying you should love less, so you won't feel hurt? Absolutely not! Sometimes, people are too eager to protect themselves and their hearts are hardened. It is the worst thing that can happen to our souls. Jesus cherishes vulnerability, and as Christians, we can love without fear because we know who defines us. It is not how much love you get from your spouse that defines you. It is God who defines you. That's where our security lies."

"Security..." Caius murmured, his thoughts drifting back to the day he tried to convince Vita to become his mistress. He had even offered to transfer half of his property to her. And he remembered vividly the shock and fury he felt when she turned down his "generous" offer.

Now he realized why his offer looked ridiculous in Vita's eyes.

"May Jesus Christ become the mediator between you two," Peter said loudly. "Marriage in Christ is like a triangle, with God as the highest point. The more you two are drawn close to God, the more you grow closer to each other."

The message sounded new in Caius' ears.

"Interesting," he said to himself. "But if I marry Vita, I won't need any mediator between us. When I draw her close to me, I'll never let her go."

Peter continued, "And I'm going to tell you a funny story that inspired me most about marriage. Long time ago, there was a man called Jacob. He was the father of twelve Jewish tribes. When he was young, he offended his brother and had to escape from home. In a faraway land, he fell in love with a girl named Rachel. He worked seven years for her father to get her hand in marriage. But on the wedding night, his father-in-law tricked him. So, the following morning, when the sunlight spilled into the tent, he suddenly realized the bride lying beside him was Leah——Rachel's less attractive sister."

Caius burst into laughter. "If I were him, I would beat that old rascal to death. But I wouldn't mistake anyone else for Vita in the first place," he murmured.

Peter went on, "I heard this story as a little boy, and I couldn't help but imagine Jacob's funny face when he found his bride was swapped. I used to believe that if it had been Rachel, he'd have been the happiest man in the world."

Caius thought of holding Vita in his arms, imagining the joy he would experience at that moment. The mere thought sent a warmth coursing through his veins.

"But when I grew older and experienced lots of things in my life," Peter reflected, "I realized it may not be the case. Even if he had wed Rachel on the first night, there would still be a day sooner or later in his life when he would wake up and find it was still Leah."

"How can it be?" Caius felt perplexed. "That makes no sense at all."

Peter emphasized, "Every good thing that used to make us excited will finally turn into Leah, the plain boring Leah, if we don't look to the source of those blessings, our God."

No way! My Vita will never turn into Leah. Not even a bit! Caius asserted angrily in his mind.

Younger voices in the room sounded just as confused as him, but most older people seemed to hum sounds of assent. He wasn't sure, but it sounded like Elaina was one of those expressing their agreement.

"I wonder if Elaina was rightfully offended by Peter's speech," Caius murmured, feeling a hint of secret amusement.

As days passed, Caius found himself worrying less about being bored when Vita wasn't by his side. The constant stream of visitors brought him endless surprise and amusement, making the time without her a little more bearable. Yet, each day he still fervently anticipated the brief moments he could share with Vita.

One night, she didn't appear.

Upset and worry prompted him to leave his bed and sneak out of his room, even forgetting to feign his usual limp. As he ventured into the hallway, he caught a cascade of laughter emanating from the adjacent room. Without hesitation, he hurried toward it, yanked open the curtain, and discovered Vita engrossed in play with a little boy, approximately five years old. Their laughter and affectionate embraces were so infectious that he couldn't help feeling a twinge of jealousy, even though he was just a child.

"Do you want your patient to starve?" he barged in, clearly annoyed.

Vita jumped in surprise when she saw him. She hurried to grab his arm. "I was on my way to your room, but we've got guests, so it took me a little longer. You shouldn't have tried to get up yourself, you know..."

He pouted like a little boy. "Well, it doesn't feel like help when you forget all about me."

Suddenly, he realized there was a man stood nearby. In the dim light, Caius could still recognize him as the man Vita had spoken to at Peter's night sermon, and his gaze seemed unfriendly.

"Thank you for saving Vita's life, my able prefect," the man uttered emotionlessly.

Before Caius could say anything, the young boy rushed to him and gave him a big hug.

"Did you save Miss Vita? If you did, then I love you because I love Miss Vita the best. Daddy said she will be my mommy someday!"

He lifted the boy off the ground and said in a stern voice, "Listen, little rascal, that is never going to happen, never! Miss Vita can never be your mother!"

An awkward silence descended in the room, and Vita's face had turned totally red from embarrassment. Marcus then rushed to the boy, yanked him away from Caius, and scolded him, "What did I tell you? Don't babble on! And some things are private, for grown-ups to know and not for children to speak about like that."

Tears welled up in Achilles' eyes. "But... But I didn't babble. You told me that yesterday. You said Miss Vita and you can serve God together and would make a great couple."

Marcus grabbed a chunk of bread, stuffed it into the boy's mouth, and gently pushed him out of the room. "Go play outside."

He turned and said with a blush, "I'm sorry. My son was just talking nonsense. I'll excuse myself." Then he vanished into the darkness.

In the room, Caius stared at Vita and said in a pitch higher than intended, "Is that why you never planned to come back? Did you desert me for this man? You know how much I worried about you. How much I still will worry if we are not... if I cannot..."

He trailed off, wary of giving away the true strength of his emotions. He was not yet well enough to experience the horror of rejection for a second time.

But he did find some solace in hearing her say, "No, there is nothing between me and Marcus." However, a sense of dejection washed over him when she continued, "And you have no grounds to question me like that. I'm neither your slave nor mistress."

"I thought you could at least consider me your friend," Caius said, disappointment evident in his tone.

"You are a friend. A very dear one."

"Is that the way you treat a dear friend, by leaving without looking back?"

"You don't understand, Caius," Vita replied, her voice nearly breaking.

"What do I not understand?" Caius felt blood rush into his head. "Appraise me of it, Vita, so that I may learn. Vita, I can't believe it. After we've been through so much together, you still won't open your heart to me." The boy's words echoed in his own mind. "Fine, I'm still an outsider after all." He pushed the curtain aside and stormed out.

The next morning, Caius was woken by two little hands poking his nose. Marcus' son was standing there staring at him, pouting his face. In his hand, he held a tiny bow and a single arrow.

"Why are you here again?" Caius said, agitated.

"To challenge you to a duel!" the boy replied with a serious tone.

"A duel? For what?"

"If I win, and surely I will, Miss Vita is going to be my mother," the boy declared.

"Well, although it's not for us to decide, I'm glad to accept the duel," Caius replied with a smirk. "And if you lose, you're going to shut and lock your little mouth forever."

"Deal," the boy said and brought out his tiny bow formed of sticks of wood. "Let's see who can shoot the apple on the table," he said and pulled the bow in full and released it. The arrow went straight toward the apple but missed by barely an inch.

"I'm impressed. You're very skilled for your age," Caius remarked genuinely, and the boy beamed. However, his expression shifted from shock to admiration when Caius threw the arrow with his bare hands, piercing the apple and pinning it to the wall.

"Can you teach me? Please!" If he'd had a tail, he'd have been wagging it for sure.

"You have to practice some basics first, to build up the strength in your arms and torso," Caius said. "That's the secret to everything I've learned. Now do a rear lunge, little man."

"Hey, I have a name. Achilles!" the boy protested, but still followed Caius' instructions.

"And don't forget your promise. Never bother Vita with your stupid requests again," Caius said as he grabbed a broom and tapped on the little one's head.

"Doesn't matter," Achilles said. "She will choose my father anyway."

"Let's wait and see," Caius said with a small chuckle, giving the boy's shoulder a playful squeeze. "Now hold your leg straight."

Suddenly, he sensed a secret joy. He'd never been so close to a child before.

Is this how it feels to have a son? If so, it is a wonderful thing.

While they were talking, several boys appeared seemingly out of nowhere, all around Achilles' age. Caius vaguely remembered seeing them arrive with their widowed mother seeking shelter from Elaina.

"Can we also join the drill, master?" one of them asked with a little shyness. "We all want to learn to protect our ourselves and our mom."

"Yes, but you have to work hard, and never complain," Caius said. "If you complain and whine like girls, I will stop teaching you immediately. If you beg to sit down when your legs have not yet buckled, or if you constantly cry out for help, you will go. Do you understand?"

It was the first afternoon on which Caius felt time passing without noticing. When he heard Vita's voice calling for dinner, the boys were all sweaty and dusty.

"Oh, my word! Look at them! They look like they have been playing in the gutters all day. Whatever did you do to them, Caius?" Vita exclaimed, her eyes wide and round.

"Master Caius was teaching us to fight!" Achilles said proudly.

"Caius! Tell me you didn't. He is only five. He will get hurt!" Vita protested.

"My father started drilling me at this age." Caius laughed and ruffled Achilles' hair. Then he called out to the boys, "Let's call it a day, little men. It's time to return to your parents."

"Marcus has gone. Achilles has to stay with us for a while," Vita said, holding the boy in her arms.

"What do you mean?" Caius asked, looking concerned.

"Yesterday, Marcus came to bid me farewell. He went with Elaina and Peter to help the Corinthian church. Achilles is too young, so he needs someone to take care of him," Vita said. "They will probably be back next month."

"That is great news, at least for me. He's lost his chance," Caius said with a chuckle.

"And that doesn't mean you have one, sir!" Vita blushed and gave him a nudge.

Fifty

The Disease

THE PAST FEW DAYS had been very delightful to me, since Caius and Achilles were getting along so well.

"I told you to raise your arm higher!" Caius' voice sounded from the courtyard when I was cleaning the room.

"I'm doing my best. I'm not feeling well." Achilles' voice was shaky. "My head hurts."

"Stop whining! I know you want to skip the drill," Caius scolded. "What did I say about moaning and whining right at the beginning of our training sessions? And I'm not going to let you skip today's drill. Do you honestly think that on the battlefield, the enemies would lower their weapons and leave, just because they hear you whine that you have a headache?"

"No, but even so, my head really hurts." Achilles sounded as though he was about to cry.

"Come on! Laziness won't make you a good fighter."

I couldn't bear it any longer. I hurried to the courtyard, scooped the little boy into my arms, and sent the others away. The warmth emanating from his body made me want to slap Caius' head.

"He is a child. He won't lie. If he says he has a headache, he means it!" I scolded Caius with an irritated glare before taking the boy to the bedroom.

"I have a bit of a headache too!" Caius dramatically exclaimed as he watched us depart.

"Oh, Lord, how can such a strapping man be so childlike," I whispered under my breath.

The boy's fever got worse as time passed. Caius summoned his house physician.

The physician said in horror after he had checked Achilles, "This is not good. I heard that a contagious disease has spread from the palace. And I'm much afraid this looks like it."

My stomach twisted into a knot. "It must be the one the princess got. She gave me a wooden horse and Achilles found it, so I gave it to him—"

"What horse?" Caius asked.

"Do you remember the day I met Nero's daughter in the palace? She gave me a little wooden horse after I retrieved the kite for her. Achilles saw it the other day and I gave it to him as a gift. I should have thought of it. When Nana was sick, the villagers did say items used by sick people can pass disease." I sobbed. "Oh, I'm so sorry. I shouldn't have given it to him. His illness is all my—"

"It is not your fault," Caius said and put an arm around my shoulder.

"Can you do something?" I looked at the physician and asked in desperation. "*Anything* to help him."

"There is nothing medicine can do," the white-bearded physician said with a sigh. "But over time, a few patients just get healed by themselves. All you must do is to keep the patient hydrated and cool and leave the rest to the gods."

"Great!" Caius said. "You stay here and look after the child. I'll give you 100 gold coins in ten days, whether he survives or not."

The physician's face suddenly drained of color. His lips trembled, but no words escaped.

"Did you not hear my order?" Caius bellowed.

The physician flung himself before Caius and pleaded desperately,

"My lord, I'm seventy years old. Even a minor infection could be fatal for me. Please, have mercy!"

"I'll take care of him," I asserted firmly. "I made a promise to his father, and I'm going to keep it."

"No, you can't do this!" Caius protested. "I served in the military, and I've seen people die from this kind of disease. It's excruciating. If it were to happen to you, it would devastate me!"

"I will be careful. When Nana was sick, I took care of her and was spared. I believe there is something in me that will keep me from this kind of disease."

"Nonsense! It was just luck. And nobody can be lucky all the time!" Caius scowled. "If I am honest, you seem to think your faith will always protect you. Well, let me tell you, plenty of the faithful, of all beliefs, die from this kind of scourge."

"What do you expect? That I leave him to die? Elaina is not here, and all the poor widows here can barely care for themselves. Besides, I'm the one who may have caused him to get sick. I can't let the poor old physician take the risk for me."

Caius fixed his gaze on me, holding it for a prolonged moment before releasing a heavy sigh. "I won't argue with you," he conceded. "But I can't let you take this risk unless you let me share it."

"No, you have never been exposed to this kind of disease before. You'll get infected!" I protested, my voice rising uncontrollably in pitch.

"Now you know how *I* feel?" Caius smiled bitterly. Then he just stared at me without a word and held my hands tightly.

"I guess it is no use if I say no," I finally gave in.

"Precisely."

"Shall we pray together?"

"I am at your disposal," Caius said, tugging my hands and we knelt at the window.

"I do agree, after so many days mingling with your people, I believe your god does have some power," Caius said. "Please, forget what I said and let us pray."

Even knowing he had not given his heart to our Lord, the fact that he was beginning to admit the power of my God made me happy enough. I knelt down at Caius' side and prayed.

"Dear God, we don't know why you let this happen, but we know you are in it with us, not forsaking us in all circumstances. Please heal Achilles and protect us in caring for him."

That night, however, Achilles' condition only worsened. I was really worried about the little innocent boy who was suffering, but also, ashamedly, I couldn't shake the fear of Caius ridiculing me if my prayers for the boy didn't work out.

Now, he had a high fever and vomited frequently.

We took turns placing wet linen on his forehead to help bring down his fever. By dawn, he had finally fallen into slumber, his temperature lowered, and he seemed far better.

We both fell asleep sitting at the table, having witnessed the passing hours of the night while staying awake.

This happened on most days, and every night, we knelt and prayed.

In the following days, Achilles' condition was up and down, as were our hearts.

But finally, on the tenth day, he awoke and asked for some soup. When he finished the soup, he asked for bread. Caius' physician had told us how to look after him and how to detect if he was improving. Knowing his appetite was back, we knew he would survive.

I burst into tears of happiness as I embraced Caius.

"Hey, stop it. You smell," he teased as usual.

"You stink even worse!" I laughed.

Following a peaceful dinner, our evening abruptly shattered with the noisy swing of the door. Marcus stood at the center of the disturbance, his eyes bloodshot and his tunic haphazardly worn inside out.

Top of Form

"How is Achilles? We heard the news and hurried back." His voice was shaky.

"Marcus, thank God, your son is fine now."

Before I could tell him more, he rushed to the inner room and threw his arms around Achilles. "I don't know how to thank you, Vita. You saved my son's life," he said with tears.

"No, it is God's grace, Marcus," I said. "Oh, and Caius helped too."

Marcus' eyes flickered, and his complexion paled further as he uttered, "Thank you too, prefect."

"I did it all for Vita," Caius remarked with a smirk, draping an arm around my shoulder. My immediate impulse was to recoil, but reflecting on the days we had spent risking our lives together, I couldn't bring myself to do so.

Marcus' gaze flicked from Caius to me and then down to the ground. "You both must be exhausted," he remarked, his voice devoid of emotion. "I'll take my son home so you two can rest." With that, he made a move to scoop the boy up, avoiding our eyes.

"No, I want to stay here! I want Miss Vita. You said she is going to be my mom!"

"That's not going to happen," Marcus stated firmly, lifting the struggling boy and exiting through the door, the boy kicking and screaming all the way.

"Well, looks like he's back to full strength." I smiled in the direction they'd disappeared. As I turned back, I found myself locked in Caius' intense gaze, feeling a sudden flush rise to my cheeks.

"It's late. I think I should go back to my room now." I fumbled for words. Ten days of risking our lives together had put a special intimacy between us, something I couldn't bear.

"Marry me, Vita," he said as I walked off. Not loud, but enough to shake my world.

I was speechless.

"I think we discussed it long ago," I said after a long, intense silence.

"When I say marry me, I mean to marry me legally and publicly."

"But how is that possible?"

"Yes, legally, I am prohibited from marrying a freed slave as a senator. Furthermore, it is unthinkable for a patrician to unite with a plebeian. However, I am prepared to relinquish my position as a senator, even if it means becoming a subject of ridicule among the patrician elite. Thus, let it be so."

"You're willing to do that for me?" I couldn't believe my ears.

"Yes, I can't imagine my life without you. And all these days, I've been thinking what it would feel like if we got married and had a son together, a son just like Achilles. We'll take care of him and love him together. Just imagining that melts my heart."

His gaze was burning like fire when he continued, "Now I know how important this faith is to you. I still don't fully understand it. But since this is so important to you, how can I make you offend your god by being my mistress?"

"So, He is still *my* god?" Something in my heart crashed silently.

"Don't worry, Vita. You can worship your god freely in our future home. I know your god doesn't like shrines or idols, so I'll prepare a room dedicated to your prayer time."

"Caius..."

"But please promise me one thing, Vita. Can you put your husband a little above Jesus in your heart? Just one palm length and I will be happy. It tortures me to think my wife's heart has another man more important than me. You won't reject my request, would you?"

"Caius, I see God is doing work in your heart. Can we be patient and wait for his timing? We can start as friends."

"Not friends!" he shouted, like a five-year-old boy. "We can never be just friends. Friends means platonic love. What I feel for you, Vita, it burns!"

"Caius, you need some rest. Why don't we talk about this after we both get some sleep?"

"No, I can't wait even one more moment." His eyes darkened. "Give me your answer now! I'm willing to give up so much for you. Won't you even want to do this little thing for me?"

Oh, Lord. I collapsed on my knees. *Why do you tempt me so hard? Please give me strength to do what's right. And please, do not pressure me; I cannot stand it!*

"Caius, I'm sorry, but I can't accept your proposal right now," I stammered, my body shaking uncontrollably. "I won't deny I have feelings for you. And yes, before you remind me of it, I know an offer like this is a once-in-a-lifetime chance for a girl of my status."

"You know I never saw you that way," Caius said. "Well, maybe in the beginning, but now, I regret it so much. Such an ignorant fool was I then."

"No, Caius. I didn't blame you for that. Please let me finish," I said. "To me, marriage is more than protection and providence. It is even more than affection and attraction. It is more than desire or the burning love you describe. To me, it is the union of the two souls." I felt my whole body tremble when I uttered these words. "Please give me more time and give *us* more time. Let God finish the good work He has started in your heart until we can share the deepest joy and adoration in Him. Please, please don't force me to make any commitment before His timing."

"*His* timing," he sneered coldly and looked at me, stone-faced. "All you care about is your god. When did you ever care about my feelings?"

"I do. I just…" I didn't know how to explain it to him.

After an awkward silence, he said, "I guess you've expressed your opinion clearly. I've been a fool to think you have even a little love for me in your heart. How foolish was it for me to expect true love from any woman! Least of all you, the cold-hearted one!"

Then he turned and walked out of the door, disappearing into the dark of the night.

Elaina came in not long after, and I threw myself at her, weeping bitterly. She stroked my hair gently just the same way she had done the first time.

Saying nothing, she just held me tightly.

Fifty-One

Journey to Greece

"My lord, how was the new wine from Tuscia?" a courtesan in a yellow wig asked Caius, holding a glass of wine to Caius' mouth, her kohl-rimmed eyes hooded by long curled lashes.

"Lovely, but not as sweet as your lips," Caius said and planted a kiss on the woman's lips just as a Thracian gladiator sliced the throat of his opponent.

"Good fight! Such savagery!" Caius let go of the woman and shouted.

"You promised to give me a kiss when the Thracian won," another girl beside him said in a thick northern accent.

"I thought my proposition was the opposite. Kiss when the Thracian loses." Caius laughed. "Sneaky, but I'll kiss you anyway." He planted a vigorous kiss on her parted lips.

"Hey, you bruised me!" the girl said teasingly. "But I like it."

"This is Rome. This is life!" Caius exclaimed. "What's got into me that I let go of such fun for so many days?" he asked aloud as he settled back into his seat.

"Congratulations on getting back to your old self." Theophilus came from behind with a plate in his hand. "What did I say? Vita might be a good girl, but she doesn't suit you. Look how gawky you became at that slum." He handed Caius the plate, filled with olives and candied almonds. "Enjoy life, my lord," Theophilus said, playfully mimicking the girl's foreign accent.

"You're right, my stooge," Caius said, and they both laughed. "I must have been bewitched. But now, I'm back to my senses." Caius casually picked up a candied almond, popping it into his mouth. Then, he swiftly seized the wine cup from the hand of the woman with the yellow wig and downed its contents in one gulp.

·▾·♥·♥·♥·▾·

Back at the villa, Theophilus carefully supported Caius as they entered the atrium.

"I'm not drunk. Give me more wine!" Caius demanded, his voice slurred, just as a slave arrived bearing a papyrus scroll wrapped around a golden central baton.

"The court messenger sent it this morning, my lord," the slave reported.

"I'll hand it to him when he's awake." Theophilus took the scroll from the slave.

Caius remained oblivious to their conversation, persisting in his demands for more wine.

"More wine coming up, but we need to get there first," Theophilus replied, leading Caius to his bedchamber. Shortly afterwards, Caius dozed off into the dreamy embrace of the night.

The following day, one of the slaves brought in a goblet with fresh ginger juice and honey. Theophilus helped Caius drink a little. Caius sat up, rubbing his temples.

"Here is the letter from the palace," Theophilus said, handing him the scroll.

"When did it arrive?"

"Yesterday. I asked your slave to give it to me because you were as drunk as a sailor on shore leave."

Caius unfolded the scroll and his mouth spread into a broad smile. "This is just what I need," he exclaimed.

"What is it?"

"Nero is leaving for Greece, the entire court accompanying him, including me," Caius said. "He has been planning this for a year, but I've never been so excited about it until now."

"Rumor has it that a messenger of the goddess Muse told Nero that he needs to go to the east to get inspired for his great poem," Theophilus added, leaning in to examine the letter himself.

"Poem or no poem, I don't care. All I need is a diversion from..." Caius' eyes dimmed. "Well, whatever."

Theophilus put his arm around Caius and gave him a comforting pat. "You will have it, my friend."

"Get my luggage ready. The ship departs tomorrow," Caius said with a blank look.

・▼・♥・♦・▼・▼・

At the break of the following day, Caius didn't linger at the villa. He rose early, providing Theophilus with instructions on what to look after while he was away.

Shortly, arriving at the harbor, the grand royal ship towered over everything around it, polished and glistening in the early morning sun. Its port side was decorated with images of nymphs and goddesses traveling by water with Neptune as their captain.

It was still early; most patrician guests hadn't yet arrived.

"Take my luggage to the ship," he said to the slaves carrying two huge trunks behind him, and he walked toward the east side of the harbor.

The morning sun was still half hiding sheepishly behind the roof of the temple of Juno. Bakers were taking down the planks they had used to block their shops during the night.

Mules clip-clopped along, pulling creaking carts loaded with fresh goods from the boats moored at the harbor. Sellers called out to attract customers to their makeshift shops, while others roamed the area, hawking their wares.

"Get your fresh fish!"

"Pomegranates just picked this morning!"

"Marzipans! One silver coin for a dozen," an old woman in red called out enthusiastically from her shabby stand, proudly displaying freshly baked marzipans in a neat pile.

The image of Vita as she'd once overstuffed her mouth with marzipans invaded his thoughts, hopelessly making his mouth curve—before it swiftly turned down again.

Oh, forget it. You idiot. He shook his head violently and quickened his pace.

However, a few steps along, Caius set his eyes upon a jewelry store. A girl emerged, her wrists adorned with several radiant bracelets. Caius let out a sigh and turned away. Even this sight reminded him of sweet Vita.

"Perhaps it's better to board that ship right now," he muttered to himself. "Everything I see here, everything I do... it is all a blight, bringing that troublesome woman back to my mind."

As Caius arrived at the enormous ship simultaneously with Nero's entourage, the empress' face lit up when she saw him.

"Caius, I'm glad you could make it." She smiled broadly.

"How could I miss such fun?" Caius replied as he smiled back. He noticed the ecstasy that crossed her face at his response.

"Are you here alone?"

"Well, unless you count my luggage." He decided on the spot not to refuse any advances that might come his way. He needed to put Vita behind him and move forward with his life. However, had he not vowed exactly the same previously, in the days just passed? And had it worked?

No. Not a jot.

The empress laughed heartily at his joke then cast him a sly glance as she boarded the ship. Caius and the other guests who had been waiting for the emperor's arrival followed suit.

Guests now occupied the deck, nothing but the top brass of Rome. Matrons wore draped gowns made of light, flowy fabrics in shades of blue or green, reminiscent of the sea's colors. Most adorned their necks and hair with pearls and shells; Sabina had even put a tiny gold-coated seahorse pin on her wig. Passing by his side, they all blushed when he smiled at them.

Slaves were distributing goose liver-wrapped olives to the guests while they waited for Nero's address. The guests engaged in conversations, forming small groups and clustering around the deck. Then, suddenly, Nero's voice resonated through the air.

Everyone became silent at once.

"Greetings! I would like to thank you all for accepting my invitation. Your presence brings me much joy to have you here. Take your time, relax, and enjoy the ride."

The guests cheered. Nero's slaves and the crewmen collected the luggage, leading the owners in batches to the cabins prepared for them.

Caius was escorted to his cabin, which was remarkably spacious and adorned with beautifully crafted sea nymph-themed frescoes. As the slaves bowed and exited the room, a sudden sense of emptiness enveloped him.

He dropped down onto the bed, already in a posture of defeat.

"I'm here to forget about her. I'm here to forget about her," he murmured, as if trying to convince himself.

At that moment, a slight knock on the door accompanied by laughter caught his attention. "Come on in," he said, and three young matrons sallied into the room.

"Caius! We haven't seen you for a long time," one giggled and sat by his side.

"Why didn't you bring your lovely little bird with all her pretty plumage? Is the rumor true that she left you for a gladiator? Has she *abandoned* you, my sweet? Aw, so sad..."

She ran a feather across his arm, trying to tease him. Instead, he was sorely annoyed.

"Nonsense! I was just tired of her!" Caius yelled. "Why—why do you people keep going on and on about it? Why must I keep asking you—nay, telling you—to let this matter rest?"

"Oh, my sweet, I am very sorry..." She tickled him again. "In that case, we shall not again mention the pretty-faced girl with the sweet laugh and all her bright clothes... And we shall not mention how red-faced you always appeared around her, even when she was giving you the brush-off. No, we shall not mention a word. Hush, hush. That is how it is from now."

She looked at the second girl. They chuckled, making fun of him as if sharing a private joke. The second looked up with her big eyes beneath fluttering lashes, saying, "Of course, how right you are. We shall not mention the darling girl who was scented like a divine being, who wore his jewels with such panache, and whose voice was always heard, 'Oh, Caius!'"

She placed a mischievous finger across her lips as they giggled together.

Caius' expression was displeased. He moved toward the door, wrenching it open.

"Please, if you will mock me, here is the way out. Feel free to use it."

"Oh, shush," the bolder of the two women said with a teasing smile. "We're here to lift your spirits, darling. That's our mission tonight." With a gentle touch to the small of his back, she insinuated her intentions.

He closed his eyes, a wry amusement flickering through his mind.

What's become of me? Once, I reveled in the company of women like these. Their curves, their captivating voices, their seductive gestures—all held a potent allure. But now, beneath the surface allure, lay only a dull ache of boredom, gnawing away at me.

Nevertheless, they may well aid me to forget, given time, he pondered with an inaudible sigh. *It is worth a shot.*

"Come on! Forget about gossiping. Let's go and have some fun!" he exclaimed, leading the girls out of the cabin.

It was another world on the deck, the sun descending toward the horizon, making the sea shimmer in beauty. The gentle breeze caused the silk dresses to cling to the matrons' bodies, revealing their alluring curves.

Later, the empress came out of her opulent cabin, its walls adorned with gold foil, the door opening directly onto the deck. She glided onto the deck dressed in a radiant white stola, its fabric billowing gracefully in the wind with each step she took.

Heads turned in her direction, most of the guests appearing captivated by her beauty. She basked in delight, waving greetings to some as she scanned the deck from end to end.

When her eyes met Caius', a smile tugged at her lips as she advanced toward him, commanding the attention of all around. "The breeze is invigorating, isn't it? I guess it brings people to their senses." The empress' voice dripped with honey as she spoke, her eyes tracing the contours of his shoulder and chest with an unmistakable hunger.

Suppressing a flicker of nausea, Caius responded with a knowing smirk, "You're right. I should have let the refreshing wind blow into my villa earlier."

"It's never too late," the empress said, her expression turning sheepish as she used her hand to cover her mouth. "Caius..." she provocatively slurred his name, and he responded with a grin.

"I hope you're having a pleasant journey," he said, leaning slightly forward, his eyes locked onto hers.

"I've not been one to enjoy traveling by sea, but having you here has made this much better."

"You flatter me, Empress." Caius endeavored to conceal his inner turmoil, willing himself to bask in the admiration of this formidable woman. However, he couldn't help but notice Tigellinus standing not far away among the guests. His gaze bore into him with a mixture of jealousy and something darker.

Music started. Nero emerged from the cabin door, ascending the central stage just as he had done during the royal feast.

"Emperor, sing for us!" people shouted, knowing what he was expecting.

He kept his silence, a restrained smile lingering on his lips, until the clamor of shouting grew loud enough that the dolphins on the other side of the bay could hear it.

"Very well, my dear family and friends. Despite the sea wind not being ideal for my throat, I shall sing just one song for your sake. But it will be a brief one." The *short* song lasted an unrelenting, painful hour, with everyone clapping and cheering until they were utterly exhausted.

By midnight, the cacophony had finally ceased, leaving most of the guests collapsed on the couches, snoring softly. Matrons busied themselves with having slaves scrub stains from their dresses.

Caius lay in the dark, listening to the sound of the sea and the chatter of guests on the deck. The aroma of spilled wine mingled with the scent of sweat and vomit, assaulting his senses.

Suddenly, he felt a strong yearning for the humble hut of Vita and her Christian companions. He longed for their simple meals, prepared with love, and shared among people who genuinely cared for each other.

He missed their conversations and genuine laughter, untainted by flattery and crude flirting, emanating straight from the depths of their hearts.

Most of all, he missed Vita. He missed her plain dress stained from days of hard work in the kitchen, her face flushed and sweaty from toiling all day, and her eyes brimming with tears but still resolute whenever she spoke her mind.

Somehow, he even missed her stubbornness.

He hopelessly realized how deep this girl had been stamped on his soul.

Caius staggered to his feet and grabbed a large jug from a slave, emptying the contents down his throat, desperately wanting to drink his sorrow away.

The following days passed rather slowly since no matter what he did, he couldn't escape thinking of Vita. Thus, he spent most hours in his cabin, dodging the empress and her circle of friends.

Four days had elapsed since he embarked on this sea voyage, and Caius was already consumed with regret over his choice to join. He had hoped to escape the thoughts of Vita, but every aspect of this journey only intensified his longing for her. He couldn't shake the question from his mind: should he have heeded Vita's advice and granted her the time she had asked for? Was it truly so challenging to do? Yet, as he recalled her unwavering resolve when she declared that she could not prioritize anyone over her god, jealousy seared through Caius' chest.

·♥·♥·♥·♥·♥·

It was the early hours of the morning, and the ship was already buzzing with activity. Caius didn't wake until the booming voice of the captain reverberated through the vessel, heralding their imminent arrival at Antium.

The empress' slave knocked on the door. "Lord Caius, the empress invites you to tour the city with her and the emperor."

"Tell her I am sick," Caius bellowed.

Sick of her and her gang. He finished the sentence in his heart.

After the slave left, Caius rose from his bed, stepped out of his cabin, and made his way toward the deck. The long-awaited sensation of fresh air and warm sunshine sent a shiver down his spine. He scanned his surroundings with half-closed eyes, and his gaze landed on the shimmering golden beach.

"The beach is good. The sand is good. The open sky is good, and the wind... is good," he proclaimed to himself loudly. "No marzipans, no jewelry shops, no memories," he muttered under his breath before descending the ladder leading to the dock.

Wandering aimlessly along the beach, he took leisurely steps, immersing himself in the wholesome and invigorating environment. The cool, salty breeze from the ocean was refreshing his lungs.

Not only that, but it was also freeing his burdened soul.

Just ahead, Caius saw children playing happily with each other. Achilles' little face and his stubborn expression flashed in his mind. He missed the few days spent with the little boy.

How wonderful it would be to run the length of this beach with...someone. A sense of melancholy descended on him as thoughts of Vita flooded his mind once more, making his gut squirm.

But this time, he didn't attempt to shake off the thoughts. Instead, he gazed up at the vast, gray sky and whispered, "If this is your will, god of Vita... then I submit. For what other choice do you offer me?"

He sat down on a bench, watching two boys drawing pictures with sticks on the sandy shore. He didn't know how much time had passed when the boys' parents called them away. With giggles and intertwined hands, the boys scampered off, leaving behind their drawing tools. Caius reached for one of the sticks and began to doodle on the sand himself.

He drew a fish.

He stared at the fish for a long time, then a woman's voice sounded from behind.

"Jesus Christ, Son of God, Savior."

Caius spun around, caught off guard by the sight of a pale woman standing behind him. It was Acte, Nero's ex-lover, who now served as a palace slave.

Despite his frequent visits to the palace, Caius had rarely engaged in conversation with this quiet lady. The last time they had a brief encounter was at Nero's extravagant feast, when she had conveyed the message requesting his presence on behalf of the empress. People gossiped that the empress made her carry that peacock fan for her just to humiliate her.

Caius attempted to smudge the drawing, but his hand paused as he locked eyes with Acte's kind, warm gaze. Oddly, he felt secure in the presence of this woman who had traversed the corridors of royal power.

"I did not expect us to cross paths here. Did the empress grant you a day off?" Caius inquired.

"No, my lord. My ailing health won't allow me to carry the fan for the empress, so she relieved me of that duty. I thought I'd take some time to pray on the beach instead."

He nodded, and she went on, "Then I spotted you, and figured I'd show some courtesy, only to walk in on you drawing our sign."

Somehow, the way she said *our sign* did not even irk him. He enjoyed the sharing.

"So, you are... one of them?" Caius asked, hardly able to let the word *Christian* drop from his lips another time. It had not carried him to glory so far, so it was better not spoken.

He noticed Acte's eyes dimming at his last word.

"Yes, my lord, I have been a Christian since I was very young."

"You mean when you were Nero's mistress? I'm glad to hear that not all Christians are so stubborn about being chaste outside marriage." Caius smiled bitterly.

"No, I was a new Christian then, blinded by passion. I betrayed my faith," Acte said with a sigh. "But when I realized that I wasn't as dedicated to my faith as I should be and that I was not setting a good example of Christian faith for Nero, I left him."

"You left him?" Caius visibly recoiled.

Everyone in the court thought Nero had left Acte because of his affair with Poppaea.

"Yes, and he has hated me ever since. But I still love him and pray for him every day. That's what brought me here," Acte said plainly.

Caius felt his frustration and anger brewing again.

"I don't get you stupid Christian women. We worship the gods to make our lives better, do we not? Why must you so-called Christians put such shackles onto yourselves?"

"You're mistaken, Caius, misguided. Romans may worship gods in the hope of improving their lives, but Christians worship God for God Himself. We strive to obey, even when His commands seem inconvenient. We trust Him because we believe He has good intentions for us. He knows what He's doing," Acte responded firmly. "Worshiping God has nothing to do with what we gain by it. That would be mere selfishness and conceit, both un-Christian traits."

"Worshiping god for god himself..." Caius murmured. "You blindly trust his purpose for you is good. But look what you got from him. You became a laughingstock in the palace as well as Poppaea's fan bearer, and a fan bearer who cannot even hold a fan properly."

He was surprised by how insensitive his words sounded, but at that moment, the only thing that mattered was to prove the absurdity of her supposed faith.

"You may not believe it, but I won't trade this life for all the luxury Poppaea has. There's a peace within me, unshakeable, untouched by anyone or anything. It's a peace Poppaea never knew, not even for a fleeting moment, my lord," Acte said calmly. "Even if people see me as a deserted woman, I know I'm not. I'm loved and cherished by the creator of the universe, and His love won't fade when my beauty fades away and my body decays in the earth. Even if they see me as hopeless, I know He has a grand plan for me, something beyond what my eyes can see and my mind can comprehend."

Caius sighed, loudly and deeply. "Then let me just say I totally give up on you people," he remarked with a tone of frustration.

He continued to gaze at her, his sense of bewilderment growing.

Not just because of her words, but because when she had said the last sentences, there was visible contentment on her face. He remembered seeing that contentment on Vita's face when she was praying. Now he knew what that was. It was the assurance of believing she was loved, no matter what.

He sighed again.

And even as he had hurled his spiteful words at her, still she smiled and rested a warm hand upon his forearm. "Whatever you say of me, my lord," she said, "it is mine to accept from you, because my God has shown me otherwise. Whenever I feel that He has forsaken me, He always comes to show that it is not so. Thus, words cannot hurt. Only losing my God can hurt, and that—with certainty—shall never happen to me."

"You surely do remind me of someone," he said softly, a hint of annoyed resignation in his tone.

"Is she the reason you are here alone? Is it all due to the lady you admire—for whom you beat yourself as is plain to see?"

"Yes."

It was as simple as that. Caius was surprised by how easily he opened up to a woman with whom he had hardly spoken before.

"She is a Christian girl. I loved her—" He swallowed and paused for a while. "I love her. I love her with all my heart. But she rejected me because I couldn't share her faith. And I knew from her eyes she had strong feelings for me too. Wasn't she stupid?"

"No, *she* is not stupid. You see, you still can't stop thinking about her, can you?"

"I hate to admit it. I tried to compete with her god for the first place in her heart. But I lost," Caius said dejectedly. "I lost miserably. I asked her not to put her god before me, but she would not."

"Maybe that's why you were attracted to her in the first place," Acte said with a soft smile. "Caius, what are you *really* afraid of? Losing the first place in her heart or losing your heart to her God?"

Her words struck him like a thunderbolt. Before he could utter a word, she added, "I must go, Caius. I have preparations to make for tonight's big feast." With that, she stood up and made her way toward the ship. Caius caught sight of her limping form and remembered that people said she had inherited a rare disease from her family and would not live much longer.

Watching her struggle, his heart ached for this unique woman. It seemed to be an unjust god who would take away the ones who seemed most righteous, most deserving. This only added to his increasing sense of bewilderment. Would this faith ever make sense?

He sat there and sank into deep contemplation, reminiscing about every moment spent with Vita. He remembered them all so vividly, and the days with her Christian friends made him miss everything even more. And in these moments when he was feeling so ashamed of his petulance, at his unashamed demands and his rudeness about her faith, something slowly came to him. It was that the reason she would not take him as he was now... it was because she already *had* everything, and he had nothing to bring into the marriage, at least not compared to her. Because he did not have her god. Or rather, her god did not have him.

He was not a man of faith in this god.

This was the difference. She would not marry him because although she did love him, he was lacking. She would not marry him as he failed to understand and unite with her soul.

They were not two souls united, far from it. This was why she'd been so sad when he always mentioned "her" god—when he'd never included himself. Now, he felt so stupid.

Yet he had spent enough time with those who were not Christians to also see a marked difference there. Compared to what he saw and experienced these days, he was now experiencing a longing to be part of the community Vita loved, and as one of the family, not as a bystander. The longing became so strong that it overruled his Roman ego that strongly objected to the thought of taking a religion of the lower class.

He rose from where he sat. "I want to go back to Vita," he said to himself. "I'll tell her I want to be united with her, in body and soul, even in her God. If she will even consider me after I made such a fool of myself."

He had already made up his mind.

Fifty-Two

Leaving Rome

"I've lost Caius. It's over. I'll never see him again." I sank into Elaina's arms, my body trembling. This was the second time I had broken down in tears since Caius left the night before.

"What happened?"

"He asked me to marry him. He even promised to renounce his senator status so he could marry me legally. But there is one condition, that he wanted me to place him above Jesus in my heart. I begged him to wait until God finished His work in his heart, but he refused. And I guess we are probably never going to see each other again."

"I know. It's hard." Elaina stroked my back gently and rocked me like a newborn. "Do you regret it?"

"No, but I feel so much pain here." I sobbed again and put my hand on my chest.

"I know. It must've hurt so bad," Elaina said gently. "But trust me, God will heal the wound someday."

"But why can't it be well right now?" I wept louder. "It may take me forever to forget."

"It'll happen in God's time."

"But it's too hard!" What she had said was not what I wanted to hear. Thinking about "God's timing" was the last straw that made Caius leave, my sadness grew even more.

"There, there, poor girl," Elaina said, handing me a linen cloth. "And before God's timing happens, I'll be there for you. Have faith, my daughter."

"I'm trying," I said through shaky breath. "But I'm just not so sure about this anymore."

"So sure about what?"

"Do we... I mean, do Christians always have to be so hard on ourselves? He loves me. He respects my faith. And he's even willing to sacrifice his social status so I won't do things that offend my God. Isn't that enough? Will God really get angry if I choose such a good man?"

"My dear daughter, I totally understand how you feel. The problem is not whether God will be angry or not. It is about whether you are willing to settle for less. If God is with you, I can't imagine it being easy to choose a man who lacks faith. So, will you settle for less... so much less?"

"Less..." I pondered Elaina's words, finding it difficult to associate this concept with Caius, the ideal man sought after by almost all Roman patrician girls.

"Caius is handsome, rich, and loves you deeply. But are you willing to accept a husband who won't understand the deepest part of your being? Or are you willing to wait until God brings the best to you? Remember, our God is a loving father always, wanting the best for his beloved daughter?"

Elaina's words brought me endless comfort, and even though I had assured myself of the same thing many times, I still doubted them when the real trial came. Now when these words were spoken from her mouth, it was like listening to God Himself speaking to me.

"The best..." The remaining doubt tried not to let go of me. "But what if God wants me to marry someone I don't love?" I murmured.

"Oh, Vita, don't worry about that. God cares about your feelings more than you do," she reassured, enveloping me in another embrace.

"Besides," she continued, "God doesn't just put you in this world to have romantic relationships. Don't forget your dream, girl. Did God ever put any vision in your heart to serve Him in any particular way?"

Her gentle reprimand acted as a fresh breeze enlightening me.

My vision? Yes, I did have one. Writing. To write my own stories about my walk with God. How long since I had stopped doing that?

Even so, God had preserved my parchment and ink throughout all kinds of circumstances.

"Let us just pray." Elaina tugged my hand, and we both knelt by my bed. "Dear Lord, we know that you are the master of the universe, and you know why all things happen. We trust you to lead Vita in your gracious will. We pray that you grant Vita strength in this trying time, strengthening her faith to overcome the storm and stand firm in you. Give her the strength to pursue the vision you put in her heart, for your glory. In Jesus' name."

"Amen." A peace like never before washed over me.

"All right. Now eat something. You haven't eaten anything since last night. When our bodies are weak, our spirits suffer too," Elaina said, handing me a plate with baked bread.

"I need to go check on the new girl, Vabiana. She was cast out by her family and will give birth any time," Elaina said. "Please eat something, or you'll faint tomorrow."

I nodded and watched as she left the room.

That night, I slept fitfully, haunted by a dream of Caius on a sandy beach, walking away from me. I stretched my arm out to reach for him, but he remained just out of grasp.

I screamed his name, but the sound was swallowed by the void of silence around me. Struggling to move, I tried to run towards him, but it felt as if my feet were trapped in quicksand, refusing to obey my commands. Caius continued walking, oblivious to my cries, his figure slowly fading into the distance until he vanished from my sight altogether.

"Caius!"

I awoke drenched in sweat, gasping for breath, and hastily wiped away the beads of moisture on my forehead. Determined to shake off the lingering remnants of that haunting dream, I propelled myself out of bed and strode over to the desk. With trembling hands, I lit the tallow candle, its flickering flame casting dancing shadows across the room. From my satchel, I retrieved the parchment paper and ink, feeling a sense of urgency to capture every detail before they faded from memory.

As I began to write, I poured my heart onto the page, chronicling every recent event, every dream, and every prayer. Surprisingly, the memories flooded back with remarkable clarity, each word flowing effortlessly from the tip of my pen. In the act of writing, I found solace, a semblance of order amidst the chaos of my thoughts.

Eventually, as weariness crept upon me, I reluctantly extinguished the candle's light and retreated to bed once more.

And this time, no more dreams.

At some point, a gentle knock on the door roused me from my sweet sleep. "It's me, Vita. Can I come in?" Elaina's voice floated through the wooden barrier.

"Yes," I replied, my voice still heavy with sleep.

"How are you feeling?" She walked over and took a seat on my bed.

"Better." I sat up and smiled. "Thank you, Elaina."

"You are doing great, sweet child." She reached out and wrapped her arm around my shoulder. "A brother working at the Ostia harbor brought me news today. A ship heading for Cyprus departs in two weeks. It will stop at Paphos or a nearby harbor depending on the weather. Your service here is enough to pay your ticket."

"Oh Elaina, thank God!" I exclaimed, but immediately felt a wave of sadness. "If I leave, who's going to do all the work here?"

"God will provide. A change of environment might do you good." She ruffled my hair and pulled me close, enfolding me in the warmth of her embrace. "Peter and I will pray for you as always." When her glance fell on the parchment on the desk, she smiled. "I guess God has a special way of healing His children. By the way, have you any plans when you arrive in Cyprus?"

"I'll find a job first. But not in Paphos or my village. I need a new place to start. When I collect enough money, I'll return to give Nana a proper burial."

"God be with you wherever you go."

"I don't know how to thank you, Elaina. I was too focused on myself yesterday and didn't ask you about your trip to Corinth."

"Thank God, the trip went very well. We delivered the letter to the Corinthian church. Marcus even helped them fix their gathering place," Elaina remarked warmly. "He is such a faithful Christian brother. If not for his son, he'd probably follow Peter as he continued on his mission trip."

In the following days, I did my work without saying much and spent the rest of my time writing. Even though I believed Elaina didn't disclose any information, the news of Caius leaving spread quickly. Most widows were kind and considerate by not asking questions.

Well, except for Bellona.

"Congratulations, sister. That evil man finally left. You should have told him to go earlier, sister. May God forgive your sins. Please come to me if you need someone to pray with you." She smiled with glee.

"Thanks, I will." I forced a weak smile and prayed in my heart. *Oh, Lord, help me to be calm and not punch her in the face.*

Thank God I had enough work to keep myself busy. Vabiana gave birth to a beautiful baby girl with the help of Elaina and me, and the little one brought us all lots of joy.

Marcus came to help us every other day, and Achilles never mentioned Caius; I guessed Marcus had warned him not to. *Life was bearable.*

Then, one day, I received word that I had a visitor at the door. For a fleeting moment, a faint hope stirred within me that it might be Caius, but I immediately mocked myself for such a thought.

When I got to the door, there was an elegant woman standing there, dressed in a sapphire-colored silk dress, wearing her hair up as a married matron.

"Cassia? H-how did you...how did you find this place?" My words stumbled out, barely forming a coherent sentence amidst my astonishment.

"Long story. A Christian friend of Aurelius told me."

"Oh, please come in. Can I offer you some water?" I was surprised that seeing her didn't make my heart ache anymore. Maybe it was because the source of pain had changed.

"Yes, please." She nodded.

I went to the kitchen and got her a bowl of water.

"How have you been? How is Rufus, I mean Aurelius?"

"We're both well. I'm glad to see you in good health." I could see she was struggling to manage a calm tone.

We made some small talk for a while, then Cassia suddenly stopped. "I'm sure you must hate me," she said, her gaze fixed on the ground.

"No. I have hated Rufus for a while. He broke the promise he made to me when we were young. But I never hated you."

"Even after what I did to you?"

"Rufus chose you over me. It's not your fault," I said with a sigh.

"How could you not hate me? I never should have forced him to marry me when I found out what was between you and him." Cassia's voice quivered, on the verge of tears.

"No. You treated me so well when Diana and Gala bullied me. I owe you my life," I said sincerely. "Besides, I do trust God has His plan in everything."

"Your god, I'm sure he is the one punishing me." She began to sob.

"Did anything happen?"

"It's Aurelius. No matter what I do, I feel that he still cannot give me his heart completely. I have decided to accept my fate and live with it."

"Cassia..." I was left speechless. "That's not true."

"Oh, what do you know?" Cassia yelled. "You were not there when Rufus wept in his dreams. I knew he was lamenting about losing you."

"Cassia, maybe you're overthinking this."

She ignored me and continued, "Remember that story you told me of the two sisters, Rachel and Leah?"

"Yes, but what does that have to do with anything?"

"I don't know who was luckier. Leah got to spend more years with Jacob, but Rachel remained to be the deepest pain in Jacob's heart."

I was at a loss for words. We sat together in silence for a long time.

"I should return home. But I'm glad I came here today, Vita," Cassia said. "Letting it out made me feel better." She stood and approached the door. But before leaving, she turned to me and said, "I am pregnant now, Vita. When our child is born, we'll leave Rome and move to Philippi. We'll be very far from Rome and start a new life there. It might be the last time we see each other. Take care, Vita." With that, she exited the room.

I retreated to my room and sat on the bed for a while, not knowing what to make of Cassia's visit, so I decided to say a short prayer for her.

"Dear God, I pray that you grant Cassia and her house peace and love. In Jesus' name. Amen." Throughout the rest of the day, her visit kept coming to mind.

The thoughts pained me, not because I still loved Rufus in the same way I once did, but because they were on the path to building a happy family of three, while I was left all alone, about to embark on a journey to an unfamiliar city, beginning a life full of uncertainties.

Lord, all I have is You. Please never desert me.

After a day filled with chores, I found myself on the verge of sleep when Elaina knocked on my door late at night. "Vita, Marcus wants to see you. He is in the living room. Would you like to meet him?"

"Of course," I said, rubbing my sleepy eyes, then tidied my clothes and headed for the living room.

Marcus looked really neat, his beard shaved and his hair shining with olive oil. "Vita, I hope I-I didn't interrupt your... your sleep," he stuttered.

"No, not at all. Where is Achilles? Why didn't you bring him here?"

"He's at home. I have a neighbor looking over him," he said. "I had to come alone, Vita, because I have important things to tell you."

"What is it?" I was a little nervous.

"Shall we take a walk outside? Elaina was saying you haven't gone out of this building for a while. You need some fresh air."

I hesitated but then nodded. "You're right. I do need fresh air. Where shall we go?"

"Just follow me." Marcus grinned and reached for my hand. I didn't reject him because he was like a big brother to me, making me feel safe around him.

Leaving our neighborhood, he led me down a few lanes before arriving at a river.

"Is that the Tiber River?" I asked.

"Yes, it is," Marcus replied. "Do you remember the day we ran away from Tigellinus' soldiers and went all the way here and across the river?"

"Yes, I do!" I exclaimed. "But it was so dark that night, and I didn't get to look at the river closely."

"Let's take a walk along the river then. It's such a good view here." Marcus beamed.

So, we strolled along the riverbank, surrounded by vibrant dahlias, cosmos, and hydrangeas, their blossoms in full bloom, filling the air with their delightful fragrances.

"I'm leaving Rome tomorrow," Marcus suddenly said.

"Leaving Rome?" I always thought I would be the one to bid farewell to everyone here. "Where are you going?"

"To Corinth again," Marcus answered, "but this time, I'll be going as a missionary, and I won't be back for a while."

"But what about Achilles? Is he coming along with you? It must be tough for a boy his age to leave his friends behind for such a long journey." My heart ached as I considered the challenges that lay ahead for the boy who had lost his mother.

"Achilles is a strong boy now, especially after the training he did with... well... you know. Anyway, he will do well enough with it." Marcus smiled and cleared his throat. "Vita, I know this might be an embarrassing question, but I can't have peace until I get an answer from you."

"What is it, Marcus? If you need any help, I'll do my best."

"Do you want to come with me?"

"What do you mean? My ship departs in two days..." My voice trailed off as I vaguely got his point but still couldn't believe what he was saying.

"I... what I mean is... do you want to be my mission partner and... and... wife?" His last words were almost inaudible.

"But Marcus. I-I don't..." I struggled to find any form of words that wouldn't hurt his feelings, "I mean, I respect you as a good Christian brother, but I just—"

"I know I don't have the same wealth and good looks as your prefect suitor. But we have the same faith. Isn't that the most important in marriage?"

"Yes, but..." I didn't know what to say.

"Vita, I have always prayed that God will give me a helper for my mission. The first day I saw you, I had the feeling that you were the one. Although it broke my heart when I saw the way you looked at Caius, I never gave up waiting and praying. So, do I have a chance now?"

His round moist eyes resembled those of a deer.

"What would my life be like if I became his wife?" I pondered. It must be a life steeped in holiness and piety. We'd commence each day with our morning prayer together and conclude it with a nightly devotion. We'd worship and serve side by side, embarking on mission trips together. And our future children would be raised in faith and love.

Sound amazing?

Yes. Kind of. Well, a bit. But why was there no joy in my heart?

After a long silence, I said, "Yes, Marcus. God delivered me from the temptation. I won't marry a man who doesn't share my deepest belief. But I'm sorry, I still can't love you as a wife loves a husband. It's not fair for either of us," I said, feeling a deep sorrow as I noticed the light in his eyes dimming. "I'm sorry, Marcus. I owe you my life, and you'll always be my dearest brother. But you see, though I love you, it is wholly platonic."

He took a long breath and rubbed his reddening eyes. "Well, I guess I've got your answer. Thanks for being honest with me, Vita. It's getting late now. Let me walk you back home."

We walked back to Elaina's house without saying another word.

"I'll go home now to get ready for the trip. If God wills, we may see each other in the future. Or in heaven, at least," he said as we reached our destination, giving me a gentle hug before he departed.

After he disappeared at the end of the lane, my heart was sore, as if my brother had really gone from me.

I went straight for my room, collapsing atop my bed and tossing and turning for a long time. It seemed that I had experienced far too many painful farewells in these past few days.

The man I loved, the man who loved me, and the girl who had once been my friend and sister... I had lost all these dear people. And in two days' time, I would leave Elaina and everyone here, setting off on a lonely trip taking me to a place where I knew no one.

Loneliness gripped my heart. Everyone who mattered to me was either departing or would be left behind. A frightening emptiness enveloped me, nearly suffocating. But in my dazed state, I seemed to hear a soft, gentle voice.

"I will always be with you, even until the end of the world."

Fifty-Three

Fire!

THE HORSE COULDN'T GALLOP any faster as Caius pushed it to its limits. Galloping through the uneven terrain, his body and the energy poured into one word—Vita. Nothing else mattered. Not the rocky roads with the possibility of losing the horse's shoes or the possibility of a spy following him. His senses focused squarely on his mission.

He wanted to tell her he had totally made up his mind to become part of her faith—a faith he didn't fully comprehend but was unquestionably ready to embrace.

There truly did seem to be something special about it, something that made Christians all content with whatever they had in life, even when it was little or when suffering came.

There was something transcendent about the faith. Christians seemed to place their identity in being children of God, not in material possessions or status or what others thought of them. This trait touched Caius deeply and drew him closer to his desire to know this God and be united with Vita in body and soul.

The last few weeks had been like hell. Every one of the beautiful women on the royal ship meant nothing to him and all the luxuries looked like dirt and filth.

He was ready to let go of his ego. There was no point in attempting to assert power over a heart that was under the right guidance. If her God made her that pure and beautiful in all she did, who was Caius or anyone to want to exert control over such perfection?

Once filled with pride, this time, his ego had to bow for the love he held for her and the reverence he had for her God. And he was going to do it without regrets and unconditionally.

Removing one hand off the reins, Caius looked again at the parchment where the map was drawn. He had a few turns to make before reaching the long, secluded way to Elaina's home. Out of instinct, he glanced behind to check if anybody was following him. Seemingly sensing the owner's intention, the horse neighed in response.

Dismounting and with his chest heaving, Caius stumbled into a run.

"Vita!" he yelled. "Vita!"

But it was Elaina who came to the door, casting a concerned gaze over him from head to toe, particularly noting his heaving chest, as she cautiously stepped out of the door.

"Caius. Why have you come back?"

"Where is Vita?"

"She is not here," Elaina said sternly.

"It's impossible! You must be hiding Vita somewhere. Let me in!" Caius grabbed Elaina's shoulders, rocking them vigorously, his face almost brushing hers.

Elaina shook his hands off. "I told you she is not here. And it is not civilized to treat an old woman like that."

Feeling that he had been too aggressive, Caius stepped back. "I apologize," he said. "Please, tell me where she is, Elaina. I have important things to share with her."

Elaina paused for a long time and sighed.

"Well, all right, but I doubt she'll thank me," Elaina replied hesitantly. "She left this morning for the dock on the Tiber River. From there, she planned to take a boat to Ostia harbor, where she'd board a ship bound for Cyprus around this time. However, she didn't tell me where she intended to disembark from the ship. Hurry! Ride alongside the Tiber River to Ostia, and perhaps you can still catch up with her."

Sprinting back, Caius mounted the horse, galloping away without a word. He simply raised his arm in a silent farewell as he departed.

Top of Form

Elaina watched him disappear and murmured, "Oh, Lord. If the vision you showed me last night is their fate, please be with them and strengthen them with your power."

The Tiber River was exceptionally beautiful in the summertime, but Caius had paid no attention to the view. The horse's gallop turned into a trot when they reached the most crowded area of the harbor.

The harbor was rowdy, with people peddling all sorts of goods. Vendors yelled out their wares, buyers engaged in lively chatter, and sailors barked orders at the highest volume. Caius scanned the crowd frantically in search of Vita.

"Vita!" he yelled, pushing past a cart, almost toppling it over.

"Watch your step, you dim-eyed fool!" the old man who was pushing the cart cursed. However, when he raised his head and saw Caius dressed in fine attire, a flicker of fear crossed his eyes. "My lord, I apologize for my rudeness. I didn't mean to be impolite. Did my cart damage your clothes?"

"No, the apology is mine," Caius replied, astounded by his own response.

"Vita!" he called again, his head swiveling rapidly as he arrived at the area where all the ships were ready to set sail. Passengers were queuing up to board.

Grabbing whoever he bumped into first, he asked if the stranger knew which ship was heading to Cyprus. Unfortunately, that person didn't know it.

Did the ship already leave?

The idea of losing Vita forever sent shivers down to his toes.

In his moment of deep frustration, a familiar voice reached his ears. He turned frantically to locate where it came from. By a ship two steps forward stood a familiar figure; there she was, haggling for the price of the journey. Caius noticed she was a lot thinner than before.

"Vita!" he cried with joy. She turned to his direction in bewilderment.

Her eyes widened as he rushed over and scooped her up in his arms.

"My Vita. Oh, Vita. I almost lost you," he said, squeezing her with passion. The man she'd been haggling with stared at them in consternation.

"I could have lost you because of my stupid ego. My stupid, empty ego. I have learned my lesson, Vita. Nothing comes between us again."

He gently pulled away, holding her at arm's length.

"I swear on my life, I will never make you choose between God and me. He has been the source of your existence. He is why you are so beautiful inside and out. He is why you shine above all others." He stared deep into Vita's eyes. "Therefore, no. Never would I make you choose between Him and our love. I am ready to do anything just to make sure I don't lose you. I cannot lose you. Life without you has been utter misery. Do not take my heart away to Cyprus. I'll rot in Rome, rot, do you hear? I'll die from heartbreak and perish from sadness."

Vita's face was wet from the tears streaming down.

"Speak to me, my love. Do not cry. I plead with you. End my misery and say something."

"You really would let me put God first?"

"Yes, and not just that. You *will* put God first. And I will share in your faith. I will get to know this God of yours, why you love Him so much and how He has made you so divine. When I was away, I realized how much I had missed you, and also your God and the family."

"Oh, Caius, you speak too highly of a human being."

"My faith might be shallow at this moment, but I will learn and grow. And I promise I won't ask you to marry me until God finishes his good work in my heart. Didn't Peter say the husband should be the spiritual leader at home? Someday, I'll prove I'm qualified."

While Vita was still reeling from the surprise, Caius continued, "Vita, please don't leave Rome. You can go back to Elaina's house, and I'll visit you all every week when I'm done with my job in the barracks. And I'll attend worship with you and serve with you whenever I have time. When Elaina and Peter think I'm a mature enough Christian, I'll ask them for your hand formally. Please promise you'll never leave me, Vita."

"I promise." Vita drew him into another heartfelt hug.

They stood lost in their world, oblivious to the mindless buzz around them, Caius feeling his world realign. Fear was receding as he breathed in her scent. He would protect her from the whole of Rome, fight the emperor if he had to, and keep her from the claws of the venomous women of the upper families.

But right now, he didn't want to think about all those things. He just wanted to enjoy every moment he had Vita by his side. He helped her onto the horse and rode together with her up the Tiber River. This time, there was no need to rush.

Every flower on the riverbank seemed to be smiling at them—and he smiled back.

Soon, the Gate Aurelius was right in front of them, and Elaina's house was right at the corner. "We're almost here," Caius said.

Suddenly, two young men rushed out of the gate, almost bumping into his horse.

"What's wrong with—" His anger was cut off by a sudden scream.

"Fire!" one of them shouted without slowing down his pace.

He looked toward the gate, a huge crowd rushing out from it, all shouting, "Fire! Fire!"

"Out of the way! Out of my way!" The crowd had gone into a frenzy.

"Look over there! Caius, look at that smoke!" Vita exclaimed, pointing. Before she mentioned it, he'd already caught sight of huge clouds of smoke rising far away from the inner city.

"Vita, I need to go into the city to check what is going on. I'm sorry, but I can't escort you to Elaina's home now."

"Don't leave me! I'll go with you. Last time, I helped you solve your problems. Maybe I'll help you this time too."

Caius looked into her determined eyes, well aware of her stubborn streak from their days together. He finally caved. "Fine, just hold onto me in all circumstances."

However, as soon as they entered the city, Caius instantly regretted his decision. The fire was far more extensive than he had anticipated, with thick smoke billowing into the sky and buildings crumbling amidst the flames.

"Nero has taken two thirds of the praetorians with him on his trip. I need to head back to the barracks and rally the rest of the men to put out the fire."

Dark columns of smoke billowed as they moved in the midst of chaos, bumping into people on the way as they hurried in different directions. Their horse, spooked by the dense smoke and the turmoil around them, stubbornly refused to budge.

"I've never seen fire spread so quickly in Rome," he murmured, dismounting the horse with Vita, holding her hand and pressing forward.

"We are nearly surrounded by fire. What should we do?" she asked, her distress evident.

"Let's make our way to that basilica," he said, guiding Vita toward the building that remained untouched by the flames. "We can cut through there and reach our barracks more quickly." Just as they reached the enclave, a deafening crash echoed through the air as a three-tiered building collapsed nearby.

Without hesitation, they sprinted up the basilica's stairs and paused briefly to catch their breath.

"Fire! Fire! There's fire on the left!" someone screamed as the fire roared forward, aided by the abundance of dry wood in that vicinity.

"We need to hurry," Vita said, soon discovering that many others shared their sentiment. The crowd thronged through the huge building, pushing and shoving in their urgency.

"Arghh!" Vita yelled in pain, Caius instinctively pulling her to his side. The bustling crowd had already moved on, seemingly unconcerned about the potential for a stampede.

"I-I twisted my ankle."

"I'll carry you," Caius said, lifting Vita into his arms and maneuvering through the chaos. However, amidst their hurried progress, Vita suddenly cried out, "My satchel! It's gone!" Caius turned and noticed it lying on the ground a short distance behind them.

"Let me get it for you."

"No, let's go! It's too dangerous here!" Vita urged.

Gently placing her back on the ground, Caius insisted, "This is too important to be lost. I'll be back in no time." He swiftly made his way to the fallen satchel, snatching it up, and hurried back toward Vita. But just as he almost reached her side, he saw terror in Vita's widened eyes.

"Caius, run!" she screamed as a plank of wood and debris came crashing down.

Caius shielded her with his own body, taking the blow on his back.

He bellowed in pain, his hunched posture shielding her from further falling debris until he finally succumbed to unconsciousness.

Fifty-Four

Baptism

HE FELT LIKE A boat in troubled waters, a swirling of several incoherent things at the same time running around his consciousness. He felt pain in all his joints, his skull throbbing severely. Trying to move his body left him feeling overworked as if he had been at war all night. Voices filtered through reality into his ears.

After several tries, he was able to open his eyelids, his vision fogged as every object meshed together with no clear definition.

"Caius! Caius!" a familiar voice said.

He opened his eyes, squinting at the onslaught of light.

"You are awake," Vita said, her voice trembling with joy when she called other people in the room. "He's awake! Caius is awake!"

"Praise be to God," someone said.

Memories rushed back. The fire. The rushing crowd. The satchel. And the falling plank. "Are you hurt, Vita? How is the fire now?" Caius said, struggling with his words.

"I'm fine. The fire is over. You need to rest," she said as others left the room. "And the satchel is fine too." She raised it in her hand, and her eyes glistened with a blend of relief and guilt. "You are so stupid, Caius. If you had died because of this, how would I ever forgive myself?"

"I just thought you'd be sad if it was lost," he said, hissing with pain. "And I guess there are pages about me in there too."

"Silly." She placed a hand on his shoulder. "You need to rest. Now please lie down."

"No, I can't. The Praetorian Guard needs me to take control."

"Don't worry. Theophilus visited yesterday, saying rescue and repair work is being carried out everywhere. And those emergency tents you requested from the emperor helped a lot."

Caius heaved a sigh of relief.

"I can't believe I'm still alive. When the plank collapsed on us, I thought I was doomed. But I'm happy I got to be with you at the last moment of my life."

"I thought the same way too. The basilica collapsed; many people were buried beneath it. Praetorians were digging for the ones still alive, but there were not enough hands.

Elaina and Peter heard the news about the fire, so they brought men to look for us and other brethren lost in the fire, and luckily, they found us."

"I asked Nero to recruit more men just in case of any emergencies, but he wouldn't listen. He'd rather spend the money on his banquets," Caius remarked angrily. "If we had more praetorians, we could save more lives. But I owe Peter and your Christian friends my life again."

"Oh, Caius." Vita looked at him tenderly and said, "You have done your best as a prefect. I just feel so sorry you were wounded twice in the past few months because of me."

"And not to mention hundreds of times my heart got wounded by your tongue," Caius teased. "Aren't you glad I'm still alive so you can pay me back somehow?"

"Stop joking!" Vita exclaimed. "The plank falling on you was the scariest moment of my life."

"Silly girl, I won't die. I promised to protect you all my life." He held her hands tightly.

"Greetings," a deep voice boomed from the doorway.

"Apostle!" Vita replied in awe, quickly retrieving her hands from Caius' and blushed. "I didn't know you would be coming."

"Yes, we were busy visiting families with members who had been wounded or killed in the fire," he replied. "The loss is great. Elaina is also here with me today. She brought some medicine and supplies."

"Elaina and Peter, we owe you for saving our lives," Caius said, looking toward them.

"It was all in God's hand, brother." Peter grinned.

"Would he really have cared if I'd died or not? I was not His follower back then, at least, not officially."

"Do you want to be one now?" Elaina asked with a smile as she placed a tray on the table along with a bowl of chopped herbs.

"Yes," Caius said earnestly. "I've made up my mind to serve Him before I came back for Vita. And I have not changed my mind."

"Do you understand what it means to follow Jesus?" Peter asked.

"I'll do whatever He asks me to do," Caius said resolutely.

"And I dare say you probably don't know what you are talking about, young man." Peter chuckled. "But it is fine. I told Jesus the same thing when He asked me to follow Him."

"What happened then?" Caius was curious.

"Well, then, when temptation came, I denied Him three times in a single day," Peter said with another laugh. "It took years of trial and difficulty to know what it really meant to follow Jesus. I still can't say I understand it fully right now."

Caius grew silent and Peter placed a hand on his shoulder.

"Don't worry, young man. Jesus knows our weakness, and He promised to walk with us on this journey of life. Since you made your decision to follow Him, there is no reason I can't get you baptized."

"Baptized?"

"Yes. Immersion into the water to signify the death of the old body and the rising of a new body in Christ," Vita said.

"Are you ready for this journey? It is a dangerous journey, but never boring, I promise." Peter grinned heartily.

"Yes. I want to experience this joy and share with you the divine peace you always carry around, even in the face of great trouble. I want to be able to talk to God like you always do. He listens to your voice, so I want Him to hear mine too."

"Praise the Lord. You're still recovering from your wound, so we have arranged your baptism in a couple of days," Peter said.

"No, I can't wait a couple of days. I want to do it today."

"There is no need to hurry, Caius. You still need rest," Vita protested.

"I must return to my duty immediately. Before I leave, I want to openly confess my faith through baptism. If possible, I'd like to be engaged to Vita right now. However, as a new believer, I understand that I am not yet worthy to be the head of a family. Therefore, I will patiently wait." Caius gazed fervently at Vita, whose face blushed crimson. He then turned to Peter, saluting him military-style, and said, "Apostle, you are like a father to Vita. After my baptism, may I seek Vita's hand in courtship with your permission?"

"May God reward your humility, Caius. I grant your request. The only person you need to ask now is Vita."

All eyes turned to Vita, her cheeks flushing even deeper as she bowed her head.

"Vita, after my baptism, would you be willing to enter into courtship with me, with the intention of marriage?" Caius asked.

"I would love to," she replied.

Caius rushed to hold Vita in his arms before she could finish her statement. "Vita, you have made me the happiest man in the world."

"I think it's time we prepare some water now." Peter let out the brightest laugh.

Fifty-Five

An Unexpected Encounter

WE SETTLED IN A modest villa on the outskirts of Rome, spacious enough to accommodate Peter, Elaina, and the homeless women with their children. Caius had to leave to handle post-disaster repairs, so he suggested we temporarily relocate to one of his properties. Theophilus stayed with us briefly, but after my persistent encouragement, he eventually departed to join Caius at the barracks.

Bellona lost a leg in the fire, but thanks to the physician Caius sent, her life was saved and the other leg was spared.

Each time I changed her bandage, her eyes flickered and her lips trembled, yet no words escaped her. This morning, as I delivered her food, she suddenly said to me, "Vita, I'm sorry for having said so many mean words to you. I'm... ashamed of myself."

"Don't be too hard on yourself, Bellona. I pass judgments in my heart all the time. I simply don't always voice them." I smiled and patted her shoulder gently.

"You know why I did that? Because I was jealous. I was jealous the first time I saw you when the prefect carried you on his shoulder walking past the tavern in which I worked."

"If you knew how I was feeling at that moment, you probably

wouldn't be jealous." I chuckled.

"I would still feel jealous, Vita. Can you imagine living alone for twenty years? My first husband passed away when I was just eighteen, and my second followed suit two years later. No man would dare to marry me after that. It was fair that people despised me for my gossiping, but does anyone truly comprehend the depth of my loneliness all these years?"

I was speechless at Bellona's confession. Of course, I had never liked her, but at this moment, there was a deep sorrow for all the judgment passed on her in my heart.

"Your leg is still recovering. Tomorrow, Theophilus will bring additional herbs to dress the wounds." As she sobbed softly, I gently pulled her blanket high around her.

In the afternoon, when I checked on her, her fever had grown worse.

"Elaina, I don't think I have time to wait for Theophilus to bring the herbs tomorrow. I must go out and buy some before sunset," I said in a hurry.

"It's very dangerous outside." Elaina sounded worried. "The mobs are robbing all the taverns and shops."

"The herb store is only two blocks away. I'll be fine."

"Let me go with you," Elaina said.

"No, the wounded need your care, Elaina. You mustn't leave. I promise I'll be back in no time," I said and rushed out of the door, covering myself with a ragged cloak that served as my disguise.

The once bustling street now stood in eerie silence, lined with half-burned shops. As I walked down, my gaze fell upon a resilient herb store at the end, marked by visible scars from the recent blaze, showcasing its fierce battle against the flames.

The face of the marble sculpture of Aesculapius, the god of medicine, was veiled by soot while his snake-twined staff lay broken in the middle.

Despite the damage, the store continued to operate, defying the odds.

"Five gold coins in total," the shopkeeper said when I pointed at the salve I needed.

"It was only two silver coins last week!" I exclaimed.

"Do you not keep your ears open, young lady?" the owner jeered. "Ours is the only herb shop open in this district. If you don't want it, tons of people are waiting, so stop wasting my time!"

"Here is your money," I replied, not daring to argue further. Thank God, Theophilus had left us some money before he went.

Stepping over the threshold of the store's gate, I caught the sound of heated quarreling from across the street.

"Leave my inn! Do you think I run this place for charity? I've been patient enough!" a short woman snapped, her mouth tight, a toothpick poking out the side as she planted a hand on her hip and pointed firmly at the couple in front of her.

"Please, if you could just give us one more day, we'll find another place to stay. Have pity on my pregnant wife."

The voice... Can it be? My heart skipped a beat in surprise.

A closer look proved my guess right. There stood Rufus, his beard unkempt, hair disheveled, and posture slightly stooped. His clothing was in tatters, worse than what even the lowliest slave would wear in Eubulus' household. Beside him was Cassia, looking miserable as she held onto her back with her stomach protruding, heavy with her pregnancy.

The innkeeper continued her tirade. "I showed you pity when I took you in on trust. You claimed one of your servants would bring the money. It's been nearly a week. Where is it?"

"We... I will..." Rufus stuttered.

"Stop stuttering and get out of my sight! I need this space for people who are ready to pay!" the woman barked, slamming the door shut.

"What do we do now? I am feeling pain all over my body," Cassia grumbled.

"Let's not worry. We'll figure out a way." Rufus gently rubbed her back and put another hand under her protruding belly to give her some support. "Does that feel better?" he asked softly.

Unable to hold back any longer, I called out, "Rufus!"

Four eyes looked in my direction.

"Vita?" His eyes squinted in disbelief, revealing the deep wrinkles etched across his forehead. "I don't believe it," he murmured.

"It *is* me," I said, managing a small smile.

Cassia glanced between her husband and me, a frown creasing her brow. Rufus' face was half joy, half guilt, as he tried to get across the street. But Cassia tugged on his sleeves and groaned, "I don't want to move. My feet hurt."

"Stay there," I called out to her and went across the road.

"What are you doing here?" Cassia asked, a tense emotion written on her face.

"Just bought some salve from that shop." I pointed to the herb store.

"It has been so long, sister." Rufus looked at me from head to toe and stammered out these words. "I-I'm happy you look so well."

"Of course, she is not ugly and fat like your pregnant wife," Cassia spat out. "Girls like her always know how to get the best in life."

"May I ask what has happened?" I asked, realizing the source of her emotion and trying to ignore her poignant remark.

"As you have witnessed, we just got thrown out of an inn. How do you think we are doing?" Cassia replied in a clipped tone, bitterness exuding from her.

Rufus reached out to Cassia, but she recoiled, rejecting his touch. He sighed, shaking his head, and explained, "Our villa was burned down, and we lost all our fortune. We had recently made a substantial purchase from a merchant at sea. The goods had yet to arrive, but all evidence of our payment was consumed in the fire. Now we are deeply in debt, forced to release all our slaves. And here we stand, with nothing."

"Sounds like you can keep them anyway since all their deeds were burnt," Cassia said sarcastically.

"Slaves? What about Julia? Where did she go?" I found myself rocking Rufus' arms. In Elaina's house, Caius had told me Julia went back to Eubulus' house after her ankle healed.

"How would I know? All those ungrateful dregs left in one night!" Cassia cursed.

"She left? How could she support herself without a penny?" I heard my voice crying.

"Don't worry about her. That cunning vixen knows how to make a living with men," Cassia jeered.

"Stop saying that! She's my friend," I couldn't help but cry out.

"I bet you've already found out what a natural prostitute she is, then," Cassia mocked again. "Did you used to do it too? Were you two of a kind in everything?"

I closed my eyes and took a deep breath. It was not a good time to fight.

"See, I understand how tough this is…" I tried to divert the conversation. "What I was trying to say is that I can offer you help."

Cassia huffed with derision. "What can you do, sleep with your master to favor us?"

The word stung me to my bones.

"Would you… please stop?" Rufus tugged his wife's hand hopelessly.

"Oh, Lord, please give me strength. I don't want to argue with a heavily pregnant woman and regret it later." I clenched my fists and fought against an onrush of rage, thanking God that I was not hungry at this moment.

"Please, whatever help you can offer, we are ready to accept," Rufus said earnestly.

"Would you mind staying at my place for a few days? It's Caius' house. He graciously offered us shelter until our homes are rebuilt. He has been baptized, and we are courting with the blessing of Apostle Peter."

A brief flash of pain crossed Rufus' eyes, vanishing as quickly as it appeared.

"Ha, this will be the scandal of the year," Cassia laughed. "How am I worthy to be sheltered by his noble property?"

"Cassia!" Rufus yelled angrily again.

"Don't you dare yell at me, you spineless man! I should have never forsaken our divine Mother Juno and accepted your carpenter god who couldn't even save himself from the cross. Now Juno's hands are heavy on me!" Cassia then turned and pointed at me. "And for you, do not think because you are hitched to a rich patrician, you'll be free from all the woes. The divine Roman gods will punish you for polluting Rome with your poisonous religion!"

Before I could react, Cassia continued her tirade, "And speaking of revenge, our divine Mother Juno has never spared anyone who dared to affront her authority!" Spittle flew from her mouth as she yelled in anger.

"Cassia! Enough!" Rufus' face flushed with frustration. "I've been putting up with you for too long. Do you think we have other choices? Today, you're going to accept a favor from Vita. Otherwise, we'll sleep in the street tonight, and the mobs might deal with us at night! Think about our unborn child if you are even the slightest bit worthy of being a mother."

Awkward silence.

I started walking toward the house, and they followed me all the way without saying anything.

Fifty-Six

The Arrest

THE GIRL THREW HERSELF on the floor with her legs kicking and her little fists pounding on the atrium's marble ground. I lifted her and tapped her back in a rhythm for comfort.

"What's bothering you so, little Fabia?"

"They chased me away."

"Who?"

"The kids," she said, pointing outside. "They would not let me play with them."

"Why? What happened?"

"Their mother came and told me to leave her children alone. She said we made the gods angry and brought a curse on them."

"What is wrong with the child?" Theophilus said, coming to my side.

"It looks like people have already started to blame us Christians for the fire. Our children are being bullied. Yesterday, it was poor Claudius and Linus. And today, Fabia got picked on," I replied in frustration.

Fabia slipped out of my embrace and ran to the inner room for her mother.

"Christians are not well-liked in Rome, and this is not recent news." Theophilus shook his head. "And people need someone to blame when they feel out of control."

I couldn't refute his observation. "Oh, I wish Peter and Elaina were here. At least they could pray with us and give us comfort," I said dejectedly.

"Don't worry. No one is going to hurt a prefect's beloved woman and her friends." Theophilus' sentence was barely completed before a loud crash sounded outside.

"What is that?" Theophilus looked sideways, alarmed.

"Omen-bearer! Cursed people!" a voice smoldered from outside, each word flickering and crackling like burning embers floating in the air. I hurried toward the door, but was abruptly stopped by Theophilus, who pointed toward the opened window instead.

A small crowd had gathered there.

"Every good Roman celebrates Vulcanalia so the fire god will be pleased and protect us. We heard that you never participated in the festival, and persuaded others not to go! Now Vulcan is punishing us, and other Olympian gods might not be happy as well. Get ready because we will surely make you pay," a woman with a scarred face yelled.

"Is that not the same woman who came begging for herbs the other day?" Theophilus asked.

"The very one," I sighed.

"We will return soon! Wait here like cowards in a borrowed home," a venomous voice lashed out. "We heard one of you harlots slept with the prefect who owns this place. We will come back for you and your harlot!" A surge of anger coursed through me, but I stood resolute, unyielding to their threats.

"Who are those idiots yelling outside?" a groggy-looking Cassia said, waddling to the atrium. Rufus followed her, his eyes heavy from lack of sleep.

"Hold your peace, lady; these people outside are without reason," Theophilus said.

"Who are you to be talking to me like that?" she replied, her voice already rising.

"Mom, I'm scared of her." Fabia's little head suddenly popped out from behind a curtain.

"You need to calm down, Cassia," Rufus said, laying a hand behind her back.

"Do not tell me to calm down. Nobody gives me respect anymore. I, daughter of Eubulus, being disrespected by derelicts and scrawny children." Her eyes were watering and her lips stretched in a cry.

"If you have not noticed..." Theophilus started, but I cut his sharp retort short with a firm hand clamped over his shoulder. Cassia attempted to make her way to the door, only to be intercepted by Rufus.

"Folks are losing their heads, pointing fingers at us for the fire. It's not safe for you to leave," I cautioned her.

"I blame you too! I blame all of you! You, you, and you! People like you angered the gods and brought us this disaster," she said, bursting into another round of tears.

"Please, Cassia, be kind to these people when they've been kind to us," Rufus begged.

"Do not tell me to be kind," she roared in anger and stormed back into her room.

Theophilus shook his head and shared a look with a dejected Rufus.

"She gets on my nerves every time, even more than those outside," a lady remarked from behind us.

A few occupants rushed to the atrium after hearing the noise. "Glad someone finally says it," another old lady chimed in agreement.

"I just feel sorry for Rufus; he seems like a good man," the first added.

Hearing their whispered conversation, Cassia pivoted and headed back to the atrium. She charged toward them, hands waving in frustration. Rufus swiftly intervened, grabbing her shoulder from behind and enveloping her in his arms, gently guiding her back to their unit.

·•·♥·♥·♥·♥·

"I cannot keep doing this, Vita." Rufus found me the next morning as I made my rounds and was on the way to check what they needed.

"Doing what?"

"Thank you for your kind gesture, but it is obvious that if I keep my pregnant wife here, there will soon be more problems for all of us."

I wanted to comfort Rufus, but my words couldn't escape my mouth. He was right. Cassia was becoming too much of a burden for everyone here.

"I'm sorry. She wasn't like this before. Ever since she got pregnant, she's become very paranoid and quick to anger. It only got worse after the disaster," Rufus sighed heavily. "We've already packed our belongings. Cassia only needs a little more time to... to calm down before we leave."

"I understand you, Rufus. But where are you planning to go?"

"I will look for cheaper housing on the outskirts of town."

"Rufus! Rufus!" Cassia yelled hysterically from the room.

"I need to go and see what she needs," Rufus said and hurried inside.

I sighed and headed to my room, retrieving a pouch of silver coins from the money chest before returning to join them.

"Couldn't she at least help us with something? Are we going to travel empty-handed? What will we eat?" Rufus' voice roared from behind the curtain.

"Who is she to give to me? She was my slave!" Cassia protested.

"But we've already found shelter at her villa."

"The place doesn't even belong to her!"

I took a deep breath and entered. The rambling instantly stopped.

"I am sorry for bothering you, but I wanted to give you this to ease your journey," I said, extending my hands toward Rufus.

"Thank you for your help, Vita. We really need it," Rufus said, accepting the pouch. Cassia stared at me angrily without a word.

"Shall we pray together?" I suggested.

"We don't need help from a troublesome god! And don't think your money is a pity offering, just like you offered me your man!" Cassia retorted, snatching the pouch from Rufus' hand and hurling it to the ground. Then she rose abruptly and rushed out of the room. "I can't stay here for one more moment," she declared as she left.

Rufus picked up the pouch and placed it in his satchel, apologizing, "I'm truly sorry, Vita. I owe you everything." With that, he lifted the two large trunks and followed Cassia out.

Quietly, I trailed behind them, observing as they hurried out of the front door and watched Rufus' back disappear into the street.

Memories from five years ago flooded my mind. I had caught a glimpse of his back as he disappeared down the narrow lane toward the village gate. Little did I know that the following three years would be filled with heartbreak, longing, and relentless searching. Now, I stood there, watching his back fade before me for the second time, not even knowing if I would ever lay eyes on him again. I felt my heart was torn to pieces.

"Oh, Lord, please protect Rufus. Although my romantic feelings for him have faded, he will always be my closest family. Please watch over him and care for his wife and unborn child as well," I whispered softly, my tears streaming freely.

·▾·♥·♥·♥·▾·

It had been three days since they left, and I was still worried how Rufus and Cassia might be doing.

However, life in the villa became much more peaceful. We'd had fewer complaints and confrontations from the usual suspects, though it was fair to say the neighbors were still hostile toward us.

We could tolerate that, but the children were all suffering emotionally. Their mothers told them not to yell back at those mean kids on the street, so they had to bottle up their feelings. They stayed in the house most of the time and did not say anything to one another. It broke my heart to see them like this.

"Theophilus, we can't let the little ones live like this. They need some fresh air. Can you take them to a safe place to have some fun? Maybe just for half a day?" I asked.

"I have purchased a vineyard just outside the city. The kids can play there," Theophilus said. "But if I leave, who's going to protect you? Caius will be furious if anything happens to you."

"Nothing will happen. Just half a day and let the children enjoy some fresh air. I'm going to be fine," I said. "I'll talk about this with their mothers."

As expected, the widows were at first concerned about their children's safety if they left this property, but eventually, they all gave in to their begging and nagging. So Theophilus let them go into his carriage and drove off, while all the children exclaimed, "Vineyard! Vineyard!" from on board. After waving goodbye to them, I headed to check on Bellona, to whom I'd given some salve earlier.

I was intending to see how she fared when I heard a loud bang on the front door. The consistent hammering of fists pierced the quiet atmosphere.

"Open this door now!" someone shouted.

"Who's there?" I approached with caution.

"Open up! We're praetorian guards," came the familiar voice, sending my heart pounding in my chest wildly. Before I could gather my wits, the door was forcefully kicked open, and a swarm of heavily armed praetorians stormed in.

Leading the group was Tigellinus.

"Tigellinus, why are you here? You cannot just barge in here without telling us our offense." I tried to use the calmest tone possible.

A scroll was unfurled before me.

"I *can* be here with this in my possession," Tigellinus declared with a smirk. "Does a royal decree from the emperor suffice to justify my presence? Read it yourself if you're capable."

Although I couldn't make out all the words on the scroll, some enlarged ones caught my sight and sent an icy sensation along my spine.

"Christians charged with arson? Rumors abound, but there's no basis for it. Some of us were also victims of the fire!"

"That is not for me to answer," Tigellinus replied indifferently. "Arrest everyone in this building!" he ordered. "And I've got this one myself." He snatched me by the arm and fastened a rope around my wrists. I struggled, but he kicked me in the shin, and I crumpled in pain.

The other soldiers charged through the atrium and the inner rooms. Cries of women and infants could be heard as the guards pushed and shoved them out of their quarters.

"Where is that Theophilus dog?" Tigellinus looked around as the soldiers brought all captives into the atrium. "Too bad he's not here to watch the show. Never mind. Leave some of our men here to wait for him."

Then he herded us into a horse-drawn cage outside and closed the cage door.

"Why are they taking us?" one woman cried out hysterically.

"We can't leave like this. Our children are still out!" A widow was about to cry when Bellona covered her mouth. "Don't! Unless you want them to die," she whispered with urgency.

"Oh, Lord. What am I going to do? Is this still by your will? Give me guidance, please!" I lamented in the cage.

As we arrived at the gloomy prison, a sense of dread settled over us. Our apprehension grew as we were herded inside. Then, the prison door clanged shut in my face.

The guards had not been merciful in handling the people. Babies cried from different cells, and women, some of whom were fire victims, endured their pain with stifled grunts. As I was forcefully pushed into the prison, I caught a sinister smile on Tigellinus' face.

"I will see how you will escape this time," Tigellinus taunted, his menacing figure towering over me. "Pray to your gods, use your witchcraft, cast spells. Do whatever you have to do and do it quickly. Your time is limited." His chilling cackle echoed in the dark cell as he departed.

Fifty-Seven

A Royal Scheme

THE INDIGO SKY WAS on the verge of fading into white, an unusual time for the emperor to call a meeting. Caius felt unsettled when a royal slave delivered the order.

He mounted his Esperian horse and headed for the palace. Before he entered the door of Nero's library, he heard the dictator's agitated voice.

"The mobs are crazy. They are gathering outside the palace gate and protesting all day. Some even say I was the one who set the fire! Can you believe that?" Nero roared.

"I'll kill all of them at your order," Tigellinus replied.

"You can't kill them all, my lord," the empress suggested. "They will view you more of a tyrant."

Nero looked at Caius and smirked, saying, "I heard you ran back to Rome in the middle of our trip for your loved one. How touching is that!"

"Yes, my lord. By the grace of God, she accepted me as her suitor at last," Caius said. "But I returned to my duty right after the engagement. We praetorians will do our best in appeasing the people and rebuilding the city."

"How wonderful! I've been thinking of a perfect wedding gift for you," the empress said with a hand over her mouth to suppress her grimace. "A very memorable one."

Her smile, tinged with malice, tightening Caius' heart with dread.

"But the mob is not easy to appease," Nero said. "Last year, I sponsored three months' games in the arena to stop them from grumbling about the tax raise. We'll probably need a more splendid show this year."

"We can gather the best gladiators from all provinces," Tigellinus suggested eagerly.

"I have a better idea. What would please the mob more than witnessing the execution of the arsonists in spectacular ways?" the empress said.

"Arsonists?" Nero stared at her in disbelief. "But they suspect I'm the one who set the fire!"

"Unless you give them another name." The empress' voice was as cold as ice. "A name that is already defamed. People will believe it."

"And who should that be?" Nero asked, clearly excited about the empress' suggestion.

"There is a secret cult in Rome that has been hated by the public for years. People call them Christians." The empress' words sent an icy jolt through Caius' body, freezing him in place like a statue.

"Oh, yes, yes, I've heard of this name. They used to be a sect of the Jews, but now rumor says they are everywhere. Some even claim there are converts among my Praetorians." Nero's gaze cast on Caius and Tigellinus. "Have you heard of such things, my prefects?"

"Indeed. I dismissed one last year who openly confessed to being one of them. He refused to pay homage to Mars, our divine war god." Tigellinus beamed.

"But I heard they are upright people," Caius interjected.

"You are too naive, dear boy," Nero cackled. "I won't blame you though. Passion always made men stupid. It's nothing new."

"These Christians, they make perfect scapegoats," the empress continued. "They believe in one true god, so they don't participate in all the festivals. And they believe there is a final judgment day when the wicked will be thrown into a fire pit. If we spread the rumor that they are the arsonists, the mob will believe it for sure."

"Genius!" Nero exclaimed. "Who else would serve as better scapegoats than these fellows? And there are so many of them, enough to make a great show to please the mob."

Caius felt a cold sweat break out on his forehead.

How did this happen? How did things start to go in this direction?

He stepped forward and said in a loud voice, "My lord, please consider this carefully. If the people find out Christians are not criminals, how are they going to respond? I worry you will lose your prestige with your subjects."

Caius' words caused Nero's eyes to widen, yet swiftly, a subtle smile tugged at the corner of his mouth. "Prefect, I'm curious. Why do you care so much about these Christians? They are the notorious kind anyway. I'm doing a good thing for the empire to purge the dregs from it," he added with a nonchalant shrug.

"I happen to know some Christians, and they are kind and honest people," Caius said earnestly. "Punishing innocent people for crimes they didn't commit... What will the people think of you, my lord?"

"People?" Nero jeered. "The mob never thinks. They only believe what we tell them to believe. I'll hire more orators to give speeches in all the markets of Rome. They'll give people the story they want."

"You're right, my emperor. Shall I start the arrests today?" Tigellinus' hand was resting on his sword.

"Do as you please. There is no way they'd escape." Nero waved airily and yawned.

At that signal, all the people were dismissed, and Caius' heart sank.

Vita and her Christian friends!

That piece of property was very private so they should be safe for now. But it would be better to move them farther away from Rome as soon as possible.

If he had to protect just Vita, it would be much easier. But Vita would never leave her friends unattended. Maybe he needed to hire a ship tonight and transfer them to his estate in Macedonia until this turmoil passed. "Rome is not a safe place right now. If Vita were to be caught, there is no way she would deny her faith and save her own life," he muttered to himself.

He struggled to conceal any sign of uneasiness as he walked to the door. But the empress' voice dragged him back.

"Caius, I need you to check the emperor's bedchamber. Yesterday, the slaves reported that there was a black shadow around the window. Could it be an assassin?" She gave the mischievous grin again, the one which made Caius want to punch her right in her face.

"Assassin?" Nero seemed terrified. "Check carefully, Caius. It's an uneasy time and I know many people want me dead. If you find any suspects, I'll inquire about them in person!"

"That sly woman! She's trying to delay me," Caius cursed under his breath as he followed the slave reluctantly and checked Nero's bedchamber. By the time he had finally convinced Nero that everything was fine, it was almost nighttime.

He hurried to the gate of the palace and mounted his horse, heading for the east side of the city. Not even the cool summer night breeze could dry the beads of sweat on his forehead. Gripping the horse's reins tightly, Caius leaned forward and pressed the spurs against the horse's sides, urging the steed to surge with every ounce of strength it possessed.

"Oh, Lord Jesus, please let me make it in time."

In this moment, he truly did pray to the Lord, not a fiber of doubt left in him.

Fifty-Eight

A Plea to Nero

Caius' heart plummeted when he saw a familiar figure approaching him on a horse at the turn onto Saturn Street. All remaining hope dissipated into thin air upon seeing Theophilus' desperate face.

"Theophilus!" he shouted.

Theophilus dismounted hastily, rushing toward Caius. His grip tightened around the horse's reins, while his bloodshot eyes and glistening beads of sweat caused Caius' heart to sink even further.

"My lord, I beg your forgiveness. I failed to protect Vita. Please, punish me!" Theophilus pleaded, his voice choked with anguish. He told Caius how he had taken the children to his vineyards to get some fresh air and had been spared from the arrest.

"When we were heading toward the villa at sunset, the blacksmith living across the street stopped me. He told me some fully armored soldiers had snatched all of them away. So, I hurried to hide these children in my home and rushed to inform you. Do not go to that place; there must still be Tigellinus' men there."

"I must go there! What if Vita is still there, hiding somewhere in the villa?"

"No, do not deceive yourself, Caius. She was taken away. The blacksmith recognized her and confirmed it. If you get caught, even if Tigellinus were to release you somehow, we might lose precious time to rescue her."

Caius felt the world crumble around him.

Alighting from his horse, he almost lost his balance. After regaining his footing, he grasped Theophilus' shoulder firmly and said with a mixture of determination and compassion, "This is not your fault. Gather yourself. I may still need your assistance."

"Do you think Poppaea was behind it?" Theophilus asked.

"Who else except that viper?" Caius cursed. "She deliberately delayed me after Nero issued the order to catch the Christians! The only thing I don't understand is how she discovered their whereabouts."

"You should go to the palace to see Nero right now," Theophilus suggested. "He favored Vita. He'll probably release her."

"I can't," Caius said. "At this hour, Nero must be in the bosom of one of his mistresses. Offending him right now only does the opposite. I'll do it tomorrow."

"And if he refuses," he added, squeezing his fists, "I'll break in the jail to save Vita."

"I'm with you, whatever you do!" Theophilus said firmly.

Mounting their horses, the two rode home in silence.

It was barely the break of dawn and Caius had made his way to the palace.

Throughout the night, he had barely slept, except for a brief moment when he dozed off while praying for Vita and everyone else. As he waited in the palace atrium, his prayers continued silently in his heart. He had arrived before the rooster crowed, even though he knew that Nero was unlikely to be awake at such an early hour.

The once intriguing, half-naked nymphs adorning the walls only filled him with loathing.

Around noon, a chamberlain emerged, motioning that Nero was ready to receive him.

Caius trailed behind, following the chamberlain's lead as they made their way toward Nero's private study. As they approached the parted curtain, a courtesan with a yellow wig emerged, her form veiled by a silk blanket barely concealing her nudity.

With a languid gesture, she performed a slow, graceful curtsey directed at Caius before gracefully slipping away. Behind her was a floor strewn with scattered blankets and pillows, vibrant flower petals, and toppled wine cups.

"Prefect, did you suddenly remember you missed something when you examined the palace yesterday?" Nero, in his purple night gown, raised his head from a pile of scrolls and parchments.

When was he ever so fond of scrolls? A sudden spasm of suspicion pricked Caius.

"My lord, I have something more urgent to discuss with you," Caius said in the calmest voice he could manage.

"Well, if it doesn't concern my personal safety, I don't consider it urgent," Nero said with a playful grin on his monkey-like face as he leaned forward. "We have plenty of time to talk. Why don't you come and see my new plans?" He beckoned Caius to come near.

"New plans?" Caius murmured, taken aback by the delirious gleam in Nero's eyes.

Nero stood and retrieved a large scroll from the table. As he unwrapped it, it revealed several scrolls nested within each other. With care, he straightened them out and placed them on his table side by side. These scrolls contained detailed plans of buildings and roads, reminiscent of those in Rome but with notable distinctions.

"What are these?" Caius inquired, his mind racing with various suppositions, each sending a shiver down his spine.

"My plan for new Rome. Neropolis, you may call it," the emperor proclaimed with a wide grin.

He proceeded to display the plans one by one, revealing intricate details and exotic landmarks that could only be realized through the extensive demolition and reconstruction of a significant portion of the city.

"These plans, they must have taken months to draw," Caius

commented, struggling to maintain his composure amid his growing disbelief. He had heard rumors about Nero's involvement in the fire, but he had never truly believed them. He couldn't fathom an emperor being crazy enough to do such a thing. But now, he was not so sure.

Is he really out of his mind as the rumors claim? Or perhaps madness is merely his facade to mask his ambition. These thoughts ran through Caius' mind in rapid succession.

"I like to make plans ahead of time." Another grin from the royal face with which he wasn't comfortable.

"Emperor," he stuttered. "...these plans are quite detailed and accurate. Is there any chance the fire happened according to the will of my... lord?"

"Are you accusing me of something, Prefect?" Nero asked, his voice cool as the breeze before a storm.

"No, emperor, I would never."

"Good! Anyway, however it started, the fire was the will of the gods. And it is also the will of the gods that I, Nero, should rebuild Rome in its new splendor. I'm going to rebuild the city in such beauty that its past glory will look like nothing," Nero declared with fervor, his gaze distant as if he was envisioning the grandeur that would soon grace the landscape.

"Are you in it with me, my dear prefect?" he suddenly turned to look at Caius straight in the eyes.

The slight remaining hope of defending the Christians vanished. Now, Caius just hoped he could still save Vita and use his remaining years to help her recover from the loss.

Nero went on, "I know you have sympathy for these Christians. But remember I do what I must for the good of Rome. Their deaths will allow peace in the city. If they are truly loyal citizens, they should embrace such a noble role with gladness."

"My lord, what if they found out the truth? What if the Christians were cleared of these rumors and regained their reputation someday in the future? What would the future generations think of you?"

Caius held his fists so tight that his fingernails almost pierced his palms.

"The Christians will never exist long enough for that to happen, my dear boy," Nero cackled. "And I will always be remembered by the future generations as the greatest emperor, artist, and city builder." Nero's face glowed with ecstasy. "By the way, I must thank you," he added.

Caius looked at him quizzically. "Thank me for what?" he asked.

"That young lady who accompanied you to my banquet, the messenger of Muse; she inspired me to write a great poem, maybe my greatest yet. I had been struggling to put my inspiration into words for a while. Then, on the night the fire started, the words began to flow as freely as if they came from the Muse herself."

Vita? Could it all have begun that night? Oh, Lord, how could you let this happen? Vita would be devastated to know she played a role in all the tragedy without even knowing it, Caius contemplated in anguish.

"Emperor, even the one you have called a messenger of Muse is one of the people you have arrested, so she will get killed as well. If she has your thanks, at least spare her life. She is, after all, the only one who can guide you in your quest to be the greatest poet."

Nero's mouth widened as he exclaimed, "How is she among them? Is she a Christian?"

"She is, my lord."

"A Christian? With such talent, it would be a waste to see her die. As a token of my gratitude, I will extend her mercy. If she revokes her god and admits that she's a messenger of Muse as I have called her, then I will gladly let her go."

Caius buried his face in his hands.

Vita would rather die than revoke her faith. There's no way she would do that.

"Emperor, please, I beg you; I know she will never revoke her faith..."

"Then I can't help her, can I? That's obvious!" Nero cut him off with a final tone. "These Christians deny all Roman gods, such that sparing them may offend Muse herself, which is the last thing I should ever want to do."

Devastated, Caius decided to make one more attempt. He bowed his head in a gesture of begging. "My lord, I will do anything if you would release her."

"I have entertained you long enough, Prefect, or would you like to join them?" Nero bellowed. "If you have nothing else to report, get out of my sight!"

Knowing it was something Nero could do, Caius decided to leave and find another way. However, there seemed to be no other way. The only solution he could think of was to find out where the prisoners were being held. He could then break into the jail with his most faithful men to save her.

Fifty-Nine

The Empress' Offer

"We found her." Theophilus rushed into the barracks study, beaming with excitement. Caius shot up from his chair.

"Where? How is she?" His hands gripped Theophilus' shoulders.

"She's doing fine. Locked in a prison about twenty feet under the Marcellus Theatre, with all the Christians that we hosted in your villa," Theophilus said. "But the place was well guarded by the empress' personal guards. There is no way we could bribe our way in."

"Then we'll take it by force," Caius said firmly. "Are you with me, Theophilus?"

"Yes, my lord. I and all the tiger group in the barracks. We took an oath to do whatever you tell us to do," Theophilus affirmed.

"Good. It's a very dangerous task. We might not even be able to return alive. Get the tiger group to me in this study tonight. Tell them to bring their crossbars."

"Surely I will," Theophilus said and left the room.

Caius sank into his chair. These twenty men had been his earliest recruits. He'd been but seventeen, a new praetorian trainer then. The old prefect had thought he was a dandy boy from a rich family and wanted to humiliate him. So, he gave him the most hopeless bunch from the barracks. To everyone's surprise, he trained them into the fiercest warriors in the praetorian force, known as the "tiger group". From then on, they became his most trusted men. He knew they would risk their lives for him whenever he asked.

"Vita, I will get you back, no matter what it will cost me," he murmured.

As he was buried in thought, there was another knock on the door, followed by a soldier's voice. "My lord, this girl wants to see you."

He turned. There stood a girl by the door, dressed in a ginger root-colored stola.

Drusilla! The empress' most trusted slave girl.

The soldier said nervously, "Sorry, my lord. I don't dare to keep her waiting because she has a message from..."

"I know. Leave us," Caius said, signaling for him to exit.

"What does she want?" Caius tried hard to mask the anger he felt.

"My lady wanted you to read this." She retrieved a folded parchment from her sleeve and handed it to Caius. It carried a distinct scent of ambergris, a fragrance the empress frequently used these days.

Caius wrinkled his nose and unfolded it.

Dear Caius, you probably already know your little bird has been captured and is facing certain death. This time, I took a closer look at her, and I'm still bewildered by what's in her that captivates you. She may be young but totally lacks enchantment, especially with the change of looks after spending weeks in jail...

The last half-sentence made Caius' heart twitch. He didn't bear to imagine what Vita had endured these past weeks. Rage threatened to consume him, but he couldn't delay reading the rest of the scroll. It continued:

You have insulted me greatly by choosing such an uninspiring nobody over me, Prefect. But as a forgiving woman, I'm still open to hearing your apology. If you want to show your sincere apology by action, I'm always ready to see you at my private villa. Drusilla will tell you where it is. And in that case, I will ensure your little bird is released and sent far away to live out her days in peace. There isn't much time, of course. I will expect your response at once. I look forward to our time together.

Caius felt his whole body burning with anger. *The audacity! Doesn't she fear I'm going to expose this letter to the public?* he asked himself silently.

But realizing that irritating the empress was the last thing he wanted to do right now, he crumpled the parchment with his hands as if destroying the woman who had penned it.

He left his desk and walked to the window.

Theophilus was training some new recruits. Caius saw sweat streaming down from their young and innocent faces. In a daze, he felt as though he were witnessing his own Tiger Group men from eight years ago.

His heart twisted with pain. Lately, he had been too preoccupied with the thoughts of saving Vita, almost forcing himself to forget one fact: If he really broke into the jail, it would almost constitute a crime of treason. And even if he and Vita managed to escape, anyone associated with his endeavor would face certain execution.

The tiger group would be executed. His household would be destroyed, and all slaves sold. Even these soldiers not involved would face a negative impact on their career prospects.

Oh, God. How selfish have I become? he moaned silently within himself.

Without turning his head, he said to Drusilla, "Go, tell Poppaea to release Vita first and she will get what she wants. I'm a man of my word. But I don't trust her to keep her promise. Let her write down her oath and send it to me. I'll burn it at the altar of the Isis temple. She knows what punishment her goddess gives to a person who breaks an oath like that."

Sixty

Shocking Secret

I COULD HAVE COMPLETELY lost track of time if I hadn't counted all the meals. It was so dark here, with just a dim lamp in a wall niche for light. There were no windows anywhere. The walls and floor were cold, damp, and covered in moss and mold.

In the first few days, I had fervently prayed that Caius would miraculously appear and get me and other Christians out of this hideous place.

However, as I waited in the darkness for an extended period, that hope began to wane. Now, I found solace in the fact that Caius hadn't come, as it told me that he, at least, was safe.

People around me had also gone through changes like this. There was wailing and moaning in the beginning, also the hysterical crying from desperate mothers missing their children, and from the ones who couldn't bear to think about their own fate.

But now, this place was much quieter.

Through the dim light provided by the lamp, I saw women gathered around each corner of the room. Most prayed in low murmurs. Some snuggled together to form a warmer space for those who were weaker or held infants in their arms. Once in a while, someone would initiate a hymn and all women in the cell would sing together in a not too loud but firm tone.

Every time, I joined them and felt a strange peace surpassing all fear in my heart. I was amazed at how I could feel so peaceful in the face of imminent death and horror.

I missed Elaina and Peter but was so thankful that they were spared.

I missed Caius ten times more. I had missed him before, of course. But this time, I could dwell on it as long as I wished, with no fear or guilt in that wistfulness.

When I thought of him, I prayed in my heart each time, "Dear Lord, please strengthen him and protect him. Please grant him wisdom to make the right decisions."

In a moment, the clank of the chain on the door disrupted my thoughts. I turned and saw in the dim light two figures being shoved into the cell by the guards.

"Be silent, wretches, or I'll hack you with my dagger," the guard shouted, his voice filled with menace. And then, the clunking sound echoed once more.

"Do it, you filthy pig!" the figure shouted.

Oh, the voice... It can't be!

I moved closer and nearly gasped in disbelief as I recognized the faces before me.

"Rufus! Cassia! How can it be? I had hoped you were both safe away from the city." I tried to embrace them but was pushed away by Cassia.

"We heard the news that the raids started in your neighborhood, so we rushed back to warn you," Rufus explained, his head bowed. "But it was too late, and they left some men in that house to trap anyone who might come back."

"Why are you so stupid?" I shook Rufus' shoulders, sobbing. "Look what you've done to yourself and your wife and your unborn child! Nana will be heartbroken if she sees this in heaven! You should never have come!"

"No, Vita. You don't understand. I had to."

Tears ran down his face. His mouth quivered, wanting to say something, but he stopped himself once more. I cast a quick glance at Cassia, and to my surprise, she seemed quite silent this time, a stark contrast to her previous state.

Something's happened.

However, profound sorrow overwhelmed me, leaving me with little strength to probe further. "What's done is done. God, grant them some peace in their final days," I prayed with a heavy heart. In despair, I continued, "Come with me. I'll show you the most comfortable spot we have." I gestured to Cassia and guided her to a corner of the cell where women with babies were seated. There was some scattered hay on the floor. Cassia followed silently, her face with no emotions.

"Your feet must be aching. Have some rest here," I said to her.

Then I turned to Rufus and said, "I'm sorry, Rufus, we have some women who are breastfeeding here. You might have to stay in another corner."

Rufus hesitated for a moment before choosing a spot not too far from his wife. His gaze remained fixed on her, a mix of sadness and tenderness in his eyes, along with something I couldn't quite tell.

The young moms looked at Cassia first with disdain and hostility, but still, they let her take a decent spot. The following few days were quite peaceful, to my surprise.

Cassia never uttered a word. All she did was stare at the dim lamp, lost in thought.

The food was scarce here, with just a bowl of thin porridge for each meal. Rufus always made sure to save half of his for Cassia. But even so, Cassia kept getting weaker, her beautiful eyes sinking deeper into their sockets.

One day, having heard her stomach grumble, I offered her half a bowl of porridge, saying, "I don't feel well today. Here, have some leftovers." However, Cassia remained motionless.

Rufus came over, took the bowl from me, and said, "Thank you, Vita. I know you're just pretending to be sick so we can have this. But

I've got to be selfish this time. We'll take it because the baby needs food, and Cassia too."

Cassia suddenly grabbed the bowl and flung it to the ground. The bowl shattered, sending splatters of porridge in all directions. "Why are you humiliating me?" she shouted hysterically.

"Why? I'm not!" I was taken aback.

"What's the point of eating? We are dying anyway. I'm guilty enough that you are here. And now you are showing kindness to me so I will look ten times worse than I already am."

"You are guilty that I'm here?" I murmured, struggling to digest her words.

"Because I'm the very reason you are here! How do you think those praetorians could find that place? It's because of me! I told them!" she yelled, her voice laced with frenzy.

"No! Please! For God's sake! No!" Rufus moaned, his hands on his head. "Can't you at least allow us to die in peace?"

Cassia's words were like pouring a cup of wine into sizzling oil.

All the women rushed toward her, shaking her and screaming, "Why did you do this to us? Go to hell, you evil woman!"

Vabiana, who was holding her baby girl, punched her from behind, crying hysterically. "How could you do this? My daughter is only two months old. And now, because of you, she will be torn to pieces by the lions!"

Others quickly joined in, attempting to strike Cassia, while Rufus desperately tried to shield her with his body. The furious fists of the women pummeled his back. He groaned under the weight of their relentless blows, pleading for mercy in the name of God.

Eventually, the widows grew weary and ceased their assault. The cell then filled with another wave of hysterical wails and curses.

The dark cell walls started to spin around me, so I tried hard to clear my mind and make out what Cassia meant. Yes, it made sense. I had suspected someone must have given away our whereabouts, because Theophilus said that Caius hardly ever told anyone about this place.

But I'd never—not for a moment—thought it could be Cassia.

Yet there'd been that encounter at Elaina's place; now, the reason why Cassia hated me so much was within reach.

"And you remember the assassin? Ha! It was because of me too!" Cassia continued with a hysterical laugh. "I told the empress where you were hiding. And if you wonder where I got that information, ask your closest girlfriend!"

Another shocking revelation. I couldn't even support myself to stand.

Julia? How could it be?

Sure, I knew she had hard feelings about me and Caius, but the thought that she'd actually want me dead was too much to believe.

"Oh, Jesus Lord, why is this happening to me? I'm not like you. I can't handle all the hurt and betrayal like this. My faith is not strong enough. And these women, they might have had peaceful lives with their children if it weren't for me." It felt like my heart was being pierced in so many places.

My legs buckled, and I slid down to the floor, leaning against the wall for support.

"I'm so sorry, Vita," Rufus said in tears. "It was my fault. I should have kept a closer eye on my wife."

"Oh, please. Just stop. Stop, stop!" I pleaded, unable to bear any more.

I turned my head away, torn between wanting to hate Cassia and aching to forgive her, but I couldn't manage either. This woman had shattered my life, my hopes, and my dreams of a future with my beloved Caius.

All I could bring myself to do at that moment was to turn away, vowing never to look at them again.

"Oh, Lord," I whispered internally, "let the execution come quickly, so I don't have to endure this agony any longer."

Sixty-One

A Visitor to the Jail

THE WEIGHT OF DESPAIR pinned me to the ground, and I sat there for days, totally losing track of time. The four tall, grim walls closed in on me as though I was in a tomb. I couldn't sing. I couldn't pray. The idea of a swift execution became more tempting with my every breath.

Suddenly, a hysterical cry pulled me out of my solitude and thoughts.

At first, I assumed it was Cassia's voice, but a more focused look made it clear—it was Vabiana who was wailing.

"My baby! Hadrianna! My poor Hadrianna is dead!" she shrieked.

Other women woke up and all rushed to Vabiana's side. In the dim light, I saw Vabiana holding the little figure, tears streaming down her cheeks.

Her face contorted in grief, Vabiana moaned through her tears, "Oh, no, God, why are you taking her away?"

"How could it be? She just had a slight fever this morning," another woman murmured in disbelief.

"Poor child, maybe God wants to spare her from a crueler fate in the arena," another woman suggested, reaching out to hug Vabiana. But Vabiana pulled away.

"Please! Please go. I know you mean well, my dear sisters, but please leave me alone with my daughter," she wept bitterly.

All the other women slowly retreated to their places and knelt down in silent prayer. I glanced over at Cassia and saw her sitting there, hand resting on her belly, deep in thought.

After a painfully long moment, I heard Vabiana's shaky voice, "Vita, come here, please." Surprised that she called for me, I moved closer as she requested.

"Come and sit down," she said, her voice now steadier. "Hadrianna loved you the most. I wish you could be with her at this moment."

Looking down at Hadrianna's lifeless body, a deep sense of loss engulfed me. The tremendous joy I experienced when I helped deliver the baby flooded my memory. Tears I had been trying to hold back slowly rolled down my face.

"I know it is better for her to die right now than to be torn by the lions, but I just can't..." Vabiana managed through her sobs. "Oh, God, my heart is torn to pieces. She is so little. She should have the chance to grow up and have a life... I know I need to pray, but I just can't..."

I wrapped my arms around her, holding her for a long while. "You don't have to pray, Vabiana. The Lord knows everything. He knows the unuttered words. He sees all your tears."

Lord, what can I say... We are all about to die. May your peace dwell among us, the kind of peace no one could take away, I murmured in my heart.

Then, abruptly, the sound of the door chain clanking echoed through the space. The guard's voice rang out, "Which one is Vita? Come out!"

At that, I sprang to my feet. *Lord, please, not Caius. It's too risky for him to be here,* I silently prayed.

I trailed behind the guard to a separate room. There, a woman cloaked in a cape stood beneath a small window high up on the wall, her hair styled in a lofty braid. As she turned, she unveiled a smile that was both beautiful and sinister.

Poppaea.

Poppaea eyed me for a moment, then sneered, "I still don't see how this gaunt face has snared his heart."

"Caius... Is he well?" I knew this was not the person to ask, but still, I couldn't help it.

"He is more than well, except he is not your lover anymore. Actually, he is now warming my bed in my private villa."

"No, I don't believe it. He would never have done that," I said firmly.

"Well, he did it to save you, in the beginning," the empress said with a smirk. "But after a while, I think he forgot why he was there. He told me he should have come to me earlier and I'm the most charming woman he ever met in his life."

"No! You're lying!" Though I didn't believe her, my body quivered involuntarily.

"I'm lying? How do you know? You know nothing, stupid young girl, and more importantly, you know nothing about men." The empress gave a satisfied grin. "You Christians are so hypocritical. You let your man go without pleasures of the flesh for months. How cruel is that? No wonder he loves me *so much.*"

She emphasized the last words.

"Stop it!" I yelled.

"Ha, you can't stand it?" Poppaea cackled. "I might have considered tormenting you further, but not today. Yet, remember, you're his ex-lover, so he pleads for me to spare you from the arena execution."

"Is that so? I doubt you will release me."

"Well, at least you are not completely stupid," she said mockingly. "Of course, I have no intention of releasing you. I want to have your head right now. But your ex-lover made me take an oath before my goddess. So, I'm sending you off to Farasan Island, thousands of miles from Rome. And you'll live there for the rest of your life."

The room fell into silence.

Then, unexpectedly, I burst into laughter.

Poppaea's eyebrows shot up. "Why are you laughing? Don't you dare mock me!"

"Oh, my lady. You are not a good liar. If Caius has already forgotten me, why do you care if I live on some remote island or in Rome?"

"Because I don't want to see your loathsome face. And I haven't forgotten what you did to my daughter with your witchcraft." She managed a calm enough tone.

"We both know that's not the reason you hate me."

"It doesn't matter now." Poppaea seemed to have collected herself. "You are now in my hands, and I have said all I have to say. My men will take you to a carriage out of this building, and in a couple of weeks, you'll be on Farasan Island."

Silence descended, a thousand thoughts filling my head. My anxiety peaked, so I bowed my head and offered a short prayer. Miraculously, my racing heart started to slow down. I yearned to live, but to be exiled to a faraway island for the rest of my life, with no hope of seeing Caius again, what kind of life would that be?

Suddenly, Hadrianna's lifeless face and Vabiana's grieving tears flashed in my mind. To my great surprise, these visions were followed by Cassia's bulging belly and Rufus' sorrowful eyes.

"No, my Lord, I can't do this," I begged. "I don't have the strength to do this. You are asking too much of me."

"No, my daughter, you are stronger than you think," an almost inaudible voice whispered. "Because I'm with you."

I closed my eyes and infused all my remaining strength into this one short prayer.

"Then be with me, my Lord."

I turned to the empress. "I think I should thank you for this generous offer, my lady," I said calmly. "But I choose not to accept."

"It's not up to you," Poppaea said impatiently. "If it weren't for my goddess, I'd have your head right now."

"Let's make a deal. You took an oath to release me, and now, I'd like you to release someone else instead of me. In return, I personally release you from your oath."

"What do you mean?" She glared at me in shock.

"There is a pregnant woman in this cell; release her in my place. One life for another. You will be innocent in the sight of your goddess."

"Why should I listen to you?" Poppaea's voice took on the tone of a rebellious child. "Who are you to know anything at all about my goddess?" She turned and strode to the door, instructing the guards, "Bring this girl to the carriage outside."

The guards approached me and firmly grasped my arms.

"My lady!" I said loudly. "Your daughter visited me in a dream. She's happy where she is, and all she wishes is for you to be a kinder person. Just in case you don't believe me, there is a diamond-shaped mark on her back. You know what she was wearing on the day she met me, so there was no way I was going to notice it."

Poppaea halted abruptly, her silhouette rigid. Though she refrained from turning, a subtle twitch of her shoulder betrayed her stirred emotions.

"That's one life for two. Not so fair." Her voice was as cold as the prison walls.

"What do you want then?"

"I can make it fair," Poppaea declared, her expression morphing into that unnerving smirk. "You'll stay here. My maid's going to bring a potion. It's a special blend from the ancient temple of Isis, meant for priestesses who swear not to have children in this life or the next. But fair warning, it's really painful to take. You asked for this, so it's yours."

With those words, she left the cell.

My Lord, isn't this too much to ask of your daughter? I sank to the floor, my prayers a silent plea. *Grant me the strength to endure this, Lord.*

Hours after, the servant girl came back with the potion in a small bottle, engraved with the ankh, a symbol of life.

She waited until I had consumed every drop before she departed. Moments later, an intense pain erupted in my belly, plunging me into an abyss of darkness. When consciousness returned, I couldn't discern how much time had passed. I sat up, my hands instinctively moving to my aching belly, a shocking coldness gripping me.

No children in this life and the next?

I'm confident that I'll spend eternity with God in the New Heaven and New Earth—a place where there's no need for marriage or childbearing. But still, sadness crept into my chest silently. Caius' face appeared in front of me, a vivid memory from the day he had said he wanted me to give him a son, a son like Achilles. He dreamed of training him in combat while I would pass down the stories Nana once whispered to me.

"Lord," I murmured, the words heavy with despair, "now I've been stripped of everything. I'll die with no husband, no children. Even my satchel and writings are lost. When I'm gone, it'll be like I never existed in this world."

When the guards shoved me back into the dungeon, Cassia was no longer there. Rufus rushed to me, his trembling hands descending on my shoulders.

"Why? Why?" He sobbed and pulled me into his arms. "You are my little sister. I should have protected you. You didn't have to do this."

"I hope you had time to name your unborn child," I said before I lost consciousness again.

"Yes, yes, I did." Rufus' words sounded far away but I could still hear him.

Sixty-Two

Apostle is Back

*T*ODAY IS THE DAY.

Caius sat at his desk in the barracks study, his gaze fixed on a piece of parchment filled with handwritten words. Among them was a date, the date he was supposed to meet the empress in her private villa.

At least Vita should be outside Rome safely right now, he told himself. *Maybe someday I can find out where Poppaea sent her.* But he shook his head right away. *What are you going to do then? Go to see her when you are sharing a bed with the empress? Forget about it. All I can do is pray day and night that Vita will move on and start her new life.*

Pain snatched him and made it hard for him to breathe.

Abruptly, the curtain of the study swung to the side and Theophilus came in.

"Prefect, there is a riot at the Gate Fontinalis. The guards there can't handle it."

"What happened?"

"It is said that there are hundreds of people coming from Arretium and they want to enter from Gate Fontinalis to beg for food because there is a shortage in their province."

"At this time? Rome has enough trouble," Caius responded, exasperated.

"I understand, but these people are desperate, and they've even clashed with the gate guards," Theophilus added.

"Fine, get my horse ready, I'll go there right away," Caius said, his fingers massaging his temples. He had been busy with work for many days and hadn't had much sleep.

"Caius, I'm worried about you," Theophilus said. "Promise you'll take some time to rest after sorting this out?"

"I will," Caius replied, offering a weary smile to his friend. Yet, the thought of rest seemed distant. How could he relax knowing the hardships faced by the people of Rome, who depended on his service? And, though he wouldn't admit it aloud, immersing himself in work was his only escape from the constant worry about Vita and the ominous night that loomed ahead.

Upon reaching Gate Fontinalis, Caius and Theophilus were met with chaos. Ragged men, armed with prongs and hoes, were thrusting at the guards' shields while the air was filled with the shouts and cries of women and children behind them.

Spotting Caius, one of the guards hurried over. "Prefect, these mobs are out of control. Shall we suppress them by force? What would you have us do?" he asked, his hand instinctively moving to the hilt of his dagger.

"Hold on, let me speak to them," Caius interjected, quickly dismounting his horse. He walked toward the crowd and called out assertively, "Attention!"

The chaos momentarily subsided as all eyes turned to him.

"Men of Arretium, I'm prefect of the Praetorian Guards in Rome. I've heard your misfortune, and my heart is with you," he called out loudly. "However, as you've probably heard, Rome has just suffered a big loss, and the city is still recovering. We are short of resources everywhere."

"But we have to live too," a man clutching a prong called out.

"Isn't the emperor of Rome the protector of all the provinces?"

"Yes, he is," Caius agreed. "Let me finish. We will not leave you unattended. We don't have enough room to accommodate more homeless people. But we'll bring bread and tents so everyone may eat and take shelter here, right along the path outside the city gate.

"For the next two days, we'll make sure you're fed and then send you off with some coins. After that, head east to Ancona. Reports show there are extra grains imported there this year."

The crowd started murmuring, discussing among themselves. Finally, their apparent leader addressed them, "Fellows, even if we enter Rome, we're probably not going to get any food to feed ourselves. Let's camp here tonight and go to Ancona in a few days." Then he led them to the side of the Via Flaminia and called for them to sit down. Caius also ordered Theophilus to bring extra food for the women and children. Gradually, the commotion died down.

"Good thing you had the foresight to ask the emperor for extra tents earlier this year, Caius," Theophilus remarked.

A bitter smile touched Caius' lips. *Years from now, no one will remember these tents I provided. They'll just call me "the empress' toy"*, he mused ruefully.

With a heavy sigh, he turned to the gate guards and instructed, "Treat these people with kindness."

Suddenly, the voice of a guard echoed from the other side of the gate, loud and clear. "Cyrus, we've caught another Christian! This old fool turned himself in!"

At that, Caius spun around, and his heart almost stopped beating for a moment. His eyes widened in shock as he saw Peter, the very man who had baptized him and blessed both him and Vita, now in the grasp of the guards, his arms being bound.

Beside him stood Elaina, an old woman bravely extending her hands to the guards to be tied up as well.

"There must be some misunderstanding here!" He rushed to them and blurted out, "I know this man personally. There is no chance he is one of them." His eyes darted to Peter, silently urging him to play along.

"Thank you, Prefect," said Peter calmly. "But I've made up my mind this time."

Facing the guards, he declared, "I'm Peter, a devoted follower of Jesus of Nazareth. I've promised my Lord to take care of His lambs. Now take me to the prison where my fellow Christians are held."

"No, Peter. You don't know what you are doing!" Caius pleaded. "Let me have a private talk with this man," he said to the guards.

"Not to go against your authority, Prefect," one of the guards hesitated, "but the empress and Tigellinus were here this morning and strictly warned us not to let go of any suspicious men."

Caius' hand moved to the hilt of his dagger, his tone firm and commanding. "If I hear any more objections, you'll answer to my sword." The guards, recognizing the seriousness in his voice, stepped back, complying with silent obedience.

"Apostle, please listen to me. You don't know the cruelty of the emperor. There is no way you could save your fellow Christians from his hand. The church needs you. I'll risk my life to see to it that you safely leave here today," Caius implored with deep sincerity.

"No, my dear brother," Peter said with a gentle smile. "Your kindness and bravery have humbled me. But there is a place I must take."

"What kind of place?"

"To be with my people."

"But your... *our* people are in a dire state. There is no way you can save them."

"When the news of the arrest reached me, Elaina and I were in a town two miles from Rome," Peter said. "Brothers there urged us not to go back. And I listened, taking the road to Capua. But on the way, a vision of our Lord stopped me. I asked Him, 'Where are You going, my Lord?' He told me, 'I'm going to Rome to be crucified again because *you* have deserted my flock.' I was so ashamed; I knelt and confessed my faithlessness. And that's what brings me here."

Elaina chimed in, "I was there too. Though I only heard a

resounding boom, I knew it was the voice of our Lord."

Caius, taking in their testimonies, found himself at a loss for words.

"I am ready for whatever might come, Caius," Peter said, placing a reassuring hand on his shoulder. "But I'm worried about you, my brother. Your eyes look so weary. Is anything troubling you?"

Caius was taken aback by Peter's astute observation. He inhaled deeply, gathering his thoughts.

Finally, he broke the silence. "The empress proposed a deal to me. She said she'd free Vita if I became her lover. I agreed. I know it's a grave sin, but the thought of Vita dying... I couldn't bear it."

Feeling Peter's grip tighten on his shoulder, Caius sensed a mix of understanding and concern from the old man.

"My son, thank you for being so honest. I understand your struggle. All I ask is to think twice before you choose this path. Will Vita be truly happy when your plan is successful?"

Before Caius could say anything more, Elaina continued, "Caius, Vita's faith is strong, and her love for you runs deep. She'll stand by whatever choice you make, as long as it's guided by faith. We'll keep you in our prayers from the prison."

Suddenly, the guards called out, "Time is up!"

"We're on our way," Peter and Elaina responded. They waved Caius goodbye, and approached the guards with a calm grace, as though they were meeting old friends rather than facing captivity.

Caius stood rooted to the ground, watching the receding figure of the apostle and his wife. Their white hair fluttered in the breeze, their postures stooped with age, yet their steps were unwaveringly firm.

In that moment, Caius felt a profound shift within him, a newfound strength welling up from deep inside, starting at his feet and rising through his entire being.

Sixty-Three

Confronting the Empress

Caius' villa was filled with an uneasy hush.

In the dining room, all the slaves gathered, their attention riveted on their master and his friend Theophilus. They had been given orders to prepare a lavish feast, but the curious thing was that no guests had arrived. A sense of speculation filled the room, as each person wondered silently about what could be happening.

Caius broke the hush with a solemn tone. "Many of you have been with this household for generations. My heart is full of gratitude for your service." Bewilderment flickered across the faces of the slaves as they absorbed his words.

"You've been serving me for years, but we've never shared a table," Caius exclaimed. "Tonight, let's break that tradition and have a feast where all of us can sit together and enjoy the meal."

A ripple of shock and murmurs swept through the room at his words. However, as the kitchen slaves began to serve the feast, the enticing aroma of the dishes quickly overcame any lingering doubts. The table was laden with succulent boar stew and spiced wine, fried dormice encrusted with pine nuts, and an array of Rome's finest wines.

Appetites piqued, everyone began to savor the delectable spread, eating heartily and drinking freely.

However, a hint of uncertainty still hung in the air. Eventually, Caius lifted his goblet and addressed the gathering with a smile. "Some of you may have noticed changes in me lately. The truth is, I've met someone who has completely changed my life."

There were knowing smiles around the room, and several girls couldn't help but giggle.

"You may think I mean Vita, whom you probably miss a lot. Yes, she did change my life," Caius said with a wistful tone. "But there is someone else who means a lot to both Vita and me. He was a plain carpenter and died as a criminal thirty years ago because He claimed to be God Himself. Not one of *our* gods, but the one and only creator of the world."

A low murmur rippled through the slaves.

Caius went on, "I wish I had more time to explain about Him. But there's one important thing I want to leave with you, my final words: If you ever encounter this man in your life's journey, don't just walk away. Give Him a chance. Trust me, getting to know Him is something you'll never regret." He observed their perplexed faces and silently prayed in his heart that God would one day open the heart of each one of them.

"Let's raise a toast now," he declared, lifting his goblet. His eyes met a few puzzled gazes around the room before he took a sip.

"I will take a long trip tomorrow and won't be back for years," Caius announced. "So today, I want to grant all of you freedom."

They all gasped. Tears welled up in the eyes of the slave girls. "No, Master, we will wait for you. No matter how many years," they implored.

"You girls are still young. I won't forgive myself if you wait for me and end up an old maid. You've served me for years and served me well. You've been more than just servants to me; you've been like sisters," Caius continued. "And as a big brother, I will not only give you your freedom but also your dowry." He then turned to address the male slaves, "And I will also give *you* enough gifts so you can find a proper free-born wife. Who knows, perhaps one day, a son of yours will rise to be a senator."

Seeing them not moving, he continued, "I've made up my mind, so don't argue. Now go in an orderly fashion to the treasury, each of you. Marcellus will meet you there and give you your certificates of freedom and the money I promised."

The room fell into stillness, interrupted only by the muffled cries of a few distressed girls. "Now, go!" Caius bellowed. "If you still see me as your master at this very moment, do as I say! I've been too lenient with you, and it seems you've forgotten that a master holds the power to discipline a disobedient slave as he pleases," he said, pulling a sword out of Theophilus' sheath.

After the last slave had exited, Caius let the sword fall and slumped heavily onto the couch. Theophilus joined him, sitting down beside his friend. Caius, gathering two goblets, handed one to Theophilus. "Now it's just us. Let's head to the atrium for a drink," he suggested.

Side by side, they made their way to the atrium and settled on a bench near the pool. Theophilus sipped his drink in silence, the tranquility of the moment hanging between them. Eventually, he placed his goblet on the bench, turning his gaze toward the pool. "The moon is particularly bright tonight," he remarked softly, his eyes reflecting its glow in the water. "I've always loved how it dances on the surface of your atrium's pool."

"Yes, it's the last night I'll see this moon here," Caius said with a hint of melancholy.

"I figured as much."

"I knew you'd figure."

Their laughter briefly filled the air.

Caius then reached for a wooden box, intricately decorated with ivory. He opened it and pulled out a key, tossing it to Theophilus. "Inside are the deeds to the two properties I bought this year. I haven't registered them with the city council yet, so they might escape Nero's notice when he seizes my assets. Consider them yours now."

"What's the catch?"

"Of course, there is one," Caius replied with a slight smirk. He finished his wine in one long gulp and set the goblet down with a firm thud. "Those children... you can't hide them in your room forever. They need a home."

"I have a vineyard west of the city wall. They will live there safely."

"And they need to be provided for and educated."

"I'll send food to them every day and hire the best tutors to teach them."

Caius smiled and clapped Theophilus on the shoulder. "I knew I could count on you." His eyes then drifted to the statue of his mother across the garden, bathed in gentle moonlight that softened her usually stern features. "Just make sure Nero's men don't get their hands on her," he said, pointing at the statue.

"You have my word," Theophilus said.

Caius retrieved a token from the wooden box, its surface intricately engraved with the head of a tiger. "When the tiger group sees it, it's like they see me in person. They will do anything for whoever holds it."

"You want us to break into the jail to save you. Is that right?" Theophilus sat up straight, his eyes gleaming. "As that's what I have in mind!"

Caius let out a weary sigh. "It's no use. I don't want them to lose their lives in vain."

"What do you want them to do then?"

"When I'm gone, Tigellinus will take control of my men. They are fiercely loyal to me. Show them this so they will listen to you and not lose their lives in revenge."

"I want revenge too!" Theophilus grabbed the goblet from the marble table and smashed it on the ground vigorously. Tears streamed down his angular face. "And I don't care about losing my life! I want to crush that bearded monkey, that treacherous viper, and that beast Tigellinus!"

Caius rested his hand on his best friend's shoulder, patiently waiting as Theophilus' tremors of anger slowly subsided. He knew that despite Theophilus' fury, his friend would faithfully execute his wishes without question.

"Nero's administration is rotten from top to bottom, and he has squandered too much money on his endless banquets. So now, he's had to cut the pay of the Roman legions. I heard news that the military leaders from the northern provinces, especially General Galba and Otho, are planning to overthrow him. When they arrive, our twenty strongest warriors armed with Parthian crossbars will serve as a formidable ally."

· ♥ · ♥ · ♥ · ♥ · ♥ ·

The moon cast a blood-red glow in the sky when Caius entered the small but elegant villa at the secluded end of Venus Street.

At the gate, two young slave boys noticed Caius and bowed respectfully. The timid smiles on their faces filled him with loathing and pity.

Crossing the threshold, Caius stepped into the atrium. He was greeted by the sight of walls festooned with flower garlands. Several well-built male slaves acknowledged his presence with bows, their heads lowered in deference.

"Our lady is waiting for you in the inner chamber at the end of the corridor," they said and tried to take the praetorian armor off Caius' body.

"Get your filthy hands off me!" Caius roared, forcefully pushing through the corridor, and striding toward the inner chamber. The torches lining the walls illuminated the place, casting a glow on the floor adorned with rose petals and glistening gold powders.

A sweet fragrance of musk and myrrh permeated the air as Caius approached the embroidered curtain. With a determined tug, he pulled it aside and stormed in. Poppaea reclined there on a lavish couch, clutching a golden goblet in one hand. Her emerald-green stola draped provocatively off her shoulder, revealing her radiant skin.

"I'm pleased you didn't keep me waiting," she purred, flashing a flirtatious smile. She let down her hair, a cascade of shimmering gold descending down her back.

"I heard you had a preference for blondes," came her words, dripping like honey. "So, I bleached my hair just for you. How do you like it?"

"You look even more like a prostitute than you ever did," Caius said. "Even less classy."

Poppaea's face turned from white to red then white again in an instant. "How dare you! Don't you forget your little bird is still in my grasp! I can fetch her from the place I sent her to. One more word like this, and I'll put her back in the arena."

"Poppaea!" Caius said calmly. "If you think you can crush our souls by threatening our lives, you know nothing about us Christians."

"You? Christian? Do you even know what you are talking about?" the empress hissed.

"Yes, I know what I am talking about," Caius declared. "I'm ashamed I didn't do this earlier. Like I said, I do not wish to be your lover anymore. No matter what you plan to do, I'll remain faithful to Vita and to my Lord Jesus."

"Think carefully before you go on, Prefect!" Poppaea yelled.

Caius brushed her off and pressed on, "I'm a Christian too, just like those folks you've locked away. I believe in the one true God and in His son, Jesus, whose blood redeems us from our sins.

"You, along with every high and mighty lord in this city, are the true arsonists. You make life unbearable for the common folk while you sit on your thrones and high positions, thinking you're divine but acting like pigs!"

"You talk as if you're not one of us."

"I used to be. But now I refuse to live a life of cruelty and greed. And I'd rather die in the arena with Vita than share a bed with a royal prostitute!"

Poppaea's eyes grew darker with every word. Finally, she let out a wild, hysterical growl. "Who are you to judge, you hypocritical man? Everyone thinks I'm promiscuous, but where were all the senators and patricians when Nero forced Otho to divorce me just so he could have me? Where were you, the so-called pillars of the empire?"

A tinge of pity stirred in Caius' heart. All he had known was that Poppaea had left her husband to marry Nero, but her side of the story shocked him.

Speaking in a gentler tone, he said, "Poppaea, I did not know that, and I'm sorry for what you've been through. You're right. As a sinner, I have no right to judge you, and I apologize. But believe me, even the greatest sinner can find hope for forgiveness in God who I serve."

"Shut your mouth! If anyone needs forgiveness, it's not me!" Poppaea shrieked, followed by a hysterical laugh. "You want to die, but I won't grant you that satisfaction! I swear on my daughter's grave, I'll make you watch your precious 'little bird' from the front row as she's mercilessly torn apart."

With a final, chilling laugh, she bellowed toward the door, "Guards, seize him!"

Sixty-Four

The Arena

It had been months since the devastating fire that engulfed Rome, and the air still bore the lingering scent of destruction and decay. The streets, now scattered with makeshift shelters and piles of accumulated garbage, reeked of the pungent stench of unwashed bodies, human waste, and rotting food.

Caius sat, his hands bound, in a carriage winding its way through Rome's bustling streets, en route to the Marcellus Theatre, the city's most famed arena. Tigellinus sat beside him, a dagger gleaming in his hand, a weapon he boasted of sharpening just the day before.

This was the day the arsonists would be executed.

Sadness and anger permeated Caius' chest to a point where he felt he might burst.

He prayed fervently in his heart, "Oh, my Lord. I'm at my wits' end. Please do something to save these innocent Christians. They love you so much. And if you are willing to spare Vita's life, I will serve you all my life with all my heart."

The carriage made its way through the Forum, a place once bustling with vendors and eager buyers. Now, it was transformed; tents housing fire victims sprawled across every open space. Orators stood on elevated stages, addressing the passersby with fervent speeches. Caius, seated within, didn't need to hear their words to know what they were talking about.

An old man with skinny arms and a white beard, reminiscent of Peter, sat begging in a corner. Caius felt a surge of pity as he observed him. However, the moment was shattered when two drunken men stumbled past, jeering at the old man, "Christians to the lions! Why don't you join us at the arena to watch those wretches torn apart? Maybe you'll earn some coins there!"

To Caius' dismay, the old man leaped up and began to echo their shouts, "Christians to the lions!"

The fleeting pity in Caius' heart turned to rage. He thought to himself, *My Lord, if the rumors are true and you intend to cleanse this world with fire, let it come swiftly. These senseless mobs don't even realize what they're doing.*

The grand Marcellus Theatre soon towered before them, with crowds converging from all directions. Caius was ushered into the royal box, flanked by Tigellinus on his left and guards on his right. He attempted to loosen the ropes by rubbing his hands together, but Tigellinus, quick to react, pressed the dagger against his waist.

"Behave yourself, my dear boy," Tigellinus warned. "The empress' orders are clear. Make any wrong move, and I can end your life without a second thought."

Caius stared at him as if he could swallow him with his gaze.

Inwardly, he sought solace in prayer, *Lord, help me calm down. Grant me wisdom, please.*

Nero and Poppaea soon arrived in the arena in full ceremonial garb worthy of a celebration, driving the crowd crazy with frenzy. They ascended to the royal box and sat in front of Caius. Poppaea turned and gave him a triumphant smile.

"You look well, Caius. Today's show will be exceptional. Open your eyes and watch."

Caius cursed silently, *Oh, Lord. Women like her should be thrown into the arena, not my Vita, not these kind Christians. Show your justice, my Lord. My faith is not enough to hold me through such pain.*

I have so much to learn as a Christian; my faith is not enough yet.

As more audience members filled the empty seats, the theater transformed into a tightly packed olive press. The air turned stiflingly hot, making each breath a struggle. Slaves tirelessly fanned their wealthy masters with peacock feather fans, while those less fortunate fanned themselves with the edges of their tunics, only adding to the already sweat-laden atmosphere. Amidst this, Nero rose abruptly, lifted his hand with dramatic flair, and spoke with a booming voice.

"People of Rome, I welcome you to this gracious day of judgment in which we are finally bringing the heinous scourge of evildoers to justice." The crowd went into another round of cheers, and Nero's face was almost split with a wide grin.

"We have seen this cult of evildoers parading as holy, worshiping a dead man, going wild with fallacies and strange visions. We have all seen what they have done to our precious city!" he yelled, his stomach heaving as he tried to catch his breath.

The crowd hailed at his statement.

"Kill them off!"

"Kill them off!"

"Kill them off!"

"Not just yet, my people, not yet," Nero interjected. "We shall do this in the same fashion with which they ruined our lives and properties. These Christians have an old saying: 'an eye for an eye and a tooth for a tooth'. That's how we shall repay them! We shall destroy them in smoke and fire, just like what they did to our beloved city!"

Nero's well-trained voice carried to every corner of the theater. "And after they are executed, every one of you here will get fifteen copper coins as a gift for your witness."

"Long live Caesar! Burn them off, burn them off!" The crowd descended into another rancor of shouts and yells.

"Now let the show begin!" Nero said loudly and raised one hand to the sky.

A cacophony of fanfare blared brassily. Slaves entered the arena, carrying crosses to place beside pre-dug holes. The clanking of chains echoed as the gates opened, and the Christians were ushered in, intensifying the crowd's frenzied, bloodthirsty clamor.

A young mother, clutching her baby, squinted as the long-awaited sunshine shone on her face. Her frail, spindly legs barely supported her, and her ribs were sharply outlined against her skin due to malnutrition. The sight of the Christians, with their raw, reddened skin and faces marred by dust and fatigue, almost brought tears to Caius' eyes. He couldn't help but wonder if Vita was enduring even worse treatment.

Some Christians collapsed to their knees in the red dust, while others stood with slumped shoulders, struggling to remain upright. Caius scanned the faces of the prisoners, relieved yet anxious to find Vita was not among them. His gaze, however, settled on two faces he recognized——the couple from the wedding officiated by Peter. Caius' mind briefly revisited their encounter at Elaina's house, where he had first met them face to face after the wedding. At that time, they were adorned in attire befitting newlyweds, exuding joy and celebration. Now, those vibrant garments had been replaced by worn, ragged clothes. Yet, their hands remained firmly clasped together.

Amidst the grim scene, a mournful melody began to rise from the Christians huddled in the arena's center. Gradually, some of the weakened prisoners found the strength to stand and add their voices to the sorrowful chorus.

"Are they singing?" whispered those around Caius.

"These people must be lunatics," someone remarked, sparking a wave of jeers.

Yet, amidst the scorn, Caius recognized the melody. It was the same hymn sung at the wedding he had attended. Peter's words from that day echoed in his mind: "Our relationship with our God is like marriage. When we believed Him, we got engaged. But we waited patiently for the wedding day. Nothing can separate our union with God, even death. And death may even be the prelude to our wedding, the day we can finally live with our God, forever, never parted." He didn't understand these words when he'd heard them for the first time, but now these words hit him like lightning.

The guards forcibly extended the arms of the Christians across the crosses and secured them with nails. Screaming, crying, and blood filled the arena. Once nailed, the crosses were hoisted upright into the prepared holes. Guards then stacked bundles of wood at the base of each cross, reaching up to the feet of the victims, and set them ablaze with torches.

"Oh, Lord, send rain and quench the fire. Save your sons and daughters," Caius whispered in agony.

This time, no miracles came to be. The flames quickly enveloped those on the crosses. Around Caius, cruel laughter erupted. Senators flung their wine goblets in mockery, while plebeians threw their dice, their shouts and jeers piercing the air. "They've sung their last song now. If their god holds any power at all, why didn't he put out the flames?" they taunted.

Merciless leeches! Caius seethed inwardly. Then, a faint whisper brushed his ears, "Yes, but weren't you just like them?"

He stood still, struck by the truth in those words.

Indeed, he had been just like them mere months ago, perhaps even throughout his entire life. Caius recalled countless visits to this arena with friends and lovers, occupying seats of privilege, sipping wine, and reveling in the brutal spectacle below. He vividly remembered joining in the chorus of "Kill!" as defeated gladiators pleaded for mercy, feeding into the same bloodlust he now despised.

"Oh, Lord. Forgive me," Caius whispered, his voice heavy with remorse as he gazed through the smoke at the convulsing figures, tears blurring his vision. "I'm such a sinner who deserves death."

Meanwhile, the crowd's chants of "More! More! More!" swelled around him, their voices rising with the smoke that curled upwards into the sky.

The burnt bodies were taken down, and more Christians were brought in, only to be set ablaze. With each new group paraded into the arena, Caius' heart threatened to burst from his chest in dread. He longed to shut his eyes, terrified of spotting the familiar face among the condemned.

Yet, he compelled himself to watch intently.

Each time Vita wasn't among them, a faint sense of relief breathed life back into him, if only momentarily.

But a fresh wave of terror gripped Caius. Peter and Elaina were now among those being led into the arena, their figures aged and frail, bent under the weight of their impending fate. His heart clenched as Elaina was nailed to the cross, right before Peter's eyes. He saw the old man's body shake with tremors. Despite his apparent weakness, Peter's voice, surprisingly strong, carried across the arena.

"Caesar, I'm Peter, a devoted follower of Jesus. May I say something before I die?"

The murmurs from the crowds grew louder.

"What is this old wretch going to say?" The guard beside Caius seemed curious.

Nero remained silent for a moment. Then Caius overheard Poppaea whisper to Nero, "My lord, let him speak, otherwise people will think you fear him."

"Fear him? Nonsense!" Nero sneered. Then he raised his hand, gesturing for Peter to go on.

"I'm not worthy to be crucified the way my Lord was. I want my cross turned upside down to signify my nothingness before the only Son of God, the prince of heaven whose power dominates the earth."

"Blasphemy! He dares to claim a power greater than Caesar's!" someone behind Caius exclaimed in outrage.

Peter turned toward his fellow Christians, raising his voice so all could hear, "My sisters and brothers, this is a glorious moment. Hold onto your faith and the angels of the Lord will come to welcome you into the feast of the Lord. Tonight, we'll sit together at that feast. I cannot wait to die for my Lord and savior!"

"Silence him and give him what he wants," Nero bellowed furiously. "Do it somewhere else. Don't burn him. Let him die slowly." At his command, the guards swiftly gagged Peter, silencing his proclamation.

Then, as they dragged him away, Caius caught Peter's gaze from afar. It was a look filled with tenderness and encouragement.

Suddenly, Caius noticed that Tigellinus and the guards, engrossed in the events of the arena, were no longer paying him close attention. Seizing the opportunity, he subtly began to rub his hands against the fence behind him, working to loosen the ropes. They gave way slightly but were still far from breaking.

"Lord, help me," Caius whispered under his breath, sweat beads forming rapidly on his forehead.

The sun had passed its zenith in the sky, casting longer shadows from the obelisk as the hours went by. The fires had been put out, their smoke vanishing into the air. Among the spectators, the patricians seemed disinterested, lost in idle chatter, while the plebeians bartered with vendors and bought food.

Caius' heart pounded even more rapidly because Vita was still nowhere to be seen. *What plans does the empress have in store? How will she torture my girl and rip my heart apart?* These thoughts tormented him with every passing moment.

Driven by frenzy, he rubbed his wrists against the fence with even greater force, only to feel blood oozing out.

The empress rose gracefully before she proclaimed with commanding authority, "People of Rome! Now we have executed most of the arsonists. But there is one evil woman I saved for the last. This woman is a witch, and she even corrupted the backbone of our empire, our ex-prefect, Caius Amelius! So today, we will make her execution the climax of our show!"

Sixty-Five
The Final Battle

"No!" Caius cried out when he saw Vita being brought to the center of the arena. He hadn't seen her for almost two months. She was attired like a goddess in a scarlet silk dress with her shoulders bare, flowers adorning her hair.

But she looked gaunt, pale, and like she could almost be blown away by the wind.

The slaves put up a high swing on the ground and bound Vita to it. Then they smeared red paint on the two poles of the swing.

"What are they going to do to her?" Caius heard people around him murmuring and his head began to hum. The world started to spin, and his knees trembled when he saw the gate of the arena was open and two raging bulls were released into it, running wild.

The bulls were double the size of ordinary ones and each was tied by a strong rope, with the other ends inside the gate.

"This is going to be fun. Let's cast lots about when the girl will fall to the horns of the bulls," two guards chatted behind Caius, unleashing a torrent of panic within him. *No, my Vita! God, please help me!* he pleaded silently, rubbing at the rope in frantic desperation. However, even with all his effort, the rope remained unyieldingly tight.

However, just as despair was about to engulf him, a flicker of hope arose as Caius felt the rope give way slightly. Astonishingly, he soon realized his hands were free. He quickly turned and saw a woman wearing a hooded cloak behind the fence, a knife trembling in her grasp.

It was Acte.

"Go! Save her!" she muttered, her lips pale and quivering.

"How dare you!" a soldier's voice thundered from behind Acte. In an instant, Acte's body convulsed. Caius watched in horror as a dagger protruded from her chest, a fountain of blood gushing from her mouth.

"No!" Caius bellowed, his voice choked with horror, words failing him.

"Assassin!" the guard shouted. "That woman has a knife." Tigellinus and the other guards swiftly advanced, delivering more stabs. Acte collapsed, whispering her final words to Caius.

"Go! Save her!"

The guards instantly redirected their focus to Caius, lunging toward him. Reacting swiftly, Caius snatched a dagger from a nearby guard and darted between the seats, nimbly evading anyone who tried to intercept or pursue him. He leaped into the arena, landing with a solid thud, rolled to break his fall, and then sprinted to position himself protectively in front of Vita, arms outstretched.

"Let me defend her!" Caius faced Nero and yelled defiantly.

"No, Caius! Don't do this! You'll die!" Vita cried out in desperation.

The crowd inhaled sharply in unison, their collective gasp rippling into a wave of murmurs that swept through the audience. Soon, cries of "Let him fight!" burst forth, swelling in volume and fervor. Among them, several patrician matrons dabbed at their eyes with handkerchiefs, visibly moved by the scene.

In that moment, Caius caught a fleeting glimpse of hope as he observed a hint of fear flash across Nero's weasel-like eyes.

He glanced at Poppaea, whose face contorted with fury as she exchanged whispers with her husband. The audience hung on the edge of their seats, anticipating Nero's verdict. After a tense moment, Nero declared, "You will fight! But when you fail, you and your woman will meet a fate so gruesome that it defies imagination."

Caius bowed in acceptance of the challenge, prompting a thunderous cheer from the crowd, eager for an entertaining spectacle.

Closing his eyes, Caius uttered a swift prayer, "Lord, I beseech you for a miracle!"

"You don't have to do this, Caius," Vita sobbed. "Please, Caius, let me die for my faith. It serves nothing if you are taken too—nothing at all."

"No, it's our faith now. Besides, I promised that I'll protect you," he said as he turned to the bulls. This time, they were released without any restraints. They charged directly at him, flaring their nostrils.

Caius circled the pole swiftly, skillfully evading the bulls' attempts to catch him. However, their speed was formidable. One bull closed in rapidly, delivering a powerful blow with its horn that sent Caius crashing to the ground, agony coursing through his body.

"No!" Vita's scream reached his ears.

Struggling to his feet, Caius felt warm blood streaming down his shin.

As the bulls charged again, he summoned every ounce of his remaining strength. In a desperate move, he jumped onto the back of the nearest bull just as it closed in on him. The animal bucked wildly, trying to dislodge him, but Caius clung on, determined not to be thrown off.

In one swift, decisive movement, Caius plunged his dagger into the bull's heart. The mighty beast stumbled and then collapsed onto the ground. The crowd erupted into frantic cheers at the dramatic turn of events.

Before Caius could retrieve his dagger, the second bull charged at him with full force. Reacting swiftly, he struck the bull's left eye with a powerful blow, even as its horn impaled his left shoulder. The massive creature dragged him several feet before flinging its head violently, snorting and pawing at the ground. This action hurled Caius to the side. The bull, driven by its momentum, continued charging forward.

Caius tumbled to the ground a few paces in front of Vita. He struggled to reach for his dagger in the dead bull's body but couldn't move. The remaining bull was running aimlessly in the arena, seemingly maddened by the pain in its eye.

But finally, the beast seemed to resume its focus on him and got ready for a lunge. Its gait became haphazard, likely impaired by the loss of one eye. Yet, it was just a matter of time before its horn pierced Caius' chest again.

"Sorry, Vita. I've lost this one," he whispered, resigning himself as he closed his eyes, hearing the bulls' thundering hooves nearing.

Suddenly, Vita's loud prayer pierced the air. "Lord, protect Caius as you did David from the lions!"

David. The thought sparked a memory, a story from long ago. Inspired, Caius, despite his agony, hastily removed the belt Vita had woven for him.

Frantically, he began scouring the ground for pebbles. "What are you trying to do?" Vita shouted, her gaze fixed on him from above.

"Looking for a miracle, like David did," he replied.

With determination, he looped the belt around his arm, transforming it into an improvised sling.

But it was too late. The bull was one foot away from him. There was no way he could shoot at such a short distance.

"Come on, friend. Toss me farther this time," he yelled at the charging beast. In the next instant, he was in the air, flung effortlessly by the bull as if he were nothing more than a ragdoll.

He crashed onto the arena's edge as the bull charged onward. His eyes refused to open, and blood flowed from numerous wounds across his body. Yet, amidst the haze of pain, he was acutely aware of one thing: The sling was still clenched in his hand, and within its fold lay a small, round pebble.

The bull pivoted sharply and charged with renewed fury.

The sling whirled around with immense velocity.

The frightful whooshing sound of the pebble took away the breath of everyone, the bull's mighty bellow changing into a loud shriek, a sound of agony and the throes of an impending death. With a thunderous thud, the beast's massive frame collapsed onto the ground.

A hush fell over the arena, quickly followed by an eruption of deafening cheers from all sides. For Caius, though, these sounds of triumph and excitement soon receded into a faint echo as he slumped to the floor, succumbing to unconsciousness.

Sixty-Six

Epilogue

Reader, I married Caius 267 days after our harrowing ordeal in the arena.

The day he was carried out unconscious, the physician said he was probably not going to survive. It was the third time he got himself wounded for me and I blamed myself so much.

But God showed us great mercy by saving Caius from the brink of death. He woke up after a seven-day fever. When he was drifting in and out of consciousness, I remained steadfastly by his side, clutching his hand, tears streaming as I pleaded, "Don't leave me. What am I going to do without you? You are the only one I have."

He struggled to move his lips and murmured, "No, Vita. You have Jesus. And He is far more worthy to stay with you than I am."

And those words comforted me to no end.

Finally, he recovered but his right arm lost all sensation. It was, in the view of everything, a small price to pay. I had him back—and he, at last, had me.

Our lives were spared, largely due to the profound impact of Caius' bravery on the audience. It marked a miraculous victory, compelling even Nero to refrain from provoking the crowds who fervently pleaded for mercy.

However, given Caius' treasonous status, Nero decreed the confiscation of all his possessions and ordered the destruction of his villa by fire.

Fortunately, Caius had dismissed his slaves before confronting the empress, thus sparing them from the tragic events that followed.

Only Decima chose to stay in that villa no matter how hard Caius persuaded her to leave. She intentionally cut her wrist, sitting next to the sculpture of the old master, allowing her lifeblood to drain before the arrival of Tigellinus' men.

In the aftermath, her body and the house were set ablaze together. Once the fire had subsided, we gathered her remains and laid her to rest beneath the very ground where the villa used to stand.

With the assistance of Theophilus and Caius' other companions, we also managed to retrieve the remains of my fellow Christian friends who had been executed that day, including Rufus. We ensured they received a proper burial, and Rufus found his resting place in the backyard of Eubulus' house, marked by a stone bearing his name.

If ever Cassia was to return, she could easily find him.

When Caius was recovering, we had to move into Theophilus' apartment room and be provided by him. It was such a humiliating experience for Caius, but I was glad to see how he had grown in faith and diminished in pride. Now, he cared not for material things, though it still irked and shamed him when he could not provide even a simple sum of money for his wife.

As for me, reader, I did not care. I had at my side and in my heart all I needed.

There was one more thing that filled me with profound gratitude. My satchel, containing the initial pages of my memoir, was miraculously recovered by Theophilus amidst the debris of our former dwelling place, which had been reduced to rubble after the arrest.

I thought about the trials and challenges those pages went through, and how they were preserved, and couldn't help but believe that it was God's will for me to write down these experiences. But after all this, I had a sense of immense, overwhelming relief that even if all my stories had happened to be blotted away, God would remember every drop of my tears.

We had a small quiet wedding at Theophilus' vineyard outside of the city, attended only by Theophilus and all the children he had saved on the day of the arrest. Caius said that he felt sorry for not giving me a luxurious wedding. But as he saw the happy smiles on the faces of those kids, he too felt it was God's best plan.

Those children had never smiled so brightly since they'd lost their mothers.

Although Theophilus urged us to stay, we made the decision to depart from Rome. The young ones needed a fresh start to heal from their severe injuries, many of which had left lasting scars on their hearts and minds.

We took them on a ship bound for Cyprus. Isn't that funny? I'd been waiting for that ship for so long, but never imagined I'd ever get to board it with Caius, now my husband. And you probably guessed where we were heading for? Yes, my home village.

We arrived in January and the House of Darkness became our new home.

Of course, its plaintive condition was still the same as when I had left the village. We spent three months cleaning and renovating it, transforming it from a mere skeleton into a structure with sturdy walls, a solid roof, and bricks. We all worked together, including the youngsters and even my old neighbors.

In the first month, we had to huddle together in the only room that didn't have cracks in the walls.

However, when summer came, it turned out to be a stunning place with tons of flowers. Most of all, gladioli, of course. Now, no one would dare call it the House of Darkness.

We happily renamed it the "House of Grace".

Oh, and I nearly forgot to mention that we had a guest join us here. It might not be entirely accurate to label her as a guest, considering she once belonged here a long time ago——the marble sculpture of Caius' mother, the one he had initially hated but now cherished. We returned her to her original spot in the atrium.

Theophilus offered to send us money, but Caius refused; we could provide for ourselves and the children by living off the small plot of fertile land behind the house. It was a great challenge for Caius especially when his left arm was still slowly recovering, but he made it through lots of prayers. Now, he could proudly call himself a good gardener.

Do you remember Marcus? He somehow found where we lived and visited us two years after we moved here. He brought little Achilles. I couldn't call him little Achilles now, because the boy had grown almost as tall as me! He and Caius had a pretend fight in our yard and had lots of fun. Marcus said he had been ordained as an elder in the church of Macedonia. Knowing he was as resourceful as he always had been, I pleaded with him to look for Julia and Cassia, who should have a two-year-old child by now.

He said he would keep this in mind.

In the sixty-eighth year of Nero's reign, which was four years after we moved to Cyprus, as Caius had predicted, General Galba and several other northern provincial governors rebelled against Nero. The senate, who had hated Nero for a long time, declared him a public enemy. Nero fled Rome and drove a knife into his own throat with the help of one of his freed slaves, all on a hot summer's day outside the city.

Hearing the news of Nero's death, General Galba led his army into Rome and claimed the throne, with the help of the praetorians, especially the "tiger group".

However, Galba clearly lacked wisdom in his dealing with money, causing him to lose Tigellinus' support quickly. In desperation, Galba returned all Caius' property, resumed his patrician status, and wrote an earnest letter to him. In this letter, he implored Caius to return to Rome to assume the role of the new prefect and provide his support.

We prayed about the situation but didn't sense that God was guiding us in that direction.

"Don't you miss Rome and all the feasts and luxuries?" I asked Caius one day.

"After three years enjoying the fresh air in Cyprus, I don't think I can stand the terrible stench and the mosquitos of Roman summers," he said with a smile and held me tighter. "Besides, going back to the palace would mean less time spent with you."

So, we didn't go back. After all, why would we?

Did we not have everything we required here? We had each other, safety, security, good food, a plot of land, and most of all, we had—and shared—our love for God.

Meanwhile, Caius asked Theophilus to take care of all his properties and use the earnings to support the churches in Rome and nearby towns. Theophilus had always possessed a natural talent for management, so it was a pleasant job for him.

In one recent letter, he told us that he had sponsored the Church of Rome to make hundreds of copies of Luke's two letters to him.

I hope some of these copies will be preserved and future generations will see me being called "the most excellent Theophilus", he said in his letter.

Galba's reign on the throne proved short-lived.

The following year, he was assassinated, marking the beginning of what came to be known as "the Year of the Four Emperors". Each of these rulers met a similar fate, their reigns cut tragically short. The years spanning from the latter part of Nero's rule to the conclusion of the fourth emperor's reign were nothing short of a nightmare for the privileged elite of Rome.

Countless patrician families were uprooted, their masters subjected to gruesome executions and their properties seized by the state. Reflecting on these events, we could not help but thank God for His miraculous protection that shielded us from such horrors.

"His ways are higher than ours. Now I believe it," Caius would often say.

As for Poppaea and Tigellinus, what became of them?

Well, according to Theophilus, Poppaea died in summer the same year we moved to Cyprus. Rumor said that she had a quarrel with Nero when she was heavily pregnant, and Nero kicked her in the belly which accidentally caused her death. And Tigellinus, who was hated by his own soldiers and colleagues, survived Nero and Galba's reign through lots of schemes and bribery. But when Otto became emperor, his bribery only bought him a little time to cut his own throat with a razor before the death order arrived.

Every time we read those letters, we were just grateful that we and the children could live in a peaceful place far away from the center of the swirl of violence.

These years hadn't been entirely easy for me, however. I was still healing from the sorrow of losing my beloved Christian brothers and sisters, as well as my dear Rufus.

At times, I felt guilty for being the sole survivor. However, one night, while caring for five sick children with Caius, it struck me that God assigned each person a unique mission. Living for Christ every day was just as challenging as dying for Him once and for all.

The children grew amazingly fast. We taught them reading, writing, sewing, planting and most importantly, the word of God.

Sometimes, I would feel sorry for not giving Caius a child of his own, although he never complained about that. But I still prayed that God would heal me miraculously and grant us a surprising joy.

I know you're probably curious about how Caius and I were doing in our married life. Well, let me tell you, it is quite different from what I imagined or expected. It is a wonderful thing to love, serve, and commit to someone for a lifetime. But I won't lie; it hasn't always been easy. We both have to learn and grow together.

Sometimes, I wondered why a man who'd risk his life for me in the arena couldn't be bothered to put his dirty clothes in the laundry basket, even after I reminded him hundreds of times. Maybe Caius had similar thoughts too. But in those moments, we remembered Peter's words, recognizing that we were both sinners and in need of

God's grace and each other's.

We would turn to the Lord, confess our sins, and renew our commitment to each other.

And even in the intimate moments behind closed doors, we still had to put in the effort and learn along the way. I had to admit I had too many illusions about those moments, and God had shattered them one by one. Beauty is fleeting, and passion as well. Gradually, I learned that intimacy between husband and wife is not about satisfying the desires of flesh and eyes; it's more about reaffirming our covenant before the Lord in a "touchable" way.

But it was all worth it. The challenges we'd faced and the journey of overcoming them had only made us stronger and brought us ever closer, such that we became as one, man and woman as God made us, to be together and grow in His glorious name. Our trials deepened our understanding of what the apostle Peter meant when he said, "Love requires patience and perseverance."

As my time is running short, dear reader, allow me to conclude my writing with a heartfelt prayer. May the name of God be exalted through my words, and may you, the reader, come to know Him and journey alongside Him throughout your entire life.

The Story Continues...

If you've enjoyed this tale, I invite you to join my email list, because the story doesn't end here. As mentioned in the preface, this narrative originated from my plans to create a webcomic. Now that the book is published, I'm considering revisiting this project in the near future. By joining my email list, you'll receive updates about the webcomic. Perhaps I'll even ask for your input, such as voting for your favorite scene's storyboard or choosing Caius' hairstyle.

In the meantime, I'm planning to write a spin-off book featuring two secondary characters from Vita's Prayer: Julia and Achilles. I have a deep affection for these characters, yet their futures remain untold in the original story. Here's a hint: during a fire, Julia cunningly acquired a significant portion of the Eubulus family's wealth by stealing their deeds. Twelve years later, at the age of 27, she rose to become Rome's most prominent gladiator school master.

Though no longer in her youthful prime, Julia retained her charm and attracted numerous suitors.

Albus, another gladiator school owner, finds himself indebted to Julia for a substantial sum. Unable to repay, he offers Achilles, a mute yet exceptionally strong and attractive gladiator, as payment. Despite Julia's initial doubts about Achilles' value compared to the debt owed, her greed prompts her to accept the offer.

However, Julia's plans unravel when Achilles unexpectedly speaks the next day, revealing himself as a Christian who refuses to engage in violent arena battles. Julia realizes she was deceived by Albus, who used a temporary mute-inducing medicine on Achilles to prevent him from disclosing the truth before the transaction.

Despite this setback, Julia discerns Achilles' untapped potential and offers him a role in her school, replacing her deceased accountant. Little does she know this decision will ultimately overthrow her entire life.

If you're curious about what unfolds next or if you'd like to stay updated on the Vita's Prayer webcomic, please visit www.vitasprayer.com and sign up for the email list.

To my dear husband, who may not have risked his life for me in the arena or be the biggest fan of my book, but he's the one who's always there, expressing his love in the most caring and practical ways, cooking our meals, and making sure all dirty dishes find their way into the dishwasher.

Author's Plea

Dear reader, as an indie author, your review is incredibly important to me. Please consider leaving one on Amazon or Goodreads. Also, as a first-time writer who is composing in her second language, I'm open to corrections. If you happen to spot any grammatical mistakes or wording issues, please don't hesitate to send me an email at grace@vitasprayer.com.

Please, please, please give this book a review on Amazon or Goodreads!
My mom worked so hard on it.

Made in United States
Orlando, FL
27 April 2024